HEMLOCK AND SAGE

A Coyote & Crow Novel

by Tali Inlow

Coyote & Crow LLC

This book is a work of fiction. Any reference to historical events, real people, or real places are used fictitiously. Other names, characters, places, and events are the products of the author's imagination, and any resemblance to actual events or places or persons, living or dead, is entirely coincidental. Text and artwork, copyright ©2022 by Coyote & Crow LLC. Illustration by Mackenzie Neal. All rights reserved, including the right to reproduce this book or portions thereof in any form whatsoever. For information about special bulk discounts, uses in educational settings or other inquiries, please send an email to info@coyoteandcrow.net. This novel is set in the fictional world of Coyote & Crow, created by Connor Alexander. For more information on Coyote & Crow please visit our website at: www.coyoteandcrow.net.

Dedication

*To all the youth of Makasing,
may you never stop discovering who you are*

TABLE OF CONTENTS

wanzi | how owl & raccoon came to be............5

- wanzi 6
- pit 29
- tahood 49
- hawa 62
- zapataan 77
- sakpi 87

pit | how owl learned to fly 108

- pitsika 109
- nishaawi 114
- hisika 123
- pina 141
- kawanzi 157
- kinapa 170
- wantikinapa 176
- pitikinapa 194
- tahootikinapa 199
- hawatikinapa 215

tahood | when owl chased raccoon's tail 223

- zapatikinapa 224
- saktikinapa 230
- pitsitikinapa 243
- nishaatikinapa 255
- hisitikinapa 273
- pinatikinapa 283
- kawatikinapa 291
- pidii 298
- pidii doba wanzi 306
- pidii doba pit 327
- pidii doba tahoo 344

pidii doba hawa 356
pidi doba zaptaan 368
pidi doba sakpi 376
pidi doba pitsika 383
pidi doba nishaawi 391
pidi doba hisika 400

hawa | the day owl bled & raccoon fled 406

pidi doba pina 407
pidi doba kawanzi 411
tahodii 428
tahodii doba wanzi 440
tahodii doba pit 445
tahodii doba tahoo 453
tahodii doba hawa 474

Acknowledgements 477
About the Author 481

wanzi | *how owl & raccoon came to be*

WANZI

End of day is signaled by a low two-tone chime.

There is not a mad rush to leave, not exactly. But there is certainly a different energy in the air the moment instruction for the day is over.

For one seventeen-year old, the excitement is more than just the temporary feeling of freedom brought about by university's close or the fresh breath of warm afternoon air.

For Niya Suwatt, the end of this day means one thing and one thing only: she is that much closer to *tomorrow*.

Though there is still a lot of today left.

Niya pushes herself up from where she's been kneeling, her bare knees coated in a light dusting of rich dirt. The soil pod that she has been working in is a twelve-by-twelve-foot square filled with delicate cedar saplings. Their variegated leaves are full of promise, but Niya finds herself only mildly intrigued by the prospects their unusual coloring offer.

She knows she should care more, knows even that she should be proud of this achievement. After only one year working with the horticulture elders and ecological tinkerers alike, she might already be on her way to bringing about an entirely new variety.

Instead, Niya only wonders about time. The time she's wasted flitting from one university specialty to the next these past three years. Average to compellingly skilled at everything from gat programming and wuyi transcription to herbalism and hydrology, underwater work and exploration—and now, apparently, horticulture. Her parents' wishes, perhaps finally fulfilled!

Niya knows and is grateful that these trees are a gift from the Creator. She whispers a silent prayer in thanks as the thought strikes her.

But Niya also knows that she feels restless, like an itch at night.

She would call it boredom if she had only a slightly rasher streak to her. Oh, how her parents would love to hear that. Nearly three whole years of freedom to make up her mind about what specialty she will pursue, freedom that many her age are not afforded. There is always work to be done, more and more of it by the year, it seems—and more and more abundance to go around, which serves everyone. Niya reminds herself of this again and again.

Her parents have had remarkable success; not as ordinary farmers, not any longer. They have risen in the Cahokian social scene because of their abilities to grow unique varieties of vegetables. Many a chef clamors for the favor of the Suwatts and their choicest selections on market days. Who but the Suwatts can manage to grow cold weather squash that is both resistant to freezes *and* that tastes like the sweetest nuts? Not one year ago, a fight had nearly broken out over the most unique crop of Suwatt corn that the market had yet seen—when roasted over the fire, the entire batch managed to taste like sweet, grilled meats. A delicacy that Cahokians far and wide were still hoping to see repeated this year or, better yet and somehow in the grasp of the Suwatt family, improved upon!

Farming, however, is not what plucks at Niya's heartstrings. She knows that for certain, even if she isn't entirely sure what *does* pluck at her heartstrings—or, worse still, whether or not she will find it anytime soon.

And it isn't boredom that Niya suffers when studying with the horticulture elders and working in the grow pods, she knows that much. She derives a very real sense of satisfaction from the cedar saplings and other fauna experiments. Instead, she believes it to be a very clear sense that farming simply is not her destiny. Unfortunately, all of her other stints in various programs yielded the same results: dissatisfaction and an ache for something different. She excelled in multiple areas of study, but which was the one that would really light a fire in her heart, that would keep her sated for years to come?

It is a question for another day, a conversation that Niya will inevitably have to have with herself and her parents, who are itching in their own rights for their only child to join the family business. On top of the familial expectations, if Niya changes course again, she'll be the oldest student in whatever program she pursues this time next year by far!

Standing up and brushing a few loose chunks of hair from her forehead, Niya sighs. But her indecision and restlessness are wiped away by the shouts of her friends.

"A-yo! Niya!"

Adasi and Nampeyo run up to her, all excited energy and big smiles.

An easy grin emerges in spite of Niya's unresolved musings. Although she may be uncertain about what the future is supposed to look like, for now, it can wait its turn.

For one more night, that is.

Adasi is days away from graduating out of the Hapaki Mininan schooling district of Cahokia, of finishing his trade education and completing university studies, and his eagerness is writ large across his every feature. His smile is wide as are his broad, strong shoulders. He is a solidly built young man destined for adventure. The past three years while Niya has been waveringly indecisive about what on the Creator's green earth she should be studying, Adasi has been learning everything he can about trade, economics, and the farthest-reaching markets of Makasing. Niya is sure that he will set off before next winter's end on a journey to who-knows-where: the lands of the Ti'Swaq or the Ezcan Empire or somewhere farther flung than even those places. Time will tell, and Niya looks forward to Adasi's inevitable adventures.

Their friend Nampeyo will have it the hardest, being away from Adasi. They will be a good sport about it, of course, because Nampeyo is nothing if not the consummate friend and unwavering support of them all; the backbone of their friend group. But the two young Cahokians have always been particularly close. Best friends since a young age. Niya and Tusika came along later, after Adasi and Nampeyo had already forged an unbreakable bond between them.

They will miss one another immensely, Niya is

certain. They share the sort of bond that makes goodbyes difficult and greetings sweet.

The path of study that Nampeyo follows is one that has been set for them, it seems, all their life. Always tinkering with this or that, Nampeyo yearns for a different sort of exploration than Adasi: that of technology. Science. And their passion for discovery has always been strong, uniquely guided by Nampeyo's own spirituality and deep connection to the earth.

Adasi is going to discover new lands, have incredible adventures. Nampeyo is going to change the world, right here from their backyard. Her friends are going to move mountains and tame wild rivers, unlock the secrets of the Adanadi and create things altogether new and previously unimaginable.

Niya will find her own way. In her own time. But time feels remarkably short. And while this may not truly be the case, Niya feels herself resenting its inevitable passing.

Perhaps time wouldn't be so scary if she knew what in the Creator's name she should be doing—next week, next month, next year!

Adasi tugs on the end of one of Niya's long braids, the gesture one of brotherly affection. Nampeyo extends a hand for a quick fingertip shake of greeting. The three friends' movements are practiced, easy. Niya brushes the dark dirt from where it is pressed into her knees. It has left damp stains of earth on her dusky skin. She straightens herself, tugging her black shorts down from where they've ridden up a bit and brushing her wristband across the line of sweat that has formed on her forehead. On her other wrist, she adjusts her pale, translucent green niisi so that she can better see its face in the bright afternoon sun.

"You two ready for tonight?" she asks.

"Hey, girlie!" Adasi exclaims, his mouth wide and teeth sparkling in the early afternoon sun. "You know we are. Right, 'Peyo?"

"Always prepared, of course. I anticipate that Niya and Tusika will not achieve an ideal amount of rest before tomorrow's ceremony. What do you think?"

"Oh, ho ho," Adasi throws his head back and laughs—a bark-like sound followed by a series of short coyote-yips. "*That* is a bet I would hate to take. I think any of us will be lucky to get rest of any kind tonight, eh, cousin?" Nampeyo is not his blood relation, but this is a common phrase of endearment and easy affection between their friends and many others besides.

"Excuse me, but I'll ask you not to take bets—either for or against us. Not tonight, at least." Niya pauses, wrinkling her nose up as she thoughtfully frowns. "Or tomorrow, come to think of it. There's enough pressure as is. Me and Tusika, we don't need you goofs wagering on who will have an allergic reaction to the Adanadi solution or, I don't know, trip and fall in front of Kaatii Patak!"

The friends share grins, their feet shuffling in the lush grass just outside the soil pod. Niya's well-worn moccasins point slightly inward, "pigeon-toed", the stance an inheritance from her noosoo—her father— and the footwear a gift from her niisi. Adasi wears a sturdy grayish boot on his left foot, the right foot having no need—he lost his left leg in a childhood accident. The prosthetic he wears now is merely his most recent, as the Cahokian healthcare system has ensured a replacement every few years—as he has grown and as the technology has advanced. Nampeyo's feet are covered in a biologically-replicated, gat-printed, second skin of a sort, dyed a bright and exuberant orange to match the streaks of color in their hair that they are sporting this week. The material on Nampeyo's feet is preferred by their instructor—low-impact, quiet, and repellant to dirt and other microbes that could be carried into their laboratory.

"Eh, you're not worried about tomorrow are you, cuz?"

Adasi's tone is playful yet sincere, a balance he has always struck easily. That's his Path of Coyote at work, and his own natural tendency towards camaraderie and empathy.

"Wouldn't I be just a little crazy to *not* be worried at all?" Niya shoots back, suddenly imagining the looks on the faces of her family and friends if she comes out of the Adanadi ceremony tomorrow with a bloodshot eye and swollen face.

Nampeyo clasps her shoulder in their hand, their slender fingers strong. "It doesn't even hurt, little sister," they say, this term, like "cousin," not really an indicator of a familial blood relation but more a familiar term of endearment. In fact, Nampeyo's ancestors come from the opposite coast as Niya's. Adasi and Nampeyo both hail from big families whereas Niya is an only child. This had led to them adopting her as their kid sister a long time ago. "And the healers will have antihistamines on hand, should you experience a reaction."

"Hey, but don't I know that already?" Niya chides in return. She nudges Nampeyo slightly with her hip, chuckling as she does so at their pragmatic advice. Their own Path—Falcon—is apparent. Whereas Adasi has a penchant for levity and jokes, Nampeyo tends to be sharp-eyed and to the point.

"You'll probably just want to sleep after," Adasi offers with a shrug.

"Perhaps it also helps to remember that only one in five who take the Adanadi develop an Ability, but we all gain a connection to our Path animal." Nampeyo lifts one hand into the air, an eyebrow tilting upwards as well, as if to say: *And isn't that nice!*

Niya puts on an expression of faux-thoughtfulness. "Hmm...I'd like those odds if my own family hasn't gone without an Ability in seven straight generations. One in five sounds reasonable, but it seems to not apply to the Suwatts."

"Oh, what's the problem, cuz—afraid to join the no-Ability crew? It'll be fun, we'll get matching tattoos and have secret meetings where Tusika isn't invited."

Adasi's comments are kind-spirited, having received only a Path connection from his own Adanadi ceremony. No extra Ability imparted. But Adasi was born to scout and travel and adventure, Ability or no. They all know it. When his two-week period after his Adanadi ceremony had come and gone, no Ability having been made manifest, it was no great thing, not to Adasi.

Niya moves across the underside of the covered pavilion to gather her things. "Don't poke fun at Tusika. She can't help her family's good fortune, can she?"

"Seven generations strong," Adasi says, pointing out the fact that they all know—whereas the Suwatts have gone seven generations without an Ability from the Adanadi, Tusika's family has a long line of gifted firstborn children, all having received Abilities going back seven generations into the past.

"The Pataks are blessed." Niya laughs, humbled. "However it is that the Adanadi works, it is not destined to be so for me." She stands up straight, the strap of her pack now slung across her chest. "Believe me, my friends, I have peace for tomorrow and the weeks after. I will not be losing any sleep over what will or won't be."

The three friends go their separate ways after affirming their previously made plans for the night. As she walks toward the docks, Niya knows that this last confession has not been her most honest.

She knows the likelihood of receiving an Ability is low. But how she wishes she might receive one—how she longs for anything that might make her decisions about the future easier.

Perhaps she could receive Gecko's Heart and become a trail runner, delivering messages from one corner of Makasing to another. Or Mender's Touch which would make her a remarkable healer, in conjunction with her already half-decent herbalism skills. Something totally unexpected for someone of her shorter stature might be Power of the Bear—she could get into

Tawaraton or even Gatchoo! Either school would leave her parents beaming.

Pah, Niya thinks to herself. *Best to leave that sort of daydreaming to Tusika.* The name flooded her heart with warmth, and a sort of slow-burning excitement.

It is easy to remember that seven generations of her family have gone without an Ability while seven generations of Tusika's have been blessed: it is right there, everytime she says her best friend's name: Tusika, sweet and a little bitter on her tongue.

In the common tongue of the land of Makasing, Kag Chahi, Tusika means *eight*. Tusika will be the eighth generation of the Patak family to take the Adanadi, and Niya is sure that her friend will be the eighth generation in their long, unbroken line to receive an Ability.

The rational side of Niya's brain tells her that the lack of Abilities in the Suwatt family is no failing on her part, or her parents, or their parents before them. But another thought echoes right behind that one, as it always does.

What if I am different? Niya wonders. *What if this time, the Adanadi chooses me?*

"Ahh..." Niya scoffs under her breath to herself. "Silliness and nonsense."

And yet, she does wonder.

The Adanadi had changed the world after the Awis, that long ago time when the world had been swept into darkness, humanity dragged right to the brink of extinction. Seven-hundred and ten years ago, now, the stories say that hope, for a time, had been all but lost. Fires and quakes and flooding alike. The Creator, forsaking the people of Makasing—and, perhaps, the world beyond, though none alive now knows the truth of what lies beyond the sea. But then something peculiar sprang up in the aftermath: a curious, purple light, a mesmerizing substance. In the leaves of plants, the fur of animals; nature, touched by the divine.

It had taken time, as all advancements do, but great minds had come to cultivate, harvest, concentrate, and apply the substance. It became known as the Adanadi, perhaps the ultimate sign that the great Creator had not abandoned them in the wake of the Awis after all. And all around, the reminders of the dark but also the light served to cultivate gratitude, and thoughts of the future. How much brighter could it be? And how dark...

Niya makes her way to the water's edge on the western bank of the island she is currently on. Hapaki Mininan is but one small piece of the Cahokian landscape. Here, much like the entirety of the great city, the evidence of the Adanadi makes itself known.

The trees lining the water's edge are patchily luminescent, even in the bright afternoon sun. Their leaves are coated in a fine filigree of violet-streaked patterns amongst their own more common greenery. Two turtledoves take flight from a nearby garden, and Niya watches as they twist and turn around one another, tumbling gracefully and gleefully through the air; their purple-tipped wings tossing back the sunlight that hits them, returning it ever so slightly altered before it dissipates into nothing.

The world of humans, too, is suffused with the gentle touch and inevitable influence of the Adanadi. The lights along the path are powered by technology wrought from its study. The tall buildings along the opposite shore are held aloft by its power. Adasi's prosthetic. Nampeyo's feet coverings.

Niya's inevitable disappointment.

Alas, Niya knows that she is allowing herself to mentally indulge in an unattractive streak of pessimism. She will focus on what she *can* control, and that will be enough. Whatever the Adanadi brings, she decides, it cannot possibly help her fix this restless, out-of-sorts feeling regarding the trajectory of her life. Only she can do that.

She ruminates on Nampeyo's comment from before. *We all gain a connection to our Path animal.*

And wouldn't that be a nice thought, Niya thinks, *if I had chosen one yet!*

Walking along a smoothly paved pathway at the water's edge, Niya approaches a set of docks. There are many in this area, meant to offer quick ease of access from the schooling district to other parts of Cahokia via the Mizizibi's water ways. Niya has a small canoe tied up alongside others in a slip, and her fingers expertly work the knots loose that she had tied that morning. Nearly every school-age child of Cahokia crosses the narrow river to get to Hapaki Mininan on days of learning in one form or another—personal canoes, multi-person skimmers for some of the older students, or even scheduled trips on large, specialized skimmers to get youngsters across at the start and end of days.

Niya has been canoeing since she was a small girl, sitting between her noosoo's legs while he taught her how to navigate waterways large and small, overcome a spill, avoid obstacles in her path. Nampeyo had completed a build of their own personal skimmer a few months ago, and it is big enough to carry all four of them across the short distance to the university's shores—but Niya only accepts rides when the weather is poor, for she loves to sit low in the water, powering her wooden and delicately green-painted vessel with her own movements.

With a strong push and the agile motions of climbing into the canoe, Niya is off. She extracts her paddle and begins to cut a deft path through the river's currents. She breathes deeply, savoring the fresh air as it fills her lungs and the freedom that comes from traversing the great waters beneath her.

As she is navigating between two islands, she passes beneath a series of bridged walkways. The fine hairs at the back of her neck start to prickle in anticipation. She can't be quite certain, must wait a moment longer; she won't know for sure until—

"Niyaaaa!"

A figure lands in Niya's canoe, having jumped from one of the walkways overhead, a height of at least two men. Niya gives a mockingly startled shake and yelps. Clutching the side of her face with one hand and her paddle with the other, she steadies the canoe. It helps, of course, that the canoe possesses a magnetic system, a small piece of yutsu tech, that prevents the sides from dipping below the water. It had been a gift from her noosoo at the last Winter Rebirth.

"Tusika, you sly creature," Niya chides with a click of her tongue. "You really scared me this time."

Niya's best friend leans eagerly forward, face flushed from the run to the canoe, balanced with a superior sure-footedness, as she asks, "Did I really?!"

Face absolutely straight, Niya delivers the truth drily. "Certainly not. It's been at least three full moons since you managed to give me even the slightest surprise. Are you losing your touch?"

There is a moment of pause, with hardly a sound but the susurrus of the water against the bow of the canoe, and then the two young women burst into shared laughter.

This is a game they play. Tusika is excellent at it, truly she is—but no one is more perceptive, more in-tune with her surroundings, than Niya. It had been a very long time indeed since she had been successfully caught off-guard by anyone, even cunning Tusika.

"I'm determined," Tusika counters with a grin. "You know me better than anyone, but I know you the same. I'll just have to be even more agile next time, to sneak up on you properly." She lowers herself into a crouched position, sitting on bent toes with her calves pressed up beneath her—like a bow ready to spring at a moment's notice. "Now that I have found you, answer me this: how much trouble are we going to get up to tonight?"

Tusika has a smile that Niya believes she could never tire of. Her cheekbones are gloriously appled, rosy and sweet—sweeter than that mischievous glint in her eyes, that is for certain. Niya's own cheeks possess little of Tusika's volume, are instead sharp, smooth structures more fitting for thoughtful contemplation than merry-making, surely.

Struck by the comparison, Niya makes another, and another, and another.

Tusika's front two teeth have the slightest gap between them; Niya's overlap a tiny bit. Tusika's skin is the dark red color of rust, like a cliff face in the setting sun; Niya's skin is lighter, like the shoal rock beach of a lakeshore with the winter sky cast down upon it. Besides her plump cheeks, Tusika is all straight lines and narrow hips and long, lean features, her chin coming to a point and her nose more narrow; Niya is curves and wide hips, fat-dimpled skin and stretch marks, and short but strong limbs.

And in a lightning-fast moment, Niya comes to a conclusion that she is certain she must have come to many times before: nearly everything about the two of them exists as a study in opposites. No one would ever mistake them for relations.

That's the thing about opposites: one cannot exist as it does without the other. Adasi and Nampeyo are cut from the same cloth, but Niya and Tusika are two different halves of a walnut.

"Tusika, getting into trouble is your standard, not mine."

"But getting me out of trouble is yours!"

Niya chuckles, the sound sweet and easy, unlike her inner feelings of today. "I will not argue with that."

Tusika smiles that smile of hers, leaning towards Niya from the seat she's taken in the front of the canoe. They communicate that way, sometimes—with little more than a smile, a glance, a touch of fingertips against a wrist or a held breath shifting the air between them. It's natural, the way they interact. Like the way the far-away lights in the heavens of the night sky shift in ever-changing but predictable patterns.

It has not always been this way. Oh, the girls have known each other their whole lives long—born nearly side by side in the same hospital, their manas—their mothers—found their close births particularly auspicious. For much of their lives, they were forced together in various ways: playing on the same teams, sharing classrooms and teachers, shadowing one another's parents. Tusika learned the fruits of manual labor and the value of a gentle touch in the Suwatt fields, and Niya saw firsthand the power behind the right word spoken at the right time, the intensity of a mere look, by watching Tusika's mana at work as a member of the Council of Twelve.

But no river is perfectly smooth. And sometimes unseen obstacles make for rough waters.

In their earliest years, there always seemed to be a sense of urgent competition between Niya Suwatt and Tusika Patak. As if they could not peacefully coexist—as if they had been born so close together for no other reason than to antagonize one another. For their manas in particular—Ahyoka Suwatt and Kaatii Patak—it was reason enough for celebration when finally the tides turned and the two girls began to see one another less as adversaries and more as...

Well, as friends.

As Tusika chatters about her afternoon, Niya paddles them along, watching the sunlight play across Tusika's face, and *feels*. Only in the past few years have the now seventeen-year-olds begun to operate under the understanding that perhaps they are better off together than they are alone. That the things that made them clash in the past—like Tusika's penchant for trouble and Niya's for escape, or Niya's fanciful thoughts of the *what ifs* in life versus Tusika's strongly grounded sense of reality—are, in actuality, precisely the things that make them so well suited for another, once the irritation stopped and the urge to connect surged..

As friends.

The word doesn't quite feel right to Niya, but neither is it wrong. Tusika is her best friend, beyond a shadow of a doubt. But the intensity of her feelings for the other girl go beyond admiration, loyalty, or friendship. Tusika is a natural born leader, and though Niya is not necessarily built to follow blindly, she believes she could all too easily—if Tusika were the one leading the way.

Niya brings them swiftly to the eastern bank of the Mizizibi, where a long row of slips for community use makes for a quick place to dock. While she is moving the canoe carefully into place, Tusika stands, jumping up with tow rope in hand as they reach a free space. Pulling them in the rest of the way, she smoothly and securely loops the rope into place before extending her hand. Niya takes it gladly, hoisting herself up onto the dock to stand next to her friend.

"What is the name of the place we are going tonight?" Niya asks.

"Ah, I cannot recall. I can pick it out on a map though, so we'll get there."

"Eventually," Niya jokes.

"And a rowdy time we'll have on the way, eh?"

"Another new place," Niya clicks her tongue against the backs of her teeth. "You would think by now that we have visited them all—every single club in the city, let alone our district."

"New places to explore every day!" Tusika crows, spreading her arms wide. "I love that, don't you?"

Her friend really does love the city of Cahokia, Niya knows that with great certainty. It isn't merely the influence of Tusika's politically-minded mana speaking—or even Tusika's own political aspirations. But sometimes Niya wonders exactly what it is that Tusika loves more about Cahokia: the city itself, or the power it promises.

"I love exploring with *you*," Niya replies, bumping her round hip against her friend's thinner body.

Tusika laughs. "Our last night before the Adanadi." They move through the people who share the path with them, walking the busy streets of the Mataawi District. Here, politicians and artisans alike mingle, the latter making good nizi off of the former as they bustle from this meeting place to that. There is clear evidence of more lavish living in Mataawi than some of the other Cahokian districts—and more lavish spending, based on the wares, foods, and tech on display around them.

The smells alone are nearly mouth-wateringly distracting—but the girls have had years of practice walking these streets, smelling and tasting its delights, and their sights are set elsewhere.

When Tusika continues again, her tone is much quieter now, less exuberant. The voices of merchants nearly drown her out. "I could hardly concentrate on my school work today. The only thing that got me through it was knowing that if I was not at university, I would be helping my parents with preparations for tomorrow."

The two friends exchange a very pointed look before grinning wryly at one another again. The Pataks can be overbearing at their best and downright insufferable at their worst.

"I'm sure your parents are showing as much enthusiasm for this as for anything else their first-born does," Niya offers with a smirk.

"And that, my dearest friend, is exactly the problem. The Patak family does not know how to do things small. Everything is big and shiny and gratuitous. It must be memorable and the talk of all in attendance for months and, and, and...! You know?"

Niya knows, Niya has always known. Tusika's parents hold positions of great prestige in the Cahokian social echelon. Her mana is a member of the Council of Twelve—the reigning political body of Cahokian life and the highest-powered members of society in this city that has become the cultural epicenter of all of Makasing, like the reigning eagle over all the other birds of the sky. And her noosoo, Thakashan Patak, is an engineer of renown, known for crafting some of the most amazing and landscape-altering pieces of technology and architecture in the past two decades—in this political district in particular, the elder Patak has erected a particular set of skyhigh walkways between three centers of the Cahokian government that travelers from far and wide visit for the experience they offer of standing amongst the clouds.

Though Tusika bemoans her parents' anticipation of the approaching ceremony, Niya knows that not all of the young woman's complaints are grounded in truth. Because the fact of the matter is that Tusika wants all of those things, too—the glamor and prestige, to be the talk of the town, to be known. She simply wants all of that out from under the shadow of her parents' legacies. To be a wonder of her own volition.

Niya, on the other hand, has no interest in being in the spotlight. And while she does not spurn the idea of taking over the Suwatt agricultural business in the future, neither does she relish the idea.

With a nod, Niya placates her friend. "I wish we could be together the entire day, not just for the ceremony and the celebrations after."

Tusika dramatically gasps. "Niya! No, Love. I would not wish that on my worst enemy, and you are my best friend of friends! I can only imagine that the time with your family beforehand will be so much more heartfelt and personal than mine. I have jealousy in my heart, I will admit that." She says this last line with a smile and a return bump of her hip against Niya's. "But we're lucky, aren't we? It's rare to be able to have a dual Adanadi ceremony. Can you imagine—if we were going through it even a few years ago, we would have made each other perfectly miserable, and on such an important day, too."

"Yes, good thing you grew up and saw the light—and how wonderful I am."

"Please, I saw no such thing. Only that befriending you instead of fighting you would make you more tolerable. And I was right!"

Niya laughs loudly at Tusika's selective memory. "Funny how quickly you seem to misremember the past. I think it was *me* who called for a truce, wasn't it?"

"Hmm," Tusika sarcastically strokes her chin as if thinking hard. "But *I* was the one who got you out to your first dance club. Do you remember that?"

Smiling down at her own feet, Niya nods. "Of course I do." And how could she forget? That night under the lights, with the music and the dance and the heat. She had seen a carefree Tusika, a Tusika whose smile was her own and not for those around her. Niya had fallen in love a little bit, then—or perhaps recognized a long buried feeling for what it truly was. "Let's call us even then."

"Oh, okay," Tusika grins. "I'm just glad for tomorrow. For us."

"A dual Adanadi ceremony. It will be special indeed. And you can get through half a day of Patak formalities for that, yeah?"

"Yeah," Tusika agrees, her eyes bright and shining, her voice almost breathless.

They've reached the entrance to the yutsu train station. Niya reaches out and gives Tusika's hand a reassuring squeeze before turning to head toward the twisting slope of a descent down to the yutsu platforms below, but Tusika begs off.

"Go on without me," she says, and Niya turns back. "I have an errand to run."

"Ah. Would you like me to come with you?"

A sly look snaps into place on Tusika's face. "You can't. It's a surprise."

"A surprise? Hmm..." Niya wonders, pursing her lips and narrowing her eyes. Then she widens them in very real delight. "Is it for me?"

"You could say that."

"Will I like it?"

That sly look morphs into something different—something confident and powerful that leaves Niya feeling eager for the night ahead.

Tusika replies, "I think you will, Kakooni. I think you will."

They part ways, Niya's cheeks warm. Tusika has that effect on her. Calling her by her nickname—Kakooni, *pumpkin*—doesn't help one bit.

There are other things to think of as Niya stands on the yutsu platform, awaiting the smooth, super-fast ride that will take her around the district and to her home. Many other things, important things: what the night ahead holds, the needs and expectations of her own family for tomorrow, the Adanadi itself and the Path Niya must decide upon in less than a day...

Instead, she finds it difficult to think about anything besides how clear Tusika's path through life appears. And how muddled her own has felt for some time. And the lingering feeling where Tusika's hip had touched her own. This thought she shook off as quickly as she could.

But things will work out. Niya believes this.

By the grace of the Creator, if by no other way.

PIT

The yutsu trains emit a low, pulsing thrum through the air, so thick and visceral that Niya can practically feel it in her bones as she makes it to the platform. She's just missed a south-bound train, but another will be by momentarily. The yutsu stations are home to the highly regular loop of the levitating trains that circulate the city of Cahokia. The fastest way to get from one end of the sprawling city to the other, to traverse its five-hundred square-mile breadth, is by the yutsu rail system.

Yutsu technology is one of the major scientific boons of the Adanadi. The discovery had been made that tissues rich in the purple glow of the Adanadi, when exposed to focused electromagnetic energy, gain the near-miraculous ability of levitation. This technology opened up the world of Makasing in uncountable ways. Personal transportation is more accessible than ever before, and massive undertakings like the train Niya steps onto make travel quick and easy, with minimal impact on the environment around them all. Moving walkways, accessibility devices and more are common applications of the yutsu tech.

At this moment, Niya is mostly grateful that she doesn't have to navigate the traffic and neighborhoods of miles and miles of Cahokia to reach her home. After a long day of university studies, the train affords a few sweet minutes of respite. Niya presses her forehead to the panoramic window and watches the terrain blur by. Her eyes slide shut, and just as she is slipping into daydreams about the next day's ceremony—

Her niisi lets off a gentle tri-tone ping, the device buzzing at her wrist.

Niya glances down at the tiny computer that so many Cahokians sport. Recognizing the attention of her eyesight, the device projects into the air above its surface a message from her mana.

[Mana] Have you passed through the market yet?

With a swipe and pinch of her fingers, Niya brings up a syllabary map and types out her response in mid-air. Once she finishes punching the syllables into place, she double-taps the message and it fades in a conical spiral downwards, back into the niisi's facework, disappearing. The trouble with her mana's message is that, if Niya had received it but five minutes earlier, she could have gotten whatever was needed. Her home district's market has one of the most conveniently situated yutsu train stations to the schooling islands, but its selection is mediocre at best.

[Niya] Left Mechim ga Wayoopike already.

Even as she sends the message, Niya can practically hear the regret in her mana's sigh.

As surely as the moon pulls on tidal waters, Niya's mana replies.

[Mana] Ahh, my girl. I would have preferred Eeko goods as is.

[Niya] I can ride around to that stop if you like, Mana.

[Mana] No no, come home, yes?

[Niya] Home soon.

Eeko goods are largely tech-based. What could her mana be wanting from there? Something for tomorrow's celebration? Niya will find out soon enough. She just hopes that her mana does not need her late into the evening—she and her friends are likely to have a late night, but the sooner they are able to start their merry-making, the sooner this antsy feeling inside Niya's chest can be squashed, ignored, until the time comes for it to truly matter.

She crosses her arms and looks back out the window once more.

A majority of the train's track takes it through underground tunnels, a massive loop beneath the city of Cahokia. But occasionally it does go above ground. Niya would know this path with or without the visual cues, the familiar landmarks.

The train moves south for several miles and then turns east, passing beneath many of the buildings of the outer ring of the Mataawi district. The tunnels steer clear of a majority of the district's more important buildings—like the public aid house, the hanayan, and others. Instead, much of the ride traverses the outskirts of the more populated areas, cruising along beneath farmlands and mounds and the woven heart of nature that still beats throughout the city.

Several stops are made along the way, every mile or two, and primarily at sports stadiums, or markets, or other places meant for public gatherings. When the train turns north again, the shift in the rails is subtle, but Niya has taken this journey so many times that she feels it in her bones. Home approaches, marked by the train station for the Maaitu'Tuasu Plaza—one of the proudest new public works for Cahokians. Tusika's mana and especially her noosoo both like to lay claim to the reconstruction efforts with only the slightest prompting—and sometimes without even that.

The plaza is beautiful indeed, a sight to behold for anyone emerging back aboveground from the yutsu station—staircases gleaming purple and brilliant swirls of blue worked into the stone now overlaid with glowing orange from the last shreds of daylight, the edges of the plaza rising impressively towards the sky, drawing the eye to the stars. The sun is low on the horizon at Niya's back as she turns east. The sounds of the district are quieter here, at this time of day. There is no great ceremony happening at the plaza or sporting event or any sort of celebration for the time being. Only people, going about their daily routines. And less of a crushing populace here on the far eastern side of the district where the Council of Twelve resides. Simple sounds of light footsteps and chattering voices, shop windows being shut for the day, children playing in the distance. And all of that, silhouetted by the great, smooth stone walls of the plaza, which has been suffused with many years of use for protection and warmth since the Awis.

Niya's home is only a few hundred meters from the station, though she has to circumnavigate much of the plaza to get there—better to walk around the plaza itself than to have to endure the construction that went on for two solid years before the thing was finished. "Pah!" Niya makes a quiet noise beneath her breath as she remembers the nuisance. She smiles at herself once she realizes she has done this, thinking that it is precisely what her late daadoo—her grandfather—would have done.

He did not live long enough to see her take the Adanadi, to become the woman he always thought she could be. But Niya will make him proud regardless, right? He's watching, from the great Beyond, she is quite certain. And the rest of her family will fill up the empty space he left behind over a year ago, swelling with pride and duty as the ceremony approaches.

Even before Niya gets to the entrance of the Suwatt family home, she can tell that she is in for a restless few hours from the furniture and normal daily implements jumbled outside the door, moved temporarily to make way for celebratory preparations. She flinches a bit, knowing that she and her friends are planning a splendid and spectacular night, that they will probably be out *beyond* late—and knowing at the same time that her presence tomorrow, likely bright and gods-forsakenly early, is not only expected but requisite. And this evening? Surely a great deal of planning, prepping, cleaning, cooking, and more—the Suwatt household feels abuzz from a distance, how must it feel inside?

Standing before her own front door, Niya steels herself. Her mana, exuberant and energetic on any given day, when on a mission is a force not to be taken lightly. And it is no small thing for your only child to be taking the Adanadi, to be crossing that threshold from youth into adulthood. It deserves to be celebrated with all the energy and vigor her mana could muster. Niya puts on a smile and pretends like she isn't still totally undecided about her Path choice.

Niya believes her parents and her living grandparents

might deny it if hard-pressed, but she knows it to be true: they hold out hope. They hold out hope that Niya, for the first time in so many generations, will be a Suwatt with an Ability, that the Adanadi will bless her with a special gift beyond her chosen Path.

It is no small responsibility, that of carrying an entire family's hope.

Niya always reasoned, often to convince herself as anyone else: Even if she gets an Ability, what will it change? Her parents are well-known farmers, and her maternal niisi is a skilled herbalist. On her noosoo's side, her niisi is a teacher and her daadoo, a long-ago retired trader. They live a comfortable life, are well taken care of by the society that they are so integrally a part of.

But to have an Ability *would* be something special.

"No pressure," Niya says to herself, breathing in, holding it, then releasing it on a long exhalation.

Just as she reaches forward to press open the front door, it swings outward. She senses the motion just before it reverses its expected course, jumping out of the way.

"Child!" Niya's niisi—her grandmother—exclaims.

"Why are you yelling at me?!" Niya laughs, moving to step inside, wrapping the elderly woman in a side hug as she passes her. "You are the one who almost hit *me* with the door."

"Ah, you!" her niisi laughs, eyes crinkling up from the smile that shifts the muscles and skin of her entire face, from the tip of her chin to the line of hair atop her forehead. "I couldn't hit you with the door if I tried. Pah!"

"And she has tried, hasn't she?" Niya's mana says, stepping into view. "That strength, she gets it from her Path, you know." Niya swallows hard at the not-so-subtle implication.

The two women, though separated by twenty-five years, strike a stunning resemblance. Niya knows that her own high cheekbones and sharp facial features are reflected in front of her, that here stand three generations of serious faces. The three of them also stand at an almost uncannily identical height.

Niya's mana, Ahyoka, moves to cup her face, patting it thrice with her warm hands. Dark brown eyes catch Niya's own, and Niya thinks she can almost see the source of the earth's power growing there, in the deep. Her mana is a strong woman, and immovable. Proud. Loving. And warm.

And their resemblance does not reside only in their physical looks. When each of them took the Adanadi, the tissue used in their ceremonies was that of Eagle. While neither of them gained an Ability from the process, Niya recognizes a sharp, kindred look in their respective gazes. Something wise and best not crossed.

As if she would ever consider such a foolish notion.

"Manaaaa," Niya says, drawing out the second syllable, a good-natured smile on her lips as she playfully rolls her eyes. "I'm sorry I couldn't get to the market for you."

"Well, we do what we can with what we have."

Even as she speaks, Niya's mana is moving back around the corner and out of sight, the indigo fringes of her skirts swishing just behind her. Her niisi shakes her head fondly before producing a rounded cornmeal cookie topped with a touch of maple syrup from somewhere in her own skirts. She uses both of her hands to place it delicately in one of Niya's before shuffling after her daughter, mumbling loudly enough that Niya can hear her perfectly.

"As if what we have isn't plenty for us and all the other kiddos taking the Adanadi for the next month!"

Depositing her bag near the front door, Niya follows, the sweet falling apart deliciously in her mouth. Keeping her mouth closed in order to enjoy the nutty and sweet aromatic flavors is the only thing keeping her from snorting with laughter at her niisi.

Their home is much like any other Cahokian home. Simple, comfortable, and unique to the individual family who lives within its walls. There is a small walkway from the front door that leads around a corner to the more open and airy primary space for gathering. When Niya follows in her niisi's and mana's steps, she sees exactly what they have been up to all day.

Since Niya left for university that morning, the entire space has been transformed. There are purple streamers, purple flowers, purple ornaments dangling from every fixture and random spots along the ceiling. And, last but certainly not least, wafer-thin purple paper covering all the gaps in the mound structure, causing the entire place to be cast in a violet hue where the external light passes through. There is even a purple *smell* to the place—Niya's eyes cut across to the table where a bouquet of full-stemmed lavender sits, a small dish with some of the pressed leaves next to it.

Niya can't help herself. Her home had never looked like this in all her seventeen years. She finally bursts out into laughter.

"My family—you have truly outdone yourselves, haven't you?"

Ahyoka is standing in the middle of the living space, pride writ large across her face. Niya can smell more baked goods and freshly chopped vegetables, simmering stews, and slow-cooked meats.

"Your only child takes the Adanadi once, Love. Only once."

Niya's lips curve upward in a soft smile as she walks towards her mana. They embrace in a gentle hug, and Niya basks in the warmth, the safety, the familiarity of the moment.

Still hugging, Niya whispers, "Is that roast bison tenderloin that I smell?"

"Ah," Ahyoka breathes, pulling back to swat at her daughter's shoulder. "Go on," she says, by way of inviting Niya to continue in her excitement.

"Everything looks absolutely wonderful. What could you possibly need from Eeko?"

Her mana begins bustling around again, hanging—somehow, someway—even more decorations. Her niisi is seasoning a dish in the cooking area not far from the table.

"A few weeks ago I passed a storefront where they

had special Adanadi-themed bowls and cups—"

"Oh, mana, no."

"—but I realize that would be an unbefitting extravagance. Your having already departed the market made that clear."

Niya chuckles at her mana's eagerness. "Where are my noosoo and his parents?" she asks, inquiring as to the whereabouts of her noosoo, her daadoo, and her other niisi.

"Wrapping up with the latest offerings for the next big market day. Don't you worry, tomorrow will be distraction-free, only about you."

A blush creeps up Niya's neck, warming its way to her cheeks. "You know me well enough to know that is not what I want. The less attention, the better."

Her mana scoffs, lifting three fingers into the air. "The day of the Adanadi, a guarantee," she says, ticking one finger down. "A binding ceremony, if such a day is meant to be," she continues, ticking off another finger in recognition of the ceremony wherein two or more people bind themselves together as one unit. Ahyoka gestures with the final finger, saying, "New life, if the Creator so blesses it upon you. These three days are the most important. Any reason to celebrate is worth our time and effort, yes?"

Niya nods in agreement, not merely appeasing her mana, she makes an effort to express her appreciation for the older woman's sincerity.

"You're right, mana. It will be a wonderful celebration."

"Hmm," Ahyoka gives a satisfied hum before going

back to her work. Without looking up, she says, "And the Pataks, you know them—"

"Oh yes."

"—they can't do things small. Kaatii certainly wouldn't let a first-born of a new generation take the Adanadi without a hullabaloo bigger than your daadoo's chunkey tournaments, would she?"

Niya tilts her head thoughtfully, maybe hopefully. "Would you prefer if Tusika and I were to have separate ceremonies?"

Ahyoka stills for a moment before turning her gaze briefly on her daughter. "No, no. It's not that, my love. It's...well, it's more complicated than that. And I think it's wonderful that the two of you are so close, that you will take the Adanadi together. It is a rare, special thing!"

"It is," Niya agrees easily, all too aware that this *rare, special thing* has been planned for years, has been decided down to the last details—time and place and who will be in attendance and what sort of party afterward and on and on—by Kaatii Patak, with Ahyoka Suwatt steadfastly holding her ground wherever she could.

Niya's mana approaches her, pressing those warm, calloused hands against her cheeks once more. "I mean it—I am glad that you and Tusika seem to have really grown close these past years. It means a lot to our family and to the Pataks. So interwoven from birth," she muses, her voice growing quiet and her mind taking her to a faraway place—some place seventeen or so years in the past, Niya speculates. "You girls were tied to one another in a way, and that meant our families were to be the same."

"It's been good for us, hasn't it? The Patak connection...it certainly didn't hurt yours and noosoo's business."

Ahyoka makes a sound in the back of her throat that Niya knows well. She might normally be chastised by it, but she is one sleep from adulthood. She can face down this slight, if imposing, woman who bore her, can't she?

"One might say that the Pataks lifted the Suwatts up, but one might also say that the Suwatts were rising on their own. Pah! An easy lift, if a lift at all." Ahyoka shakes a finger in Niya's face, and Niya rolls her lips to keep from smiling, funny as she finds her mana's light chastisement. "One might just say that it is the *Suwatts* who have helped the *Pataks* in this city—we have certainly made them more relatable!"

"You're right, you're right," Niya concedes, moving to hold her mana's hands in her own. "I meant no offense."

Ahyoka playfully shakes her hands loose before shooing Niya off. "Please, so serious, when there is more work to be done, daughter of mine!"

Niya presses her hands together and then spreads them wide before her. "Please—what can I help with?"

Ahyoka throws her arms up, clapping her hands excitedly above her head. She does a sort of jump followed by a little jig that leaves Niya filled with that simultaneous and odd feeling of affection and embarrassment.

"Follow me!"

Niya spends about two hours helping in the kitchen,

preparing untold servings of appetizers, kneading dough, shelling beans, seasoning, dicing, slicing, and more. She is certain, when her mana finally deems her assistance complete, her hair is as curled and wispy as her diniisi's, working its way from her own long braid. It is with something nearing exhaustion that Niya retreats to her private room, a modest space down a short hallway from the cooking and living areas.

The room that Niya calls her own is much like any other private space of a seventeen-year old Cahokian. It is suffused with the things that make Niya herself, coated in the remnants of a life lived within its walls. There are paintings representing comedians and artists that she loves. A desk down low to the floor where she can sit cross-legged on a cushion—this is where she utilizes the daso connection with her personal home terminal and their home gat to print various new wuyis. She has completed many assignments on that desk over the years. The color palette splashed across the walls, the bed, the three-tiered chest where she stores her clothes, is flush with vibrant blues and rich, dark greens. Splotches and streaks of violet intermingle with the shapes and colors that abound from every surface.

Niya bypasses her desk, beelining straight for her bed. She falls down onto it, sprawling out atop the messy assortment of blankets. Her arms are spread to her sides, and she flexes her tired hands. How do her mana and niisi do it, all that kneading? Their bread is delicious and utterly worthwhile, Niya knows, but it simply must be the inner and outer-strength alike of Eagle.

She groans quietly into the silence of her room. Of all the animals across Makasing, she must choose *one*. The memory of the choice she must make slammed back into her. A singular decision, made once and forever. Somehow, Niya dodged any talk of her choice—or lack thereof—during their preparation session this evening, but Niya has no doubt that if she had remained but a moment longer, she might have run out of subtle diversions.

There has been much fervent discussion about this within the Suwatt household the past fortnight and more. The choice of a Path animal is no small thing. Often one's family will weigh in, with influence and expectations based on one's tribe, their legends and heroes, epic tales of fortune and misfortune alike.

Any animal with concentrated Adanadi in the tissues of their body can be used for the ceremony. But trends have emerged over time, some animals much more frequently utilized than others. And study has provided many an insight into how the Path animal influences and alters the human's body, mind, and spirit after.

In Niya's family, her mana and diniisi both chose Eagle; her mana's late noosoo had chosen Bison, and there was something particularly harmonious about their marriage. Her mana likes to say it was because her noosoo's Bison disposition provided her own mana with a solid foundation on which to perch. On Niya's noosoo's side, both he and his mana are Beaver whereas his noosoo is Fox. Her noosoo's noosoo, even in his elder years, has always been tricksy and fleet of foot, whereas her noosoo's mana doesn't miss a trick, however clever.

Each of them has a strong connection with their Path. The Adanadi grounds its taker, almost like a spiritual touchstone that belongs to that person alone—but still serves as a shared social experience across all of Makasing.

Much has been said about Niya's inevitable and fast-approaching choice. Will she follow the Eagle like the matriarchs in her family? Or will she choose Beaver, and truly be her noosoo's daughter?

Or might she choose something else altogether? Something different, something unexpected...

Niya mops her hands over her sweat-sticky face, her hands smelling of squash and earth. She has never wanted to do the unexpected thing, has never been the daughter intent upon causing her family any sort of grief relating to the unknown of last second choices. But she has learned, over the years, that she often does the unexpected thing regardless—changing university course time and time again, or deciding with her best friend to undergo physio-locks so that they can take the Adanadi together.

What is more unexpected than still not knowing which animal's Path she will follow the very night before the Adanadi ceremony? Her friends find her charming. Her family wishes more sensibility upon her. And Niya? Well. Niya would like at least one thing in her life to feel set, decided, resolute.

Really, the Adanadi ceremony is so rote nowadays, so simple in the grand scheme of things, that making a choice of Path can happen at the very last minute and still go off successfully. Does Niya want to be so uncertain at the final hour? Of course not. But she has been hoping for a sign, an inkling, some clue from the Creator, if They could be so gracious, to help her figure this out!

Niya thinks that it must always have been this way. At least for as long as the Adanadi has been part of the mainstream culture of Makasing. Her parents stress the importance to her because it was stressed to them, and so on.

One thing Niya knows for sure: for all her dodging and fretting over her lack of a decision, her family is markedly less intense about Paths when compared to Tusika's.

For the entirety of the seven generations leading up to Tusika's Adanadi ceremony, the Pataks have chosen the Path of the Deer. Every last one of them—from the most politically irrelevant cousin to the current member of the Council of Twelve, they have shared one singular Path. It is not merely expected that Tusika will be the eighth generation to choose Deer, the anticipation is very real that she will receive an Ability. The greater question is: how rare will her Ability be, how special, how spectacular?

Niya believes that Tusika is meant for something special—and not just because that is what Tusika's family has been drilling into her head pretty much her entire life. Tusika is her best friend and confidante; they have shared everything together in life, and Niya sees what is beneath the surface, in those rare moments when Tusika pulls back the facade, disrupts the projected image. And Niya knows this: her friend is destined for something bigger than even her ambitious mana and driven noosoo have cooked up in their minds and expectations.

The wind shifts outside of Niya's bedroom window, fluttering the curtains. A light rain begins to patter against the roof above and the ground just outside. Niya basks in this moment—that freshness, that wholeness, that smell of disturbed earth and the giving of life. One of her favorite smells in the world.

She inhales deeply and clears her mind. She decides to no longer think of tomorrow, nor of the two-week period after the ceremony wherein she may or may not receive an Ability. Instead, Niya thinks of the press of hands in soil, the touch of cool water to seed, the effortless way the land yields to human influence. Something rises up in her: the taste of freedom. In her mind, her late daadoo speaks to her. Niya's throat tightens a little as, in her mind, she can hear his voice as clearly as she had that last time they'd spoken, before he passed. Can hear the pride in his voice, the catch of emotion there on the tip of his tongue.

No one chooses for you, my girl. The choice is yours and yours alone—and that is what makes it so powerful.

A tear slips from the corner of Niya's eye. Her breathing is deep, even, slow.

And then, she sleeps.

Trees surround Niya in her dream. An endless forest. Fruitful and vibrant, lush and looming with a darkness to one side and an impenetrable light to the other.

Different but alike. Neither welcoming nor repellant. But Niya's heart feels torn in two all the same.

She takes a tentative step forward. But the step feels oddly heavy, like the pull of the earth has been intrinsically altered. When her foot meets ground, she isn't sure that she has gone anywhere at all.

She isn't sure that she hasn't gone—

There is a sound in the brush. A soft rustling. Crunch of dry leaves, snapping of tinder.

Deer? Coyote? Bear?

There is a rustling higher up, up, above her head. A low whistle, a swoop. Wings in the night, in the light.

Eagle? Falcon? Crow?

No, no, something else. Someone else. Unknown, unknowable—yet. Niya's feet lift again, and she feels like flying. She feels like nothing can hold her down, hold her back. Not once she discovers the secret. Not once she partakes of the forest's knowledge.

That pull from the earth, it crawls up her body, starting from her toes. Crawls like gecko's sticky feet, inching along and up and up and over. Inside, too, but that's a different feeling entirely.

And as the earth's pull changes, shifts, becomes Niya's, her heart fills, full to bursting. A cry leaves her lips, complete and wondrous and terrifyingly good.

She crashes back down to earth, and the earth crashes with her.

Flat on her back, she looks up to the sky above her. It is light; it is dark; it is everything and nothing. And alternating between those two states, there are wings.

Swoosh.

A cry.

The creature approaches, ever closer, and closer—

― · · · · ―

Niya wakes to the incessant chiming of her niisi at her wrist.

With a bolt, she sits upright. She curses under her breath as her fingers swipe at the incoming call, pulling the image up into a three-dimensional projection above the device. From her open window, she can see that dusk has come on while she was napping—which means that she is on the verge of being very late to meet her friends.

Hence the call at her wrist.

She hits a digital button while also jumping out of bed, making a deliberate choice to answer only via voice and not video.

Nampeyo's voice echoes up from her niisi.

"Niya, did your mana forbid you from coming out tonight?"

"Ah ah, no! No, 'Peyo. I'm coming out with you all, of course I am!"

Adasi's voice this time, and it sounds particularly close and clear. Niya can practically picture him pulling Nampeyo's wrist right up to his mouth to speak into it.

"You forget us, cuz?"

Niya is bouncing about her room, grabbing a neatly folded outfit from a shelf. She sorts through her jewelry box, fingering over some half-finished beading projects before selecting what she'll wear tonight. Bounding back over to her bed, Niya nearly trips over some gat projects she had been printing up and assembling. She jumps over them at the last second but has to fall onto her bed in order not to stub her toes.

"Are you okay over there?"

"She forgot us, cuz."

"I didn't forget, I'll be down in two blinks. Bye!"

She hangs up on her friends with a downward swipe towards the niisi's surface.

Then she goes about getting ready for her last night of adolescence before crossing over into adulthood—as quickly as she possibly can.

TAHOOD

If she hadn't foolishly fallen asleep, Niya would've had more time to prepare herself for their night out. As things stand, she thinks she did a fairly decent job—the outfit she's sporting is one of rich and supple leather strips, dyed in alternating sky grays and forest greens, the colors lightening as they move down her body. She feels at home in her skin in this outfit, a perfect way to spend the night. With the little time she had, she kept her makeup simple with iridescent green stripes down her arms, turning into delicate spirals on the backs of her hands. Two squares of black broken into quadrants on each of her cheeks. Golden, beaded earrings hanging from her lobes, just daring to brush against the bare skin of her shoulders. She left her hair simple—she had undone her braid, combed it out a little too quickly, then tied it back with a strip of supple leather at the base of her skull, her long hair falling down, cascading in a straight wave to nearly brush the hem of her skirts.

She kisses her mana goodnight, her noosoo still not yet back from what must have been a very long day of work. With a last call of advice to not wait up for her, Niya laces up her shin-high dark leather moccasins at the door and then departs into the cool air of the encroaching night.

Her friends are not far from her home. She finds them easily, just west of her family's dwelling on the side of one of the nearby mounds that are built to provide warmth in the winter and cool dwelling in the summer months.

As Niya approaches, she first sees Adasi and Nampeyo. Adasi is wearing rugged, handsome dark green pants and a short green vest, his bare chest exposed and painted with multi-colored symbols; the whirling shapes are every shade from splashy yellow and brilliant green to deep indigo and shimmering turquoise. Nampeyo is wearing a long, knotted skirt of deep orange that clashes artistically with their dyed hair; the rest of their body is naked but for the intricate white and sparkling orange designs that they and Adasi must have spent all afternoon painting across their chest and back, arms and face.

When Niya is close, Adasi whistles his admiration. Nampeyo stands with that straight posture of theirs, clapping enthusiastically with a wide smile.

And then the first two open like a door on a hinge, revealing Tusika and allowing the two young women to come face to face.

Niya knows that her eyes light up when she sees her best friend from the way her heart leaps.

Tusika is wearing an outfit the likes of which Niya could not have imagined. Niya can see the infusions of Tusika's personality throughout the piece—from the golden streaks of light that are dancing across its edges as if alive to the finely embroidered lavender-colored petals all down the arms. Skin-tight across her arms and chest, dipping low along the lines of her collarbones. Then down, down, flowing outward. There are tinges of purple glinting throughout the entire outfit, and as Niya gets closer, she can see the finest thread she has perhaps ever seen woven into every bit of it—glowing with a violet intensity, as if infused with the Adanadi itself.

Knowing the Pataks and their penchant for indulgence and splendor, it might just be.

Tusika's pristine eye makeup, and the intricately beaded accessories dangling from her wrists and hooked to several of her fingers complete the outfit. An auspicious blending of the old and the new—a single Second Eye clipped before her left eye which digitally alters the world around her; white makeup on the backs of her eyelids; concentric circles patterned across her hands; feet bare with matching patterns across their tops, but with a protective skin no doubt molded to the palm of her feet for comfort and protection.

Niya is certain that her expression says it all: the dress is stunning, and her best friend is beautiful. She can't wait to see how the garment sways with Tusika's movements. She feels like her heart might kick out of her chest and dance along with them.

"These two," Nampeyo grunts, breaking the moment like they have a thousand times before.

Adasi punches them lightly in the arm by way of agreement, barking out a laugh and then turning it into the sound of a coyote's enthusiastic yips up at the night sky.

"Let's go!"

Nampeyo and Adasi lead the way to the yutsu stop that will take them to the heart of the Mataawi district. Niya isn't sure what type of club they're headed to, but the type of music isn't necessarily the point. Not tonight, when adulthood is so close she can reach out and caress it. It's a feeling of palpable energy and youth and plenty, like nothing can go wrong and anything at all might be possible.

Niya and Tusika bring up the rear, a few feet behind their friends. Niya reaches out, her fingertips dancing along the beautiful, torn edges of Tusika's dress.

"Your errand," Niya asks, "it was this?"

Tusika looks over, her eyes shaded behind the fashionable combination headpiece and second-eye she's sporting. But those accentuated eyes, Niya can see them regardless. Can see them as clear as day.

"It was," Tusika confirms.

"For me?"

A low chuckle reverberates outward from Tusika's chest. She looks up into Niya's eyes through eyelashes that are long, eyes that are hooded—but if they're hiding something, what is it?

"It certainly is not for Adasi, is it?"

Tusika's lips purse in a way that Niya is sure only happens for her. It's not flirtation—no, flirtation happens on its own between the two of them already, naturally enough. It's something else, like a soul-deep contemplation. A ponderance that no one else could possibly hope to explore fully. And when she looks at Niya like this, Niya isn't sure if the ground is preparing to open up, swallow her whole—or if the sky is expectantly waiting on her to take flight.

Niya does not reply, not before Tusika speaks again.

"And you—" she starts, her hand trailing down to grasp Niya's from between them. They continue walking a few steps more, then Tusika is spinning Niya, spinning her as if they're dancing to the silent music of the night. "You look like this even after we wake you up from a nap, hmm?"

But there is a certain sort of musicality to the night around them. The hum of yutsu transports, the swell of the masses around them, no matter the hour. A taste in the air of brewing tea and late night cookfires, the pulsing sounds of different clubs. An automated door hydraulics up to accept a couple into the building within, and the sounds of laughter echo out of the comedy club as the friends pass by.

Niya blushes beneath her makeup, a blush imperfectly concealed by the atmosphere that surrounds them.

"Ah," she says, "how did you know?"

Tusika winks. "I know my Niya."

The clubs are not a habit so much as an occasional, well-anticipated release. A way to explore the boundaries of fashion, technology, music, dance, and more. The quartet of friends go out once or twice a week. Elders like to pretend that the clubs are not for their generation, but Niya knows well that her daadoo and niisi have a favorite location for dancing, for singing, for seeing their friends and acquaintances alike—and many other elders besides. One of the greatest facets of the Cahokian night scene is the diversity, the sheer volume of choices, and the appeal to people of all sorts, all ages.

Before long, they reach the front of an unobtrusive building not far from one of the smaller gatchoo stadiums in the district, primarily used for some of the league's practices. There is a bright sign out front that reads "Two Goals", a nod to the nearby gatchoo stadiums and the gameplay that happens therein. Niya spies no windows, no other indication of what sort of club they're headed towards.

Turning to walk backwards for a few steps, Adasi bobs his eyebrows goofily, shifting into a sly grin. "Ready?" he asks. Then, failing to await their inevitable chorus of yeses, he gives a coyote-like yip. Nampeyo chimes in, performing a mimicry that somehow manages to sound like a coyote and unlike one at the same time.

When the door opens, music pulses like a living thing, pouring out onto the ground in front of Niya's feet. She can feel it in her stomach, in her bones. In her head and heart. There are throaty cries and pounding drums. Sounds of ancestors, borne across hundreds and hundreds of years. A sharp clap, a darkening sound; the Awis, made manifest in waves that punch at her eardrums and the space behind her eyes. Then a swell, a rebirth, the changing and growing, shifting and knowing tones of new, new, *new*.

Niya does not turn her head, but she does reach out, taking Tusika's hand and wrapping it up in her own. A reassuring squeeze meets her. She returns it, as natural as anything in the world.

"Stay close to me tonight, will you?" she asks.

Tusika's reply is easy, immediate. "Always."

And her friend might have said something else, might've uttered some other word or phrase, something important; something inconsequential. Whether she did or not, the sounds are lost on the wind, the waves, the magnetic aura of the club.

Before the door can shut behind their friends, the girls step forward. Tusika's fingertips catch its edge, hauling it back open.

But in the instant before they head inside, Tusika shifts her grip. Her fingertips move to encircle Niya's wrist, her jewelry brushing up against Niya's skin. She pulls, pulls, and Niya yields, *yields*.

Tusika's breath is warm, familiar. She dips her head the couple of inches between them, and Niya feels herself grow in response. As if her body is compelled by some external force.

But it isn't that at all, is it? It's inside of her. Always has been. Even back before they grew close, when their relationship was all competitions and comparisons, pointed glances and cold shoulders. It had grown lukewarm, then more and more comfortable—and before Niya had known what was happening, it had smoked and sparked into a living, breathing flame. A pulsing beneath her breastbone that beats in time with the other girl, that thrives in her presence, that *lives* for her.

Niya feels the brush of her best friend's lips against the edge of her own, quick as rattlesnake's strike but faint as a feather. So struck is Niya that she cannot tell the feather's touch from the snake's venom.

Tusika pulls back just so, letting Niya look up into those sparkling, mischievous eyes that she so loves.

In this moment, if there is one thing Niya wishes to know—more than the right choice of Path or what course of study to take or even if she should follow in her parents' footsteps with the family business—it would be this: *does Tusika Patak feel even a fraction of the love for me that I feel for her?*

The lack of words could go on indefinitely, and Niya would still be sated. But when she does dare to speak, she speaks from her heart.

"One more night," Niya says, her wrist still firmly but gently gripped between the other girl's middle finger and thumb, "before the Adanadi changes us forever."

Tusika says, "It would take something far less commonplace than the Adanadi to do that."

"Our physio-locks will be removed." Niya thinks about the blockers Kaatii Patak, Tusika's mana, had suggested a few years ago—the simple medical device that would allow Tusika and Niya to effectively align their growth and development, to be perfectly in sync. To be ready to receive the Adanadi in the same instant, to walk into adulthood side by side. A rarity, a blessing—a choice not lightly made but one neither girl has grown to regret. "And who knows what will happen after that."

"It doesn't have to change us," Tusika counters. "It certainly doesn't have to change everything." Her face, so powerful and sincere. Niya feels the kiss still lingering on her skin, regretting the moment the feeling might fade.

"Some things will change."

Tusika is still, then she nods once, sudden and sure. "Some things. Not us."

Then Tusika juts her chin towards the pulsing light and energy of the club's interior, gesturing with her smirking lips.

Their friends are waiting. And so is the night. The last night. Before things change.

Or don't.

Niya steps forward, leading them inside. She pulls Tusika along behind her this time, her hand shifting to hook the tips of her fingers into the tips of Tusika's—or is Tusika doing the leading somehow, even from behind?

Niya can never be certain. But what she does know is that Tusika feels like an unstoppable force, she always has. More than a mere counterbalance to Niya's thoughtful yet indecisively measured steps through life, Tusika is the center of a hurricane—all stillness and eerie calm, with the tipping point into chaos moments away at all times. Niya loves her, because to be close to Tusika is to love her. But Niya has thought, on more than this occasion alone, that Tusika may not be capable of loving her fully in return.

She knows one thing to be true: even a slice of love from someone like Tusika? Intoxicating.

The club envelops them, the music swells, and Niya's feet are bouncing to the beat, her heart free and full in her chest.

"Yo, cuz!" Niya shouts, dropping down onto a seat cushion and squeezing her way between Adasi and Nampeyo. She is sweating from all the dancing, vigorous and unrelenting as the beat has been since they've arrived.

"Water, eh?"

Niya hums her appreciation, reaching for the tall cup of water that Nampeyo pours for her. The pitcher is a polished copper color, and the drinking vessel is a special printed material, designed to perfectly cool whatever liquid touches it almost instantly. Nampeyo cannot hear many of the thankful sounds Niya makes as she downs the refreshing water, but they can see her thanks on her face. They grin jovially before leaning back, arms crossed behind their head.

The club is dedicated to the sounds of napanait hubya—music that is energetic, experimental, and derived from traditional dances from many different cultures. In the short time they have been here, Niya has already picked out some familiar words and phrases, even particular beats, cadences, rhythms, that belong to cultures other than her own.

Niya's family are Tsalagi, and that is their language, too. All Cahokians are fluent in the common tongue of the continent of Makasing, Kag Chahi. And many people hail from various tribes, some knowing multiple languages. Or none unique to them, as happens more and more nowadays—true Cahokians, no one definitive tribal identity beyond the one created by the Awis, when the peoples of their continent were pressed together for survival.

Niya has heard Dinadayapi influences and Hopi beats; Kiowa samplings and Lakota tonal vibrations. The musicians and mixer have been working the crowd together, bringing in tracks from artists of the Diné Republic, the Keetoowagi Federation, the Haudenosaunee Confederacy; some popular already, mainstream, while others are new, must be from up-and-comers that the friends have yet to discover and share with one another. A blending of traditional songs—for hunts, blessings, ceremonies—juxtaposed against newer songs focusing on things like love, freedom, riches. Music from all tribes and yet, somehow, no tribes.

A rare pause happens in the music, then one of the drummers starts pounding out a steady, singular beat. The dancers are still in anticipation of what is coming. Like switches being flipped, one at a time, different sounds are layered atop the drumming. A rattle shakes, its beat like bones buzzing, incessant and driving. The drum continues, every fourth beat emphasized now with a shout from its drummer, baritone-low and rumbling. Next, another voice, wavering and haunting, musicality made manifest in the air. The dancers begin to stir, to step, feeling the music coming alive. A flutist adds the next layer, then another voice. Every instrument, including the voices, is a response to the others. Projections begin to emerge on the walls and the ceiling—bright, iridescent colors. Neon and sharp. Odorless smoke rises up into the air, taking on shapes of its own as well. Rabbit and Wolf. Buzzard and Crow. Hummingbird and Turtle.

Even as Niya feels the song building up inside her chest, pressing to burst free of her, Adasi beats her to it. He jumps to his feet with a shout, a glorious cheer. He steps his way around their little corner of the club, his feet bouncing in an intricate set of steps. His hands turn one over the other, his body spins about, and always he is constantly propelled forward.

Nampeyo leans over, laying their slender fingers atop Niya's shoulder. They speak into her ear so as to be adequately heard.

"I better capture this song for him, he will be upset later that he failed to do so himself."

Niya nods in agreement, pressing her forehead against Nampeyo's.

They smile before reaching their left hand over to swipe upward on the surface of their niisi, orange of course. After a few complicated but familiar gestures through the digitally projected interface, Nampeyo is utilizing a program of their own creation to capture the entirety of the song from the club. Niya has seen them use it before—it renders the song into a digital, shareable file, and uses an algorithm to flesh out the pieces that were missed from the original performance, cross-referencing other searchable tracks to find comparable material. Before tomorrow morning, Nampeyo's program will have created an entire track list based on this sample performance, and they will share it with Adasi, who adores finding new music and artists. The songs will keep him company on his inevitable adventures.

Niya and Nampeyo are swiping through the musical recommendations that are coming up on their niisi's display when their friends return in a whirlwind.

"Hey, yo!"

"Cuz, you have got to get out here, these performers are lighting the place up!"

Niya catches Tusika's eyes, sparkling as they are with the spirit of the night, the heart of the music. Over her shoulder, Adasi is already spinning away again, dancing with strangers in the crowd, his face alight with joy

60

and the freedom of being young and Cahokian. There is diversity aplenty, no two individuals dressed exactly alike, no two precisely entwined styles, nor even two people in the entire club feeling this night, experiencing this night, in the same way. Despite this, there is a cohesion to the masses, a unity amongst them all.

Perhaps it is Niya's perception of her best friend, the magnetism she feels towards the other girl—but the entirety of the shifting, jubilant masses seems to ebb and flow with Tusika at the center. Eyes upon her, movements in tune with her, almost as if it happens without anyone quite knowing the how or the why of it. Tusika Patak, surrounded by dozens, by hundreds—but still one in a million.

All around them, dozens and dozens of youth and elders alike partake: of the music, of perception enhancers if they so choose, of dance, of each other, of the shared, palpable energy.

Niya hops up, following quickly in Nampeyo's light footsteps. They join their friends, and the four of them dance, dance, dance—and all of the rest of it, too.

This may be the first time they have visited this particular club, but Niya is certain it won't be the last.

Because things aren't going to change. Not all things, at least.

Not this, Niya tells herself, as the four of them join hands, weaving in and out of the crowd around them, an unbroken circle. *It couldn't possibly.*

HAWA

By the time they leave the club, the dark of night is shifting into that far away light of onrushing day. It is far enough off that it doesn't feel like tomorrow yet, might still pass for today.

They head for an all-night tea house on the way back to the yutsu stop. Adasi will eventually have to head back across Lake Etesi Gami to the north to get to his home; he'll take one of the overnight skimmers on the crossing. Nampeyo lives to the south and will walk, though they may be able to catch a ride on a sunwing, solar-charged and speedy. And Niya and Tusika, while not direct neighbors, live fairly close to one another, in the eastern portion of the Suumar Wahat district.

Niya's skin tingles with the energy of the night and the remnants of the club's effect as they enter the tea house. The lighting is vivid and demure at once, all purples and blues, bright but soothing.

"Ah, let me order," Tusika pleads with the smile of a wolf pup on her face, hands clasped together as she positions herself between the other three and the counter. "Please, go—sit! Tonight, I treat you all. Grab seats, yeah?"

She winks at Niya, who rolls her eyes playfully in return.

Adasi picks out a low table and plops himself down on one of the cushions. The expression on his face is one of dazed delirium; pure bliss. Nampeyo excuses themself to the toilets.

Folding herself down neatly onto a cushion opposite

Adasi, Niya steeples her fingers together, the heel of her palms resting against the table. She leans forward, positioning her chin on the tips of her touching fingertips. Eyes closed, she breathes, breathes...

When she leans back, opening her eyes, Adasi is looking at her with a gaze almost unfamiliar in its intensity.

"What—" she begins.

But he interrupts. "The ceremony, Niya—" She sits up straighter, surprised as she is by his tone. "—when you take the gift of the Adanadi, you must remember that it is about you. Not you and Tusika."

Nose scrunching in confusion, Niya says, "It's always been about me and Tusika. We're a packaged pair, have been since we were born in the same hospital wing so close together. Even when we hated being talked about in the same breath, it was still the same. You know that."

"I do know that, Niya. I know how special it is, how special you *both* are, to be taking it together."

"Yes, a ceremony that Kaatii Patak made sure we could carry out as one! She wants it to be unique for her daughter, of course, but that also makes it so for me."

"Yes," Adasi hums, "yes, I know..."

"Why am I sensing a 'but' in there, brother?"

Adasi's forehead draws down, and he purses his lips in thought. He weighs his words before speaking them into existence. "But...when have the Pataks ever given something without expecting something greater in return?"

Niya almost laughs but for the seriousness in her friend's face. "The Adanadi is for everyone, Adasi—the whole of Makasing. The Pataks do not give it or take it away, and they cannot use it for influence or renown, both of which they already have in excess. They have been blessed by the Adanadi for a long time, yes, but so have many others. What is it that you fear for me?"

Intense eyes on Niya's, Adasi says, "The Pataks expect their daughter to be something certain and true and particular. But this is not about what the Pataks want their daughter to be, nor is it about who the Suwatts know theirs is. The Adanadi is about the person taking it and nothing else, it is about the person you are before and the person you are after. Believe that Tusika knows exactly how important and special it is for *her*. So, you must not forget: you are special, too, in your own right. You can stand alone, as a person separate from Tusika. Whether Kaatii Patak likes it or not."

His voice, so serious, leaves Niya without a response. Of course she is a person separate from Tusika—but does Kaatii Patak respect that? Would the Suwatts be worth anything to the Pataks if not for their daughters?

Before she can fully process the meaning behind Adasi's words, the others are joining them.

"Dandelion mint for you, hmm?"

With a grateful, if slight, smile, Niya accepts the offering from Tusika. Their hands brush for longer than is necessary in the passing off of the hand-carved, wooden cup. Niya wonders if this was her doing, or Tusika's. Her best friend's face gives nothing away—even if it did, would Niya be able to translate those subtle cues, those meticulously refined hints, into meaning?

Niya ruminates as they each drink their teas and share a light meal of smoked salmon, fresh fruits, and quinoa. The chef's meal for the late-night club-goers is delicious and well-chosen. The four friends are somewhat subdued as they sip their warm drinks and eat their seasonal meal. The night is late, closer to morning than anything else. Without saying it aloud, they all know the truth of the matter: no one wants this night to end.

Adasi and Nampeyo have already gone through the Adanadi process, and it didn't change the dynamic of their group in any sort of negative, irreversible way. But the girls' joint ceremony tomorrow is something altogether different and Adasi's words have shaken her a little on the decision. Tusika is destined for something greater than the average Cahokian. Anyone who knows her can see that and see it clearly—and if they didn't see it or understand it or, daringly, not accept it, then Tusika's mana could certainly enlighten them. And Niya, too, while from a family ungifted with Abilities, still has high expectations on her own shoulders from her family and community both. So why did...

"You girls," Nampeyo says, their voice pitched low and strange, cutting off Niya's thoughts. The other three at the table freeze, mouths in various states of fullness, to stare at them, unblinkingly. Their slender fingers are drumming against the table in an unrecognizable beat. Nampeyo draws the moment out for a long time, the suspense building—like a professional comedian or storyteller, but not one of the really good ones. Finally, they speak, an unfamiliar husk and a drawl to their intonations. "Proud of you."

They bark the words out, in the worst imitation of a gruff elder that any of them have ever heard.

Their facade breaks, face crumbling into a fit of laughter. And then all of them are guffawing, heaving in and out great breaths of laughter.

Niya wipes her eyes with the backs of her hands, likely wreaking havoc on her painted face. But tears of mirth are streaming from her eyes anyway, and the night—

The night is near complete.

"Aren't we all, oh great and wizened elder 'Peyo," Adasi jokes. He reaches over, wrapping an arm around his best friend's shoulder. They rest the sides of their heads against one another as the laughing dies down. "Aren't we all."

— . . . —

They head out of the tea house, prepared to go their separate ways.

"Until we meet again," Niya says. Then she repeats it in Tsalagi, her family language. "Donadagohvi."

In rotating pairs, they grasp one another by the opposite wrists, meeting in tight, one-armed hugs.

Adasi heads towards the skimmer platform. Nampeyo heads off in their own direction.

Niya and Tusika begin to walk east with plans to meander at their own pace.

Silence follows them for a while, even the busiest

parts of the district falling into something resembling a slumber at this time of the night.

Then Tusika shoos the silence away.

"Can I stay over at yours tonight, Kakooni?"

Her voice more closely resembles Niya's namesake— *quiet*, in Kag Chahi—than her usual energetic, confident manner. When Niya looks sideways at her, out of the corner of her eye, she is certain that her friend keeps her gaze turned ever so slightly away.

"You are always welcome, Wanzi." Wanzi, meaning *one* in Kag Chahi, is Niya's own nickname for her friend. Since Tusika, meaning *eight*, is quite literally an homage to her family's gifted lineage, Niya has always used this pet name as a way to put distance between who Tusika is and the person her family expects her to be. "Are you alright?"

In a flash, Tusika's demeanor changes. Her smile lights up her eyes. Rosy, full cheeks lift upward. Her shoulders lower ever so slightly, as if momentarily relieved of some burden that they have been holding up.

"More than alright, Love. We both know my mana will still be awake, despite the late hour. I do not want to answer to her, not tonight."

"And you like my mana's breakfast."

"She does make the best sausage and cornmeal mash in the city!" Tusika pleads with a quirk of her lips.

"Hmm..." Niya hums beneath her breath.

"What?" Tusika asks, brow arched.

"That is it? No other reason— besides that inquisitive mana of yours and that skillful chef of mine?"

As Niya asks, her fingertips itch. To reach out and touch Tusika's wrist. To pull her close. To breathe in the same molecules of air. Or, better yet, to have Tusika do the reaching out, the pulling close—to take whatever it is that has linked their lives all these years and turn it into something new.

To turn it into the something wonderful that Niya believes it can be.

Instead, Tusika remains looking ahead, and she nods once. "That is all. And that I want some of that amazing Suwatt cornbread for breakfast."

Niya cocks her head to the side, this time gazing more pointedly at Tusika's grinning profile.

"Is it?" she asks, determined to hear the truth from her best friend's lips. She puts as much earnestness into her tone as she can summon, pleading for Tusika to quench whatever fire it is that Niya experiences for her best friend—or else match it, if she can.

But just because it is a truth Niya wants to hear does not mean that it is a truth that Tusika shares.

Unanswering, Tusika turns abruptly as a low humming vehicle approaches. It's a nighttime resupply cart, moving along at a decent speed through the city streets. The girls have hitched rides on such carts countless times in the past, sitting on the vehicle's edge as long as it continued in the right direction.

"Ah! Our ride approaches," Tusika crows, ignoring Niya's last question whether by chance or purpose. "To home!"

They won't have long to sleep, most of this night already gone as it is. But sleep will come after taking the Adanadi—a process that has been greatly refined over the last hundred years. However refined and even with veritably no discomfort, there is still a lot of drowsiness after the fact. The body changes, for one thing, and the spirit does, too. Energy must be expended for that to happen, even if the happening is subtle.

All of Niya's family members are already asleep when they get inside, probably for hours. She and Tusika step quietly across the open hearth area so as not to make any noise. Above them, the raftered ceiling opens up to a skylight that has been left ajar for the night—the sky is quickening towards sunrise. There is just enough light to guide them across the room that they will avoid any stubbed toes.

The girls change for the night, Tusika slipping into some spare clothes previously left over—patterned matching shorts and shirt made of thin, breathable material—and Niya opting for a light sleep shirt and a pair of comfy underwear that stretch partially down her thighs. Plopping into bed with a tired yawn, Niya lays on her back and looks up at the ceiling. Projected against it from a device plugged into her terminal is the entirety of the milky way, the trail of cornmeal laid out amongst that giant, unknowable blackness by Dog all those years ago. Tusika climbs in after Niya, crawling over her to claim her usual side of the bed closest to the wall. She curls into Niya's side, her forehead pressed against Niya's bare shoulder.

Her friend is asleep in moments, leaving Niya alone with her thoughts. Tusika's voice from earlier echoes in her mind.

It doesn't have to change us.

The minutes pass. Tusika lets out a quiet breath in her sleep, then she rolls over. Her long, lean legs kick against Niya's ankle. Niya smiles at the familiarity of it. Fighting off her restlessness, Niya rolls over as well, gripping one hand in the soft material of Tusika's sleep shirt.

Some things will change.

And this is how Niya falls asleep: clutching her friend, and wondering, not for the first time nor for the last, if the coming ceremony will be the beginning of something that will pull them apart forever.

Not us.

Or, perhaps, more optimistically: something that will bind them together, more strongly than ever before.

———

This time when Niya dreams, she is sitting cross-legged on the forest floor. Her eyes are closed, but she can see through her eyelids to the world beyond. There is a trail of ants walking in circles around her, part of their trail climbing up and over her bare foot to get access to the valley between her knees, then another foot—up, and over, repetitious in lost or otherwise unknown meaning. The ants circumnavigate her body, and Niya isn't sure what they are doing behind her. But when they come back around, they are carrying something, something meaty, something red. Something of her. But what? And why?

She feels nothing until she feels everything, and her

dream eyes snap open. Her jaw drops in a silent gasp. Before her is one large, black eye. It blinks, long and slow, taking up the entirety of the forest. She cannot see what it belongs to because it overshadows itself, consumes the world to the horizon and perhaps even beyond.

Who are you? Niya asks. But she has no voice here. Maybe that's what the ants are carrying away—her voice box, chopped, dismantled, gone.

The voice answers her: Who? But its voice is not like Niya's, reverberating only in her skull. The eye's voice fills her eardrums, rattling, shaking, pulsing from everywhere and nowhere at once. It rumbles across the entire forest, stirring up dead leaves and moss cover, picking them up into the air like a tornado's whims at play. The bark on the trees themselves quiver with the mightiness of it. Who? The voice speaks again, and Niya's heart skips a beat.

Yes, Niya asks, this time speaking only with her mind. She closes her eyes again, this time seeing the great, slow-blinking eye behind closed eyelids. The black eye is everything, everything and more. Who?

You, the eye replies.

Me?

We.

We...

The eye moves. It shrinks away, disappearing and taking the horizon with it. In a flash, it is coming back towards Niya again—rapidly closing the distance. She opens her eyes again to see it fully, to see it fully and to know it better. To remember it, maybe even to take it with her when she leaves this dream. If it will have her, if it will let her.

A thought races across her mind. A thought fueled by sleep and dream and exhaustion: what if it takes her, what if it does not let her leave this place?

Then a face makes itself clear, makes itself known. And Niya feels something inside of her come alive.

A second eye, black as night, to match the first. White face. Tufts of brown. An auburn ring around a wise, ancient face.

Oh, she thinks.

Aloud, she says: We are—

Niya should be exhausted, but she isn't. When she wakes to the smells of sausages and freshly baked bread, her stomach growls. How can her body be concerned with anything besides the dream that she'd just had? So disconcerting, it has left her feeling shaken. Not like herself. A strange feeling, coupled with the fact that she should be utterly exhausted but somehow instead feels invigorated.

She can feel that Tusika is still in bed. Her backside is pressed against the other girl. She rolls over slowly, carefully. But her caution is unnecessary. Tusika is already awake and staring unblinkingly up at the ceiling.

"Tusika," she says. Never does she call her best friend "cousin" or "sister". Those terms have never felt right to Niya. Tusika is closer than blood to her, something altogether different—sacred and exceptional in the lone spot she holds in Niya's heart. A closeness between the two of them that not even their families could fully account for, present since they were born and placed side by side in the hospital's nursery, futures intertwined by something bigger than either of them, perhaps.

The girl turns her head sharply to look Niya in the eye. Niya is almost certain that Tusika is blinking back tears. Quick blinks, purposeful and rigid. Her brow is tense, her breathing shallow. She seems almost panicked, like a doe preparing to flee from a hunter's arrow.

Or worse: like a hare, caught in a trap. Alive, but facing certain demise.

"Tusika," Niya says again, this time her voice holding a firmer quality to it, more demanding.

"I..."

But Tusika does not finish her sentence.

"What is wrong? Has something happened—are you okay?"

Niya is beginning to worry, her tone edging closer to nervousness, to panic. Always so perceptive, Niya cannot interpret her friend's emotions at the moment. And that scares her.

Almost as if this shift in Niya has triggered a sudden, equal shift in Tusika, the girl begins to change. The cloud of dream that had been hanging over her dissipates, planting seeds of doubt in Niya's mind that it had ever existed in the first place. Tusika's face turns light and confident now, that charm that is so typical of her, so ordinary, back in place.

Like a mask, Niya thinks. A thought that she does

not dare voice aloud.

"I must go," Tusika says. She leans forward and kisses the tip of Niya's nose before hopping out of bed.

"But—" Niya falters, propping herself up on one elbow as she watches Tusika get dressed. She watches those even, measured movements as if trying to spot any little weakness, any sign to give away what is going on in that head of Tusika's. But no cracks emerge. "Breakfast," she finishes lamely.

It is true that Tusika prefers Ahyoka Suwatt's breakfast to that of her own mana's. It is also true that she prefers the Suwatt household over that of the Pataks', perhaps in every conceivable way.

Niya decides not to bring that up. Not now, when she knows that there are pressing familial duties on a day like today.

"Enjoy it for me," Tusika begs off. She gestures at the niisi she wears at her own wrist, a newer, shinier model than Niya's "A message from the Patak clan—much to do at home before the ceremony."

"Wish you didn't have to go."

"We'll see each other soon enough, yeah?"

"At the choosing of the Path sample," Niya confirms. "Deer for you—"

"And what will it be for you, my friend? Will you follow your noosoo to Beaver's waters, or your mana to Eagle's heights?"

Tusika's eyes glint. Not with mirth or amusement, Niya believes, but with a deep sense of understanding.

Odd, Niya thinks. She does not allow her brow to

furrow in confusion, though she wants to.

Because the choice of Path in Tusika's family is easy. Expected. *Known.* They have always belonged to the Path of the Deer. How can Tusika possibly understand the choice that is before Niya?

Instead of any of these thoughts, Niya says, "Still deciding."

"Time is short," comes Tusika's reply. She walks close to Niya's bed before dropping down to her knees at the edge of the overflowing blankets. She leans forward, reaching out to press her palm flat against Niya's chest, just above her breast. Niya's heart thuds against her best friend's touch. "You honor your *own* heart." Her voice is intense, persistent. "You follow the path that you are meant to follow. Right?" It is as if she is trying to convince herself as much as Niya.

"Right," Niya says, repeating Tusika's words back to her. "Honor your own heart."

With a singular and defining nod, Tusika gets to her feet, her movements fluid and strong.

And then she is gone, Niya's door sliding shut behind her. But not before she hears greetings between Tusika and Niya's family in the rooms beyond, that charm of hers dialed all the way up, jovial and easy, like she belongs. Tusika has so rarely ever failed to belong, wherever she finds herself.

Niya sighs, confusion laying heavily on her shoulders. Not just because of Tusika's actions and words, but because of her dreams.

Which Path will she choose?

As Niya rises from bed, she realizes the truth with a jolt: she did not know the answer upon waking.

But she does now.

— . . . . —

The outfit Niya wears is one that she and her niisis picked out especially for the day. Niya is proud of it, proud that it highlights her Tsalagi roots but also her own personality. It also has highlights that are very Cahokian. The primary colors are bright and buoyant—red and yellow mixed into stark, beautiful patterns with black and white. And then that techno-touch of Cahokia, with purple lights and metallic shapes and tint mixed in. The back of the outfit goes high up Niya's neck, fanning out to create a small, tight silhouette behind her head. The lights cast a strong glow, one that would almost throw her face into darkness if not for the illuminating makeup painted across her face and neck, her arms and legs—painted skin that lights up seemingly of its own volition. The rest of the outfit is form-fitting, supple and comfortable despite its rigid, almost armor-like look. Her arms are entirely bare, and the pants are draped over with a long skirt patterned after traditional tear dresses of their ancestors.

Niya feels like she can take on the world while wearing it.

Armed with her decision of Path, Niya finds herself capable of believing that anything is possible.

She exits her room, leaving her childhood as she goes.

ZAPATAAN

Within seconds of leaving her room, Niya's noosoo is crossing the room in four great strides to meet her.

He cuts a well-built but squat figure. Niya knows that she gets much of her physical strength from him. He smiles when he first sees her, those slightly-overlapped teeth of his the mirror image of her own. And when he embraces her, she feels safe in powerful limbs that squeeze her tight, lifting her feet off the ground. When he places her back down, they are nearly eye to eye, nose to nose. Yona—grizzly bear in their Tsalagi language—is his name.

Names, so important to many tribes across the whole of Makasing, hold meaning. And the name of Niya's noosoo held much meaning to his parents, indeed. Often the stories of family members' names would be retold at important events, and Niya is certain she will be hearing one very shortly.

"Granddaughter," Yona's own noosoo, her daadoo, chimes from the hearth as soon as she enters the large, wide-open living space of the home. "You know how your noosoo got his name, don't you?"

Niya chuckles, indulgent and happy on this special day.

The happiness comes easier than it would have even half a day before. The two dreams she has had, they have unlocked something within her—an easy understanding, a sense of peace. She knows which Path she will choose, and so she can approach this day with ease instead of angst.

"Please, daadoo—tell me the story. I've heard it before but would gladly hear it again."

"Ah," he says, "you indulge me. Wado!"

He thanks her, then spins the tale.

All good Tsalagi tales begin the same:

This is what my daadoo told me, when I was a boy.

And so her daadoo tells Niya how her noosoo got his name.

Generations ago—back when flesh was broken to take the Adanadi, when the process was anything but painless or simple or commonplace—there was a great man, a Tsalagi man. His last name was Suwatt. His first name has been forgotten by memory.

He was strong of mind but meager of body. He knew then, as many would come to know, in time, that the Adanadi's gifts are imparted but once. He knew that he had to make the right decision. Not for himself, but for his tribe. For his family. For the babies not yet born, and for the future yet unseen.

Times were hard, after the Awis. The Adanadi, the Creator's left-behind gift, is the answer for progress. Progress and perseverance.

Suwatt knew this. While many in his village would not take the Adanadi, he was brave enough to endure the trial.

When he came out the other side, he had chosen the Path of the Bear.

And the Bear had chosen Suwatt right back.

In less than a fortnight, he had attained the grizzly's might—the power of the Bear! Suwatt's strength came to be known far and wide. He became a builder of inimitable speed, getting entire villages housed before the next winter's freeze.

He became a legend. We remember his deeds, even now.

As Niya's daadoo concludes the story about their ancestor, she claps her noosoo on his shoulder.

"And yet you chose the Path of the Beaver, noosoo. Despite this great namesake."

Across the room, both of Yona's parents chuckle. From the cooking fire and meal area just across from the primary hearth, Niya's mana speaks up.

"I believe you inherited a bit of that Beaver spirit yourself, daughter—sharp of eye and mind. And no one can work longer or harder than you and your noosoo when it comes time for harvest."

Yona links his arm around his daughter's, where she has it extended between them. He pulls her close, sharing words only meant for her.

"And I have not regretted my Path, not for one single day. Neither will you, whether you follow me, your mana, or one of those mazakaska kooks over there. Or," he pauses, his eyes shining with love, "strike out on your own Path altogether."

Perceptive, indeed—a trait that Niya is pleased to share with her noosoo. He seems to know, without her saying a word, that she has made up her mind. That she knows which Path she will follow for the rest of her life. A decision and a process that, once completed, cannot be undone.

"Come!" Ahyoka calls. The tail end of the noosoo-daughter moment fades gently away. "Breakfast, my girl. Eat up! And then we will begin our family preparations."

― ▪ ▪ ―

The morning flies. Before heading to the ceremonial mound where the Adanadi will be given, Niya's family partakes of private traditions.

The central tradition that Niya's parents make sure is part of the specialness of the day is the smudging.

To begin, they turn off all artificial light in their home. Only the fire in the hearth and the mid-morning sun from the sky-opening in the center of their home illuminate the space.

Her family sits in a circle with Niya at their center. In front of Niya and to her right-hand side, her mana; to her left-hand side, her noosoo. Completing the circle are her niisis and her daadoo.

A smudge bowl is handed around the circle to her mana. The bowl is large enough to hold the four sacred medicines for the ceremony but small enough to fit comfortably in any of the family members' hands. It is made of a smooth, polished stone, dark blue in color and worn down into a bowl shape from hours of meticulous movements. Niya knows that her family has been handing this bowl down for generations—maybe even from as far back as the great grizzly bear Suwatt's days.

Ahyoka holds it purposefully in hand, extending it towards Niya's noosoo. While the ceremony itself is traditional, the tool that Yona uses to light the bundle is anything but ancient: a piece of tech made household commodity in the last few years, an instant source of light and heat. He takes his time, lighting a couple of small fires in the bowl, ensuring that each of the four medicines is able to catch.

The medicines are carefully chosen for any smudging, and oftentimes they will only use one or two of them at once. But for an auspicious day like today, Niya's family has included all four: several pieces of loose sage for purification, a braid of sweetgrass for healing, loose leaves of tobacco for peace, and a small bit of cedar for protection.

After the fire is lit, her daadoo produces a beautiful feather, one that Niya has never seen before. He must have gone out hunting for it in the forests surrounding their farmland on the outskirts of Cahokia. Perhaps he searched all week, waiting for the perfect dropped feather for his only granddaughter's pre-Adanadi smudging. Niya thanks him with her eyes and a nod of her head. His smile gives her heart warmth.

Yona takes the feather with both of his hands. It rests gently in his palms.

Ahyoka waves her hands above the smudge bowl. The little flames dissipate. In their stead, plumes of dark gray smoke waft up and away from the bowl to fill the air before her face. The contents of the bowl fade to a warm black and orange glow. Like the embers of a ceremonial pipe's end.

With a nod, Ahyoka turns to her partner. Yona bows his head and uses both of his hands to place the quill of the feather into her grip. She smudges the feather with purposeful movements, cleansing it first and foremost—one side, and then the other. Ensuring that the smoke touches the entirety of its surface.

Niya admires the feather. It is largely white with a swath of light brown along one edge. Irregularly shaped lines of a darker brown cut across it at regular intervals.

Those colors, Niya thinks, her mouth dropping open with the slightest hint of surprise, *are familiar to me.*

Familiar, and new. Familiar, and old.

The ceremony continues, her mana smudging herself. Then they each partake. And finally, Niya concludes the smudging by cleansing herself with the medicinal smoke, much like each of her family members have done.

But smudging is special and unique for each person in different ways. Niya's mana and her mana's mana and her noosoo's mana—they all taught her their ways. Her daadoos, too—and her noosoo, of course. Each and every one of them followed the formula, the ritual. But each and every one of them said their prayers the littlest bit differently.

That's the power of it, Niya thinks. *That's where the magic comes from.*

The first part of herself that Niya smudges, when the time comes, is her heart. This is the vital organ that pumps life from her head to her toes. Next, her mouth—inhaling the sweet smoke so that every prayer she speaks is pure and good. Her eyes, to see the goodness around her; her mind, to think good thoughts; her hair and arms and chest, to keep sacred the parts of her that reflect her history, that hold it close and dear.

Niya says her prayers as she always has: silently, her lips moving without producing sound. The words that leave her are not only for her, they are for those she loves—for the people inside this room and beyond its walls, too. But only Niya needs to know the words that she speaks. Only Niya, and the Creator. And the Creator does not need her to shout from the rooftop for her intentions to be known.

A few minutes more and Ahyoka concludes the smudging. The Suwatts stand. And together, they leave their home, walking to the public building atop a great mound that is dedicated to Adanadi ceremonies.

— · · —

The path is smooth beneath the soles of the ceremonial boots Niya has chosen for today. She made them herself, a combination of gat prints, basket-weaving techniques from her niisis, and leather work from her daadoo. Her mana helped her with some beading designs on the tops and sides, and her noosoo helped her procure some tech-enhancements from the Eeko market—those, she worked into the backs and soles. When she walks, patterns flash up from the ground and along her heels, roll up the backs of her feet, and almost seem to light the fringes of her tear dress on fire.

She is proud of the final product. She feels truly Tsalagi in this moment, walking towards the Adanadi—and truly Cahokian, too.

"Is Tusika excited?"

Niya turns to her mana.

"Yes," she says, the answer almost rote. But then she pauses, remembering this morning. The strange bout of urgency and anxiety that was rolling off of her friend in waves. "Well. I think so."

"Tch," Niya's noosoo clicks his tongue, waving one of his large hands in a frustrated motion. "Such pressure do they put on that girl."

"Yona," Ahyoka clicks right back, the second syllable of his name hitting hard from the back of her throat. "Not our place," she says. "The Pataks have high expectations, that is all. Tusika is a strong young woman, she can handle herself."

His name may hit forcefully in Ahyoka's mouth, but her tone is one of gentle chastisement. They reach out and lace their fingers together.

"She is strong," Yona agrees. "They forged her in a fire of their own making, didn't they? Pah, I don't envy her, I'll tell you that much. Thakashan and I, our monthly community meetings that we host are enough for me to see the Patak expectations at work. And every once in a while, Kaatii shows up to see what sorts of talk ends up on the agenda." Yona gives an over-exaggerated, fake shiver. "That marriage is well-suited, I'll tell you that much. Those two, they can really get going on treatises to be written or disputes to be settled. Everything is always so *important*."

Niya stares at their conjoined hands for a moment before she speaks again.

"There is a great deal of pressure that comes from being a Patak."

"Yes, daughter. But they are able to do a great deal of good for the community—for Cahokia."

"Pressure forges diamonds, eh?" Yona says, squeezing Ahyoka's hand before spinning her around in a circle, as if performing a dance step. "You know what else pressure does?"

"Enlighten me," Ahyoka replies with a chuckle.

Yona leans in closely, conspiratorially. "It blows gaskets."

"Noosoo," Niya groans as her mana elbows her noosoo right in the gut. She places her forehead in her hands while avoiding her makeup, keeping it smudge-free. "It is a stressful time, and *yes*, Tusika has a great deal of pressure on her. But I also know that Tusika…" Niya trails off, not sure how to properly voice what it is she is trying to say. Her parents wait patiently for her to continue. "Tusika enjoys the pressure, in a way. She wants to be successful, she wants to be…" Another pause. A few more steps. The word that Niya uses to finish her sentence, her explanation of who Tusika is as a person, it feels right as it leaves her. "Important."

"Ah, my girl," Yona says, his voice deep and booming. He leans over and kisses her atop her head. "None of us have any doubts that she will be exactly that."

"It is in her blood," Ahyoka agrees.

And what is in my blood? Niya asks herself as they fall back into an easy silence, their destination fast approaching.

Niya already knows what her future is supposed to look like—honing her already advanced horticulture skills, improving upon the business her parents have already had so much success with, taking the Suwatt name into the future of fine foods all across Cahokia and perhaps even beyond.

Yes, she knows what her future is supposed to look like. But she does not know what it will be.

And therein lies the confounding nature of choice, of free will and its inevitable and oftentimes unenviable consequence: the unknown.

What comforts Niya as her family climbs the long set of steps up to the entrance of the Adanadi building where it sits atop a prominent mound in their district, is one small fact: she knows what Path she is about to take. This one question, at least, has been answered.

Many questions remain, of course, primary among them the question that won't stop dogging her every thought...

Where will this Path that she is about to choose—this Path that, it seems, has chosen her—lead?

Only time will tell.

SAKPI

The Adanadi ceremony for Niya of the Suwatt family and Tusika of the Patak clan is planned for precisely midday.

But first, both girls must have their physio-locks undone.

The two families meet in the great hall of the building, massive stoneworks around them leading up to wide windows inset with a biologically-printed translucent film from industrial-sized gats—a material resistant to high winds and hail, and that blocks the more harmful of the sun's rays. The space is airy and cool—inviting, despite the serious nature of the ceremonies held here.

The contingent of Pataks significantly outnumbers the Suwatts. But this rarely ever bothers either of the girls. They know who their families are, even if they are still figuring themselves out.

As respect and traditions dictate, Niya and Tusika each greet the matriarchs of the other family first.

The eldest woman on Niya's side is her noosoo's mana, and Tusika greets her with a warm embrace—as if they hadn't probably shared a hug and an exchange just a few hours ago, when Tusika was leaving the Suwatt home.

Niya moves directly to Tusika's eldest living relative in Cahokia, a beautiful and regal two-spirit Patak who stands head and shoulders above Niya. They greet each other very formally, much more so than the greeting between Tusika and Niya's niisi. But this, too, is expected—Tusika hugs Niya's niisi because that is the relationship between the young woman and Niya's family; Niya, like everyone else in the whole of Cahokia, is expected to treat the Pataks with deference at such occasions as this. Never is the status difference between the Suwatts and the Pataks clearer than when a ceremony is afoot.

The two-spirit elder of the Patak clan is deaf and communicates almost entirely via Plains Sign Language, or PSL. Most Cahokians can communicate in PSL just as readily as in Kag Chahi. Niya respectfully greets the elder, who bows their head in return, greeting Niya with the faintest of smiles drifting across full lips, like a secret. Finally, she shakes wrists with the two-spirit elder, her head deferentially bowed. Then she proceeds to work her way around the entire Patak congregation.

Once finished, Niya meets Tusika where the girl is standing between Niya's parents and her own. She greets Tusika's parents—Kaatii and Thakashan—with reined-in enthusiasm, attempting to keep her eye on the Pataks without straying to her friend.

When she finally has the chance to properly lay eyes on Tusika, Niya feels her breath catch in her chest. She all but audibly gasps, catching herself at the last second to reel back into the proper decorum.

"Hello, my friend."

They grasp one another's hands, both smiling. There is a shining light in Tusika's eyes, almost a sheen of tears—but none fall. Niya searches that familiar face, eyes darting to and fro, trying to make sense of what she sees.

Is there something else there? Niya wonders. *Does she feel how hard my heart beats? Does she feel how it beats for her?*

And, most pressing of all—and painful, if Niya's heartbeats are unrequited: *Could Tusika's heart beat back for Niya just the same?*

A quirk of lips, a darting tongue, a playful grin. That's just it, isn't it? Niya loves Tusika, and Tusika is her dearest, closest friend. But Tusika was born to lead, to be the center of attention. Why would she choose to partake of the Adanadi with Niya? A few short years ago, Niya had thought Tusika's feeling of self-importance to be irksome; now, she knows her better—knows that Tusika does not care only for herself. She cares with all of her heart, and she cares for many. Today is but one manifestation of how much she cares for her best friend—for Niya. And that is why they are taking the Adanadi together. The cloudy thoughts of earlier that morning, the questions of why she would share her special day with anyone, are laid to rest in this moment.

Niya's smile feels tremulous at best, but Tusika's appears strong, firm. She squeezes Niya's hands once, twice, then turns away, looking between the two families gathered before them for this auspicious day.

Tusika's attention is turned elsewhere, but she still holds Niya's hand. Her skin is warm but not clammy, her grip strong but not constricting. Niya feels grounded.

As Tusika continues to chat amicably with everyone around her, Niya eyes her friend's garb for the day appreciatively. The deep purple, form-fitting piece that swaths Tusika from neck to ankle is beautiful and rich. Niya's fingers reach out instinctively to touch the high collar, and she relishes its softness while also wondering at it—lined with some sort of synthetic material to stiffen the lines of the garment, it appears almost metal-like in nature from afar but feels plush up close.

A quiet falls across the two gathered families as a door at the center of the hall slides open.

Tusika gives Niya's hand a rapid series of gentle squeezes before turning to her mana. "Ready?" she asks, deferring to Kaatii.

Niya knows that there is very little love lost between the two Patak women, but this trait is one that they share: respect given for respect earned. And Tusika does everything she can at all times to earn it.

Kaatii Patak says nothing, merely inclines her head, her hair wrapped in a ceremonial bun at the back of her head, her features so similar to Tusika's—narrow, thin, sharp. She wears a dress of black. The fabric has an effervescent sheen to it, and her moccasins, black and yellow-beaded, are laced up to her knees. A sharp, small smile graces her lips. Niya sees the same regality multiplied across the whole family as she surveys them—Patak relation after Patak relation, all lifted chins and haughty airs. Her noosoo stands out, wearing a shirt and trousers of sunshine yellow with black accents, artfully paired with his wife. Tusika's round cheeks come from him. Much of him is round in nature, like he was a ball who might fall and roll and roll for having no sharp edges to catch the ground. And with Tusika at the head of them all, looking like the glorious embodiment of the future that she is—the embodiment of *their* future, of the Patak name, reputation, and creed.

Not for the first time, nor for the last, does Niya wonder at the burden of expectation on her friend's shoulders.

But today is about the two of them. *A day for Niya and a day for Tusika,* she thinks in a mental response to Adasi's words the night before. And from here on out, the two girls will be walking mostly alone. Once they enter the Adanadi chambers, the wait will begin for their families.

This taking of the Adanadi as a pair is not common among Cahokians. It is possible that some tribes across Makasing have dual or larger ceremonies, but Niya is not familiar enough to know whether or not it occurs regularly. The Adanadi is timed precisely to the peak of adolescence, that tipping point from child to adult. It happens at the very crest of development.

Niya and Tusika are a special case, and one that both the Suwatts and Pataks agreed on long ago. Though their daughters were not always the best of friends—Tusika's competitiveness and Niya's stubborn streak saw to that until only a few short years ago—there was never any denying that the two girls were meant to be in one another's lives.

Seventeen years before, Niya had been born at the close of one day while Tusika came with the dawn of the next. Their manas were in the same healing ward throughout their respective labors. With the Pataks in a place of high honor due to the Council of Twelve seat and the Suwatts providing produce and custom-grown greenery to many of the great houses of the district, the two girls were destined to grow up close to one another.

Niya sometimes wonders at the odd pairing of the Pataks with the Suwatts. But she thinks back to those new mana ward days, when both Ahyoka and Kaatii were coming into motherhood at the same time. The bond that must have been inevitable. Holding their suckling babes close while sitting around the healing hearth. Evenings listening to comedians' stories and songs, universally profound. Laughing together at jokes despite their sore bodies and weary eyes. And that story Niya has heard enough times to know by heart: the way both manas had caught their daughters on the sleep mat in one of the nurseries, holding hands—or the closest semblance to such an act that newborns might accomplish.

Yes, they were destined to grow up close to one another. And it's funny, Niya thinks, how a supposed destiny can be self-fulfilling: how two babies holding hands meant they were destined to be close, and that destiny made their parents see it through to fruition.

She is not upset by it, not now. She might've been, back when she was more of a child, caught in the shadow of this Patak girl who seemed an inevitable, unmovable fixture in her life. But once both Niya and Tusika stopped being at odds with one another long enough to see the wisdom in their families' choices, they realized the truth of it: sometimes two people fit together so well precisely because of their differences. This is, after all, the theory behind magnetism—and doesn't it apply to Niya Suwatt and Tusika Patak, if no one else?

The physiological hold, or physio-lock, was a natural next step, once the dual Adanadi ceremony was arranged. The lock has allowed them to time it all perfectly. It will be removed simultaneously from both girls. And then the Adanadi will be taken at once.

In this way, they will go down their paths at the same time. They will cross the threshold from childhood to adulthood together.

An auspicious day, indeed. And Niya knows that she would not have it any other way, even as Adasi's words of wisdom from the night previous ring briefly in her head once more.

When you take the gift of the Adanadi, you must remember that it is about you...The Adanadi is about the person taking it and nothing else, it is about the person you are before and the person you are after.

And his warning about the Pataks swirls in her mind, too.

When have they ever given something without expecting something greater in return? You can stand alone, as a person separate from Tusika. Whether Kaatii Patak likes it or not.

But she knows herself, doesn't she? Knows herself enough to trust in the Path decision that has come to her, and also to trust in her own heart. Because loving Tusika couldn't possibly be the wrong choice, not when she feels so strongly about the young woman standing beside her, taking these steps forward with her, now, into the future.

Niya and Tusika walk hand in hand up the grand staircase in the center of the room. At the top of the stairs, they turn back to bid farewell to their gathered families. When they turn back to the doors that lead to the private suites where the physio-locks will be removed and the Adanadi administered, the giant doors *swoosh* open with an audible, hydraulic hiss.

Together, they enter.

— · · · —

"This way, girls."

A short, round woman leads them down the hallway. She is the same woman who put Niya's physio-lock in place. She recognizes the three tight and high buns atop the woman's head and the way she lisps over certain words.

The girls sit next to one another while the healer removes a sterile tray of instruments from the mobile cart that wheels about the room. The cart is linked to the niisi of whichever healer is on duty, connected on the daso network of the center; as soon as the healer enters the room, the cart proceeds to follow them, producing any necessary tools, medicines, or supplies that may be needed.

Removing the physio-locks is simple. In a nearly painless procedure that takes only seconds, the woman removes the implanted device that has been modifying specific hormone and corticosteroid release from each girl's upper arm. Next is a quick injection in the same location that will cause a near-immediate breakdown of any remaining medicines from the implant that may be lingering in their tissues.

In less than five minutes, both Niya and Tusika are

ready to receive the Adanadi.

The healer escorts them from the room and hands them off to another staff member, this one a fairly young man of dark complexion and strong features. His hair is remarkable, impressively long and stark white—unusual coloring for his age, but striking and beautiful nonetheless.

"Follow me, please," he says with a smile. They walk down a series of hallways, wide enough to easily accommodate a personal mobility device when needed. "I have been assisting with the preparation of Adanadi solutions for several years now, but I have never had the honor of preparing two solutions for a single ceremony."

Tusika, who has been uncharacteristically quiet up until now, responds. "Oh, friend. You will do well to remember us—today is the day you prepare the Adanadi for the ceremony of Niya Suwatt and Tusika Patak. We will do great things with this gift that we are about to receive."

He laughs, the sound tinkling and joyous. "Is that so? I will remember it indeed."

The man turns one last corner and guides them into a beautiful room. The walls are alive with plant growth, and the ceiling is convex, bulging almost like a living thing down into the room from above before curving back up and up and up—to a cylindrical opening to the world beyond. Birdsong can be heard emanating down the shaft-like structure in the middle of the room, echoing from just beyond their line of sight. Though still nervous, Niya appreciates the smell of green in this room, and the songs of the skies.

Set about the room at evenly spaced intervals are sixteen pedestals—fifteen for the most common animals chosen for the Adanadi in all of Makasing, and one pedestal where another animal may be selected from the database of all available species. Each is outfitted with its own three-dimensional display, very much like the miniature displays of their personal niisi devices but much grander in size.

"Please, explore the room. And take your time. Once you have made your Path selections, you can lock in your decision at the station of your choosing." Their guide inclines his head towards the girls in a sign of respect for the decision they are making, the decision that he gets to be a part of for so many. "If you have any questions at all, please do not hesitate to ask."

Both girls offer him thanks. He turns away to give them privacy. Niya and Tusika look one another in the eye, then turn together to face the room at large.

"Yo, my friend—we only get to do this once," Niya says, a shine to her eyes, her mouth dry and her heart fluttering in her chest. "Some time alone to check things out, you think? I know the Patak connection to Deer is strong, but this beautiful place. We may not have another chance to explore it again."

And there that look is again, that solemn, nearly fretful look, coloring Tusika's eyes and cheeks in uncertainty or worry most unfamiliar.

"Hey—" Niya begins, pulling Tusika closer by their conjoined hands. "Are you—"

But Tusika shushes her, the veil of familiar confidence

and easy authority falling quickly back into place. As if it had never wavered.

"Hush, my friend. I am well. We will take some time alone, yes—I think that is best."

The girls walk in opposite directions from one another. Niya heads towards the nearest pedestal. As she approaches, an image projects up into the air above and around it, the complex machinery inside having sensed her nearness and activated the deck.

The simulated voice of a Cahokian elder emanates gently from Niya's own niisi. Since her personal device is automatically on the same daso network as the building, the communications are routed straight to her for ease. When she walks up to the first pedestal, it also starts generating a hologram individual performing PSL for her, possibly a setting left on for a previous Adanadi-taker who needed it. Since Niya does not, she makes a swiping gesture on her niisi to turn the PSL off.

Niya watches as the floating pixels coalesce into various images, the images fading quickly from one to another, creating a video that she is able to walk around, taking it in from every angle. As she watches, the simulated elder voice tells her about this path.

Bison is a mighty creature, the voice says. A cloud of billowing dust blows up into the air, the impressive projection going as high as the ceiling. The sounds of stampeding hooves echo up from Niya's wrist. *Strong and protective, the manas watch over their calves. The bulls fight for their place in the hierarchy of the plains herd.* The image zooms across the wide open stretch of prairie grass to focus on a large group of bison. They are running full out, fierce and determined. *Bison is a key part of everyday life for all peoples—providing meat and furs that are used for sustenance and warmth. Their bones are used for ceremony and structure.* The scene pulls back, shifting. Now, the herd is at rest, grazing. A calf nurses from his mana's sack. Young bulls run and kick in playful, testing circles. *Those who take the Adanadi of Bison are often granted unique strength and will.* A group of young adults take the place of the playing bison. They toss rocks a great distance, playing catch with them as if they weigh very little at all; they partake of a game of tug-of-war that nearly results in the rope itself fraying down the middle. *A powerful combination of mind and body...*

After a minute or two, Niya walks away from this pedestal and towards the next. As she goes, the sounds fade from her niisi and the image dissolves into nothingness. The Bison pedestal falls back asleep.

Across the room, Niya catches sight of Tusika, moving away from one pedestal where a pair of twin fawns are grazing under the watchful eye of their mana. She approaches another, and a great tree sprouts up to the ceiling, and an agile fleet-of-foot raccoon scampers across a long branch.

Turning back to her own side of the room, Niya moves on.

The next pedestal is for the Path of the Spider.

There is hardly another creature capable of creating more unique and masterful structures in nature than Spider. The voice this time is different, though still artificial. An image appears bit by bit before Niya and in the space above and around the pedestal, this time a vast and intricate array of webbing. Though the coloring of the image is a mix of bright and iridescent pinks and blues, purples and deep grays, Niya can almost convince herself that the spider webs in the air before her are a striking silver, glistening with morning's dew. *Spiders' strength comes from her ability to create—structures that give off the false appearance of fragility, ensnaring her prey with cunning artistry, geometry, and optical illusion.* The image shifts, honing in tightly on a large wolf spider. Numerous eyes shine back at Niya, purple and blue, midnight black and sunset pink. *With Spider's many eyes, no secret remains hidden for long...*

Niya visits the pedestals of Bear, Falcon, Badger, Eagle. She and Tusika cross paths. Fox. Snake. Crow. Raccoon. Deer.

There are only a few pedestals left, when a great and glorious night sky positively erupts upward from the one nearest to Niya.

Silent are the wings of the great Owl in the night. The darkness envelopes her, until the very moment before she strikes. Niya steps forward, a feeling of reverence resting atop her shoulders like a comforting hand, a familiar shawl. The flapping of powerful wings is silent as Owl's flight, but a faint vibration pulses up her wrist from her niisi. The sensation feels like it is coming from inside her own body. The beautiful and haunting form of a dark-feathered owl soars into the projection. *Hardly any other animal endures and excels in the night like Owl. No other creature so calculating, so wise.* The owl above the pedestal suddenly turns his head, one of those big, yellow eyes blinking. And it catches her gaze. Niya is sure of it. Even though no other pedestal's path animal had done any such thing. *The sounds of Owl hold meaning for and sway over all Peoples. The majestic creature flies across the night skies, and she keeps a silent, watchful eye during daylight, too.* The image cuts to the owl dive-bombing its prey, swooping down with the precision and velocity and power of a perfectly-aimed spear. *To befriend Owl is to befriend Death herself,* the disembodied voice of an artificial elder woman says. *To befriend Owl is to live on a path of endurance and cunning.* A small screech owl now sits in the branches of a tree. The lights from the projection indicate daytime. The owl appears to be sleeping. But then it, too, opens its eyes, turns its head, is searching, searching, until it finds—

"Niya."

She jumps at the interruption. The pedestal deactivates. Turning her head, Niya comes face to face with Tusika. She glances across the room and sees that their guide is watching them out of the corner of his eye. As soon as Niya spots him, he turns back to the corridor outside, caught.

"Whoa, you okay?"

"Yes, I..." But she trails off, uncertain how to answer.

"Have you chosen?" Tusika asks, glancing curiously at the pedestal that Niya has stopped at. "Is it—"

"Go on," Niya says suddenly, her voice choppier than she intends for it to be. "Let me meet you in the corridor, if you have made your choice." She begins walking away from the pedestal and toward the door. "I need only a minute more. And you have made your choice, haven't you?"

Tusika smiles, and it's that charming look of hers that flips Niya's stomach. Because it is both the Tusika she knows and loves, and it isn't. And she is both people at once, somehow.

"I have. Take your time," Tusika says, going towards the exit after squeezing Niya's elbow gently.

Once Niya is truly alone, she casts her eyes across the room. She can't help but wonder which Path her friend has chosen.

Ahh, silly, Niya thinks to herself. *A Patak never falters.*

The thought leaves her mind almost as soon as she thinks it.

And she turns her intentions towards the Path of her choosing, moving forward in a few quick, purposeful strides.

"Your preparations have been made ready," the man says.

He extends his hands, palm up. In each rests a small oblong cylinder made of a special gat-printed material. It is opalescent in hue, catching the light in a mysterious way. As Niya reaches forward to grab her vessel, the material is almost squishy, yielding to her touch. She looks at it closely and can see a light etching in copper and turquoise—a faint outline of her chosen Path animal. She smiles in reverent acknowledgement.

This is her Adanadi. The small dropper contains the aqueous solution that will be instilled into the corner of her eye, where the cultivated, concentrated material from the source animal of her choosing will become a part of her.

She will be forever changed.

With a smile of eager excitement, she turns to her friend. Tusika is looking at her own dropper with a surprising stoicism.

"Tusika—"

But the other girl gives a short, almost imperceptible shake of her head. Niya does not finish her question.

"You will each complete the giving of the Adanadi for the other." He continues, appearing slightly less confident after the unexpected interruption from Niya, but he soldiers on regardless. "At least three drops from your vessel must make it into your eye. Do not worry, there is plenty in each. And there is no harm if you administer extra drops."

"How will we—" Tusika starts.

This faltering in her voice at all is something new and strange for Niya to witness. Her friend is a guide in maintaining absolute confidence in the face of any adversity. And this... this is not adversity, is it?

She continues. "Will we know when the process is complete?"

"Oh, yes," their guide nods along with his words, as if to drive the point home. "You will know."

Niya does not know if the peculiar man has a mysterious streak about him or if it is simply a byproduct of working here, where he does. Seeing people go through the Adanadi process day in and day out, handling and mixing all the various solutions. If she were not so excited for what is about to happen, she might dwell on it more, or perhaps partake of some light teasing. She still had time to change paths at university...

Instead, she places her dropper, her vessel, in her left hand, extending her right hand to her friend. Tusika swallows hard before giving Niya the smallest of smiles and mirroring her actions.

"Ready?" Niya asks.

Tusika looks her right in the eye. Her nod is swift and forceful, and Niya is nearly sure that the girl means it.

A panel to the side of the door before them is engaged, and it slides open with that magnetic yutsu hum that accompanies so much of the movement in Cahokian life.

As one, they enter.

─ . . . ─

The room is of modest size. The lack of decoration is distinct and purposeful. Niya quickly recognizes the heptagonal shape of the space, not having to count the walls to know that there are seven. There is simply a way about the space, something welcoming and familiar, that lets her know that it is a sacred seven-sided room. The shape to the walls is abstract, giving it an almost limitless feel to it, despite its average size. It does not feel any larger than perhaps the common living area of most Cahokian homes. The walls themselves seem lit from within, a pulsing vibrancy to them that fills the space with an artificial but comforting warmth.

In the middle of the room are two cushions, also seven-sided. They are each in the middle of a slight recess in the floor, this, too, heptagonal. The cushions are elevated on their own columnar shapes up and out of the recessed floor section. The girls walk towards them. It seems obvious that the space can be shaped and altered to fit any particular Adanadi taker's needs. For the girls, it has been set up to allow them to either sit cross-legged, kneel, or face one another in some other way of their choosing.

Niya takes up the left cushion; Tusika, the right.

"Are you ready, Kakooni? Truly?"

Niya hums back, low and deep from the back of her throat. "I should be asking you that, my friend. You seem spooked."

"I am ready," comes Tusika's response, no small amount of haughtiness lifting her tone. Her shoulders thrown back, her chin raised high. Her face is all seriousness for a moment before she lets loose a sly grin. When she speaks this time, her tone is for Niya alone—not for some imaginary audience that needs convincing. "I am ready," she repeats. Calm. Slightly quieter. Niya's Tusika.

This time, Niya believes her.

Reverently, they swap droppers. Tusika inspects Niya's. Her eyebrows lift.

"A strong Path," she says, nodding in approval. "I can feel it, Niya. This is the right choice for you."

Niya glows at these words. It is not up to anyone else to approve her choice, but she loves Tusika dearly. To have her approval means much to her.

Looking down, Niya rotates the small dropper between her thumb and first two fingers of her right hand. She is turning it, twisting it about in the light to get a look at the deer engraved there, the Path animal that every Patak scion for seven generations previous has chosen.

And when she catches sight of the engraving, she can feel her breath catch in her chest.

Tusika has not chosen Deer at all.

She has chosen Raccoon.

"Our ceremony, together," Tusika says, her voice solemn and low again. Niya's head jerks up, and their eyes connect with intensity. "This secret, ours alone."

Suddenly, the speech about "following your own way" that Tusika had given Niya that morning makes sense. Her angst upon waking. Her hesitancy at times, even today, leading up to this moment.

You honor your own heart. You follow the path that you are meant to follow.

How strange, comes Niya's first thought. How strange, indeed—not only for Tusika to seek a Path other than the one traditionally followed by her family, but to keep it a secret? Secrets, not a common part of family life. But Niya acknowledges that the Patak and Suwatt families are each very, very different. In some ways that are more significant than others.

How brave, comes Niya's next thought, close on the

fleeting wisps of the first. Brave, for Tusika to follow a Path wholly her own.

And then a traitorous thought, an unwelcome thought, flits across Niya's mind.

How worrisome.

Not the Path, but the secret of it. Not the Path, but whatever Tusika's reasoning for deviating from her family's expectations might be.

With a soft smile, Niya reaches out to lay her hand over Tusika's clenched fist, the one not holding Niya's dropper in it.

"Safe with me," Niya says. "Both your secret, and you."

And she means it. Because she would try to keep Tusika safe from this secret, from her family, from the end of the world if she needed to. That's what Niya would do for this girl, for her best friend, for the person she loves. She knows it to her bones.

With a smile now that seems more genuine than any other she has offered today, Tusika unclenches her fist and holds Niya's hand in her own.

"Let us begin."

Niya says a prayer to herself in Tsalagi. The words echo in her mind. Her eyes are closed while she prays, and Tusika is respectfully silent. Her friend is not particularly spiritual and has never been the first to initiate prayer, even preceding such an auspicious event as this one. Tusika participates in things such as smudging within her own home or ceremonies in the community for which participation is expected, but she does not live and die by the sacredness of such things.

Once Niya's prayer—to the Creator, to her ancestors, and to her soon-to-be Path animal—are complete, the girls take turns placing several drops into the other's eyes. Niya goes first, instilling several drops into Tusika's left eye. Then, after a few necessary blinks, Tusika does the same for Niya.

A few seconds pass, then Tusika speaks.

"He said we would know when—" But she doesn't finish that sentence, instead opting for another as the Adanadi takes over, doing what it has done for so many before. "Oh."

"Tusika," Niya starts, "What does it feel li—"

And then Niya, too, is gone.

It feels like flying, because it is. *Niya* is—flying.

On the back of a great white and brown barn owl. Powerful, majestic, silent in the night sky.

Niya does not know what a right Path choice feels like, does not know if she would have been better suited for another Path animal.

But Niya knows that this, *this*...this feeling of flying, this feeling of connection, this lightness...

It is the most important and most beautiful thing she has ever before felt.

Niya flies now on the Path of the Owl.

And she knows not what heights await her.

pit | *how owl learned to fly*

PITSIKA

Niya does not feel so different, not really. Once she surfaces after the Adanadi runs its course, she feels very much like the same Niya who awoke earlier that day.

Except for all the ways that she is no longer that same girl.

A young woman now, walking on her chosen Path.

She and Tusika stand from their cushions, embracing one another. The other girl's arms around Niya feel like vice grips, tight and unrelenting. Niya leans into the feeling, suffusing whatever warmth she thinks she has to offer across their bond in an effort to offset the tension rolling off of her best friend in waves.

"What is done is done," Tusika whispers. Then she says it again, and again.

What is done is done.

As if saying it will make it true. Or less true—Niya is not sure.

"It is done," Niya affirms. "Should we go to our families now, or—?"

"Our families." Tusika repeats the phrase, an odd intonation on the second word. As if it tastes foul, in her mouth, or unfamiliar.

"We can wait a while longer," Niya assauges. "Here, we can sit—"

She pulls Tusika towards her, sitting them down side by side on the cushion that Niya had occupied during the brief taking of the Adanadi, during the moments after, when her Path animal—Owl—had carried her through the skies above Makasing and beyond like she was the lightest of burdens. Like she was no burden at all...

"Tusika," Niya says, more firmly now than ever. "Sit." She pauses. "Tusika, are you alright?"

Her best friend is silent. It has a stillness to it, that silence, a solemness inappropriate for what should be an abundantly joyful moment, and Niya feels out of sorts. She decides to sit in the quiet and listen—not just with her ears, but with her heart. Reaching out with a perception that grows from both her head and her heart, hoping to understand Tusika's somber silence better.

Niya does not know why Tusika has taken the step that she has taken, why she has gone down the Path of the Raccoon rather than the Path of the Deer, as is expected of nearly every Patak family member in living memory. But she clearly felt compelled, and isn't that reason enough? Niya has no familial ties that she knows of to Owl, no one in her immediate family who was rooting for this choice. And yet, here she sits. Not Beaver nor Eagle, nor Fox nor Bear. But *Owl*.

The difference between the Suwatts and the Pataks is all the difference in the world: status. Expectation. Position and power. And by choosing Raccoon, Niya knows that Tusika has explicitly denied every expectation of her family. The ramifications could be...well, *everything*.

Or nothing.

And it seems that Tusika has come to this same

conclusion, has probably been ruminating on it for days or even weeks herself.

"They do not have to know," she says. Niya's eyes snap up to her friend's face. Tusika continues. "My path is my own. No one else's."

"But your Path traits, surely they will make themselves manifest. And when you develop an Ability, it may be obvious what animal's Adanadi you've taken." Biting her lip, Niya reaches out and rests her hand lightly atop Tusika's where the other girl's fingers are digging into the cushion. "Wanzi...it is going to be a hard secret to hide—"

"But I will!" Tusika interrupts, her voice rising. She throws her hands up forcefully, pushing Niya's away. She breathes in sharply and then releases it just the same, before a terse calm settles back over her. When she turns towards Niya, her eyes are shining. Tusika reaches out, grasping the hand she'd pushed away moments before in both of her own. No apology comes, but Niya sees it writ large on Tusika's anxious face. "I will...with your help, my friend. Right?"

Niya looks sideways at this girl, her closest and best friend. She thinks back to the night previous, when lips had pressed gently against the corner of her mouth. How they had slept in tangled limbs; grown up together with purpose and fortune tangled, too. How they have grown in confidence as confidants over the years, and none of it by chance...

Bowing her head, Niya thinks of the differences between Deer and Raccoon.

"Not so different," she whispers.

"What?" Tusika asks, and she looks shaken, as if from a trance.

"Deer and Raccoon," she clarifies, wrapping her arm around her friend. "The animal's Path you have chosen is not so different from the one your family wished for you. Deer, she spoke well amongst her forest friends and foes alike, and she was wise in teaching people to treat animals—even those we hunt—with respect. Raccoon has rarely met a stranger, a gifted communicator; he can be tricky, but he has great intellect to accomplish his wiley schemes..."

Tusika nods, and her voice is stronger now than it has been since taking the Adanadi. "Deer possesses great wisdom while Raccoon is cunning—but both are leaders."

"See?" Niya bumps her shoulder against her friend's. "Not so different! And you're a Patak, Tusika—you'd gain an Ability from your Adanadi Path and rule the Council of Twelve whether you chose Deer or... or... Cricket! I'd swear by my ancestors in ghost country that you'd be in charge even without an Ability." At this, Niya playfully nudges her friend with her shoulder, but she is met with an unmoving cold.

Tusika, who has been looking across the room, into the distance at nothing at all, turns eyes as sharp and glinting as daggers on Niya when she says this. Niya feels taken aback, would pull away from anyone—from anyone else.

"You really think that?" Tusika asks. And her voice is as cold as a gentle stream in winter. Her voice hides a venom that Niya feels is unfamiliar and familiar at once—she has heard this tone, has watched as it was turned on others. But never on Niya, not until now. "That Kaatii Patak would even be *seen* with an ungifted firstborn child of hers?"

"Well," Niya begins, taken aback by this question, "yes, I...we both know how Kaatii can be, but she would never forsake you for something like—"

And just like that, whatever spell that had been cast upon the both of them is broken.

No, not broken—shattered.

"You were right before," Tusika interrupts, standing so abruptly that Niya's arm is thrown off of her. "We should not keep our families waiting."

Her back is to Niya, and Niya feels cold, confused.

Then, as suddenly as Tusika has become this hard, unfamiliar creature to Niya, she changes again. Spins around and faces Niya as if nothing is out of the ordinary.

"Are you coming, Kakooni?"

Even the nickname feels strange, coming out of her mouth. But Niya shakes herself and grabs ahold of the outstretched hand before her, smiles as if the world has not shifted beneath her feet, and the girls make their way out of the ceremonial room, towards whatever it is that awaits them on the other side.

NISHAAWI

There are purple and blue streamers flying through the air, draped in the trees and from every pole beneath the pavilion. The two families have gathered to celebrate the girls' taking of the Adanadi.

The Pataks, who have, for generations, had uncannily high odds of developing an Ability after the taking of the Deer Adanadi, are gathered at one end of the pavilion. They have amassed quite a crowd around them, as some of Tusika's most boisterous uncles are taking bets.

"Old great grandma Wichan was the Patak who received an Ability the fastest of all—in less than one single day, she had Far Sight!"

The crowd murmured in excitement, some of them Pataks and others merely members of the community anxious to celebrate the taking of the Adanadi by the youngsters. Some have heard these stories a hundred times already, while to some, the stories are brand new.

Another of the uncles takes center stage now, hardly having to lift his voice to be heard by the captive audience before them. "On the other hand," he says, stretching out his arms and bringing the hush of the crowd down with him. "Foolhardy cousin Koonoo did not receive his Ability until the very end of the fortnight period. It was the early morning hours of his fourteenth day when Deer's Smile came to him in a vision so strong..." Here, the uncle crouched down, paused, and then leapt upwards with a roar. "He wet his breeches!"

The people around him let out a shout, the laughter carrying to the far end of the pavilion.

Niya is surrounded by some of the women in her family—her mana and two niisis, a younger cousin, Kiyan, from her noosoo's side, and her mana's sister.

"The Path of the Owl!" her mana says. "Oh, you have to tell us how you came to this decision, my love."

"Aren't you supposed to pick an animal the same as the rest of your family?" her cousin asks.

None of the women in the circle belittle this question, as it is an important question to ask. In the Suwatt family, choice and individuality is important. In some families, traditions and family history—and sometimes no shortage of pride—determines what Path someone might walk.

This thought makes Niya's stomach clench. But as the person who has most recently taken the Adanadi, she feels it is important that she be the one to answer her little cousin.

She reaches out and rests her hand gently on the girl's shoulder. "Not necessarily, but this is sometimes the case." Her eyes dart across the shaded pavilion area to where Tusika's mana and noosoo are sitting on a bench. They look as if they are holding court of some sort, sycophants from the community and their own family alike stopping by to pay homage before departing. "The Path you choose might be influenced by your tribe, your culture, the stories you grow up with. Perhaps an experience you live through or a feeling in your gut. It might be important in your family unit to be on the same Path as one another, but it is not a requirement. There is no law that tells us what Path we must choose."

"Or that we have to choose a Path at all?"

Now, those gathered around Niya do laugh a bit. Not because this is an ignorant notion, but because the Adanadi is a gift from the Creator—a tool that the people of Makasing have cultivated and harnessed in order to make their world a better place for all. To not take the Adanadi would be to shirk a great and powerful gift.

On the breath of her chuckle, Niya says, "Well, you are not wrong, cousin. You do not *have* to take a Path, not if you do not want to. But only good comes from taking the Adanadi." She cuts her eyes up to the matriarchs of her family—her niisis, her mana, her aunt. "Right?"

"The Adanadi grew out of the darkest of nights—"

"The Darkening," the cousin, Kiyan, offers.

Niya's mana nods sagely before continuing. "Yes, the Darkening—the Awis. When the Creator places something on this earth to harm us, there is something of equal and opposite value, something to heal and make whole again. The Awis was a terrible time, and even now, we sometimes face its ramifications. But the Adanadi..."

Ahyoka steps towards the edge of the pavilion, stretching her arms out wide. The other women follow.

Between her outspread hands lies the great cityscape of the Mataawi District. From their elevated position atop one of the grandest mounds in the district, they can see the distant spires across the Mizizibi waters of other parts of Cahokia. And the buildings constructed with sturdy materials, gat-printed alongside those made from the earth—to be returned to the earth someday, when their own time comes. The hum of yutsu barges on the water, the magnetic shivering power of the rail system beneath their feet. The bright primary colors printed up or painted upon every human-made surface. The glow of the city, the glow of the Adanadi—suffusing every part of Cahokian life.

Niya glances with pride at her mana's face. That widespread wingspan of her arms, long fingers tapering to points and casting a shadow behind her from the face of the midday sun—she looks like the embodiment of the Path of the Eagle. She looks almost as if she could fly.

"This," she continues, "would have been possible in time, but the Adanadi took our progress and sharpened it. Oh!" she interrupts her own storytelling rhythm with a shake of her head and a rueful chuckle. "Would we have come to this?" She poses the theoretical question. Not even Kiyan interrupts with a theoretical answer. "Yes. I believe, yes—we would have. But in my lifetime? No. And not in Niya's, or yours, Kiyan—or perhaps even any children that either of you may someday bring into the world. The Adanadi was the Creator's gift, the Creator's way of offering balance to the world after the Awis changed it irrevocably. To not take the Adanadi would be an unusual choice, but it is a choice that a few do make. But for those of us who have taken it, we walk our Paths with the confidence given by our animal and, occasionally, with Abilities gifted to us by our Creator."

There is a pause, a long one. And then Kiyan speaks up, chirping, "I think I'd like to choose Fox! Foxes are the absolute cutest!"

All of the women burst out into laughter, with the young girl at the center of it all, hands on hips, demanding that her choice of Path be taken seriously.

Of course they will—every decision that a person freely makes matters.

Niya remembers this as her eyes scan the crowd, looking for Tusika.

Instead, her eyes alight upon her horticulture mentor, who catches her eye and smiles. Niya excuses herself from her family to greet the primary elder who has been responsible for her tutelage over the past year—and whose endless patience for Niya's questions and desire to experiment with grafting and cross-cultivation has allowed Niya to excel as quickly as she has.

As she makes her way across the large, shaded space, greeting other well-wishers, community members, friends, and family alike on her way, she subtly continues her search.

But she does not find her friend. Not for some time to come.

— · · · —

It takes a few hours for the drowsiness so typical of taking the Adanadi to properly sink in, buoyed as Niya had been by the excitement of the gathering. When Adasi and Nampeyo had arrived—late because of a traffic jam on the water—Niya had jokingly berated them for their tardiness, then given them hugs that her great grizzly of an ancestor would have been proud of. But even the boost of energy at having her friends near didn't last, and when they depart to take care of familial duties, Niya feels zapped again. The tiredness suffusing every bit of her body currently makes her feel as if she could sleep for a week.

This is the moment that Tusika chooses to reappear.

Niya is making her excuses, a politeness though all who had taken the Adanadi understand her reasons, bidding many farewells with the help of her immediate family members, when Tusika is suddenly at her side, fingers lightly pressed into her elbow.

"Niya," she says, her voice quiet but with that familiar confidence that Niya had seen waver before. Niya turns to the girl and smiles at the look Tusika is giving her—a look that says she has been anywhere but where she wanted to be, anywhere but with her best friend. "Are you leaving?"

"Yes," Niya's reply is light, an easy smile on her lips, "to sleep. And if you are half as tired as me, you will do the same." She feels grounded, just being near the other girl again, especially after all the madness of the afternoon. A part of her needs reassurance that Tusika is still *her* Tusika, not that other person she had momentarily seen back in the Adanadi chamber.

"I am barely keeping my eyes open. Do you think your family would mind..." Tusika pauses, and Niya encourages her with a purposeful tilt of her head downward, a gentle look up into those eyes, suddenly nervous. "If I were to come to yours? It's just that," she continues in a rush, "the crash after taking the Adanadi can last quite some time. I want to be somewhere..." She shrugs, her shoulders lifting in a gesture altogether unfamiliar for Tusika—or at least not a gesture she would perform with anyone but her closest friend, "where I feel safe. Like myself."

"Ah." Niya realizes she has no reason to be nervous. Tusika will always be welcome under the Suwatt roof, and her friend knows this. "Of course, Wanzi."

The afternoon has been full of people and speeches, dancing and drums, all sorts of music and food and even gift-giving. Tusika is made for crowds, was born and bred not only to be a socialite of Cahokian society but a top-tier politician, made for pomp and circumstance, built to go the distance and leave no back unpatted and no wrist unshaken.

But even politicians need rest. Even socialites need to step away from the spotlight.

Even a Patak sometimes needs to live as a Suwatt.

— · : · —

The trek back to the Suwatt home passes in a blur. Niya's mana is the only person to accompany them, her noosoo and the others staying behind to continue the celebration, feeding their guests and honoring the ceremony's success.

The celebration will go on long into the night. If there is one thing Cahokians cherish, it is the ability to honor the good times. The hard times were so common for so long that every new birth, every taking of the Adanadi, every binding ceremony or household elevation—it is all precious.

Niya hardly has the energy to change out of her

fancy ceremonial outfit and into something comfortable for sleep. But she does, shoulder to shoulder in the space of her room with Tusika. They change in silence; they have, in fact, both been silent nearly the whole way home.

Tusika is dressed more quickly than Niya, one of the sleep shirts she keeps at the Suwatts' place draped over her, so well-worn that it's got a few holes that she happily ignores. She's wearing a pair of underwear too, and nothing else. She crawls into Niya's bed, claiming the far pillow for herself, and curling into the tightest little ball that Niya might have ever seen.

Finishing up quickly to follow her friend, Niya slides beneath the mess of blankets. The two girls find each other quickly beneath the covers. Hands clasp together to rest atop Niya's stomach. Tusika presses into Niya's side, melding to her like warm clay.

Niya wonders at their fit, not for the first or last time, the Creator knows. At the ways in which they are alike—proud and fiercely protective of their friends, hard workers and generally good at whatever they put their mind to. And the ways in which they are different—Niya, slow to anger, deliberate, careful, maybe too much so; Tusika, passionate, sometimes rash, daring. And their families, similar and dissimilar, the same—the Pataks, high up in the most elite social ranks of the city, and the Suwatts, climbing in prestige year after year; Patak loyalty, hard to keep, while Suwatt loyalty, hard to earn; generations of Abilities for one family, and none for the other.

She wonders about other things, too. They tumble about inside Niya's skull like bits of rock or shiny, polished marbles bouncing from surface to surface. Jumbled and unclear.

Niya knows that she is many generations removed from those who first received the Adanadi. And Niya knows that she will be far from the last to take it. She may not be special, not in the big scheme of the Creator's making, no—but what is it, exactly, that comes next?

She has been given a gift. A common gift, one that nearly all in Cahokia and most of Makasing are able to receive, if they so wish. But it is a gift, certainly. What will she do with it? How will Owl guide her?

What comes next?

According to her teachers, her continued tutelage under the horticulture elders. Expanding her mastery of the art.

According to her parents, taking up the mantle of the Suwatt legacy, helming the business enterprise they have built for themselves over the years.

According to Adasi, something that exists beyond the confines of her friendship with Tusika.

And according to Tusika, something great. Something Niya decides, and decides for herself alone.

But which will be true, if any?

Beside her, Tusika's breathing is already deep and even. A calm lays over her, forehead smooth and body relaxed. Niya finds that same breath in herself, deep and even...

Sleep comes, and she welcomes the respite from her thoughts.

HISIKA

When she wakes, Niya does not know if she has been asleep for two winks or two solid days.

She'd only had one dream, and she remembers it but vaguely.

Flying.

Soaring, diving, lifting through the air. All on her own, as if she had been born to it.

Keeping her eyes closed, Niya hones in on the dream, willing it back to the surface. She grasps at it like so many wisps of chilled air trying to escape the morning thaw.

It is there, isn't it? Just at the edge of her sleeping memory, an image... a dark hole in the mountainside, a yawning spot of black amongst the gray rock and green foliage.

A cave.

In her dream, Niya had approached it. That gaping maw, a grotesque scar in the otherwise whole and wholesome terrain of... of... somewhere. Elsewhere. Not here.

Now, awake, Niya cowers at the thought. Shudders to think of going anywhere near that place.

Her eyes spring open, pushing the image away now instead of pulling it closer. Any good dream would dissipate, right? Any average, ordinary dream would have the good sense to leave her conscious mind alone.

But Niya is disturbed to find her experience to be

altogether different. For now that she has recalled the place, now that she has made the cave manifest in her waking consciousness, she cannot do anything but remember it.

Beside her, Tusika continues to sleep. Niya looks at her friend instead, doing her best to focus on the tiniest details in an effort to distract her unsettled thoughts.

They had taken the time to remove their makeup before falling asleep, but only so they didn't smear it all over Niya's blankets and pillows. They had, however, failed to take down their intricate hairstyles before falling into their respective heavy sleeps post-Adanadi. Niya sits up, beginning to slowly, methodically remove her braids as she gazes at Tusika.

The other girl has a smoothness to her brow that is rare—not because she is commonly troubled but because she is always thinking, always plotting and planning each step to whatever it is she imagines next. Her red skin is smooth now because Tusika is as restful as she ever is, as unburdened as only sleep can allow a person to be; but there are slightly purplish rings beneath her eyes. She needs this sleep.

Niya nearly scoffs at that thought, the slightest trace of bitterness coloring her feelings at the notion that her own sleep may have been restful and unburdened, but the waking she had experienced had been anything but that. She can still see the cave, despite her attempts at distraction.

Done with her own hair, Niya carefully repositions herself. With the delicate touch of the expert horticulturist she is training to become, Niya begins to undo

Tusika's mess of hair from the beautiful arrangement it had been crafted into for the ceremony. Beautiful now, it is not—still soft and shiny, creases from the tiniest of braids pressed into the strong fibers. But messy from the girl's heavy sleep. Loose bits have already come free from the trappings of leather ties and mesh-printed design elements that glow only faintly now in what Niya thinks is the early morning light of an onrushing day.

Once she has taken out all of the pieces that she can access without waking her, Niya arranges it in a neat looping curl away from Tusika's face.

Niya looks at that face and wonders: *What were you thinking?*

Her fingertips press along Tusika's hairline, trailing gently along the girl's temple. As if she could divine with a touch her thoughts, her intent.

But no—knowing Tusika has never been so easy as that. Nor has loving her.

As the sun begins to filter into Niya's bedroom, she notices for the first time something tangible, physically new and different about herself: her Adanadi mark is beginning to appear. Like a bruise, but more colorful—more beautiful, and distinctly Niya's own. It looks like a stain across her forearm. As Niya slowly twists her wrist, she can almost convince herself that the splayed edges of the mark look like a wing set to take flight.

"Mmm..."

Tusika's voice hums from inside her throat, her chest. Niya tears her eyes away from her arm and to her best friend. Without even opening her eyes, Tusika tilts her head, pressing her cheek more fully against Niya's hand. Then her mouth, the soft outline of her lips. A press to skin, a warm exhalation of air.

Niya feels her heart pound at the touch—the easiness of it, the simplicity. How naturally it comes to Tusika, even in sleep. Niya's breath goes shallow. Then Tusika's hand is reaching up as she is turning, presenting her back to Niya at the same time that she pulls Niya's arm over and around her body.

"Heh."

The sound escapes Niya's slightly smiling mouth of its own volition as she is naturally pulled into a cradling position by her sleeping best friend. She slides down to rest her head on the pillow more easily and to be as close to Tusika as the girl's insistent pull demands.

"Sleepyhead," Niya whispers, her forehead pressing against soft, black hair.

But even as she says it, even as she thinks how nice this feels, how familiar and safe—Niya herself falls back into an easy sleep.

"I am hoping for an Ability that centers the intellect of my Path, you know?"

Tusika's words form the shape of a question in every way but their intent. She is speaking to Niya, certainly, but her thoughts are only of herself at the moment. Niya is crunching her way through a handful of walnuts or else she would respond. But Tusika needs no engagement to continue for the time being.

"It is why I went with Raccoon after all—a certain

stature is expected of a Patak. My poise and leadership will grow, but I may achieve an Ability the likes of which my family has never seen before. Can you imagine—" her eyes light up, and Niya leans forward, intrigued, "—if I were to receive Eagle's Insight?"

Niya does nothing to repress her sigh. "Tusika," she groans. "Why this game?"

But Tusika ignores her friend's exasperation. "I would not use this word in any other company but yours: if I were to receive that Ability in particular, can you imagine how *useful* it would be on the path to achieving my destiny?" This last word is practically uttered in a whisper. "Not merely a member of the Council of Twelve," she continues, "but a leader of the whole of Cahokia. Shaping political directives and influencing the entire city?"

"Two million people, beholden to your whims," Niya says jokingly, "how will we ever manage to keep your ego in check?"

Tusika scoffs exaggeratedly, throwing a peach pit at Niya's forehead. She misses by a mile, but only because of Niya's quick reflex to duck out of the way. When she speaks, that charming demeanor of hers is lit up in full force, and her tone is playful—but, as ever, there is a hint of serious truth beneath the veneer of casual near-indifference.

"You know what I mean, do not purposefully mishear me! People would not be beholden to me, Niya, but they will benefit from my leadership, don't you think?"

Niya nods, reaching out to poke at her friend's knuckles where they are wrapped tightly to the handle of the cracker they had been using back and forth to open up walnuts, sharing the sweet meat from inside with one another in between slices of fresh peaches from the market.

"Of course they will," Niya responds, and she means it, too.

Tusika purses her lips, eyes intently boring into Niya's as she reaches for another peach. She begins cutting it into quarters for them to share. "And what Ability do you think you will receive?"

"We've been over this," comes Niya's response, accompanied by a good-natured eye roll. "Your family are the ones who receive Abilities, not mine."

She purses her lips, indicating that she wants a slice of the juicy fruit. Tusika obliges.

"Niyaaaa," she replies, dragging Niya's name out much longer than is necessary to get any conceivable point across. "What harm is it that comes from the imagination? What damage do our dreams do to us, hmm?"

Immediately, Niya thinks of the cave from her dream. Its dark and gaping entrance, ready and waiting to pull her down into unknown depths.

She shakes herself, back in the present. Tusika quirks an eyebrow at her, asking without words if Niya is alright. But Niya brushes the concern away, and Tusika lets her with a *hmmph* and an arched brow.

"Tell me this, Tusika: if you were to wake up on the fifteenth morning after taking the Adanadi, only to discover that you had not manifested an Ability of any sort...wouldn't you feel let down, after all the imagining and the dreaming, the foolishness and silly hope?"

Tusika's own lips puff out now but in a pout. Niya bites the inside corner of her lips in an effort not to smile at the easy charm of the look she's being given, the captivating pull to agree, even if all she wants to do is argue.

"Is it foolish?" Tusika asks. "To dream? To wonder what an Ability will feel like, flowing beneath your skin, only a breath away from manifesting!"

Niya pauses to think, reaches out to grab a slice of peach right off of the knife's edge where Tusika is holding it beside her thumb. Tusika watches her with a mischievous grin, moving her thumb to her lips to swipe at the leftover moisture with her tongue. Niya narrows her eyes in a playful glare.

"It is not foolish to dream," Niya finally says, her words measured and thoughtful. "But the exact same dream in your mind and in mine are different, in the end."

Tusika's grin slides away. Her lips are ever so slightly downturned when she responds. "You are right, my friend. I'm sorry to have made light of the possibilities."

She reaches out, resting her hand on Niya's thigh. Niya glances down at her friend's fingertips, the way they press into her bare skin just below the hem of her short trousers. She licks her lips and shakes her head, as if to free herself from the spellbinding effect the other girl has on her.

Leaning on her elbows against the tabletop, Niya rests her chin in her hands. "No frowning—what is it that Mama Patak says?"

The girls intone simultaneously, "A frown today is a wrinkle tomorrow, and a wrinkle tomorrow is forever."

They tip over into laughter instantly, the mocking and overserious tones they had used to mimic Kaatii's voice not helping the matter in the slightest.

"Didn't I tell you, Kakooni?" Tusika says, grinning up from where she has the side of her smiling face pressed against her arm, resting atop the table. Her hair is splayed out around her like a spread of feathers, shiny and straight. Her chest heaves with breaths that are lightened by laughter and joviality. Her hand is no longer on Niya's leg, and she feels both heavier and lighter without it.

And Niya thinks that this must be it: the moment when Tusika is more beautiful than she has ever before been.

She blinks at the question. "Tell me what?"

"Taking the Adanadi, it didn't have to change us."

Niya's mind sweeps her back to the club. That was only three days previous.

"Not everything, right?" Niya says, echoing back Tusika's own words from that night.

Tusika's eyes are bright. She does not blink. Neither does Niya. And the moment seems to stretch on, and on.

Not everything, the words come to Niya without further prompting. She keeps them to herself.

Not everything, her mind says, *but some things.*

Time will tell.

A week passes, and neither Niya or Tusika develop an Ability. But six days remain in which one may come to either of them, or both.

Or neither, Niya thinks to herself, the thought itself a little black cloud above her head as she makes her way through the marketplace.

Since Niya has taken the Adanadi, she finds it curious: she feels just as she had before.

Except in the ways she feels different.

When she paddles in her canoe across the Mizizibi to Tuboo Sokobi for university studies, she does not get tired. Well—she *does* get tired, but it is a different sort of tiredness than it was before she chose Owl. Ordinarily, Niya would be quite winded upon arrival, particularly if the water was high after a heavy rain, or if the dams further along the mighty river upstream were recently opened.

The other day during class, she caught herself forgetting to record the elder's lecture. And then she realized why: she remembers their words and instructions more easily than before, without so much need for repeat iterations and study.

Owl's enduring nocturnal hunts; Owl's sharp mind.

The marketplace is busy, the noontime meal approaching. Niya weaves her way in and out of the masses, making it to the designated place where she is meeting her friends: a cart that travels the length of the district, making the best passionflower fruit and maple syrup drink, chilled and served with a dollop of elderberry jam on top for the purchaser to stir in, completing the tasty beverage. The owner of the cart also bakes hearty rolls stuffed with spiced meats and smoked vegetables, a perfect lunch.

"A-yo!" Niya calls, waving one arm above her head as she spots her friends—easy enough, with Adasi towering over so many others in the throngs of people.

"Hey, little sister," he calls as she joins them.

Nampeyo hands her a lunch roll at the same time that Tusika joins them with a tray of the favored drinks.

"To your health," Tusika says distractedly.

"Wado, Wanzi," Niya says. Her eyes concernedly follow her friend as the girl walks along the path to a secluded seating area, off the thoroughfare. Adasi and Nampeyo share looks of surprise with her, Adasi's eyebrows raising in question while Nampeyo shrugs.

They follow after Tusika. Niya takes a bite of her roll as they move away from the cart, down the path to a copse of luminescent shade trees. The seating area has hammocks and seats low to the ground, tables and benches under shade tree cover. The group heads straight for one tree in particular, sitting among its great roots, which have been shaped by ecological architects over the years into its own seating of a sort.

Niya sits opposite Tusika, who is staring off into the middle distance, lips pressed to the edge of her cup. When Niya extends her legs, poking a covered toe against her friend's, Tusika only gives a measured smile, appeasing and lackluster, before shaking her head slightly.

While Niya is just as aware of the setting sun attached to their Adanadi window as Tusika is, she also knows that Tusika's awareness is tied much more tightly to familial expectations that none of them can quite grasp.

The meal passes without idle talk, the only sounds around them those of the city.

Once food and drink have been consumed, Adasi claps his hands together, quite possibly in an effort to diffuse the unease. "I found a new comedian for us to check out tonight!"

Nampeyo scratches at their forehead, mouth crooked to the side in trepidation. "Adasi, would I be terribly out of line to remind you that the last amateur comedian whose show you 'found' for us to attend—"

"Was a total nightmare?!" Adasi finishes on Nampeyo's behalf.

Nampeyo cringes at the brutal accuracy of Adasi's statement before nodding their head in agreement with it.

"A fluke," Adasi says, mischievous grin in place. "You will see—this one, she is the real deal. Just you watch, she will be touring all of the hospitals in the Wiijwanka district before the next harvest."

To work in the healing centers of Cahokian society is the greatest goal of nearly every comedian pursuing the noble art. If Adasi is right, then this comedian he has picked out for them to see could be truly excellent indeed.

"What do you say?" Niya asks, gently nudging Tusika again.

"I say," Tusika replies, her words slow and measured, her gaze far away. Finally, she finishes her sentence, having left each and every one of them nearly leaning forward with bated breath in anticipation. "Let's go then!"

Adasi gives another of his trademark coyote's *woop!* into the air, and the tension seems to dissolve.

Adasi and Nampeyo beg off from their lunch break first, eager to return to classes—Adasi because he is so near to finishing, and Nampeyo because, simply enough, they love learning. Niya and Tusika bring up the rear, their pace much slower.

"The Adanadi countdown is weighing on you, isn't it?" Niya asks.

They weave in and out of the crowd, making their way to the docks.

"No use trying to hide it from you, Kakooni. And if anyone could understand..."

"No Ability yet," Niya says, finishing the thought easily. "You and me both, then."

She might have hoped to be past the worrying—which was a foolish notion. All who take the Adanadi secretly hope for an Ability, wiling away the waiting period afterward, waiting for a feeling—a sign, some notion untold, that would indicate they had been chosen. The signs of an Ability were always different, always varied, unpredictable, and uncertain until the moment a person began manifesting something strange, and supernatural. Abilities could be lumped into larger categories; speed, cunning, insight, strength, but they all manifest differently, and to differing degrees. Some might have waited and were blessed with an Ability only to find it to be weak compared to someone with the same category of Ability. Such things only added to the weight of the wait. And of course, despite the weight of her own vigil, Niya is all too aware of the mountain that Tusika must be bearing.

"You know, there's a superstition in my family about this period of time, between receiving the Adanadi and the closing of the fourteen day window."

"Go on," Niya urges her friend, bumping her gently with her shoulder.

Tusika chuckles, pressing gently back against Niya and then reaching down, looping her fingers around Niya's wrist. "They say that the longer it takes to manifest an Ability, the stronger it is. Silly, yeah?"

"Well, I don't know about—"

Niya's words are cut short as a young woman nearly barrels into the two of them. Niya pulls Tusika to a stop just in time to avoid the collision. Niya's quick reflexes and curiously sharp senses, the only reason why the stranger doesn't run smack dab into the pair.

"Ah!" their assailant exclaims, stumbling a bit amongst the throngs of the bustling lunchtime rush. Tusika reaches out to steady her, and the woman's hands land on Tusika's forearms. "I didn't see you, my apologies."

"It's alright," Tusika says, the frown on her face one of concern but also wariness.

"Are *you* alright?" Niya begins to ask.

But before the words are hardly even out of her mouth, the woman is gone.

Not before Niya manages to note her appearance: dark coloring to her skin, darker even than Tusika's, with eyes a shockingly light brown, almost golden, in the light of the afternoon sun. Her black hair, wrapped in a stylish but simple knot with several braids running through it. A streak of frosted-morning blue hair dyed at each of her temples, the length of the blue woven throughout her braids and the knot. She couldn't have been more than a year or two older than them, if that. Her clothes are remarkable to Niya only because of how unremarkable they are: simple, dark pants with a midnight blue, long-sleeved tunic, cinched at her slender waist. Whereas so much of the Cahokian fashion scene is about expression and creativity, this stranger's dress seems fit for blending in. And the woman herself, a flurry of lithe limbs and quickly uttered apologies, almost frantic in her movements. Her eyes, alight, as if searching for something she hasn't yet found. Her lips, chewed up with worry.

Niya stares after her for a moment, but the mysterious and rather abrupt woman has disappeared into the crowd as quickly as she had surfaced.

When Niya turns back around, she is confronted by Tusika's wicked, wicked grin.

"What," Niya huffs. It isn't really a question, and she isn't sure she wants to hear whatever it is that Tusika is about to say, not with the way her hip is cocked to the side and with the energy that seems to have found her again.

"She bumped into me too, you know."

"And?"

"You don't see me stammering after her!"

"Well!"

"Niya has a *crush*," Tusika sing-songs.

"You are mad. Absolutely mad."

Tusika laughs, not managing to dodge Niya's hand as she playfully swats at her shoulder.

"Not as mad as you are, I think," she continues to chuckle. "I do believe she could have knocked you right down on your butt in the street and you would have thanked her."

"*Mad,*" Niya huffs. "And she was nowhere *near* knocking me down, I'll have you know. Besides, I don't have time for some inane crush."

"What *do* you have time for, then?" Tusika asks, still grinning.

Niya playfully rolls her eyes before mockingly batting her eyelashes in her friend's direction. "Only for you, my love."

It's a joke, of course, and it makes Tusika laugh. But it makes Niya's insides scrunch up painfully, all too aware that she makes time for Tusika, always. That the only silly crush between the two of them is the unrequited one that Niya Suwatt has for Tusika Patak.

They reach the dock and Niya's canoe, and she takes them back across to the university islands, Tusika intermittently chuckling throughout the journey, as if laughing at some secret joke to which only she is privy. At least her friend's mood was buoyed by the encounter.

Niya's mind is split between two thoughts when she returns to her classwork.

The first, whether or not Tusika might someday feel for her as she feels for Tusika. This, Niya thinks, less probable than her receiving an Ability from the Adanadi. The brief interaction served to raise the question between them, echoing in the opposing canyon walls of their two hearts.

The second, the woman's face as she had steadied herself in the marketplace—those eyes, that intent set to the lines of her worried mouth...

For some reason, Niya cannot unsee her, not for the rest of the day.

———

So it isn't crazy, Niya decides, when she imagines seeing the woman in the crowd later that night at the comedy club.

She hardly even hears the jokes being told, as distracted as she is. When the audience gives an uproarious laugh at something the comedian says, Niya takes it as her opportunity to sneak off to the toilets.

But she does so not from some pressing need but to try and see if she can't spot the woman somewhere amongst the bodies in the club.

When she returns to their table a few minutes later, Adasi is sure to tell her that she missed all the best jokes. Nampeyo is actively snoring, having fallen asleep in the plush cushions of their space some time ago. Adasi is riveted by the performance, especially enamored by the comedian's use of their travels as fodder for their set. Had she not been so distracted, Niya might have paid better attention for Adasi's sake; he was sure to speak of little else for weeks.

And Tusika is riveted on Niya.

"Alright?" She asks.

"Yes, yes," Niya assures her.

But is she? Or has she simply gone crazy, thinking she is seeing things where and when she isn't?

Her lackluster assurances are enough for now, and Tusika turns away from her and back to the stage. But Niya knows she isn't imagining a slight and subtle shift in her friend's behavior—Tusika's hand lands on Niya's exposed thigh, her fingertips caressing Niya's skin more sensually than is strictly fair, Niya thinks, or even usual for them. The cool brush of the delicate, metal links of Tusika's bracelet tickle, and Niya leans into the touch, the feeling, the rush.

Tusika's strategy, though, has worked. Because Niya does not think of the woman from the marketplace the rest of their time at the club, nor the comedian, nor the Adanadi. No, she thinks only of the way Tusika's skin feels against hers.

It's that word again, that feeling: *intoxicating*.

As they prepare to leave, Tusika leans close, her hand still on Niya's thigh. Her breasts are against Niya's side as she whispers, "Come back to mine with me tonight, Love?"

That word thrilling her hidden heart, what could Niya possibly do but nod her agreement?

There's something about that word, about *intoxicating*, that calls back to Niya from her horticulture lessons and old tales from her herbalist niisi about such things.

A handful of bitter red berries that ruin your insides; miniature apple-like fruits, manchineel, sweet until they close your throat; small but beautiful hemlock flowers along the water's edge, pleasant on the tongue until the seizing, the shaking, the mindless death.

Tusika's lips, painted bright, bright red tonight.

Intoxicating things can be toxic.

PINA

The air is thick as the girls make their way through the gloom to Tusika's home.

Niya looks up to the sky. "Feels like rain."

Almost as if she has summoned it, the sky opens up.

"Ahh!"

They run through the sudden downpour, passing several mounds in the night as they approach the Patak home. As the seasons change, the weather turning colder, the upper levels of homes tend to become abandoned, shut off from the rest of the structure. The living spaces within the mounds themselves stay cooler in the summer heat and warmer against winter's chill. Tonight, there is sparse evidence of life, late as it is. Faint white glowing against the gat-printed window materials. If there are other sounds in the night, they are drowned out by the thundering rain.

A lightning strike slashes through the sky as they round one final corner, splashing through already forming puddles as they arrive on the doorstep.

Tusika's home takes up only a slightly larger footprint than Niya's, but the differences are otherwise endless, starting with the front door. It is made of dark, weathered oak. Heavy and imposing but undeniably beautiful—and far richer when compared to the Suwatt's, which is made of pine.

The girls shelter under the overhang as Tusika moves to brush her niisi against the panel inlaid on the door's surface. Just as the lock mechanism *thwangs* softly out of place, a voice shouts at their backs.

"Hey, yo!"

Niya, normally so aware of her surroundings, feels caught off-guard by the voice. She wants to blame it on the rain, which has turned from a deluge to a more gentle pitter patter as the heaviest thunderclouds have largely passed by. Or perhaps, more aptly, on the way Tusika's body is pressed to hers; the promise in her best friend's voice of something more, something she has anticipated for so long but only ever dreamt might come to pass...

Yes, it's Tusika more than the rain that has clouded Niya's senses, her awareness, her good judgment.

"What—" Tusika turns around at the same time, her tone aggressive, bordering on annoyed.

"Oh," is all Niya manages.

Because the young woman from the marketplace is approaching them through the mist and light rain. The cool drops have hit the warm ground and the rushing Mizizibi waters and stirred up a fog that is rolling through now, and Niya's breath catches on the lone syllable she is able to utter.

Because this woman—who had looked so striking in the marketplace before—now looks like a goddess incarnate. Like Selu herself, or a beloved woman of old, from the stories out of the time before the Awis. Her dark brown skin almost glows from the night lights and the raindrops. She is wearing an outfit of criss-crossing overlays of green so dark as to appear black with alternating strips of blues—every color, it seems, from the sky to the rushing winter stream, the butterfly's wing to the azure banners of the marketplaces. The bodice is tighter about her middle before billowing down and out around her. Her strides are purposeful and sure, her gait solid, unwavering.

Even in the face of Tusika's glare, which is anything but measured. Anything but kind or welcoming.

"You are the daughter of Kaatii Patak, member of the Council of Twelve."

"Who are you to ask?" Tusika shoots back. Niya thinks it unwise to point out to Tusika that the stranger had not posed a question at all, had clearly been stating fact.

The woman is less than three steps from them now, and Niya shivers at the steely resolve in her golden eyes.

"My name is Inola Cato, and I must see Kaatii Patak."

"That is too bad," Tusika says. "It is late. You will have to go through proper channels." Something passes over Tusika's face, a shadow. "How did you know how to find…"

The woman—Inola Cato—allows Tusika's voice to trail off to nothing. And then she steps forward purposefully, making for the front door, arm extended.

Faster than a striking snake, Tusika counters Inola's steps, reaching out to grab the woman's wrist. She gives it a twist, a classic defensive move they are taught in their primary school classes. But Inola moves her entire body with a counter-twisting motion, using Tusika's own body against her. Inola moves them both near to the side of the Patak home, pushing Tusika near to the very door she had been trying to enter. Taking half a step back, Inola flicks her wrist. A rush of wind seems to sweep around and then past her hand, and a small dagger flies at Tusika's outstretched hand.

With a gasp, Niya steps forward. But she quickly sees that her friend is not injured—merely annoyed, and perhaps the tiniest bit relieved that the woman hadn't impaled her.

Tusika stumbles but cannot move far. The newcomer's dagger has wedged itself expertly, with a supernatural precision, into one of the links of Tusika's bracelet, right into the oak door. Mouth agape, Tusika almost immediately begins to pull at her wrist to free herself.

Around them all, the rain continues to fall.

Inola is now on the doorstep, her shoulders perpendicular to Niya's chest. The stranger turns her head slightly, eyes cutting down and to the side, catching Niya's. And Niya could swear that the woman's lips tilt upward ever so slightly.

Not a smile, no.

But a *smirk*.

Inola presses her palm flat against the door that Tusika had already unlocked.

Niya's voice is small as she says, "You can't."

This gives Inola pause. Tusika is still fuming in the rain, her petal-pink painted face running with tiny rivulets. She continues to try and pull herself free.

"Can't I?" Inola asks. Her tone and volume match Niya's—quiet, beneath her breath. Almost conspiratorial. She, too, is drenched, the strands of dyed blue hair at her temples pulled loose, dripping down her neck and collarbones.

"It isn't—" Niya starts, unsure as to how she will finish, even with Tusika spluttering next to her.

"It isn't what, little owl?" Inola asks.

Niya's lips part in a gasp. How had this stranger known her Path?

"Polite," Niya finishes. Tusika groans.

This gets Inola to turn her body more fully towards Niya. She tilts her head, looking back at Tusika.

"Sorry about the... rain," Inola says to Tusika. Then she looks Niya full in the eyes, and Niya feels every ounce of energy coming out of that amber gaze. A penetrating energy, a sense that Niya is being perceived in a way that she never has before in her life. "And I am sorry," Inola continues, "that I am unable to be polite. In this matter, I do not have the time or the will to practice such manners. You will have to find it in yourself to forgive me."

Then Inola pushes the door open, crossing the threshold into the Patak home.

Niya almost feels sorry for the woman, certain that Kaatii Patak's ire will be potent enough to dissuade any such future impositions.

— . . . —

"I am looking for Kaatii Patak."

Inola's voice is strong and steady, like her gait. She calls down the hallway, disappearing around a corner, leaving a wet trail of footprints as she goes.

Niya moves to help her friend free herself, but as she reaches her, Tusika gives a mighty grunt, pulling the dagger from the door. Looking like a mad woman on a mad mission, she follows swiftly after the stranger-turned-intruder. Niya is right on her friend's heels, uncertain as to whether or not she will have to intervene physically—what else is Inola Cato capable of?

And with the dagger clutched tightly in her fist, what might Tusika Patak be able to do?

When they turn the corner, they nearly run into Inola's back. She has stopped, her feet spread to the length of her shoulders, a puddle forming from her sopping hair and clothes. Tusika moves around the edge of the room like a wild cat, edging along so that she is partially between Inola and her own mana.

Because Kaatii Patak is awake at this hour.

Of course she is, Niya thinks to herself. *A Patak's work is never done.* Hasn't she heard that phrase enough over the years?

The elder does not stand at the intrusion. She is sitting on a lounge chair near the hearth at the center of the room. On a small table to her left, a cup of something hot enough to be steaming. In her hands, she is holding a tablet whose holographic contents she swipes back downward into the screen, all too casually. As if it isn't top secret Council of Twelve business. As if she doesn't have a strange woman in her home, dripping wet atop a magnificently large hand-woven rug.

Niya finds herself flinching as she watches Kaatii's eyes drag from Inola's gaze down, down to those moccasins where they are actively muddying the piece, and back up again.

Kaatii is not as tall as the eldest Patak living, but she strikes an imposing figure, even dressed as she is in house moccasins and a supple robe marked from top to bottom with flowing patterns of light red and white. Beneath the robe, she is wearing a loose but richly-styled red shirt with clasps done up from hem to neck, and white sleep pants.

"I am Kaatii Patak," Tusika's mana says, "but I imagine you already know that."

The woman does not waste even a moment's time.

"I am Inola Cato of the Badger Band of the Muskoke, my mana's people, members of the Keetoowagi Federation. My noosoo is of the Wild Potato Clan of the Tsalagi. I am here to request your help on behalf of my people."

Though Niya does not find it particularly easy to look away from Inola Cato as she proclaims the needs of her tribe, she does manage to cut her eyes across to Kaatii. And what she sees is a shadow of interest, largely masked behind that cool politician's facade that the Council member has perfected over half a life and longer.

"Tell me what it is that your people need, young Cato." Inola opens her mouth to speak, but Kaatii is not done speaking herself. She holds up a hand and Inola's mouth snaps shut. "But as you tell me, remember that you are here as an uninvited guest. You would do well to tread lightly and not become an unwelcome one also."

Niya watches as Inola breathes deeply, tiny

indentations in her cheeks forming as she seems to chew on them inside her mouth. Waiting, contemplating…

And then, she charges onward.

Within moments, Niya is enraptured by the story unfolding before her, by the rhythmic cadence of Inola's voice.

The woman comes from storytellers, she can tell.

And this is what she says.

One year ago, a man walked to the center of our village at midday on a day of rest, when many were congregated there for the breaking of bread and sharing of stories. He raised his voice and proclaimed that he was leaving for the hills, and that he implored all who wanted to know the truth of the Adanadi to follow him. He turned to the north and said: if you feel forsaken by your Path, follow me. He turned to the east and said: if you did not receive an Ability from your Path, follow me. He turned to the south and said: if you worry that your children—and their children, and so on—will be dependent on a ritual that does not guarantee success or advancement in life or means, follow me. He turned to the west and said: if you believe another way exists, wherein we may all reap sweet rewards, follow me.

To the horror of many watching on, the man walked away. And he did not walk away alone.

No, two others followed him that first day—a young man, and a middle-aged woman. As the three disappeared over the last hill at the village's edge, the final sight for the people left behind: the man's blood red cloak, flapping in the otherwise still air of the night, and the backs of their two family members with him.

But the whispers stayed behind. Seeds planted that day grew. And tales from the hills where the three had retreated came back to our village on the winds of change.

Not all winds are good. Not all change is sacred.

Frightful tales of the ends to which man will go to become something more. Experiments and worse. Untried and ancient ceremonies, bastardized for nefarious purposes.

And the whispers that came into homes in the night carried people away in the day. The man's numbers grow still.

Inola Cato comes before you now, seeking help—for her people, and for the souls who are wandering. For they believe they are found, when truly they are lost—or so near to it that the relentless and unceasing passing of time, any time at all, is a boon to him and a harm to us.

Help us now, before this sickness spreads from our hills and across the region. Before it sweeps across the whole of Makasing, poisons Cahokia, and chokes the peoples of our lands.

— · · · —

The storytelling abilities of the woman before her may have captivated Niya. But one glance, one syllable out of Kaatii Patak's mouth, and Niya knows that she is probably the only person in the room so enamored.

"Well."

Inola's cheek twitches. Niya holds her breath, releasing it only very, very slowly. As if to disturb the air may break the fragile peace of the moment. She can see it on Inola's face—the woman wants to say something. Is, perhaps, desperate, to speak more words into existence and make her plight strike home like an iron in a forge, sparking Kaatii Patak to action. But she holds her tongue. As any storyteller worth their salt would do in the same situation—let the words ring out, let their truth and their energy manifest in the world on their own.

"This man instigating villagers to join his cause, what is his name?"

"His name is Gishkiy."

Niya almost imagines a pause in Inola's voice before she utters the man's name—as if to say it is to invoke a power better left untapped.

But maybe there is something to the man's name after all, because it has sparked emotion strong enough to burn in Tusika's mana. Kaatii stands, her unwavering gaze positively scorching.

"You bring this story to me, now. In my home. In the middle of the night."

"Councilwoman Patak, he has sent one of my band's members home in *pieces*. How many more—" Inola begins, misunderstanding, not realizing that this was no question.

But Kaatii performs that authoritative gesture from before—a hand in the air, and silence falls like ash. Inola's mouth snaps shut, and Niya watches as the muscles at the side of her face and neck twitch, tensing from the effort of holding her tongue.

"There are proper channels, and there are improper channels. You have demonstrated that you believe this channel, my home, in the middle of the night, to be *proper*. I will now give you the benefit of believing you know this is not proper. So, speak now—and tell me what courses of action you have already taken. In what ways have you thus attempted to handle this matter on your own?" She pauses, waiting for a response with an air of sincerity that rings utterly false to Niya.

As a member of the Council of Twelve, Niya knows that Tusika's mana has spent a lifetime cultivating these words. Knows exactly how to use them to help, to hurt, and to raise high her comrades just as she brings low her adversaries.

Inola clasps her hands behind her back. Niya can see the tense line of white across her knuckles where she is squeezing her fists tightly together.

"Appeals have been made to our village Council. Our elders. Even our war chief."

"To no avail?"

"None."

"What else?"

"I have appealed up to the Keetoowagi Federation's body of government. But..." Here, Inola bites her lip, ducks her head the slightest bit, then glances back up at Kaatii as if testing the waters. "You may know that their body of power is not particularly...expedient."

Stillness, and then Kaatii's lips quirk the slightest bit. So slight, that Niya believes she might have imagined it altogether. But Inola takes it as the positive sign it might be and continues.

"I worry that there may be even less expediency placed on our plight due to the small size of our village and our location."

"Which is where, precisely?"

"We border closely the Haudenosaunee lands."

"Ahh."

Niya shifts slightly where she stands, uncomfortable but unwilling to draw attention to herself as things unfold in the Pataks' primary room. But this new revelation makes sense—the Keetoowagi and Haudenosaunee regions are, to put it very, very lightly, not particularly fond of one another, so far as Niya has always understood.

"The Haudenosaunee see us as Keetoowagi, the Keetoowagi see us as Haudenosaunee—or too close for comfort. Government forces are stagnant, and I—" Inola's voice cracks. She lets loose her hands to wipe the back of her wrist over her brow. "*We* need help. They have... my sister. She joined them some days ago."

Kaatii is quiet a moment.

"You must seek a proper audience before the Council of Twelve."

Inola barrels onward, seemingly oblivious to the utter control Kaatii is holding over the younger women in the room.

"But time is of the essence, and I—"

This time when Inola falls silent, it isn't even because Kaatii has raised her hand. She doesn't need to.

A mere lowering of her chin, a sage arch to her brow, and Inola's words fade away as the power structure in the room seems to finally sink in.

"You must seek proper audience—"

"And what would you do?!" Inola bursts out, taking a step forward that isn't threatening so much as it is desperate. "What would you do if they took someone important to you? What if they took your *daughter?*"

Her voice is ragged as it tears from her throat, and she throws her arm out, gesturing in Tusika's direction.

Tusika is standing opposite of Niya, moving ever closer to her mana as the conversation unfolds.

But as these words come from Inola, Niya watches her friend. Something crosses Tusika's face. She isn't sure what it is, not precisely and not at first—but it is not warm. And neither is it fear.

As the moment settles, Niya sees it more clearly for what it is: Tusika has heard Inola's words, and she has seen them as a challenge.

And Tusika with a challenge laid before her is like a hungry wolf fighting for a kill. The survival of who she is rests on the outcome. She will not back down, will not fade away, will not forget.

"My daughter," Kaatii says, "has no part in this. Not until she ascends the Path of the Deer, rises to the occasion, takes her rightful seat on the Council of Twelve someday in my stead."

The same call to politics and destiny as usual. Niya has heard it as many times as the other Patak sayings the family loves to lean on.

But that isn't what Inola hears, apparently.

"Deer?" Inola says, her face scrunching up in confusion as she looks directly at Tusika now, tearing her eyes away from Kaatii for what feels like the first time since their engagement has begun.

Niya swallows the gasp that bubbles up from her chest, remembering what Inola had said as she had passed her in the doorway.

Little owl.

Is it possible? Niya wonders. Can this Inola Cato see a person's Path?

How?

Niya's head snaps over to Tusika, and she sees something new in her friend's eyes. If she had been challenged by Inola's words before, now she looks as if her stare could shoot daggers; like the dagger in her hand would not even be needed—as if she could commit murder, cold-blooded and relentless. The wolf on the hunt.

No, Niya stops herself. Doused with cold realization, she sees things more clearly in a flash. *Raccoon, prowling for the precisely right opportunity. Not a predator searching for prey, but a scavenger searching for the right challenge—and the perfect way to overcome it.*

Inola shakes her head. "Your daughter has no role in this, you are right in that. But can't you see with your heart? Can't you marry the ideals of familial bonds and duty?" She takes another step forward, and Niya watches as Kaatii's fingers flex, inching closer to the ni-isi at her wrist. "Can't you help me? Knowing that you are my last hope, won't you help me?"

Without missing a beat, Kaatii says, "It is time for you to leave, Inola Cato. And hope that I do not unkindly remember this impromptu meeting when you ask for an audience before the Council of Twelve."

These last words are threatening enough that Niya can see the calculations happening behind Inola's eyes, can see her wondering at the possibility of success—can see hope dwindling, even as the four women come to a standstill. Niya can see the urge to continue imploring writ large and bald on the newcomer's face, and silently pleads with her to yield.

To no avail. One last step forward by the stranger, and in less than a blink, Tusika has crossed to her mana's side.

"A cornered beast may do anything to survive," Kaatii says.

Not to Inola, and certainly not to Niya—but to Tusika, whose fingers of one hand are still wrapped around Inola's dagger while the others are hovering in the air above her mana's niisi, blocking her from calling Suyata to their home.

The Suyata are elite guards in Cahokian society, and each member of the Council of Twelve has guards on call, day or night. But Tusika, with this staying gesture, has kept the force from crashing down on Inola like a deadly wave. For while Kaatii could certainly hold her own, and Inola has the force of her supernatural aim, Suyata defending the elder are certain to beat her bloody first and ask questions later, if ever.

Why? Why would Tusika block the call?

"She is leaving now," Tusika says, her eyes boring into her mana's. Something happens then, something crosses between them that Niya and Inola couldn't possibly interpret. Then she cuts over to the uninvited guest who is standing terribly close to the both of them, fists clenched and jaw tight. "Isn't that right, Cato?"

The air is thick with tension, muggy—as if the stormy Mizizibi fog had followed the women indoors.

All eyes are on Inola as she does the strange, the unexpected: she turns to Niya, merely the slightest tilt of her head, shift of her shoulders. And those light eyes meet deep brown, and she asks without words: *Is this the choice I must make?*

Niya's heart races. And she offers a subtle nod. Her chin dips towards her chest almost imperceptibly.

Then Inola's eyes close, her head bows, and she gives one definitive, defeated nod.

She turns to leave without any further conversation. And Niya is almost certain that she sees a tear slip from the corner of the woman's eye as she goes.

And from next to Kaatii, Niya can feel Tusika's eyes burning into the both of them as Inola departs.

KAWANZI

"Gishkiy." Tusika says the name as if it will provide some sort of clarity or resolution. "Gishkiy... this name sounds familiar, but his way of doing things does not." She turns to the stone-cold profile of Kaatii Patak, daring to ask a question as only a Patak's progeny might. "Do you think the Council will be able to help?"

When Kaatii Patak speaks, she speaks to the room at large—as if Niya and Tusika are not the only people there to listen.

"There is an order to things."

"We know that, mana, but do you think—"

"There *must* be an order to things."

She does not say more, and her tone brooks no further discussion. The three of them stand in the uncomfortable silence for a short time, and then she leaves without a word, heading down the hall and to her private room.

As soon as her mana is out of sight, Tusika collapses down on one of the sofas in the living area.

"Can you believe that?" Tusika asks, throwing her arms up behind her head. "Kaatii may be a tough nut to crack, but breaking and entering is no way to charm her. I can't believe anyone would think such a thing would get their request taken seriously."

Niya feels as if her feet are glued to the floor. She looks down at them, surprised that she hadn't even removed her moccasins. But when would she have done that? Before or after racing in after Inola Cato and her best friend, all three dripping rain water in their wake? She feels strange, out of sorts. But she looks up, looks at her best friend, and answers the question with a question of her own.

"Can't you?"

Tusika, who has been wiggling down into the plush cushions and wrapping a blanket around her shoulders, freezes at Niya's tone. The words are pleading and accusatory at once. As if on cue, Tusika sits up straighter, her feet going back to the ground. Niya watches as her facade shifts, changes, falls into place—just as it should. Just as Tusika would like the world at large to perceive her at all times.

Niya dislikes the appearance of this side of her best friend, but she knows that Tusika's mana would be proud. The two of them, so alike in this moment—whether Tusika will ever admit it or not.

Niya's thoughts, so excited and feverish on the way to Tusika's home, what might await, grow more dour and disturbing as time passes. Why does she feel like she does not know the other young woman at all? Where is the person Niya loves?

"It is a strange circumstance that her people are dealing with, that is for certain. And even though I have no siblings of my own, I can imagine the fear in her heart at the thought of her sister with such people."

Tusika bows her head, silent and contemplative for exactly the right amount of time to come off as sincere, and perfectly so. Niya feels her brow wrinkle, drawing downward as she frowns. When Tusika continues, Niya finds herself listening not for the expected words and phrases, intonations and beats, but for the cracks that surely must exist.

When she sees the cracks, hears them, *feels* them, Niya experiences the slightest breaking of her heart.

"We must give people from all lands of Makasing the respect that they deserve. Her situation, while frustrating and frightful, is not widespread enough to worry. She will seek an audience before the Council, and they will help her. Right?" Tusika lifts those shining eyes of hers up to Niya, a gentle smile on her lips. Sounding all too much like she is regurgitating Council of Twelve business, or like she is playing the part of her mana at business, she says, "Cults like this, they spring up and die off all the time out in the provincial areas. This one will be just as short-lived, you'll see."

"Right," Niya says in return, knowing in her heart that Tusika does not believe a word of what she has just said to her. She shifts from foot to foot, uneasy. Then she says, "I think I will walk home."

Tusika stands at this proclamation. "But I…" her voice trails off, and Niya believes that the hesitancy her friend is displaying is real this time—real because these are *Tusika's* expectations that are being dashed rather than those of a stranger. It is selfishness that draws her across the room to Niya's side, her hand darting out to gently grasp Niya's. "I thought you and I…well, I thought we might spend the night together."

This last word is set with a weight that Niya recognizes. It is a gift, an easy skill, that Tusika has used on their classmates or even young men or women at clubs on occasion. When she wants something—when she *really* wants it with her whole being—Tusika gets it. She is not used to being turned down. And the offer seems real to Niya, *almost*—would be more sincere if she wasn't remembering the way Tusika's eyes had burned when Niya had stared after Inola's departing figure.

Does Tusika really want to take Niya to bed? Or does she just want to keep her friend's mind off of another person?

Niya smiles, but it does not reach her eyes.

"Not tonight, I think."

A trap set and triggered. Tusika reacts quickly, and with venom.

"You don't want to stay with me," she says, her voice edging into that haughty Patak tone, "because you are worried about *her*. An absolute stranger, Niya. Is that so?"

Niya lifts her chin, unused to this particular tone being deployed against her.

"I do not want to stay with you, Tusika, because it is clear that you have no empathy towards that stranger."

When she turns to go, Tusika, still with her fingers wrapped around Niya's wrist, pulls her back around.

"What, do you think my mana is supposed to stop what she is doing for every citizen of Makasing who comes barging into our home in the middle of the night?" Tusika scoffs, barks out a laugh at the very notion. "And if I take a place on the Council of Twelve one day, do you expect the same and more? That the people of Cahokia shall employ me, but the whole of

Makasing shall take from me instead?"

Niya twists her wrist, pulling free from her friend.

"That is exactly what I expect. To lead is to serve. You want to lead, and so you serve. And you serve *all* peoples, not just the ones you deem fit to care for. You are meant for greatness, Tusika Patak. A true Cahokian, bright and intelligent and strong. But compassion is freely given, without tax or payment in return. And I fear that you have not learned that lesson tonight." Taking two steps backward, Niya finishes with, "I will see you in the light of a new day."

She feels sadness as she turns to go. But despite the shakes that she feels will be upon her shortly, Niya realizes that she has made the right decision—she cannot stay here, not tonight. Not even with a thrill and promise of something closer, something more intimate, than Tusika has offered her before. The draw to share physical intimacy with this star around which her world has always seemed to revolve—even this cannot shine brightly enough to blot out the heavy knowledge that her friend may be fatally lacking in the one thing a leader should have in abundance: compassion.

Ordinarily, to leave the offer of intimacy behind would be a choice that leaves Niya feeling uneasy. Instead, she feels more like herself as she leaves the Patak home than she has since they arrived here. The shakes she expected die down quickly as she departs.

She does wonder, though, if the offer will ever come again. The thought that it might not causes a sob to rise within her chest. The difference between the cool indoors and the muggy air outside is enough to distract her, to calm her uneven breaths. The rain has broken up, turned more to a light, patchy drizzle on the tail end of the storm system. Without a cover, Niya's skin prickles with goose flesh in the chill air of twilight, that onrushing push of the sun over the horizon threatening. She bows her head to keep the steady *drip, drip* of raindrops out of her eyes.

As she passes between two prominent mounds, taking the turn down a pathway that leads to her home, something catches her peripheral vision: a long, lean body, pressed against the side of the grassy human-made hill. The person's head is leaned back, eyes closed, face upturned to the heavens.

Niya both is and is not surprised to see her: Inola Cato, despondent and alone.

Inola has not seen Niya, what with her eyes pressed shut against the barely-there pitter patter of occasional rain drops. Niya could continue on, unobserved, leaving the other young woman undisturbed. Leaving her to fight through her emotions alone, her struggle, the plight of her people.

Niya knows that this stranger had needed the help of a Patak, but Niya is a Suwatt. Certainly not with the same political clout, but from a family with enough renown that maybe, just maybe, Niya *can* help. But there is something more important than Niya's surname: her heart, her compassion. She cannot sit idly by while this woman gives in to despair. If she does not stop, Niya knows that she will be betraying some small part of herself.

Planting her feet, Niya turns toward the other woman,

shifting her momentum in resolute movements. Each step forward is one that she cannot take back, but she wouldn't change her path.

Her steps are quiet in the semi-dark, masked by now far distant thunderclaps and raindrops and a handful of domesticated wolves howling up at the weather-laden sky.

When she is ten steps from the woman, she stops.

"Inola?" she asks, her voice steadier than her heart.

Inola takes notice of her in stages rather than all at once. First, her eyes open, still looking up at the sky. Next, her head rolls sideways against the grassy mound, looking in Niya's direction. Her hands are splayed at her sides, palms pressed against the large living hill that likely homes at least two or three Cahokian families. Finally, she pushes herself forward, her feet shifting dully in the grass in exhaustion.

"Come to salt my wounds, little owl?"

Inola's voice is steady and low. Weary. And yet it somehow holds a thread of levity, of light. Niya wonders at it, and reconsiders her assessment that Inola had been despairing at all—biding her time, perhaps, or waiting to try again in the light of a new day.

"How do you know that?" she counters.

"Why else would you have followed me," Inola asks, "but to give chase and gloat at my stupidity in this matter?"

"No, no," Niya starts, quickly stepping forward and waving her hands in the air, as if to wipe away the absurdity of Inola's speculation. "That is entirely incorrect, but it is not what I meant. I mean to say... *little owl*. You've called me that twice now. What do you mean by that?"

Inola's intense light brown eyes connect with Niya's. Then her gaze seems to move ever so slightly around Niya's face—Niya is close enough to tell, can sense that Inola is both looking at her but is also looking beyond her.

"It's there," Inola finally answers, her eyes dropping back down to her own hands. She gestures vaguely at Niya. "It's all over you, actually. You just have to know how to see it."

Niya's brow scrunches. "Is this an Ability," she asks, "something related to your Path? A gift of the Adanadi?"

When Inola laughs, Niya finds that she is, oddly enough, not threatened by it. The young woman seems genuinely amused by her question, and not in a malicious way.

"No, this is not an Ability. Well—not one from the Adanadi, at least. I was gifted an Ability though, from my chosen Path. I'm a particularly good shot, you might say." The expertly-placed dagger in the Patak's front door flashes in Niya's mind, how closely it had come to piercing Tusika's flesh while never seeming to deliver on its threat. "This is something altogether different." Inola waves her hand through the air as if to say that where her talent comes from is neither here nor there. "Something passed down from my niisi and from her own before her. It seems to skip generations, so it was my turn."

"And you can see my Path? The Paths of others?" Niya asks, oddly more curious about Inola's preternatural aura-seeing ability than her Adanadi one.

"Yes and no," Inola responds with a tilt of her head. She brushes her hand along her hairline, pushing rain water away so as to keep it from running into her eyes. "I see colors around people. An aura, I guess. Growing up, I thought everyone could see them." She shrugs. "Apparently, they cannot."

Niya knows that they are straying from the primary issue at hand, but she considers that this line of questioning may be as much a distraction for Inola as it is for herself.

"So...what color am I?" she asks. A slight pause before she says, "Owl...colored?"

At this, Inola actually giggles. A light, tinkling sound. And Niya finds herself captivated.

"Not at all! You have a faint hue of silver at your edges and a shock of yellow-orange like marigolds coming out of your ears."

"You're serious," Niya deadpans.

Inola sighs deeply. "It seems to be my curse that I am hardly ever anything else."

If Niya's resolve had been turning one way before, it is set now. This young woman needs help, and Niya can give it. The fate of Inola's mission to Cahokia—tied intrinsically to the fate of her sister and village—rests on Kaatii Patak. The Council of Twelve must decide to send help, and Tusika's mana may not be of the favor-granting persuasion. Maybe Niya's friendship with

Tusika can help, or her parents can call in a favor or two...

These thoughts enter her head and exit her mouth just as quickly.

"Will you allow me to help you?"

Inola is still and silent, disbelief writ large across her face.

"Now I ask you in return: are *you* serious?"

For some reason, the faces of Niya's mana and her mana's mana flash before her eyes. When she counts herself among them, a trio of faces so serious as to defy all likelihood of levity could they make, the thought of her absurdly offering to help but being unable is almost funny.

But then Niya pictures her mana, working at the marketplace. Discounting prices for those unable to afford their specialty produce. Slipping treats to children as they pass. Sharing her own private concoction of cream with an elder who has arthritis in their hands. Or her niisi, who was always teaching Niya the same lesson dressed up in different clothes: *if the Creator put something on this earth to harm you, then they put something on this earth to heal you, my girl.* A salve for a burn, a cure for a stomach ache. Balms for the spirit or for one's pride...

Of course Niya is serious.

She, too, is rarely ever anything else.

"I can make no promises. And I am not sure what help I could truly be. But yes, I want to be of service to you, Inola Cato."

The look that Inola levels at Niya at these words is heavy. She knows in an instant that Inola has not often in her life been offered help without asking or without a price. She flushes at the attention, her skin warming against the chill that is creeping across the city as the rain pulls away, as night settles fully into itself, embracing its own darkness. Inola looks hungry for action, desperate for results. Niya knows what she is to the woman, and she embraces it: the next step in her journey.

"You spoke your words in the Patak home, and your story came to life before my eyes. Your worry is real and true, and I do not know if I can fix anything, but I...I would like to try. To help, if you will let me."

Inola shakes her head, but a smile is firmly on her lips. "Little owl," she begins, quietly, almost as if to herself.

She steps closer to Niya. The glow from Adanadi-infused fixtures on the path behind them lights up Inola's face. Niya imagines that her own face must be concealed in darkness—or does the impossible aura that the other young woman sees illuminate Niya's profile even now?

When she is standing but a single step away from Niya, Inola stops, looks down, down, through long eyelashes and the haze of fog swirling around them. And she seems to take in all of Niya with a single, sweeping glance—from head to toe, from eyes to lips, from shoulder to shoulder. Almost as if taking measurements, assessing stock.

But measured for what sort of battle, Niya does not know.

When Inola continues, the words are so softly spoken that Niya has to reach for them, grab them before they float away in the thick air.

"I do not even know your name."

There is power in a name, and more power still in a name freely given. And Niya does give her name, giving it most freely of all to this stranger before her.

"Niya Suwatt. Owl's Path—but you know that last bit already, yeah?"

"Niya."

The way Inola repeats her name back to her leaves Niya feeling light. So intensely does the other young woman look at her, Niya wonders what could possibly be going through her head.

Suddenly, the wind sweeps up and a thunderclap comes again from the west. It snaps Niya back into focus, and she visibly shakes herself—as if shaking off the remnants of a charm.

"This storm is not done," she says. "Do you have shelter?"

Inola points down the path with her lips. "A small rest place not far from here. Though I do not know where I will start come morning..." She hangs her head, chunks of hair loose from her braid fall into her face, clinging to her skin from the rain.

Niya chews at the inside of her cheek. A decision is made in a flash.

"You will come with me, and we will get started on saving your sister, that's where you start."

Inola's eyes snap back up. "How?"

By doing what is right, Niya thinks. And is it not that simple? To stand by and do nothing would be the worst possible inaction. To know that this young woman and her people are facing a threat, unaided by outside influence—wouldn't that be the greatest disservice Niya could partake of?

"Come," Niya says, turning back to the path beyond the mounds. "Let's get you back to your place for the night. Our battle plans can be drawn up in the morning."

They will both need their wits about them, if they are to convince a Patak to do anything but be obstinate. For Pataks listen, and listen well—but rarely do they allow their minds to be changed.

KINAPA

"Why did you say what you said about Tusika?"

They are walking at a brisk pace, both eager to be sheltered before the next rain front comes through.

"Who is Tusika?" Inola asks in return, her face scrunching up into a look of confusion.

Niya nearly laughs at how backwards their entire interaction has been so far. How little Inola knew, rushing her way into the Patak home, but how confidently she had done it nonetheless. Another part of Niya wonders if Inola isn't blurring the lines of truth—keeping the extent of what she knows secret.

"Kaatii's daughter," she offers, "my best friend. The way you said what you said—Kaatii saw it as a threat, and I am not certain that she was wrong in seeing it that way."

"Pah," comes Inola's response, waving a hand. "Foolish of me to say what I said. But I...I didn't mean it. I am certain that here—" she gestures around, as if to encompass the entire city of Cahokia, "—Tusika and all of you Cahokian folk are safe from the likes of Gishkiy." Her hands fall back to her sides, and her pace quickens. She cuts a sharp glance over to Niya. "For now. He is charismatic, and he is resourceful. I do not know what he can accomplish with time and with his words. But for now, people elsewhere are safe from his thinking. And besides, I would not hurt someone, not without very good reason and a void of other options."

Niya swallows. She has more questions about the group causing trouble, about their leader, this Gishkiy, but she decides to keep them to herself for now.

"So," she starts instead, "how did you do it?"

"Do what?"

"Follow us all day long without us noticing." Niya maps out the entire day in her mind, surprised that she had only seen the young woman in the marketplace and possibly a quick sighting in the comedy club. "Among my friends and family, I am known for being notoriously difficult to sneak up on." Niya says as much not to be boastful but because it is a fact, plain and simple.

"Ah, yes. A biosynthetic tracking powder, purchased from a less savory vendor outside of the Eeko market. I applied it to your friend's skin when I bumped into her in the marketplace."

"No random occurrence, clearly." Niya makes note of the ends to which this new acquaintance might be willing to go. How much further could the woman be pushed? And who might do the pushing?

Inola turns to Niya with her smirk again. It rests easily on the woman's handsome face, despite her serious nature, and Niya feels herself offer a small smile in return.

"Clearly. I have been in the city for three days, looking for an in to Councilwoman Patak's presence. She is remarkably secretive when making her way home. Lots of Suyata. Lots of doubling back, this way and that. And what strange hours does she keep! Tracking a family member was one of my best options. One of my only options. Once I had her daughter's description, a name was unnecessary."

She says it all with an air of nonchalance. As if merely saying, *this is what I had to do, and so I did it*. But Niya is impressed with her tenacity, her spirit, her dedication. Niya is also wary, because prey once cornered may lash out unexpectedly, fiercely; and Inola Cato seems to have much that she is fighting for.

"Effective."

"Enough, yes. Which reminds me—"

Inola swipes up on her niisi's screen. Whereas the style of Niya's niisi is indicative of the Cahokian trends in design—sleek lines and neon colors, integrated holographic components and massive processing abilities—Inola's is more subtle. It clearly has similar capabilities, but it is shaped almost like bark, woodgrain evident from a few feet away, with colors more commonplace in nature—moss greens and amber sap. The young woman navigates to an application within her private system. Niya can't help but glance over, and Inola makes no effort to conceal her actions. She does not recognize the app but can discern its purpose: there is a map with two blinking arrowheads. Niya assumes that one represents Inola, the other, her mark. The powder she used to track Tusika literally makes Niya's friend stand out like fire in the dark—there is no way they would have known, or could have kept Inola from following them.

"And..." a few complicated gestures, some one-handed typing of syllabary code, and the second point on the map disappears. With one last flick of her wrist, Inola dismisses the app. It scatters in a small, false cloud of pixelated dust. "Tracking is now disabled." She glances sideways at Niya. "Will that make you rest easier tonight, little owl?"

Sneaky, Niya thinks, though without accusation. *Clever.* And wouldn't she behave similarly, if a loved one of her own was caught up in something like Inola's sister is? A breach of privacy, no doubt—but her willingness to help the woman is bolstered by the fact that Inola had promptly cut the program off.

"Who said I was going to rest any other way than easy tonight?"

"Hmm," Inola grins.

"Not always so serious, are you, Inola Cato? Despite what I think you would have me believe."

"And you, Niya Suwatt—not so worried about the ends I've been willing to go to so far, eh?"

"Hmm," Niya purposefully mimics Inola's humming from a moment before. She shakes her head, looking down at her feet. Another crack of thunder overhead and both young women speed up, having slowed down over the course of their banter. "I do not feel good about your means, but I cannot condemn them either."

"That, I understand. And—" Inola reaches out, her slender fingers touching lightly upon the skin of Niya's forearm, just above her niisi. "Thank you. Truly."

Niya gulps. As she is about to open her mouth to respond, the sky opens again, and it begins raining harder than ever.

With shouts of exhilaration, they both take off running. They come to a crossroads, and they have to yell over the rain to one another.

"I'm this way," Inola says, jerking her head to the west. She is futilely holding her arms above her to try and block some of the rain.

Niya squints through the downpour, takes a split second longer than she should to gaze at Inola through the drops that are falling fast and furious. The woman's hair is falling loose, rain running in rivulets down her dark skin, eyes catching the light of the soft blue lamps along the path.

How much must this all mean to her, Niya wonders, *if she is willing to accept help from a stranger on the off-chance that something might come of it?*

She looks into Inola Cato's eyes and tries to discern more. Who is Gishkiy really, what resources have already been expended in an effort to bring her sister home—what is the full story?

Inola steps closer, and Niya nearly stumbles backwards. The taller woman takes another step closer still, both of her arms coming down from their shielding position. She wraps her hands around Niya's upper arms to keep her from falling.

"Are you alright?" Inola asks, voice raised to be heard over the storm. Drops are positively streaming down her face and into her eyes, and she shakes her head to clear her vision, ducking her head to look down directly into Niya's face.

"I..."

But Niya doesn't finish, her mind too busy spinning in circles. What will Tusika think about her endeavor to help Inola? What about her parents—will they be willing to expend Suwatt capital in the quest? And Kaatii

Patak, will she find some way to punish Niya for intervening in the slightest? For undermining her?

"What?" Inola nearly shouts.

Niya crosses her left arm over her body, pointing towards her home. "I'm this way," she says, her head tilting slightly in the same direction as her finger. It would be comical if it wasn't so outrageous, them standing here like statues as the deluge continues, Niya's brain failing utterly to catch up with her body.

Inola, clearly much more aware of the pressing situation, lets loose one hand, the other drifting down to catch at Niya's wrist. With a few deft movements that Niya is certain she should be more suspicious of, Inola has pressed their niisis close together and shared contact information. Niya looks down at her wrist, shakes herself into a fully upright position as Inola steps back and out of her space.

"Tomorrow?" the woman asks.

Niya nods. "Tomorrow."

Inola runs off into the darkness, the rain quickly swallowing her up.

Already drenched to what Niya imagines to be her very bones, she stands still for a few moments longer.

What are you getting yourself into, Niya?

A better question still: *What have you already gotten yourself into?*

A thunderclap resounds closer than ever overhead, startling Niya out of her musings. She turns and takes off at a slow trot towards home.

WANTIKINAPA

Niya's sleep is restless and short, dreamless. None to help, none to hurt.

There is a soft *ping* from her bedside table, and Niya reaches blindly over, picking up her niisi and adjusting it in place before reading her messages.

The first is from her best friend.

[Tusika] Tuboo Sokobi suffered flooding from the rain. No classes today. Let me know if you have time to talk later.

Another string of messages in a group pod they've had going for years now.

[Adasi] Ayyyy no university today! This won't mess up my graduation will it?

After Adasi's message, there is a hastily drawn doodle—a coyote's smiling face, then an arrow pointing to another coyote, this one wearing a comical frown. He is not a particularly good artist, but he often does little sketches like this for the group. Ones featuring his Path animal, or the Path animals of each of the friends, are particularly common. After the girls' Adanadi ceremony, he has mistakenly misrepresented Tusika with a series of deer drawings wherein an owl ended up perched atop the doe's head. Niya wonders how his raccoon-drawing skills are...

[Nampeyo] Doubtful, coyote friend. We could use today as an opportunity to work on our projects from home. A change of location is often as useful as a rest, or so I have heard it said.

Niya scrolls, already imagining the message that may follow. She is not disappointed. Adasi has drawn another coyote, this one laying on its back, tongue lolling out of its mouth, with x's for eyes.

[Nampeyo] Have it your way—perhaps Niya will be on my side when she wakes. Let me know if you all make plans for later.

In the face of her other friends' buoyant messages, Niya feels that Tusika's was particularly sober. She reads it again.

Let me know if you have time to talk later.

Niya is eager to hear what is on her best friend's mind, to find out what state she is in today. Will she be all diplomacy, progeny of Kaatii Patak, politician-in-waiting? Or will she be the take-charge, charismatic friend that Niya knows her to be?

She is eager, too, for something else entirely: setting up a rendezvous with Inola Cato. Finding a way forward for the young woman's quest in rescuing her sister from the clutches of Gishkiy's cult. Bringing peace to the young woman's village.

The contact information that Inola had hastily shared the night before is stored in a particular section of the niisi's database. Niya pulls it up and is surprised to see that the near-stranger has shared her location with Niya as well. Of course, it would only be shared while they were within Cahokian borders or on the same daso network—beyond that, the signal would only stretch to the horizon anyway. Still, this is an act of trust. And when Niya thinks about what she had seen in the other woman's eyes, she can't help but wonder what Inola had seen in her own.

Niya sends three messages. The first, to Tusika. The second, to Inola. And finally, a response to her friends.

[Niya] Of course, we will talk later, Wanzi. Are you alright?

[Niya] Breakfast?

[Niya] My dear Nampeyo, no classes means rest. Or at least seeing what my parents are up to. How do you think the fields fared after last night? Always work to be done, isn't there?

She sends a holographic picture of her face that she snaps with her niisi's eyes, lips turned downward in an exaggerated frown. Nampeyo responds quickly with a frown of their own in mimicry, and Adasi finishes off with a self-congratulatory message that puts a smile on Niya's face.

The next message to come through is from Inola. Niya feels herself deflate, let down that her best friend was not the first to respond.

[Inola] Ah, foolish of me. I had not thought you would be eager to see me again so soon. I am at a teahouse now, but you could join me if your schooling allows?

Niya chews her lip, watching the message branch she shares with Tusika blink, unmoving, for some time. Eventually, she accepts that her friend will reach out when she is ready. That's Tusika's way—on her own time, and not a moment sooner or later. It's one of the things that Niya loves about her so much, that Tusika knows herself and her own mind, that a decision made is a decision she sticks by, through and through.

Nevertheless, Niya finds herself checking her nii-si every few seconds as she walks to the teahouse to meet Inola. She can only try and fix one problem at a time, especially when the one surrounding her best friend seems so clouded and uncertain.

Inola meets Niya outside with a biodegradable cup of dandelion and lavender tea. Niya accepts it with a grateful nod, sipping a good portion of it down before they even manage to make it to the water's edge.

"I hardly slept," Inola begins without preamble. "I have some ideas, but... I have to ask: how do you feel this morning? Still interested in helping me?"

Niya can see the stoicism written across the side of the other woman's face. The tightness in her jaw. The thick swallow in that first moment of silence after asking. She can't imagine what it might feel like, to be fed potentially false hope after so many no's.

"I am, I promise. I am not easily scared off—you've seen my best friend's family firsthand, yeah?" They both chuckle at this knowing statement, but the levity quiets into a silence that has Niya thinking of Tusika's lack of response. Niya forces herself back to the present with a shake. "I want to trust you. And I want you to trust me."

"I think that would be a good place to start."

"I've got some questions."

"Please," comes Inola's response. "Ask them of me."

"First, I must know more about this cult."

They walk side by side along the riverbank, the Mizizibi's rushing waters swollen from the heavy rains.

And so Inola tells Niya all that she knows.

Gishkiy has lived his whole adult life in Inola's village after his family moved there from Cahokia. As years went by, the story of why the family had fallen from social grace and fled the city was lost. Several years ago, he lost his father, his only surviving parent. Afterwards, he fell into a despondent fugue, unable to function. Gishkiy went through a period of isolation, then a time of mad, public ravings. After some time, he retreated once more. No one saw him for many weeks. And when he emerged again—dressed in an outfit of leather dyed red like blood and head of hair gone stark white as if he had been scared half to death—he radiated a calm composure totally unlike his recent ramblings and brokenness. This was when he spoke to the village. This was when people listened. It was like he had gone into seclusion a madman and came through something unknown, exiting on the other side changed both mentally and physically. The wrinkles of his chiseled face, which before had been deep as crags and valleys on his worried brow and about his sad eyes, were now gone—as if they had been filled in or erased. His voice became a steady, powerful thing, a beacon for displaced and long-forgotten hope, echoing out from the center of a village fallen on hard times and harder living still. And when he offered another way—a path forged not with the Adanadi's special bestowing of Abilities but fought for and earned—his voice had a special power to it.

"It was like watching some great chieftain speaking

to his people. Except none of us belonged to him." She pauses, swallowing hard. "Until some of us did."

Continuing her story in more detail than the night before, Inola tells Niya about the ghosts.

"Our village is haunted. The elders have seen things in the night and in their dreams that have driven them from their homes, crying out in terror and distress. They won't tell us what visions have come to them or what spectral visitors they've had, but we can guess. I've come to my own conclusions, too—that not all those who left with Gishkiy will return."

Niya asks the question that she is sure haunts Inola's every waking thought. "And your sister?"

Inola shakes her head, her eyes shining with unshed tears. "I cannot leave her to the wolves. Kas is less than two years younger than me, but she has always yearned for adulthood. For independence—to leave our sad little home and drag me with her." A deep, shuddering breath for stillness, for strength. "She saw me get an Ability from the Adanadi, and she dreamed of one for herself. Spent countless hours imagining what sort of gift might grace her body, mind, or spirit…"

As she trails off, Niya connects the obvious dots. "She did not receive an Ability, and Gishkiy offered her what she felt she needed to escape."

Tears do fall from Inola's eyes now, and Niya's fingertips itch to offer comfort. But while the other woman's tears show her emotions and inner turmoil, nothing about her stature invites physical touch. Niya leans forward, cognizant of the wall between them but wanting to lend support anyway she can.

She had asked for honesty, to establish trust between them. She is getting that and more.

"I could only offer her so much comfort, couldn't I? What weight could my words hold, as someone with an Ability myself? No comfort at all..."

"How long since she joined him?"

Inola's eyes meet Niya's. "Six weeks, three days. And all I want is to have her home again—safe and whole. After that, I'll go anywhere with her, do anything to keep her safe and happy." A torrent of words escapes Inola now, set free by this talk of her sister. "I was the same age when I took the Adanadi, Niya. The same age as my little sister is now—sixteen years old. Why did I develop an Ability while she did not?" she asks, turning imploring eyes on Niya. But she does not wait for a response, scuffing her toe against the path beneath their feet and continuing with her tale. "I do not know, none of us do. I never took it as my Path animal loving me more than hers loves her, or favoring me in some unknowable way. It wasn't my Fox who made the difference over her Badger, nor was it *me*. And I...I cannot say that I would not run off after some madman into the mountains. But I can say that I would not jeopardize my life, my family's well being...I've lived with an Ability for two years now, but I would live without one for a hundred lifetimes if it meant my sister had made a different choice or could be brought back from this madness. If perhaps my Ability could belong to her instead. She has been—" she fists her hands then opens them in a rush, as if mimicking an explosion. She grits the word out between clenched teeth. "Foolish!"

Niya nods in understanding. She does not have siblings herself, but is there anything she would not do for Adasi, for Nampeyo?

Is there any mountain the whole world over that Niya would not move for Tusika? Her knees might end up bloody from kneeling in dirt and gravel, and her nails might rip from her fingers—but Niya would do whatever it took to keep Tusika from harm.

She sees this same resolve in Inola.

A question forms after this thought of her friend, and she asks it with brow furrowed.

"Your appeals to governments failed, but what made you seek out Kaatii Patak? I don't know if she has a reputation outside of the city, but here, she's not exactly known for having an open door policy. Why not go straight to the whole Council?"

Taking a couple of steadying breaths, Inola composes herself. The tears slow and then stop.

"Here's the thing, Niya...Gishkiy's mad acts in public—hours spent shouting on and on about atrocities done to him and others, telling meandering, nonsensical stories and invented horrors of experimentation and worse...well, he would talk about Cahokia. About the Council, and about..."

Inola trails off. With imploring eyes, Niya leans forward. "About what?"

Shaking her head with eyes downturned, Inola stays silent for a moment. "I listened to him, once, really listened—not just as a passerby trying my best to ignore the local man in the square, loud but harmless.

I stopped and paid attention to his words for the first time. And through his madness, I heard the trauma of a person who genuinely believed that something powerful had been taken from them without consent. Between the nonsense and the moments of complete confusion, there was something else there: a name, and a curse."

The pair have walked a good length of the river, have nearly left the district behind. They stop and face the river shoulder to shoulder.

Looking at the high, coursing waters of the Mizizibi, Niya speaks quietly. "What curse?"

"Gishkiy spoke the name of a family, and I read between the lines to discern his meaning. It was absolutely mad, Niya, so I don't know the entire truth of it. He was half-muttering and half-shouting—things about spirit knots and aura alignment, childhood and stolen promises... I don't know, it was difficult to parse. When he returned after that time away, I never heard him speak of the family or his childhood again. He was pretty persistent before he retreated back to the foothills with his followers though—that those with Abilities didn't always come by them honestly, that he had discovered a way to at the very least tip the scales back in the favor of the many rather than the few."

"You're right," Niya breathes, "it does sound like madness."

"Yes, but...it sounded plausible, Niya. Picking through the tangled threads of his speech, I feel as if I could see what had happened to his family. Whatever it was that had driven them from Cahokia and to the village. The other family tied his spirit in some way to their eldest child. Grew them up together, had them attending the same events and running with the same crowds. The two of them must have been very close—which made it all the harder, after the two of them took the Adanadi. The girl, Gishkiy's friend—she received an Ability. He did not. And then it wasn't long before accusations were raised against his parents, something bad enough to drive them from the city... I can't say more for sure, and much of this I pieced together from other elders in the village, people around Gishkiy's age who recalled the arrival of his family after they became outcasts of Cahokia."

Niya's heart beats rapidly in her chest. The wide open sky somehow doesn't feel wide enough.

"This family... Gishkiy thinks they kept him from developing an Ability?"

Nodding, Inola says, "Yes. He believes they did something, performed some ritual, that took his Adanadi potential and gave it to their daughter."

Reaching out, Niya presses her palm flat against the bark of a nearby sycamore to steady herself.

It can't be, she thinks. *It couldn't possibly—*

"Who?" she asks. "What was the family's name?"

Niya turns her head to look dead on Inola's profile. Watches the muscle in her jaw working furiously. Without looking at her, Inola gives the answer Niya has suddenly found herself dreading.

"I made note of the only name I could make out of his ramblings. It was impossible to forget, because it was so very Cahokian and unlike the names that come from our band." She looks down at the ground, inhaling a great breath, before turning that stoic gaze back on Niya. "The family name was Patak," she says, confirming Niya's fear. The pit in her stomach grows, and Niya feels faint. "And his best childhood friend? None other than the current Councilmember: Kaatii Patak."

The world swims, and Niya feels herself swaying precariously on her feet. Unsteady, she sinks down onto her knees in the grass.

"Inola, the first-born Pataks have been gifted with Adanadi Abilities for almost as long as the ceremony has been around. If what you're saying is true—"

"Then it's possible that the Pataks have found some way to game the Adanadi."

"It's not just... insanely good luck?" Niya asks, realizing how foolish she sounds even as she says the words.

Inola shakes her head slowly, moving to sit facing Niya. "No, it's something more. If it's true! But what it is exactly, I cannot say."

"By the Creator..."

"Or against Them."

A wind sweeps across the water, pushing the rushing tide further up the banks before them. Niya watches the effects of mother nature; the ebb and flow, the push and pull. And she wonders if any part of this could be true.

Even as she feels the seed of truth take root in her heart.

Niya's body settles even as her mind races at the implications.

Hesitantly, Inola speaks after a few moments of quiet. "I know that you and the Patak girl are close. And I can see your aura, can discern your Path, so I know that you have taken the Adanadi. Tell me, did you develop an Ability?"

Niya's laugh comes out more bitter than she intends. "Not yet, but I've never expected one anyway." Inola tilts her head in confusion at this, so Niya explains. "I only took the Adanadi eleven days ago."

She briefly details the dual ceremony that she and Tusika took part in just over one week previous, all while ignoring the feeling of frogs jumping madly about in her stomach. If any part of what Inola has described is true—the Pataks tying their children somehow to other children, stealing or siphoning away their Adanadi potential into their heirs—then who is Niya to Tusika? What role has she played in her best friend's life, and what role has Tusika played in hers? *Truly?*

"Three more sleeps and I'll know for sure, but no one in my family has received an Ability from the Adanadi in seven generations." She shrugs but the nonchalance feels painfully fake. Bile rises in the back of her throat. "I do not expect one." She grits her teeth, wondering at the fantastical story that she has thus far heard from Inola. "And I would never follow a madman into his madness for something that the Creator does not see fit to bless me with."

"Are you sure about that?" Inola asks. She holds her hands out in front of her, between the two of them.

"Can you say that for certain—that you would not try and take back that which was stolen from you, if indeed that was the case? That you wouldn't be willing to pry into ancient places and seek lost rituals to undo a wrong..." She clenches her hands, pressing them down into her thighs through the dark leather shorts she is wearing today. "And what if all of this is done to you by your childhood companion—your best friend?"

Niya's mind refuses to believe the possibility. Her mouth goes dry and she squeezes her eyes shut momentarily, only to open them again wider than before. She opens her mouth as if to speak, to say something, to say *anything*—but no words escape her.

An uncomfortable moment passes, then Inola says, "Or you could wake in three days to find that you have been blessed with an Ability. And Gishkiy's ravings are nothing more than what they are on the surface: nonsense."

The air is muggy from the previous night's rain. Niya thoughtlessly reaches up, wiping the back of her hand across her forehead to remove the light sheen of sweat that had gathered there. She grips her fingers into the grass near her ankles. Breathing in and out, she tries to force her brain into thinking coherent thoughts. But everything is a jumble, an absolute mess.

She needs time to process everything she has heard. To take it and shape it, if possible, into a tale that makes sense enough for her to even comprehend.

"I...have a lot to think about, Inola. Thank you for answering my questions. It means a lot to me that you are willing to gain my trust."

"It means more to me," Inola replies, her tone somber, "that you have been willing to listen, when so many have not."

Niya smiles softly at this. "I can't speak yet about the Pa'taks. Tusika is—" her voice catches, thinking of Gishkiy and Kaatii growing up together in Cahokia, wondering how like Niya and Tusika they might have been. "She is my best friend. I need to find out what she knows. Whether or not you found truth in Gishkiy's words, maybe Tusika can help us find out more about his whereabouts, his plans. The Council may be your last chance for intervention, and anything we can find could be of use. At the center of your story is one truth that I do fear—that the teachings of a person, well-intentioned or not, can grow into something bigger and can lose control. That even a single life lost to his experiments is too much, but to see him gain power and influence could be the gravest outcome of all."

Inola's eyes begin to well up with tears, and she hastily looks away. The backs of her hands swipe at her eyes, and she gives a sniffle. Niya reaches out to cover one of Inola's shaking hands with one of her own, trying to impress upon the other woman that her vulnerability is welcome—that she is not alone in her quest, not anymore.

When she looks back at Niya again, her eyes are still shining and bright. "Thank you."

Niya gives a nod of her head and stands to leave. "How long do we have before you must return to your home?"

Inola gathers herself as well as she goes into an

account in her niisi. Whatever she sees has her pursing her lips from side to side as she thinks on her answer.

"I can make it about a week on what I have now. Ten days if I really stretch it, with just enough to get back home."

"Okay. A week, then. Preferably less. I won't see you going home hungry, that is for certain."

They share smiles. Niya looks away under the pretense of observing a turtle meandering through the nearby grass. The intricate pattern of its shell is streaked through with the purple bruise-like gleam of the Adanadi.

"I need to meet Tusika today. I feel...badly about how we left things last night. I don't know if she can answer questions about Gishkiy, but I know that she will at least help me. She is a good person," Niya says, suddenly feeling an urge to defend her best friend—from what, she isn't certain. The girl has done no wrong, not that Niya knows of or can imagine. "She is good..."

She can be, can't she?

Across the water, Niya can distantly see the islands that make up Tuboo Sokobi. As if activated by her wandering sight, the faraway sounds of the university chime tones ring out, carried on the winds to the ears of the two young women who are lost in their own thoughts. They ring daily, despite classes being canceled today due to the flooding.

Niya turns her wrist, taking in the time of day.

"Let me walk you back," Inola says, standing up and brushing the backside of her shorts off.

She extends a hand to Niya, offering to pull her up from her sitting place. And Niya stares at the proffered hand, extending before her face—stares at it for a moment too long—then she grabs it, hauling herself upward.

"Tusika," Inola says, the name spreading out to take up even more space than its three syllables should allow for. "You trust her?"

Niya answers without hesitation.

"With my life."

"Are the two of you... more than friends?"

She is surprised by this question. Surprised, too, that it surprises her at all. Haven't she and Tusika always been particularly and inexplicably close? Even closer than the holy men had proclaimed, with their entwined auras? Or was that the crux of it, the beginning and the end of it: their births, so close together; growing up, the way they have. An inevitability. Wouldn't that make sense, that they should end up as more than friends? As lovers? As two halves of one singular, extraordinary whole?

Hadn't Niya wanted that? Hadn't she been enticed—and terribly so—by Tusika's proposition one short night ago?

"We are not," Niya replies, her words clipped and hard in her mouth.

Odd, how being mistaken for something more with her best friend even a day or two earlier would not have upset her in the slightest—would have perhaps even brought her joy! Instead, she feels hollow at the thought. *She knows Tusika better than anyone else in the world, but does she really know her at all?*

Niya is determined to find out. To prove to herself that she *does* know her best friend—that something as monumental as this could not possibly have remained a secret between them.

What if it is true? Niya wonders. *That Kaatii received an Ability while Gishkiy did not because of some closeness between them? Could I be the Gishkiy to Tusika's Kaatii?*

"We are not them," Niya whispers to herself. "We can't be…"

"I am sorry," comes Inola's reply, her chin dipping to her chest. Niya looks down and sees the young woman's fingers squeeze together into fists, clenching and then releasing, as if she is considering her words carefully.

"For what?" Niya asks, voice as sharply inquisitive as her gaze.

Then Inola looks up. Bright, lustrous brown eyes piercing Niya through lashes, thick and long. Niya's mind flashes to the night before, when Tusika had implored Niya to come spend the night with her.

There is a remarkable difference between someone who wants and someone who takes, and Niya feels it sharply and at once.

With Tusika, the *want* is a unidirectional transaction. Niya fears that the only thing Tusika has known in their relationship, for far too long, has been the *taking* of things. Of love, of energy, of passion. This has never bothered Niya before, not truly. She has always had so much of those things to give.

Niya knows that she will feel better once she speaks to her best friend. She couldn't possibly feel any worse.

"I am sorry that I have caused a question to arise between you and Tusika. I hope that you find answers with her. Maybe we will even find out that all of this has been a gross misunderstanding. That would be preferable, after all—I'd like to go before the Council of Twelve and *not* implicate one of their members as being responsible thanks to some heinous crime against humanity perpetrated by their parents."

"The truth is," Niya starts but stops just as quickly, her mouth snapping shut. A few steps, and all the while, she can feel the edge of Inola's gaze on the side of her face. When she speaks again, she is not certain that these words were the words she had intended. But they are the words that she releases nonetheless. "I will be happy to mend things with her. And...I will be glad to help you, Inola Cato."

She turns her head enough to catch Inola's smile.

"And I will be glad to have your help, Niya Suwatt. I am lucky to count you as an ally."

PITIKINAPA

Niya walks through one of the fields that her family has been farming for two generations. The three sisters—corn, beans, and squash—intermingle at her feet, growing together in symbiosis. Niya keeps a sharp eye out for both pests to remove and varieties that might be cultivated later in the season in their favor. She reaches down, snapping a bean from its stem. Her fingers press into its flesh, opening it at the seams. She thoughtfully chews on its innards, savoring the *pop* as she bites down and the sweetness that follows.

She senses Tusika's approach before she sees or hears her. Unlike all those times before, when Tusika had tried to get a jump on Niya, she instead approaches straight down a row. Her hands are flush to her sides, almost stiff. Her eyes seem to stare ahead, unseeing.

No, Niya thinks. *Not unseeing. She sees only me.*

And this feels true even as she thinks it. Niya watches her friend only narrowly avoid a protruding root, an overflowing squash plant, an unevenness in the earth.

"No trying to sneak up on me today, Wanzi?"

Niya says it with a smile that is only returned at half-force.

"I have decided that it is futile to try and sneak up on you, Niya."

This inspires the beginnings of a frown on Niya's face, but she stops it from fully forming.

"Is that Raccoon talking, a newfound stripe of intelligence?" she asks. "Or simply your hurt pride?"

Niya's question is not gentle, but if she cannot be straightforward with her oldest friend, then with whom could she ever be?

Tusika smiles, and it does not reach her eyes. It almost does, but at the last second it stops, retreats.

"Can I walk with you?" Tusika asks.

Niya's breath catches. Her chest feels tight with a heavy breath that won't heave up and out of her chest as quickly or effectively as she would like it to. There is something tender about Tusika's tone, something honest. And it reminds Niya in an instant that she has been closer than blood to this young woman for years now, been in love with her for nearly as long.

Intoxicating things, Niya thinks. *Red berries and hemlock, sumac and manchineel and more.*

"Of course," Niya replies, reaching out her hand.

Tusika takes it, interlacing their fingers with an effortless sort of grace, and they walk together through the fields, the sun passing them by overhead.

They chat amicably, quietly, for some time. Then Niya decides they must get to the heart of the matter. But when she opens her mouth to speak, she finds that the heart of the matter is *hers*, not Inola's.

"I am sorry that my not staying with you last night hurt you."

"Mmm. You had more exciting prey to chase. It would be contrary of me to fault you for that."

At this, Niya pulls her friend to a stop, turns her around. "Do you speak for me? Or do I speak for myself."

"Tell me you haven't been with that girl today," Tusika

throws back at her. "That you have not been helping her conspire."

Niya does not miss a beat. "I have, Tusika. Because she needs help. Would you have me turn my back on someone in need? Is it not your goal to be a politician of renown, to lead the people of Cahokia?"

Tusika furrows her brow, dropping her gaze petulantly to the rich soil beneath their feet.

"Yes," she acknowledges. "But she forced her way into my home! She could have been a danger to my mana, to *us*—"

"You are right," Niya nods her head several times. "But do you know whose judgment I trust more than any other's?" Tusika looks back up, her dark eyes captivating and captivated alike. "*Yours,*" Niya says. "Yours, Tusika Patak. So tell me, and tell me true: were you afraid of Inola Cato when she came into your home? Or did you see her for who she truly is: a girl barely older than us, fighting to protect her sister and her people?"

There is silence between them for some time. Then an almost shy smile, uncharacteristic but charming nonetheless, begins to creep up Tusika's face.

"My friend, my beautiful friend." The tension eases, slipping away. "I know you are right in this matter. She was no threat to us. And I...well, I do understand her. That need of help, to do what must be done."

"I am glad."

"So tell me," Tusika spins them back around to the path through the three sisters' section of the Suwatt fields. "What more did you learn today? Tell me about this cult that Cato's village is facing. What are they up to? And what do her people need?"

So Niya tells her friend. Everything that Inola had shared with her.

Except... Niya does not bring up the claims that Inola has pieced together from Gishkiy's stories. She does not levy any accusations or even bring up the fact that Gishkiy was once a Cahokian himself. And for some reason, she keeps quiet about any connection between Gishkiy and Kaatii Patak.

Tusika is bright and cunning, curious and wickedly perceptive. If she senses a hole in Niya's relaying of events, she does not point it out.

At the end of their walk, Niya asks for something: Tusika's help to bring aid to Inola's people, to stop the cult of experimentation and the unnatural unlocking of Abilities, if such a thing is even possible.

And Tusika agrees, because they are best friends who would do anything for one another.

Aren't we? Niya wonders.

She does not offer the missing puzzle piece to her friend. And Tusika does not ask for it. Niya notes this but, unsure of what it could mean, locks it away in her heart. New information may come to light, either to prove Inola's story or to disprove it. No need to let such fantastical doubts worm their way between her and Tusika unless more evidence is unearthed.

As they make plans to meet their friends out in a few nights, unrelated to Inola's plight, neither girl seems to want to be the one to bring up the other unspoken truth: that they are less than three days now from their Adanadi window closing. Nevertheless, it is not lost on either of them.

And Niya wonders if—somehow, impossibly—her friend's seemingly inevitable reception of an Ability will be thanks in some part to her.

Niya's own voice echoes in her mind, followed closely by Inola's.

I would never follow a madman into his madness for something that the Creator does not see fit to bless me with.

Are you sure about that? Can you say that for certain—that you would not try and take back that which was stolen from you?

The bile rises in her throat again, but Niya forces it back down.

TAHOOTIKINAPA

Two mornings later, Niya is home but heading out early to meet Inola before her schooling starts. She stops in her tracks, a prickling at the back of her neck that tells her someone is nearby, though she cannot see them.

Half a moment later, a disembodied voice calls out to her.

"Always so busy, eh, my girl?"

Niya spins about in the hallway, uncertain as to where her daadoo's voice had just come from. Because that is certainly the voice of her daadoo, and he is a prodigious prankster—one of the only people in her life able to sneak up on her successfully, and Niya is quick to blame that on his Path animal, Fox.

"Daadoo?" she hisses, not wanting to disturb her ni-isis who may still be sleeping on either side of the hall.

A whistle low enough in pitch to almost be mistaken for wind whipping through a forest's low-hanging branches grabs her attention. She looks up—

Right into the face of her daadoo, who is half-hanging out of the entryway up into the top-of-mound section of their home.

"Daadoo," she says again, the long syllables familiar and almost teasing on her tongue this time. "What on earth are you doing up there?"

"Oh, only searching for my old chunkey spear."

"That old stick?"

Mischief is in her voice and they both know it. In his youth, her daadoo was remarkably skilled at chunkey—a Tsalagi sport of rolling stones and expert spear throwing—until a bad break in his throwing arm that never quite healed right, despite advanced medical techniques and a surgery or two, kept him to the sidelines. But he still coaches up the youngsters on a regular basis.

"Girlie, you best watch it, now. *That old stick* helped me win many tournaments back in my day. You never know when such a thing might be needed!"

Her daadoo's chunkey spear looks innocuous enough, but Niya knows that it is a sturdy, hand-carved, and perfectly engineered piece of wood that has seen many pitches and battles over the years.

Niya laughs silently, her shoulders shaking as she continues to try and be as quiet as possible in the early morning hours. "I know, daadoo. It may be banged up and a bit dull, but it's well-loved and has always served you well. But are you sure that niisi isn't using it out in the fields as part of that contraption to scare away crows?"

"Pah," he makes a gesture as if to wipe away Niya's words. "You may be right, my girl. Even though I've tried to tell her that there is no need for that sort of old way of things. My chunkey spear—"

"Stick," Niya interjects quickly in a whisper.

"—*Spear* may still be of use."

"Found a new youngin' to mentor, huh?"

Her daadoo smiles mischievously. "Maybe so, my

girl. Now, where are you off to so early as this? Those aggie elders got you planting sprouts before the sun comes up?"

Niya shakes her head. "I'm helping a friend with a—" she pauses, uncertain what to call her mission to get Inola before the Council of Twelve, to combat Gishkiy's propaganda and bring Kas home to Inola's family, "—project," she decides. "Gotta make some progress before university later. See you tonight, daadoo?"

"Always, always. Be good."

"Always, always," Niya repeats back to him with a fond smile.

Niya is climbing the long, sloping pathway that leads up from the yutsu station back aboveground. From there, she turns north and begins heading towards one of the main thoroughfares of the marketplace. Even though it is early morning hours, the street vendors are out in full force—particularly those selling fresh produce and specialty meats. The best cuts will go quickly, Niya knows, and she has seen her fair share of scuffles as well as debate as to one vendor's merits over another's. She smiles fondly at the memories of her Cahokian home, the familiarity of the place—untroubled by strange cults and unnatural experimentation. Around her are all sorts of people, too. Young and old; those just starting their days and others just ending theirs. There's long flowing hair, bald heads, a single mohawk in the crowd. Every color and texture and shape under the Creator's sun.

As she is passing from one street to the next, headed towards the meeting place she and Inola had designated late the night before, someone tries to grab her from behind. Rarely having ever in her young life been caught by surprise, Niya spins around at the last second, narrowly avoiding being caught off guard. But her own momentum is used against her, and she is pulled into an open storefront by—

"Inola!" she hisses. "What in the Creator's name do you think you are doing?!"

Inola's eyes are racing back and forth out the shop's front window, her gaze scanning the crowd outside—left to right and back again, over and over.

"Were you followed?" Inola asks.

Niya would find it funny if she weren't so genuinely concerned that her newfound stranger-turned-friend had lost some important, fragile grasp on reality.

"What are you—" she starts to answer but thinks better of it in the end. "No, Inola. I was not followed. Were you?"

Her eyes flit across the shop to the merchant, a little old man with droopy eyes and wrinkles for days. It is abundantly clear that he isn't the slightest bit interested in what the two young women who just burst into his shop are up to.

Even though Niya asked the question facetiously, Inola backs into the door jam. Her tall, lean frame is pressed against it as if to minimize her ability to be perceived. She cuts her eyes to Niya. "I think I have been. *Suyata*," she whispers, as if to say the name of the elite guards would be to summon them to the very doorway in which she is hiding. "I believe that Kaatii Patak is having me followed."

For a moment, Niya thinks through this possibility.

It stands to reason that a resourceful, intuitive person like Inola would pick up on the movements of persons who may be following them. It also does not seem out of the realm of possibility that a member of the Council whose home had effectively been broken into would engage the Suyata for protection, or even simply for reconnaissance.

But Niya also knows enough now to realize that Inola is a young woman, unarmed, who has behaved, frankly, in at least semi-diplomatic terms. Would Kaatii go to such lengths over such a non-threat?

Maybe, Niya thinks. *To teach her a lesson.*

And that is enough for her to go along. To be vigilant. But to also distract Inola from something that may ultimately have no bearing whatsoever on her time here in Cahokia.

"I know we need to plan to get you before the Council," Niya starts, "but tonight will mark the fourteenth night since Tusika and I took the Adanadi."

This seems to effectively distract Inola from her theoretical pursuers, if only for a moment.

"Oh?"

"We're going out. To celebrate. Whether we are celebrating receiving an Ability or not." She shrugs, reaching back to scratch at the back of her neck. "It will be fun. What do you say?"

"I...well, I don't want to be in the way. And won't

your best friend Tusika be mad to see the person who barged into her home invited to your social gathering?"

"Tusika is on our side—*your* side." But then Niya chuckles, not convinced that Inola isn't the slightest bit right. "Leave her to me."

"Gladly so," Inola quips back.

"*Ha-ha.* But really—it would..." she trails off briefly before barrelling forward again. "We haven't known each other long, but you're alone in this city and a friend. You should come if you think it might be a good distraction to you. That's why we're doing it! It will be a fun distraction."

"A distracted mind is sometimes capable of clearer thought..." Inola trails off thoughtfully. Niya grins while the taller woman chews at her lip. With a snap of her fingers, Inola meets Niya's gaze, her mind clearly made up. "Yes, a night out. Your invitation is welcome!"

At nearly the same moment as Inola makes up her mind, the shopkeeper snores so loudly that he wakes himself from the early-morning nap he's been having.

With two bursts of laughter, both Niya and Inola feel the spell crest and break upon them like a wave.

"Do you have time to talk about the Council?" Inola asks. "And about..." She looks around, as if seeking out any eyes or ears that could be spying on them in the shop's entryway. The shop owner gives another snore. "Gishkiy's connection to Kaatii?"

"Yes, of course," Niya confirms with a tight but kind smile. She places a gentle hand on Inola's shoulder, and together they go out into the marketplace to find a vendor selling quail egg bakes.

They spend the next while discussing how to get Inola before the Council of Twelve, in spite of whatever machinations Kaatii Patak might be up to. And they plot how they might go about finding more information about Gishkiy's past with the Patak family...

The fortnight since they had first discovered the Two Goals club had not changed the place in the slightest. Drums pounding, people stomping; flutes and rattles and lights. The sounds and smells and intensity all hit Niya at once as she and her friends move inside.

Adasi and Nampeyo head off in search of seating for their group to stake claim to. Tusika is slightly ahead of Niya, edging closer to the primary dance floor.

Inola is near Niya's side. Turning her head, Niya takes in the enraptured look on the face of this young woman from the countryside. It's easy to forget that Inola has never been to Cahokia before—until moments like these. Something about the way her eyes light up, the part of her lips, her searching eyes... Niya flashes back in memory to moments like these with Tusika at her side, rather than pushing ahead and away from her.

Has she been spending too much time with Inola the past few days? They spent almost the entire day previous inside the city archives, digging through clips and stories from decades past, trying to pinpoint the downfall of Gishkiy's family—whatever it had been that drove them from Cahokia, the turning point in the relationship between the two families.

Niya has not voiced her fear aloud, only wondered about it late, late at night as she tries to fall asleep: *if I know what the Pataks did to Gishkiy's family, I can keep it from happening to mine.* She does have to remind herself that Inola's concern for her sister is even more pressing than her theoretical fears about the future. But Niya cannot help but wonder: if they find truth in Gishkiy's story, how far back will they have to go to find the beginning?

And, worse yet—what if the story has no end? What if Kaatii is still up to tricks and sorcery, playing with incomprehensible magics and the fickle whims of fate?

Niya pulls her eyes away from the worriless, joyful expression on Inola's face to find Tusika's back in the crowd.

What if her best friend in the entire world, the person with whom she took the Adanadi, the girl she loves— is in love with—knows more than Niya could have ever imagined a week ago?

We don't keep secrets from one another, Niya thinks. *Not secrets like this.*

And close on that thought's heels, another: *you're keeping a big one from her, aren't you? Exactly like this.*

In the ebb and flow of the crowd, Tusika looks back. Almost as if drawn, like a magnet. Pulled towards Niya like an inevitability.

Tusika's lips are red as fresh blood, and her facial features are highlighted with gorgeous purple swirls and sharp points, drawn into loops that end at each of her temples. Even from this distance, Niya can almost imagine that they look like tiny claw marks—like

Raccoon, trailing his little paws along her gleaming skin. A touch so subtle that even Tusika's perceptive mana might not catch.

Her eyes are shining, blown dark from the low lighting of the club, illuminated only by the neon colors on the walls and the glowing violet shine from her own makeup. Niya knows her well enough to catch her meaning, unspoken as it may be: *get here,* she says without words, *don't keep me waiting.* And Niya feels her heart skip a beat, knowing that there is nothing that would displease her more.

She turns to check in with Inola, to help her find food, beverage, mind-altering substances if she so pleases—and she is caught by this woman's appearance as well.

Inola is wearing a light gray leather jumpsuit with a dark blue jacket atop it, the clasps undone to show the bodice beneath. Her hair is piled atop her head in an intricate mess of braids and twists that Niya had been amazed she'd pulled off on her own. The mixed Muskoke and Tsalagi woman had kept her painted-on makeup simple and bold—a series of white, wide dots across her cheeks and down the parts of her arms that are exposed, trailing down into smaller and smaller circles concentrically to her wrists.

In the flashing, swirling, rapidly changing lights of the club, Inola's eyes look as if they contain multitudes. As if the galaxy is there, inside of her mind, peaking out just to see the show. Niya is happy to see this joy on her newfound friend's face—distraction, if only for a little while, from the plight of her village and her missing sister, Kas.

Because they are friends, aren't they? Maybe they didn't start out that way, and maybe it was never the intention of either of them. But there are times in life when a connection feels preordained, destined and true. Niya smiles at Inola's happiness, because it means that maybe they are making progress. Perhaps they will bring Kas home. Gishky's clutches might soon be broken.

She just hopes none of their efforts will ultimately be in vain. Or cause rippling harm that neither of them can foresee.

Inola spins in place, her head tilted back. Her arms at her sides. Spinning, spinning. Taking it all in. A moment later and she is laughing, the soft sound lost on the waves of the crowd and the music and the thundering drums.

Niya shifts, reaching out to Inola. To pull close and say something there, in her ear, something secret and safe that might express her excitement, her trepidation—her worry, her joy.

This is the moment when her best friend turns around. Tusika's gaze performs a curious trick—going soft and hard at once. Niya swallows thickly at the sight.

And as quickly as Niya had been leaning towards Inola, she is now being swept away, Tusika's strong fingers wrapped securely around one of her wrists.

"What—"

But Tusika gives a loud cheer, her feet already

bouncing, and then she and Niya are on the dance floor. Swept up in the crowd. And Tusika is close to Niya, is filling up all of the spaces around her. And there is an exuberance to her movements that is real and familiar, that delivers a jolt of happiness through Niya like a shockwave.

"Tonight is the night!" Tusika hollers.

Niya does not have to ask what her friend means. Only one thing has consumed nearly every conversation over the last fourteen days and nights, one thing that matters more than all others—even more than the abrupt appearance of Inola Cato. Sure, there have been conversations about the troubles with Inola's village, the responsibilities of Councilmembers, the possibilities that the future holds. But more than anything else, Tusika has thought of gaining an Ability.

More than anything else, Niya has wanted to ask: *aren't we both certain of only one thing—that you will gain an Ability while I will not?* And another question: *why, oh why, is that?* Tusika may not know the answer. But if Tusika does know something, then Niya is not certain that she can bear such a truth.

In this dance and this joy, Niya indulges her best friend. All while her eyes scan beyond the crowd, looking to make sure that Inola made it to the seats Adasi and Nampeyo had found.

"You will be the most renowned Patak of all!" Niya shouts back.

And even if this is no guarantee—has never been a guarantee, not truly—Tusika loves to hear it. Tusika lives for it—for the future, and whatever gifts it may bring her.

What is it that Niya lives for?

— . . . —

Inola, though hardly older than Niya and the others, is still looking around with a childlike wonder as Niya and Tusika seek the others out after their dance. When her eyes alight upon Niya's approaching form, Inola's face somehow brightens even more.

"Niya!" she waves her over.

Niya has to tug a bit forcefully on Tusika's hand to get her best friend to come along, but they fall into the seating area side by side. Inola, Niya, Tusika. Across from them are Adasi and Nampeyo.

Adasi chuckles goodnaturedly from her side. "Yo! One last night, is it? Time to roll those cosmic dice, you know?" He imitates the shaking of his hands, as if he is playing a game of chance with bone cubes in the Mataawi district near the stadiums, releasing their futures into the air before them all.

"It is, in a way, a game of chance." Nampeyo's voice is full of that natural serenity of theirs.

"That's what I said, cuz."

"However the Adanadi works, there must be something that triggers it within each of us. We gain our Path, yes—but some of us gain more. Is it decided at birth?" they muse. "Or is it unlocked at some cosmically, random, irrevocable moment in the short days after the ceremony? Hmm..."

Nampeyo's voice fades away, and Inola's replaces it.

"This is precisely the question that is causing my village so much harm, such grief." She hangs her head, her spirits visibly lowering. "These questions have been asked for a long time, and we may never know the truth."

Tusika pushes to the edge of her seat quickly enough that Niya couldn't grab her by the wrist if she'd had the chance. She squares off with Inola, and all Niya can do is sit uncomfortably between them.

"If the answer is out there, do you disagree with the pursuit of such knowledge?"

Her voice is cool and even, but Niya wonders if there is a trap beneath the surface. Inola sits up straighter, as if she too wonders about the spaces between Tusika's words—all of the things unsaid, that reside in Tusika's bright eyes if not her sharp mouth. Eyebrows rising, Niya can see the retort growing on Inola's face before she even parts her lips.

Niya clenches her jaw, willing herself into stillness. Before her are two women, grown. Who is she to tell either of them to behave, even if she wishes she could?

"Yes, I disagree," Inola replies, the words slow and deliberate as they leave her lips. "I believe that there are ways in which things can and should be done. Methodical, sure. What I do *not* believe in are dangerous rituals in the woods, experimentation in the mountains that sends children and partners and elders alike home to their families on the wind as ash. I do not believe in soothsayers with the split tongues of serpents." A breath, then Inola says, "I do not believe in people manipulating the gifts of the Creator to their wills and whims."

Managing to barely hide the flinch that wants to spread across her features, Niya leans forward. She can see the way Inola is testing the waters between them, testing Tusika, probing none too gently to see if she can't find truth or lies in Gishkiy's claims.

But Niya doesn't have to say anything. Adasi quickly quips, "Whoa, ease up, cuz," and no one is quite sure which of the young women he is speaking to.

Niya's brow furrows, shifting a bit in her seat. As if to say, *please don't do this—let me be the one, but not here, and not now,* she presses her hand lightly against Inola's lower back, more a product of their proximity than anything else. But the effect is immediate. Tusika's eyes narrow into dangerous slits. She looks ready to lunge at any moment, but Inola has already proven to be a worthy adversary. Tusika would reconsider before anything got too far, Niya is certain.

Though she has been wrong before.

Nampeyo turns a knowing look on Adasi, which causes him to jump up with such immediacy that his feet practically leave the floor.

"I love this song!" he shouts, pulling Nampeyo to their feet. "It ended up on that mix you made me from our last visit here. Come, let us dance, my friends!"

Niya watches the clench of Tusika's jaw, the way the lights of the club dance in her eyes. Reds and oranges and yellows, blues and greens and purples; fire and ice. The tips of Niya's fingers twitch, itching to reach out and drag her best friend away. But at the same time, she does not want to abandon Inola to the press of bodies and the beating of drums, the thick swirl of air around them.

She turns her head forward, looking at neither of them but observing both of them at once, uncertain as to who in the Creator's name will break the silence first; who will lunge for the other's jugular, either with their words or without metaphor entirely.

But then Tusika surprises her, turning quickly in her direction.

"Nothing to say?"

Niya's mouth opens uselessly. "Tusika," she finally says, willing words to come. But words fail her. "I..."

"Fine, have it your way. Have *her*."

Tusika stands, hurricane unleashed. She turns on her heel, marching off—not with Adasi and Nampeyo, but to be alone in the crowd.

As quickly as the tension has built, it dissipates. Niya and Inola are alone. The brightness, the happiness that had shined so intensely on Inola's face only minutes before is gone now. Niya feels its absence like it's her own—and maybe it is, any happiness that belonged to her gone with Tusika into the night.

"Inola," she says, reaching out with tentative fingertips. "Are you okay?"

Her newest friend leans back into the sofa's cushions, pressing fully against Niya's hand. There is a pause in the music, purposeful and pronounced, and the lights change along with the pulsing of the drums and dancers and vocalists. There is silence and darkness, interrupted in flashes by alternating colors, pounding beats, righteous cries.

Niya cannot look away from Inola's face. That dark brown skin, as dark as the namesake Inola had told Niya of days before—Inola, or *black fox*, as she was born with skin as dark as night and covered in a soft down of black hair that fell away in those first days of life—her dark skin glows when the lights flash, seems to be its own living organism. The whites of her eyes are sparks against flint. The burnished glow of her makes Niya feel small and insignificant, but also grandiose, important.

How could Niya look away, when Inola seems to embody such life, such energy?

And that frown on her face, Niya wants to make it disappear.

"Inola," she prompts again.

Inola turns her head. A slow blink. And she seems to lighten, to loosen. Her lips shift and lift, turning up. Her eyes dip down, intent on Niya's mouth.

"I am all right. And tonight is not about me or my troubles. It is about you. The ending of one thing, the beginning of another." She delicately wraps Niya's hand up in one of hers, strong and calloused. "Will you dance with me?"

Hand in hand, they move to the floor.

And they dance. And they dance. And their ancestors live in them, breathe in them, *move* within them.

The night goes on. And they go with it. And Niya does her best not to worry about her best friend.

HAWATIKINAPA

"Goodnight, friends," Nampeyo says, waving Niya and Inola off as they depart with Adasi.

"Until tomorrow!" Adasi shouts, his arms outstretched and head thrown back. He yips at the sky like the coyote he is, disappearing around a corner in moments.

Left alone, Inola turns to Niya. "Are you worried about her?"

Niya knows that she is asking about Tusika. Who else? They had not seen hide nor hair of Tusika once she had fled before.

"I am not worried. Tusika is..." She tempers her words, is kinder than she wishes to be, after how hate-filled Tusika's words had come off. She finishes with, "Resourceful. I am sure to get an earful tomorrow at university for not having gone after her. But tonight, she is fine, if pouting."

Inola frowns, and her face handsome as ever despite the expression. "I do not wish to cause strife between you."

Niya does not give a response to this statement. Instead, she steps forward, grabs both of Inola's hands in her own, and says, "It is late. Let's get each other home, yeah?"

Inola looks up at the sky, quickening towards sunrise.

"My resthouse is closer," she says, snapping her head back down to connect her eyes unrelentingly with Niya's. "Come back with me."

"I—"

"My intentions are—" Inola interrupts, then pauses briefly before barrelling onward, "—quite innocent. Very much so," she says quickly with a laugh, Niya having given her a jokingly flirtatious and disbelieving look. "In my village, on the last night of the Adanadi window, the taker does not sleep alone as part of the ceremony. Whether they've received an Ability or not—sometimes we pile eight, nine, ten or more into one single sleeping place!" Her laughter tapers off, and a darkness passes over her face. "It is meant to be a joyous time. The last night before adulthood fully comes to pass. I hope your friend... I hope Tusika is not alone."

"The last night, for your sister..."

Inola pulls their slow walk to a stop. "I was with her. When I woke in the morning, she was gone. No conversation, no note. Only a small, ripped piece of red cloth on the pillow where her head had lain the night before. I didn't need words to know where she'd gone, what she'd done. Not when I saw that little scrap of red."

"Red?" Niya asks. "What did that mean to you?"

"Gishkiy's cloak. Red as a blood moon. Memorable. And for many of us, haunting."

Niya swallows hard, swaying on the spot. Her mind flashes to that first night of Inola's arrival, how she had rushed into the Patak household, dripping wet and on a mission.

How bright Kaatii Patak's robe was; how typical for her it had been.

How deep, deep red.

"Away with us," Niya says, clearing her throat. "I'll message Tusika, make sure she's alright. And then we'll fall asleep and let tomorrow bring what it may."

———

The resthouse where Inola is staying is quiet, the other guests likely already sound asleep. The two women remove their moccasins once they get inside, carrying them as they navigate the dark.

Inola leads the way through a common area and down a branching hallway. She comes to a recessed door and swipes her niisi against a small, metallic panel near the edge of its frame. The panel blurs into a cascade of violet lights, dripping from top to bottom and then back up again before the door slides open.

Once inside, Inola reverses the process, and the door locks behind them. She touches another panel, sliding upward slightly along it, and a series of lights fade up gently. Just enough to allow Niya to orient herself, but not so bright as to reverse the sleep gathering at each woman's eyes.

The heptagonal space is modest but cozy, and Niya feels more than anything else that it has come to accommodate and represent Inola's sense of self. Three of the walls are a deep green, like a forest in late summer. The other four walls are an ombre shift between variations of soft whites. A sliding door leads to what Niya assumes to be the relief area of Inola's rented rooms.

Things that Inola has done to make it her own: a

woven throw blanket of yellows and reds and blues, draped across the foot of the slightly elevated bedspace; it is well-worn, old but loved. Two pocket-sized paintings in the realism fashion; Niya touches their edges, imagining that she must be looking at Inola's family. Her mana, and the darling little sister who set her on this journey to Cahokia in the first place. She can see pieces of Inola in both of them: her mana's light eyes and upturned nose and coloring, and her little sister… so much similarity, like looking at an ever so slightly aged-down Inola. The younger girl even has two streaks of color dyed through her hair, like her big sister.

How disappointed must the girl have been—to receive no Ability when her older sister had received such a strong one?

There is a small seating area, and Niya observes the remnants of a small breakfast there. A cup for tea, a dish for a soft chestnut roll and sausage. She can picture it. And alongside that picture, herself, superimposed like a frame once lost and now found. Meshed together. Natural, simple, wonderful.

"Here."

Inola's voice catches her off guard, as soft as it is. Niya turns, and Inola is extending some sleep clothes for her. Niya takes them gladly. They change near one another, eyes respectfully averted to allow for privacy.

After they've each relieved themselves, they slide into the bedcovers together. Niya is on her side with Inola on hers, facing each other. They stare for a moment, then another, and another.

"My mana will be missing me." Inola offers it without prompting. Niya doesn't know what to say, so she stays silent. "Not because she loves me—which she does, don't get me wrong. But because I'm the best hunter in the family, and times have been...well, I can't leave them for much longer. My auntie helps, but she has pain that keeps her in bed much of the time. And my grandparents, they are proper elders. Without Kas, that's one less mouth to feed, but at what cost?"

The words come out discordantly sweet and lilting, so different from their content, and Niya is certain that Inola is asleep in half a moment. Perhaps quicker even than that. She frowns, brushing loose hair from Inola's brow before rolling over to extinguish the last light from the room.

Niya follows Inola quickly in sleep, her thoughts on nothing but the great question of tomorrow—and the unanswered message she'd sent to Tusika as they'd arrived at Inola's resthouse: *I'm sorry about earlier. Are you alright? Please let me know.*

This is how Niya Suwatt sleeps: restless, until peace finds her; worried about her best friend, until her mind takes her elsewhere.

And this is how she dreams.

Flying above the city, Cahokia is little more than an intricate series of dots of light in the vast darkness of the world. She leaves the city behind, and it leaves her behind, too.

A blur in the sky. The sun rises. On the horizon, a

black dot amongst the mountainside.

She flies towards it, speeding faster and slower at the same time, the moment infinite and infinitesimal.

As she approaches it, the black dot yawns wider, wider, and wider still. Shifts and grows, a living thing. A breathing thing. And it has her, has her tight in its grip. A never-ending inhalation.

Niya and Owl are one. And they are breathed in, in through the cave's jagged, gaping hole of a mouth. All is dark, all is still; all is silent and dead, dead, dead.

"Alive," the cave hisses back. "I am alive." Pinpricks of red and purple in the dark. Eyes reflecting light. But there is no light, not here. Nevermore, forevermore.

"Why—" Niya starts to ask. Owl lets out a screech.

In return, the cave and its keepers scream—a scream so feral that Niya's soul shivers in place, frozen and afraid of the unknown.

Then the cave, it exhales.

So forceful, so sudden, so violent. Niya and Owl tumble, head over wing over foot over beak. Up is down and down is up and Niya knows nothing so much as that this might be the end, must be the end—

And then she hits the water.

The shock of it sends water streaming into her mouth and nose. Her lungs are drowning.

"Breathe, my child."

This is impossible, Niya realizes, until it isn't.

Her body stills. And, like some divine knowledge has been imparted upon her suddenly and without *explanation, she performs the smudging motions. Her hands move, as if cleansing herself with sacred medicines and smoke and prayer. Underwater, yes—but the power builds within her.*

She pushes her hands towards her heart, cupping the water and dragging it towards her chest. The vital organ that pumps life from her head to her toes.

Next, she cups her hands and performs the same gesture to her mouth. To speak pure, to speak good into existence, to breath even and true.

Toward her eyes. Toward her mind. Toward her hair and arms and chest, her body and spirit.

In an elongating, everlasting second, Niya does all of this.

And in that same instantaneous moment, her eyes clear. She can see. She can move with little effort, as if she is one with the river's flow.

Niya can breathe.

Niya wakes with a gasp, sitting upright with a jolt, the bedcovers tangled around her.

"What, what!" Inola asks, voice slurred with sleep and confusion.

"I can't believe it," Niya whispers.

Her eyes drag over her hands where she has fisted them in the covers. She stares at them but does not see them, instead sees only a line of Suwatts marching back in time eight generations and more. She can almost hear her Grizzly Bear-blessed ancestor, roaring at her through the depths of time...

A hard blink. She shakes herself and turns to her bedmate.

Inola's voice is weak with worry as she asks, "Are you okay?"

"More than," Niya says. Her face breaks into a smile as bright as the sun. Brighter, perhaps. "Inola, I have been gifted with an Ability!"

tahood | *when owl chased raccoon's tail*

ZAPATIKINAPA

Even though it is almost unspeakably early, the first thing that Niya does, still sitting there, upright and energized and next to Inola in the woman's temporary bed, is call Tusika.

Her friend does not answer.

She tries again, and again—but to no avail. She taps out a message quickly, hardly able to work her niisi due to the adrenaline coursing through her veins.

[Niya] I need to talk to you

"She may very well be sleeping," Inola offers, glancing at the time of day on her niisi's face, indicated by a circle around which the sun spins.

"On this, the last possible night that we might develop an Ability?" Niya asks in return, her body practically vibrating with the knowledge that she, *she*, has developed one. After all these years, all these family members having not received one. She may be seventeen-years old, an adult and grown in many ways. But even just the thought that she has been gifted in this way leaves her feeling giddy and childish in a delightful way. "I'd be willing to bet good nizi on the fact that she is out right now, using the Ability she has herself received."

And yet... and yet.

Niya thinks of Gishkiy's story. It couldn't be true, could it? Their speculation has been for naught. If Niya received an Ability, then it is settled—an Ability was not stolen from her, some unseen potential siphoned from her to her best friend by the Patak clan.

The image of Kaatii Patak standing with chin up and shoulders back, red robe about her body, and a superimposed image of Gishkiy, the villain of Inola's story, draped in a blood red cloak that twists and chokes the wind.

Maybe it hasn't happened to Niya. But couldn't it have still happened to Gishkiy?

And then her niisi starts blaring the tone of an urgent message.

"Ish," she hisses, practically sliding off the edge of the bed in an effort to reach her device from where she'd tossed it in surprise.

She grabs it and flicks through the couple of messages she has received since falling asleep. Messages from Adasi and Nampeyo that they had gotten home safe. And a message from her daadoo.

[Daadoo] Come home, child. All is well, but we need you here.

"Everything okay?"

Niya sighs and slides out of the warm embrace of covers and away from Inola's welcoming eyes. "I've got to get home." She pauses as if struck by inspiration, turning on her heels to smile down at her bedmate. "Come with me?"

"I won't impose," comes Inola's quick response. "I've forced my way into enough Cahokian homes, haven't I?"

Niya chuckles as she slips into her clothes from the night before. "You won't be imposing, not at all.

Come with me, we will have breakfast and finish going through that archival footage we found yesterday."

Inola's head tilts to the side as she considers this. They had found some heavily redacted documents and videos that might have more information that could help them find out what it is the Pataks have been up to all this time—if anything at all. Simultaneously, they are petitioning to get before the Council of Twelve, a process that Tusika had helped them line-jump a few days previous.

"Alright. You drive a hard bargain. But I fear your overall bargaining skills are not so good, Niya—I fully benefit, whereas you only get my presence."

Turning to fully face Inola, Niya summons the most serious look she can to her face, delivering her words with the weight she feels they warrant.

"Then I am truly blessed, and not merely with an Ability."

— . . . . —

Niya and Inola are chatting as they enter the Suwatt household. Niya is mid-sentence, about to answer Inola's inquiry about how she will first test her new Ability.

"—was in water in my dream, so maybe that's the only place where it will work?"

Poised to answer, Inola's next words die before making it past her lips.

Niya's mana and noosoo are both standing in the open space around the living and cooking areas as the girls round the corner. They are chatting, too—but with another guest altogether.

"Tusika!" Niya exclaims at the sight of her friend.

But the smile that had defaulted upon her face at the sight of Tusika there in her family's home does not last. In fact, it fades rapidly as she truly takes in the artificial smile on Tusika Patak's face.

And it *is* artificial, Niya can see that as plain as day. She does not call her out or otherwise draw attention to it. If Tusika is in Niya's home behaving as she would in her own—with artifice—then Niya can only assume that the young woman has her reasons.

"Niya, Love," Ahyoka begins, stepping forward with a gentle smile on her own face. This one, Niya can see immediately, is true—if a little concerned that Tusika had arrived when Niya herself had not been home. The question practically asks itself: *is your friend okay?* But Ahyoka is nearly as perceptive as her daughter, more so in some ways. Instead of drawing attention to what may be an uncomfortable aspect of their collective morning, she instead says, "Tusika was just telling us the good news! She—"

"Eight generations strong," Tusika says. Her words are clipped, almost painfully formal. "On this, the last night in our Adanadi period, I have been blessed."

"Tusika, wow! I am so excited for you." Niya's excitement is genuine, but she does realize there is a trace of falsehood in it. *What would it be like,* she wonders only in the safety of her own mind, *if a Suwatt gained an Ability when a Patak gained none?* "Please, tell us more! Is it an Ability that follows the charismatic traits of your Path or—"

"I am truly sorry, my friend, for interrupting," Tusika

cuts her off. Niya's mouth shuts abruptly, and she is certain that Tusika is not sorry in the slightest. "But I cannot stay. I came merely to pass along a message for..." Her eyes dart momentarily to Inola, where she is standing just over Niya's shoulder. "Your audience is set before the Council of Twelve. Report to the Council building at the opening time two days from now."

"Congratulations, Inola," Yona says, moving forward to clap one of his giant bear paws on the young woman's shoulder.

In just the few days that Niya has been helping her, Inola has already become acquainted with her family. They were aware of her plight, sympathetic to her needs, ready and willing to vouch for Inola on her petition for an audience with the Council if needed. But the suspicious connection between Gishkiy and Kaatii has stayed between the young women. Either way, their support would apparently no longer be needed to get before the Council—their support the day of may make a difference yet.

Thanks to Tusika and whatever strings she has pulled, an application is now somehow no longer needed. And this, in spite of the confrontation between Tusika and Inola the night before.

As Niya is opening her mouth to say something, anything, she isn't sure what, Inola steps forward and around her.

"Words cannot express my thanks." She presses her palm against her chest, over the place where her heart beats beneath her breast. The action, her stoic gaze, her deference. Niya imagines that it is a noble heart, indeed, that beats there. "Your kindness will not be forgotten."

Inola bows her head, a sure sign of respect. Niya glances at Tusika only to see her friend pointedly looking anywhere but at the woman who is actively paying her thanks.

"I must be going," Tusika says without further preamble.

"Tusika—" Niya starts.

Tusika moves to pass her, and Niya reaches out, grasping her wrist with two encircling fingers.

Tusika's voice is soft and low and for the two of them alone. "I'll speak with you later, yeah?"

Something tells Niya that Tusika has no intention of this coming to pass. But she nods anyway.

The front door closes behind her friend. Before Niya has a chance to ponder her actions, she is on the move, unable to accept this ending.

"Excuse me," she calls over her shoulder, abandoning Inola with her parents as she rushes after Tusika.

SAKTIKINAPA

She catches Tusika before she is even three mounds away. Even so, Niya can tell that her friend was moving quickly. Eager to get away, to put distance between them.

But who is "them"? Tusika and Inola? Tusika and Niya's parents?

Tusika and Niya herself?

She swallows hard.

"Hey!"

With one firm movement, she spins Tusika around. Her hands remain on her friend's upper arms, thumbs pressing into bare flesh.

"What do you want?"

The words fly like magsling bolts from Tusika's mouth. Niya takes a step back reflexively.

"What has gotten into you?" she asks.

"I could ask you the same," her oldest and best friend counters, "but it seems obvious enough."

The turn of her lips, the sneer on her face, makes it immediately clear to Niya what the other girl is implying. She drops her hands as if burned but stands her ground. Her instinct is to take a step back, to retreat from the harsh words and the venom. But because this is her instinct, she fights against it.

Instead of pulling away, she leans in.

"You got her an audience before the Council, and

yet you speak with such detachment towards her. Such malice towards me. Why?"

"I did not receive an Ability, Niya!"

The words are a scream, a wretched sound, peeled from Tusika's throat like the last dying cry of a wounded animal. All of her energy, expelled at once. Held back before and now released, and Niya can see it—can see how her best friend's body sags with the effort of letting this truth loose into the world.

"Tusika, I—"

"No, Niya. You *nothing*. You couldn't understand, you will *never* understand."

"Eight generations," Niya rushes to get out. "Eight generations of pressure, all on your shoulders. And I'm sorry—I'm so, so terribly sorry, Tusika, that you did not gain an Ability. But there is no one in the whole of Cahokia better equipped to lead our people than you."

"Without an Ability, I am nothing. No—*less*."

A day before, Niya would have been unwilling to bet two nizi on the likelihood of receiving an Ability of her own. These callous words uttered so thoughtlessly sting like a slap to the face. Her eyes begin to water, and she blinks furiously to dispel them. Ordinarily, she would be free with her emotions, especially in the presence of her best friend, the girl she loves. But right now, she feels like she can't cry. She swallows hard and steps forward, intent on making Tusika understand that she loves her—exactly for who she was a year ago, a month ago, a week ago, even yesterday!

"To who?" Niya asks, her hands clenching and

unclenching as she tries to drag some semblance of understanding from the other girl. "Who values you based on this arbitrary thing? Because to me, you are—"

"My parents," Tusika interjects again, interrupting the truth that Niya is now uncertain she will ever be allowed to give voice to again. "My entire family."

"Not every Patak has an Ability, Tusika, you know this."

"But every firstborn *does*. Every single one of us." She chokes down a sob then corrects herself. "Every one of them. But I have failed."

"You have not failed. There is nothing one can do to ensure an Ability comes to them or not. Right?"

Childhood friends Gishkiy and Kaatii cross Niya's mind. She wonders what thoughts are crossing Tusika's.

"Right, Tusika? There is no way to guarantee someone receives an Ability that you know of. Or that your mana knows of." When Tusika fails to meet her gaze, Niya raises her voice to a near-shout. "Right?!"

"What are you implying—that Pataks steal Abilities?" Tusika scoffs weakly, her eyes focused tightly on Niya's. "How could you think so little of me, of my family?"

For a moment, they are both quiet, surrounded only by the sound of Tusika's heavy breaths on the cool morning air. Niya wonders if they are both thinking of Gishkiy and his attempts at gaining Abilities, with or without the Adanadi.

Niya's voice is tentative as she asks, "Do your parents know?"

Tusika scoffs more harshly this time, her eyes rolling heavenward. "No, and I do not plan on telling them."

Niya's brows furrow, and she wonders momentarily if she is being naive, unable to imagine a world in which she would not discuss something as important as this with her parents. "That is no small secret to keep."

"But it is mine to disclose or not, isn't it?"

And Tusika steps forward with these words, almost threateningly. Niya stands her ground, her furrowed brow shifting not into a look of onrushing fear but into one of deep and deserved concern.

"I would never give away a secret entrusted to me," she says, her voice measured and sure. "Especially not one from you."

Tusika lets out a laugh that sounds more like a cry, but no tears escape her eyes. Niya tries to remember, when was the last time she had seen her friend shed tears? She cannot immediately recall, so long ago had it been.

"You tried to call me." Tusika's voice is small now. She gestures at her niisi. "I'm sorry I did not answer. I was... a mess."

"Exactly the sort of time when you should answer your best friend," Niya prods, her words careful but kind as she can muster. Testing the waters, checking to see if the tide has turned. If Tusika's temperature has cooled.

Looking up, a fluttering of lashes and cock of her hip, Tusika speaks. As if to erase her harsh words. *And couldn't she?* Niya thinks. *Wouldn't I let her do precisely that, if she wanted to?*

"You're right. But if you were calling to find out what Ability I'd received, now you know that you would've been disappointed."

"I wanted to make sure you were okay," she says, her voice steadier than she can believe. "After last night, I didn't want...well, I wished you hadn't been alone last night is all. And I was calling to tell you—" Niya pauses. Then she barrels onward, lifting her chin the slightest bit with her next words. "I was calling to tell you that I *was* gifted with an Ability."

There is a silence so thick and deafening that Niya begins to hear her heartbeat in her ears.

"Does *she* know?" It is the absolute last thing that Niya expected to hear come out of her friend's mouth. So unexpected, in fact, that she cannot even formulate an answer before Tusika continues. "Does absolutely *everyone* know but me?"

"You would know if you had answered my calls!" Niya raises her voice in frustration and hurt. But she does not answer the question, not directly, because the answer would hurt her friend more.

By not answering the question, Niya seems to have given Tusika all the answer she needs.

"Huh. So that's how this is."

"You are not being fair, Wanzi—"

"Don't call me pet names while you're off sleeping with some down-and-out stranger!" Niya does take a step back now. She takes a step back, and she raises one of her hands—as if to shield herself from Tusika's vitriol. But instead of apologizing, instead of righting the many wrongs she has uttered in one fell, vicious swoop, Tusika doubles down. "What gift is it that you have received, Niya Suwatt? What useless Ability has been bestowed upon you, hmm? Or if not useless, then it will be used far less than an Ability would have been used by *me,* by a Patak!"

Niya's words are so quiet as to nearly be swept away on the light breeze. "I know that you are ambitious, Tusika, but I've never known you to be so ugly before. Do you even know what you are saying? Or realize who you're speaking to? I believe better of you. And no Ability is useless—all are sacred, as they come from the Creator."

This is what Niya says, instead of any of the myriad other things she truly wishes to say. But her hurt—and her righteous anger—keep her from saying more, keep her even from sharing the Ability that she has been blessed with, River's Flow. However, this statement in and of itself is contentious enough when said to Tusika Patak. Because Niya may be spiritual, may have a connection to the land that goes deeper than the topsoil, has practices and traditions that bind her mind, body, and spirit to a higher path and power. But Tusika? Tusika does not stand for spirituality. And when she is as heated as this? Niya should not be surprised by her friend's response.

Tusika's scoff is harsh enough to cause Niya nearly physical pain, so intensely is her heart aching. "They are no Creator of mine."

"You are upset," Niya counters. "You are upset, and I

will forgive you these nasty slights in the light of a different day."

"Should I be thankful for that, *friend?*" Tusika snaps back. "That you will forgive my transgressions, take me back beneath your generous wing?"

"You are my best friend, Tusika. My best friend, and I...I will fight for you! Do you understand that?" However hurt Niya may be, she speaks with truth. "You are strong. You are good. You do not need an Ability to lead. Take a breath and realize that you are being dangerously unkind to someone who loves you unconditionally."

Tusika's eyes do brim up now with unshed tears. She looks to the sky, her hands pressing to the sides of her appled cheeks. She opens her mouth as if to speak, but only a sob escapes.

At the sound, Niya can feel her own eyes fill up, is afraid that she will begin openly crying any second, too—that if they both cry at once, together, they may never stop.

"Look at the good you have already done for Inola," she says, realizing a heartbeat too late that this is the wrong thing to say and the wrong time at which to say it. "Look what you have done for her. That did not take an Ability, Tusika. That took diplomacy and empathy, determination and a strong sense of fairness. You did that!"

The moment Tusika hears the other woman's name, something inside of her seems to shift, turn, break.

She unleashes a growl. Her eyes blink and are clear of tears but muddled by another emotion entirely. She and Niya have moved closer to one another during their shouting match, and she closes that final distance. Moves her hands from her own face to Niya's. Brings their mouths together, pressing herself against Niya in a move that positively screams possessiveness and desperation, masking any sort of true longing that might be beneath the rage.

For a moment, Niya lets go. For a moment, Niya imagines that she is in another place, another time. That this is exactly as it was always supposed to happen between them.

And this kiss, it is everything and nothing like Niya had imagined it would be. Because of course she had imagined before, what it would be like—kissing Tusika, being with Tusika. This kiss, it feels right, because Niya has wanted it for so long. But it also feels wrong, because she is not sure that she wants it like this.

Red berries. Hemlock. Sumac. Manchineel.

It is an act of mutual desperation, when they pull apart, however unwanted that separation seems to be. But they are both still orbiting one another, still stuck in the gravity offered by the other's close proximity. Both with their eyes shut, foreheads pressed against one another, heavy breaths intermingling.

"Tusika," Niya breathes. "My Wanzi..."

When Niya finally opens her eyes, Tusika's follow moments later in a fluttering of lashes.

"I..." Tusika begins, and Niya is not imagining the tears that are swimming in her best friend's eyes. "I have always—"

But Niya does not know what words were about to leave her friend's lips. Does not know if it would have been an apology or a declaration or some odd amalgamation of both or neither or something altogether different. Wonderful or terrible or anything, *anything.*

Because a soft voice comes from behind Niya, mutters on a breath. "Oh. I'm sorry, I..."

And the moment, whatever it had been, whatever it was going to be, is over. Broken. Smashed.

Niya is mournful of it and grateful at once.

Then she turns, and she sees Inola Cato coming to a stop nearby and looking as if she wishes she were literally anywhere else in the entirety of Makasing. She has seen the kiss, because of course she has. Tusika realizes it at the same moment as Niya, her eyes shifting from Inola's face to Niya's in a flash. And whatever it is that Tusika sees there, or thinks she sees, it sends her back to that place of rage and reckless abandonment.

"I see how it is." Her words bite, slap, sting. Niya chews the inside of her cheek, her jaw tight. Her whole body is braced for the inevitable but inexplicable storm. "Your new shadow. Your new low. Hardly do I know her, but I know you, Niya Suwatt. And I expected so much more."

In a flash, Tusika turns and breaks into a flat-out run. She disappears around a corner before Niya has the chance to open her mouth and shout after her. But what would she say, if she could even find her voice? What could she say, to make the moment end differently? That Inola is a friend who needs her help, that *Tusika* is the one she is in love with? She doesn't know.

And now Tusika has manufactured whatever truth it is that she wants to believe, run off with it and her imagination alike.

When Tusika is out of sight, Niya turns her body towards Inola. It is immediately apparent that this, too, may be a conversation for which Niya does not possess the proper words.

It is not comforting to Niya that the sentiment seems to be mutual, with Inola standing stock-still in the middle of the pathway, hands awkwardly grasping for purchase on air that offers none in return.

Finally, they speak at once.

"That wasn't what—"

"Your mana sent me—"

They stop talking simultaneously as well, and Niya feels like her stomach would empty its contents if it had any contents to empty.

"She..." Niya starts, about to explain in perhaps more detail than she should, why exactly she and Tusika had been caught in a locking of lips. Then she thinks better of it. "She is having a hard time right now."

Inola nods, her hands slipping down to hang loosely at her sides. "She is lucky to have someone like you in her life, that much I know."

Niya does not understand why Inola sounds so sad as she says this. It makes her heart ache, pounding dully as it longs for the girl who has run from her. About to speak again, she is interrupted by Inola, who rushes forward to speak once more.

"Your mana did not want your breakfast to go cold.

So I came to find you."

"Thank you, I..."

But what, what is there to say?

"I should be going," Inola offers.

And she is not wrong, is she? They have no more work to do, not to obtain an audience before the Council. Tusika has achieved that for Inola. The excuses to get together, to plot and prepare and plan, they are now thinner than ever. If the Pataks have been manipulating Adanadi potential, they could continue trying to find answers—but Inola's purpose in Cahokia has always been to get help and return home. Niya knows that the woman's family needs her, and it would be selfish for Niya to keep Inola in the city even one day longer than needed. With her appearance set before the Council in less than a day's time, what else is left for them to do together?

"But, breakfast...?"

Niya knows exactly how silly it sounds even as she says it.

"Break bread with your family, and I will do the same with my own from afar. I...I cannot risk losing sight of my purpose for being here any longer."

Unlike Tusika, Inola's departure is slow and measured, her head held high. Tusika—strong, confident, vibrant Tusika—had run like a frightened animal.

How much have things changed, in less than half a day?

Niya turns and begins her short walk home.

Every step feels heavy as she goes. It feels like both

her oldest and her newest friends are slipping away from her. What should be a joyous day instead feels clouded in angst.

Shaking her head, Niya recalibrates as best she can in the few short steps she has left.

Upon returning home, Niya finds that her parents are waiting for her with breakfast. They are sitting on sofa cushions beneath the mid-morning light from the sun as it streams down over them in the sitting area. Her face must tell much of the story of her heart, for they both greet her with open arms. She falls into them gladly.

In the moment before she dives into their arms, with tears streaming down her face, she wishes to be a child again, if only for the brief respite it might offer. Or else to be an adult, and to be successful at it. Because it truly feels like she is failing on her first day.

And when their arms embrace her, Niya feels like a child in all of the best ways. In the ways of comfort and familiarity, safety and love.

I can have both, she thinks. *I can fix things with Tusika, I can be a friend to Inola, and I can have this support.*

Her tears dry up nearly as quickly as they had come. Her sadness sits heavily on her chest, but she has comfort in the proximity of her parents and the certainty that a path forward exists—she simply needs to find it.

"What's good, Daughter?"

Her noosoo asks this question in that deep, rumbly chest voice of his. The question is one that Niya is used to, having been asked it many times before. After a bad day at university. The time she broke her arm after a bad fall on the chunkey field. When her daadoo died. One or both of her parents would be there, wrapping her up in loving arms—followed by this question.

What's good?

She realizes suddenly, almost as if she had forgotten about it entirely, that she *does* have good news. This day was worth celebrating when she was awoken from her dreams by the realization of an Ability made manifest, and these setbacks with the women in her life could not detract from that particular joy.

"Mana, noosoo," she turns in their joint embrace, a smile lifting her tear-wetted cheeks. "I do have good news."

And when she tells them that she has been gifted with an Ability, her noosoo lets loose a mighty, celebratory howl towards the heavens. Her mana claps her hands with glee before pressing her palms to her own face and then to Niya's. The joy is tangible, palpable. And Niya cries again, this time the tears coming from a place of joy rather than despair.

PITSITIKINAPA

Niya is on her knees, diligently working between soil pods at university. One of the agriculture elders is making her rounds, critiquing and offering insights as the students work. Niya is one of the oldest students at this particular point in their studies, since she changed directions with university multiple times before finally settling. Only one other student in the department has also taken the Adanadi so far, and they did not receive an Ability. When Niya had disclosed her gift upon inquiry, the elder had irreverently said, "Congratulations. Now back to work."

She very much enjoys her mentors. Especially how humble they keep them all, no matter how someone like Niya might excel.

Only one day has passed since she received her Ability. She wasted no time the day previous in telling her friends about her luck.

[Adasi] Ayeee girlies! Where's the news at?

[Nampeyo] Do not feel pressured by Adasi to tell us about any Abilities received or not. You may tell us in your own time, or not at all.

Niya had told them gladly about her Ability, though she had moved them all to a private conversation stream before doing so, not wishing to inflame Tusika's mood anymore than it already was. She had also tested River's Flow briefly in her kitchen sink—breathing underwater for about half a minute before her anxiety pushed her head back above water. She hoped that, with time and practice, she could use the Ability more effectively and for longer and longer periods of time. Her brief time in the hydrology course of study taught her enough to know that River's Flow was doing some spectacular things to her body—correcting gaseous exchange, balancing the oxygen and acid levels in her blood, and more. When she resurfaced after breathing underwater for a full, easy three minutes, she was amazed at how like herself and unlike herself she felt—no ill effects from the use of her Ability except a profound tiredness in her bones.

[Adasi] And have you heard from our Tusika?

The three of them continue to use the private stream for chatting. Her friends do not know everything about the argument she and Tusika had, but they know enough to worry.

[Niya] I have, but only briefly...I won't speak for her or betray her confidence. She'll tell you all about it when she is ready.

Adasi had replied with a hand-drawn doodle of himself sporting a goofy grin and a wink; for his right-sided prosthetic, he is sporting a cartoon lightning bolt in place of the artificial limb. It had made Niya smile, even though she was worried—how long would Niya have to keep this secret? And if she was keeping it from her entire family, would she also keep it from their friends?

How large a web will Tusika weave? How long a thread will she need to spin?

And if the web collapses, if the thread breaks, who will she allow to help her pick up the pieces?

Tusika remains conspicuously absent.

Niya stands up straight, stretching towards the sky as she unfolds from her crouching position. The varieties of beans that she has been working on are doing quite well—she is pleased with the immediate results and is hoping that when they simulate drought conditions in a few weeks, they will continue to do even better.

One of the elders walks by, and Niya overhears them speaking to another student.

"The earth gives us this. What do we give back to the earth?"

"Gifts," the student offers.

"Like what?"

"Medicines. Tobacco and the like."

"What else?" the mentor prompts.

Prayer, Niya thinks to herself, moving to another station and out of earshot of the pair. *And tears, too, sometimes.*

Even after her parents had celebrated with her over her new Ability, Niya had cried privately in her room. And she had prayed, too—for wisdom and for direction, for the power of knowledge, more than anything else, as to how to make things right again. With Tusika, of course. But with Inola as well, strange as their last interaction had been.

She has not heard from Inola, not for more than a short message or two exchange. But the woman's audience before the Council is set for tomorrow, and Niya wishes she knew how Inola was faring.

When she is done with classes for the day, Niya

heads to where her canoe is tied up on the riverbank. Staring into the powerful flow of the Mizizibi, Niya wonders what it would be like to dive headfirst into the rushing waters. To breathe beneath the surface, to swim with ease and grace.

But she remembers how tired she had felt after merely dunking her head below the full basin of water in her family's kitchen. How she had used her Ability for only a quite abbreviated matter of time, and how tired she had felt as a result. A bone-deep weariness had she felt, and she had subsequently napped the rest of the afternoon away.

I will get stronger, Niya tells herself. *My stamina will grow.*

For now, she takes the canoe back across the water, securing it safely to the dock and shoving her hands deep into the pockets of the short-cut breeches she'd donned that morning. The loose neckline of her soft green leather tunic flutters against her skin in the light breeze. She breathes deeply of the fresh air, her eyes closing for a moment, taking in the sounds of the city and the Mataawi district around her.

When she opens her eyes again, she has decided that she will not descend below ground to ride the yutsu train around the district and to her home. Instead, she will walk. As she walks, she will think. And when next she prays to the Creator for guidance, perhaps she will be rewarded. She isn't even selfish, she rationalizes to herself, as she is not looking for some sort of grand and divine intervention—simply a sign that she is not so lost as she believes.

On her walk, a snake slithers its way across the path in front of her. She jumps on first seeing it, but she quickly recognizes it for the rat snake it is. Splotches of purple Adanadi hue are visible on the edges of its belly, like smeared blackberry stains from a summer haul.

Further on down the trail, a couple of gray squirrels are fighting over loose acorns in the grass. One of them has a ring of purplish fur around its left eye, almost imperceptible until the sun hits it just right. The other has no Adanadi markings that Niya can see.

Before long, she finds her way to the same copse of trees where she and Inola had sat just a handful of days ago. She stops and stares for a moment, then decides to take a seat. Sit against one of the tree trunks. Clear her mind.

When she lowers herself to the ground, the sun is on a downward trajectory through the sky and to the west. Fitful as her sleep had been the two previous nights, Niya is not surprised to find sleep close at hand. She tells herself that she will take a short nap before heading home.

However, by the time she wakes, the sun has almost finished its descent through the sky. Her niisi is pinging incessantly at her with a message from Inola.

[Inola] Can we meet up?

Niya feels so caught off guard that she simply stares at the message for some time, uncertain as to how to respond.

When she does manage to write back, she finds her eloquence underwhelming, to say the least.

[Niya] Yes

Despite this embarrassing show, Inola does not take long to respond.

[Inola] I can come to yours, if that is alright with your family.

Niya types so quickly on the holographic projection of a screen that her fingers are practically punching through the image on each Kag Chahi syllable.

[Niya] Of course! Please come. I'm not home yet but I will be—

She checks the time with a glance before finishing her thought.

[Niya] —before the top of the hour. See you then

Never one of the fastest runners in her cohort growing up, Niya impresses even herself; she gets home in record time.

After performing the most expedient superficial cleaning of her room in her life, Niya manages to greet Inola at the front door without being entirely out of breath.

"Hello," Inola says, voice quiet, gentle. Everything about her stance is so hesitant—a far cry from that overconfident, determined young woman who had barged into the Patak home only a week ago.

"Inola, please," Niya says, gesturing to her side. "Come in!"

Inola steps over the threshold, bending to remove her well-worn moccasins. When she stands, she and

Niya are face-to-face, so close that they are practically breathing in and out the same shared air.

"Oh, excuse me—"

"I'm sorry, I—"

They both stop talking over one another, pause, and then break into nervous laughter. It quickly transforms into something they both are willing and able to acknowledge.

"We left on strange terms," Niya says. "I am sorry about that. And I need to clear the air—"

"You need to do no such thing."

"But I do!" Niya delicately reaches out, resting one of her hands lightly atop Inola's. "Tusika and I...we revolve around one another. It's just that, more often than not, *I* revolve around *her*."

"Let me guess," Inola gently interrupts. "She isn't as good at being anything other than the center of attention?"

Niya quirks her lips to the side, brow furrowing. "It's that, but it isn't. She feels threatened by you, but that doesn't make sense."

"I'm stealing your time." Inola shrugs. "Maybe that is enough? A new friend who splits your attention."

"Or..." Niya's thoughts go dark. She presses her knuckles against her lips, thinking hard. How much to say, how much speculation to speak aloud? "Maybe she knows more than she is willing to admit. Maybe her mana knows something—" Inola's eyebrows lift, and the woman stands up straighter, suddenly supremely attentive.

"You think there is a truth in Gishkiy's madness, and the Pataks are keeping the family secret safe."

Niya lifts one palm up, gesturing Inola further inside.

"We've been searching for that truth. If it exists, I think we could find it—but we're short on time. And I received an Ability, Inola, *I* did while Tusika didn't! If there was something going on with the Pataks... maybe it ended with Kaatii and Gishkiy. Tusika might be keeping her family's secret, whether she wants to or not."

Inola nods, looking pensive. After a few moments of silence, she says, "That could be. But it does not change Gishkiy's past, nor does it change his future plans. He believes something was stolen from him, some sort of divine potential. The Council must hear my plea and help, or else I fear I may never see Kas alive again. It could be too late even now."

"Tusika has not returned my calls and messages anyway. I'll keep trying, but until she reaches out again, I am focused on helping you prepare for tomorrow."

As Niya begins walking towards her room, a grateful Inola falling in step behind her, the front door opens with a bang. Inola jumps in response, startled, turning around quickly to see what's caused the commotion. Niya only laughs, unsurprised in the slightest by her niisi's entrance.

Her niisi barrels inside, click-clacking her walking stick on the floor right past the two young women.

"Pah-ah-ah," she mutters, hardly even casting a glance towards either of them. "A load of firewood and bison chips, my girls. Hop, hop!"

"Yes, niisi," Niya says.

Her words are lost on a stunned rip of laughter, and Inola is following suit. They begin moving the stacks of firewood and dried buffalo chips from in front of the Suwatt mound to the eastern side beneath an overhang, where it will largely be protected from rain and snow for the upcoming cold season.

As they work, they talk about Inola's meeting with the Council—the story of Gishkiy's rise and what she will ask for in aid of her people.

As they work, Niya can't help but think of Tusika and the secrets she may be keeping.

"I have to get this right," Inola says as she despondently presses her hands into her eyeballs. "My village is counting on me."

They have been working on Inola's speech all evening. Her appeal before the Council is her last opportunity for political strength and aid for her cause. If she is not successful, she will return home empty-handed and without direction. Time is short, and her family needs her, they both know it.

Niya does not say as much aloud, but she is as determined as Inola: if the Council will not help, then Niya believes she has no other choice but to step up. In whatever way she can. She doesn't know yet what that might look like, but she knows that it is true.

"Yes, put more emphasis on this part," Niya says, highlighting a particular section of Inola's appeal on the terminal in her room where they are working. "Focus on your sister and her autonomy. Do not give Gishkiy the power in this narrative, even if he has the power in reality. It's about the lives he is affecting, right? With his falsehoods and experimentations, he is damaging your community. The people are the heart of it."

"You are right," Inola groans. "This is a full rewrite, isn't it?"

She looks close to tears. Niya eases the terminal controls from her grasp. "Not at all, let's just—" She begins restructuring parts of the speech. Moving bits from here to there, doing some light editing, her fingers flying over the keys with precision. "There! Read through that and tell me what you think."

About two minutes pass while Inola's eyes speed over this rearranged text. When she finishes, she turns to Niya, slack-jawed, with wonder in her eyes.

"Niya Suwatt, you've done it!" she exclaims. "This is good. Strong. The Council will either help me, or they won't—but this..." Inola's eyes shine still with tears as she looks over the speech again. She lifts her hands, palms up and extended before her. "This will give me and my village our best chance. I thank you."

"You're welcome." Niya says, reaching out to squeeze Inola's fingers in hers, showing her understanding through this light touch.

Suddenly, Inola leans back, a magnificent and overpowering yawn moving her entire body from head to toes.

"Oh *ish*," she curses, "Niya, I'm so sorry—"

"No, no," Niya waves her off. "You cannot stay up any

later, and we are done anyway. Your audience before the Council of Twelve will be here before you know it. We will have you well-rested and ready to face Kaatii Patak and the others tomorrow, yeah?"

Inola nods, solemn. "Yeah."

"You will sleep here tonight."

"You are kind, but I won't impose. And besides, my clothes and things are there, so—"

"Inola, please do not insult me like this. You will sleep now, and we will eat tomorrow morning with my family. Okay?"

Inola looks down at her hands where they are resting in her lap. Dark skin and pink nails, trimmed short; some bitten down in moments of worry. "I am very thankful for your kindness, Niya."

Niya stands. "Kindness is free and freely given. Now, let's get you something comfortable for the night and settled in. Then I'll head to the—" she gestures over her shoulder towards the open living area. "Sofa," she finishes with a cheeky smile.

"Now *that* I will not stand for. You will share this bed with me, as it is yours, just as we have done before." She holds up a hand to forestall the obvious argument that Niya is already opening her mouth to make. Niya snaps her mouth shut again, grinning at how quickly they've become friends. "No arguments."

When they are both in bed, each lying on their backs, staring up at the roof overhead, Niya speaks. Her voice is soft, but she does not question whether or not Inola will be able to hear her.

"Would you like me to go with you?" she asks. "When you go before the Council."

She can hear Inola's breaths. Can hear how they ease from even and deep to shallow, rushed. Niya keeps her eyes to herself, facing the stars.

"I would," Inola replies. "I would like that very much."

They fall asleep almost simultaneously not long after their exchange, their fingers interlocked atop the blanket they share, grounded and grounding in the night.

NISHAATIKINAPA

Niya does not know where she is—not in the traditional sense of knowing, at least.

What she knows is this: she is flying again, perched between the span of Owl's wings.

What she does not know is this: when or why or to where.

She sees the cave again. Sees it in the distance. Like a wound, like a mouth. That same darkness inside it from her dream just a few nights past, when it had expelled her like a shot, when she had plunged down, down to the waters below.

When her Ability had revealed itself to her.

Niya looks into the maw of the cave from Owl's back. As powerful wings flap beneath her clenched thighs, Niya looks toward the cave with awe and wonder.

And surprise. For the previously dark opening has now filled with light.

What? Niya questions aloud.

Who? Owl replies.

That, too, Niya says, bearing down and leaning forward.

Unspoken between Owl and her rider is the decision to approach. But not just to approach: to enter.

Owl alights softly upon the ground, and Niya disembarks with similar grace. She squares her shoulders and moves into the cave. But her feet do not move. As if yutsu magnetism is floating her along, her feet skim just about the dew-drop wet grass. The sun passes overhead—it rises and sets and rises again.

Niya crosses the threshold. And the bottom of the cave opens up. She looks down and sees a sprawling, impossible bird's eye view of her home. Of Cahokia. She has only seen it from this angle in drone-captured images. But this feels different. Like the energy of the city is pulsing up, up through the sky, through the soles of Niya's feet. Through her blood. To her heart.

Her point of view shifts with astonishing abruptness, and Cahokia begins to fade away. To disappear from her sights. Her mind whirls, swirls, and Niya feels what it is to leave her home behind for the first time.

But not for the last.

Back in the cave. Back in her body.

Herself but not. Niya Suwatt but not.

Who? Owl says.

I do not know, Niya replies.

The cave plunges suddenly to a blackness so complete that Niya is sure she has gone blind. But she can still hear the rustling of Owl's feathers behind her, restless and reassuring. Can feel the ground beneath her feet, firm and real. And most importantly, can sense the ba-dum, ba-dum beating of her heart.

As suddenly as the cave has gone dark, a pinprick of light begins to glow in the back-most recesses. Could it lead to a tunnel? A branching path? Treasures, traps, treachery in the dark?

Unwavering is the light. Unwavering is Niya's step forward. And in an instant, the tiny light shatters, bursts outward in a shower of sparks, then coalesces back into a single point once more.

Niya breathes, relief flooding her lungs and her bones.

Then she freezes.

The light splits in two—violent in its abrupt change. Niya leans back then forward again. Owl's rustling feathers are silent now; silent, or else gone.

The lights disappear in a blink. Then appear again.

Eyes in a face, glowing.

The head that must be there, that must be looking right at Niya through the dark, tilts to the side. The pinpricks of light, the luminous and reflecting eyes, they look at her. Niya does not know if the look is fueled by curiosity.

Or by hunger.

She steps forward. But so does it.

She braces herself. It does too.

Then they both charge.

Niya and Inola wake with two concerted gasps.

Each of their niisis are screeching with cacophonous needs for attention.

"What in the name of the Creator—"

Niya's grouchy confusion is interrupted by Inola's gasp, followed shortly by a curse.

"Ish!"

Niya turns to see that Inola is slapping her niisi on

her wrist at the same time that she flicks a video feed up into the air, projecting its stream between them. The video is nearly as still as a picture, but Niya watches as the fluff of a punctured pillow floats through the air. The only sign of any disturbance.

"Is that your resthouse room?" Niya asks, all confusion and sleep-tinged perception.

Inola nods in answer. "Your niisi," she says, "it was lighting up, too. Best to check it. I fear that something has gone wrong."

Grabbing her device from her bedside, Niya flicks through the myriad messages that have been sent to her already this morning.

"Ish," she curses again, this time beneath her breath. Then she turns to Inola. "Something has gone wrong. And not just for you—but you may be at the heart of it, warranted or not."

She swipes the messages through the air from her display and onto Inola's. Together, they read through the duplicated messages that are scrolling across each of their screens, timestamped across the past few minutes.

[Adasi] hey, little sister. have you seen Tusika???

[Nampeyo] You have not heard from our Patak friend, have you?

[Adasi] Tusika is missing, did she tell you what's up? is this just her being dramatic, or is it something more serious?

[Nampeyo] There are already talks that the Council may get involved.

[Adasi] there's word that the out-of-towner might have something to do with it. i'm trying to find out more now.

[Nampeyo] Steer clear of the Council Building. There are rumblings of Suyata being called up.

[Adasi] this isn't right, cuz. Something feels off. i'm getting 'Peyo and heading your way.

[Nampeyo] Turn your location off. Have her do the same.

[Nampeyo] NOW.

The girls do not hesitate, each jumping into their ni-isi settings to turn off any and all functions that utilize or otherwise show their location.

As soon as the task of masking their whereabouts is complete, they turn to look at one another.

"Do you think—"

"I really must—"

They both stop, and nervous laughter bubbles up and out of Niya's chest. Inola gives a short bark of laughter herself before clapping her hand over her mouth.

"What has happened?" Inola asks in a whisper, the words partially muffled by her fingers.

Niya shakes her head even as she tries to answer the question. "I do not know. It sounds like Tusika is..." She trails off, squeezing her eyes shut. What has happened to her friend? With the way they last left things, Niya feels horrible. A tense, squeezing sensation in her gut. She feels the phantom press of Tusika's lips to her own, and tears spring unbidden to her eyes. "She's missing, or she's run off, or—" she flicks hopelessly through her messages, daring even one of them to make sense. But it all feels senseless. "Whatever has happened, my friends seem to think you're considered a suspect."

Inola's eyes narrow as she confusedly shakes her head, then they widen to saucers. In a moment, she pulls back up the video stream that Niya had seen before.

"My room," Inola says by way of explanation. "I have a simple security system set up, in case of—" she gestures generically at the picture, as if to say, *exactly for this reason*. "Look—whoever broke into my room, they were looking for something."

"Or someone."

Inola's jaw clenches. "Or someone, yes. My pillow is ripped, my blanket is gone..." Her eyes squint and she pinches in on the feed closer. "Ish, they even took—"

Her voice breaks, and she looks away. Niya holds the other girl's wrist steady, her fingers meant to be comforting while allowing her to get a better look.

She had only spent one night in the room. But she remembers with clarity the small painted images of Inola's family that had been on the bedside table.

They are nowhere in sight.

Inola is not looking in Niya's direction. Instead, her chin is tucked low to her chest, and her eyes are watery with unshed tears as she looks at the surveillance feed to her room.

Niya returns to her side. Looks at the feed. Takes in the careless, cruel way that Inola's things have been thrown about, destroyed, stolen. Inola swipes her forefinger along the bottom of the window, and the feed rewinds.

They're in and out faster than Niya had imagined possible: the Suyata, with their faces covered and their intentions bared. Three of them total—one bald, one with long, braided hair, and another with a distinct mohawk. In and back out again, all in the time that it had taken Inola's alarm to sound and wake them both.

"Suyata would only be sent by the Council." Inola exhales on a shuddering breath, her shoulders quivering. "I guess this is their way of telling me that my appearance before them is canceled."

Niya makes a decision at once and with her whole heart.

"I'm getting you back to your family," she says, squaring up her shoulders to the taller woman. "You will get safely out of the city, and we will help your sister escape the cult's clutches."

She nods her head, as if this gesture is also the signing of a contract. Definitive. Binding.

"But why would they take my things—?"

A series of three knocks sounds at the door. Both girls fall deathly silent and still.

"Niya?" a voice calls quietly.

"My niisi!" Niya yelps, hopping up and moving quickly to the door.

When she flings it open, it is not simply one of her niisis, but both of them.

Her mana's mana holds out a vacuum-sealed bag full of dried goods and cured meats, sectioned off into meal-size portions.

"For the road," she says with an earnest expression, though an encouraging smile is spread across her lips. Her expression shifts, her eyebrows drawing downward, turning as serious as Niya has ever seen her. "The Patak clan, with Kaatii at their helm—they are more powerful than you know."

"Niisi, what do you—?"

Coming quickly down the hallway on light feet, Ahyoka interrupts her daughter. She gently but purposefully moves between the two elders, putting one hand on Niya's shoulder. Her other hand holds Inola's, steadying and sure.

"Powerful allies make powerful enemies all too easily. We will do what we can here, but you must stay safe. Get this girl back to her village. The both of you must stay safe until we know more of what is going on."

"Mana, you think Kaatii—"

With a shake of her head, Ahyoka cuts Niya off. "Guessing is good for no one, my love. I've known Kaatii Patak since the day you were born, but I can't pretend that I truly know her heart. Your noosoo, he and I will see what we can find out, muster support in whatever comes next. We can get by without having Kaatii Patak as a friend, but to have her as an enemy... the relationship between our family and the Pataks isn't necessary, but it exists—and we have to step lightly."

"I understand, mana."

"I wish one of us could go with you to make sure you both get home safely," Ahyoka turns to Inola. "But whatever it is that has been stirred up will need to be dealt with here."

"Ahh, and before you go—"

Her noosoo's mana reaches to the side of the doorway, grabbing something before moving it into Niya's line of sight.

"Niisi," Niya covers her mouth with the back of her hand. "Is that daadoo's chunkey spear?"

"Your daadoo says," her niisi starts before leaning forward, one hand conspiratorially gesturing for Niya to move closer. "That this *stick* will serve you well. Now—" both of her niisis move to walk down the hall, and her paternal niisi finishes by saying, "We'll hold off Kaatii Patak and her goons—you just focus on doing what is right."

Her maternal niisi hisses back over her shoulder as they both turn the corner into the living space, "The back way is clear, my girl. Be good, but not overly so!"

This last comment causes her paternal niisi to chortle, slapping her hand on her thigh.

Then the two elders of her family are gone, and Niya is left with an ample collection of rations in one hand and the hickory spear, worn smooth from use and time, in her other.

"Yes, my girls—be safe. And I know it will be hard, but do not message any details of your journey to me and your noosoo. I hate it, but the less we know—"

"The better," Niya says, nodding and reaching out to squeeze her mana into a mighty hug.

Their embrace ends as quickly as it has started, and

Ahyoka hurries off into another room, not looking back. Niya turns to Inola, her face wrought with both shock and understanding.

"I think we better get going, yeah?"

"But what of your friend?" Inola asks, her voice thick with emotion. "Where has Tusika gone?"

Niya does not answer aloud. But her eyes say everything and more: *I do not know.*

That holy and precious underlying thread, that beating heart of existence, that runs through all things living—it chooses this moment to thrum, reverberating with a sort of shared consciousness.

Niya's niisi pings.

It is a message. From Tusika.

[Tusika] You were right, but you were also wrong. I can be the leader Cahokia needs. Give me time—not much of it, but enough. I will not let you down. I will become more than I am. Somehow, someway—I will be whole.

"Niya?" Inola places a gentle hand on her shoulder. She tilts her head to read the message that Niya does not bother hiding. "She left on her own...nothing ill has befallen her? This is good news! We can show this message to the Suyata, to her mana—"

Even as Inola's hope rises, Niya is already shaking her head.

Like coarse sand on the river's edge gliding through spread fingers, the words begin to fade away.

"What...wait!" Inola grasps Niya's wrist, swipes at the fading message with a frantic gesture. "Where is it going? What happened?"

The words now gone entirely, Niya drops her arms to her side. Her head hangs low.

But only for a moment. Then she snaps her head up, looking Inola directly in the eyes.

"She does this," Niya says, voice strained with frustration and sadness. "And she knows exactly what will happen to the people she leaves behind. Stringing me along because she knows precisely how much she means to me, disappearing on the day you are set to appear before the Council...ugh!"

Inola reaches out, her touch tentative. She grasps Niya's fingers and connects their sights. "What do you think she meant—about becoming 'whole'?"

Niya inhales sharply, her breath catching painfully in her chest. She thinks of Gishkiy and his wild but oddly plausible tale about the Pataks stealing his Adanadi potential for their eldest daughter, Kaatii. And she thinks about seven generations of Pataks, all with Ability-blessed first-born children—and then Kaatii's own daughter, Ability-less, all while her best, closest friend receives an Ability after seven generations without.

Gishkiy, fueled by potential he believes was stolen from him; Tusika, fueled, perhaps, by a lust for a potential that she had believed was promised to her...thwarted, somehow. Lost.

"No," she whispers. "She couldn't think..."

Inola shakes her head, the movements short, sharp. "I didn't think my sister would do something so foolish. I thought Kas would know better, would know that it is perfectly okay to not have an Ability! But...it's hard to understand. You and I, we never will—we have Abilities. We can't know what it feels like to not have one."

Niya presses her eyes closed, leaving them shut for several long seconds. "And for someone like Tusika, with what she sees as the world on her shoulders, a destiny so rich and important..." She is fiery when her eyes snap open, and she says, "I *will* find her. And Kas, too! I will not be beholden to her actions. And I won't let you be, either. Come—let's go."

For a moment, Niya pauses, thinking of her dream. Those eyes in the dark—was Owl showing Niya her next course? Did the eyes belong to Suyata, a Haudenosaunee Mohawk, chasing them through the night? Or did they belong to Gishkiy, the man trying to convince people of the importance of Abilities—of the need to unlock them, however they can, whatever the price?

There will be time for musings and contemplations later.

"A few things..." Niya mumbles to herself, quickly bouncing about the small space of her room. "Load this up, will you?" she asks, handing Inola a leather satchel.

Inola nods, her jaw set. Niya tosses numerous things towards the other woman in rapid succession—Inola catches them all, creating a neat little pile that she then places into the bag.

"Vacuum compartments?" Inola asks with an arched eyebrow and an impressed look.

"Yep! And it unfolds into an all-weather sleeping kit," Niya confirms, her voice muffled, bent over and half submerged in a mess of clothes and other odds and ends in her closet. She pops up triumphantly, wielding a pair of reinforced moccasins, perfect for navigating all sorts of terrain.

"Very wankata," Inola says, flipping a switch on one of the satchel's inner pockets. "Haven't seen anything like this in my village yet."

The switch triggers a vacuum seal that compresses and protects everything in the relevant compartment—from the spare clothes Niya had lobbed over to the custom gat materials she'd placed in the pile. They could sort out some method of organization later. Right now, the most important thing was getting out of Cahokia—and fast.

"Anything else that you need, Inola?" Niya asks. They're both dressed and ready to head out. Niya shoulders her satchel, which has all of her things plus the rations her niisis had provided. In her left hand, she lifts her daadoo's spear.

Inola straps her own bag onto her back, shaking her head sadly. "Anything that I left in my room was..." She sighs, sniffs hard before continuing, "Replaceable. Right now all I need is to get out of this city. To get home."

Niya nods, reaching out to squeeze Inola's hand. "We're off, then."

They do not get farther than the back door, which her niisis had informed her was clear. Apparently it had been—until it wasn't.

"Whoa, cuz!"

As soon as Niya goes to push open the door, Adasi and Nampeyo are there, pushing her right back inside.

"If you go out the front," Nampeyo says, in that matter-of-fact way of theirs, "you will very quickly be caught."

"And if you go out this way," Adasi adds, thumbing over his shoulder at the door they'd just burst through, "you'll also be caught, though it might take a tiny bit longer."

Niya's friends keep the girls from crossing the threshold of the Suwatt home, and therefore keep them out of the hands of whatever guards or Suyata might be in the area.

"We've got it on good authority that a warrant is going out on the daso today."

"Ish," Niya curses under her breath. "How much time do we have?"

As if in answer to her question, the niisis of the four young friends ping with a general city-wide proximity alert simultaneously.

They each rotate their wrists, a collective sense of dread falling over the group.

Some words from within the bulletin pop out, bold and important. And all of it, a running marquee, plastered across a high-definition picture of Inola Cato.

WANTED

CAPTURE

And then a photo of Tusika.

MISSING

"Well." Nampeyo's mouth snaps shut with an almost comical pop. "However much time you had before, I'd say you have less now."

"At least they didn't put a reward on you, friend-o!" Adasi says to Inola, a grin on his face that doesn't fit the situation but certainly fits Adasi.

But his statement seems to have done precisely the sort of trick that they really did not need: their niisis ping again, and Inola's WANTED posting is updated with a juicy notice circulating around the bottom of the frame.

REWARD: 10,000 NIZI

"Ahh yo..." Inola says, her shoulders sagging.

Adasi throws his hands up. "I didn't do that, I swear!"

As if things couldn't get any worse, Nampeyo swipes through an incoming message. "A band of Suyata have been assigned the mission of tracking you down. Their missive is directly from the Council of Twelve."

If there had been any hope whatsoever of leveraging their honest truth with the Council, it was done with now.

"They won't hear reason," Inola says, her despair rightfully tainted by her past experiences with ineffectual leadership. "They won't believe that I have nothing to do with this."

Niya's stomach sinks. "We can only handle one thing at a time," she says. Pressing the heels of her hands against her eyes, she groans in frustration. "Think, think, think..."

"We could stir up a wuyi," Nampeyo says. "Print a

tracker, synthesize materials..."

Nampeyo is staring at Adasi, and both of them seem to have similar cogs working away in their brains. "Write a program to link them. We could maybe figure out—"

"—which direction Tusika left the city," Nampeyo finishes with a snap.

Adasi claps his hands together in turn. "Or if she left the city at all!"

"You are my heroes," Niya says, her voice nearly breaking. "How long do you think that would take you?"

"Half a day," Adasi offers.

"Less," Nampeyo corrects.

"Okay, okay. Wonderful, amazing." With less time now than ever before, Niya grasps for direction. "With you two on that, we can focus on getting to Inola's home in the Keetoowagi Federation. But first, we have to get out of the city," she says, turning now towards Inola, "and we have to do it without being seen."

Inola bites her lip, a sudden bout of hesitation crossing her features. "What if, instead, I go alone? You do not need to become any more wrapped up in this trouble I have wrought with my careless intrusions."

Niya's voice turns serious, stern. "Inola, your words that night to Kaatii in her home were not careless, they were impassioned. And they have now been purposefully misconstrued by a worried mana concerned for her daughter's whereabouts. I am coming with you, and perhaps I can even vouch for you if we find ourselves cornered."

Inola's eyes swim with tears, brightening. She opens her mouth—whether to dissent once more or to fully give in, Niya is not certain. For the smooth grinding of the locking mechanism of the front door distracts them all.

Before any of them can so much as move to pretend to try and hide Inola, in comes...

Niya's noosoo, Yona.

He lets silence fall over the group as he steps into the now crowded entryway. He appears to swallow a laugh at the mix of shocked and concerned faces gaping back at him.

"Did your mana tell me right?" Yona asks. "You four were looking for something to do this morning, just sitting about twiddling your thumbs, and you jumped at the chance to help with our harvester bots, eh?"

"Harvester bots..." Adasi drawls.

Niya's eyes go wide. "Harvester bots!" she says in an excited but hushed whisper. "Noosoo—I am a lucky daughter."

Yona smiles lovingly at his daughter, no other explanation forthcoming for the three bystanders.

Inola steps forward hesitantly. "Umm," she starts, "I truly am sorry to interrupt, but—"

"Our harvester bots, young one. They are out back. Just finished up some maintenance, and Niya's niisis are out there right now putting on some final touches. Ahyoka is off to run the market stall for the day. So these two—" Yona gestures towards Adasi and Nampeyo with his lips, "—can help me maneuver 'em down to the east fields, eh?"

Niya laughs through her happy tears, relieved that her parents are helping in this way. Ahyoka maintaining an alibi and deniability towards what they're getting up to, and Yona helping without saying it as such.

Nampeyo, who caught onto the scheme fairly quickly, is already to the back door, making sure the coast is clear to get the girls from the back door and to the location where the bots are sitting, both of Niya's niisis making a show of banging on hatches and tightening bolts.

When they all reach the alcove just before the back exit, Niya presses into that barrel chest of her noosoo's, and they hug one another fiercely. "Wado," she whispers. And her noosoo doesn't say much of anything else back, simply hugs her for a long moment before letting her go.

Adasi and Nampeyo have their heads tucked low towards one another, conversing in hushed tones about the engineering project they're already working on in their minds. But Inola is standing still, jaw a bit slack with brow drawn down in confusion.

The familial trio turns to her.

"Are you all suggesting what I think you're suggesting?"

Niya steps forward, a delighted, devious glint in her eyes. In answer, she nods.

Inola's face lights up. "Wow. I am very lucky to have met you all. Let's do this!"

HISITIKINAPA

With Adasi and Nampeyo acting as lookouts, Niya and Inola are carefully secreted out the back of the Suwatt household. Yona helps the girls climb into the empty bellies of the bots where grains and other produce would ordinarily go. Once they are each secure, the boys go back inside, with the plan to wait for them to exit through the front at approximately the same time Yona makes his way out from the back, heading in opposite directions.

"See you soon, cuz," Adasi whispers through the hard hull of the harvester to Niya.

"Be safe out there, little sister," Nampeyo says.

Niya raps her knuckles thrice against the insides of the harvester, her throat feeling too thick to entrust with inadequate words.

Then they are gone, and moments later, the mechanical movements of the harvesters begin to carry them away.

Niya's heart beats firmly in her chest the entire time she is enclosed in darkness. She feels oddly floaty, as if on the edge of an immense and unknowable future.

She has left Cahokia before, but journeys beyond the city's borders are infrequent for her, often tied only to festivals and ceremonies. It had been several years now since her family had traveled to their ancestral homelands for the Green Corn Ceremony or even for the Great New Moon Festival. Instead, the Suwatt family performed their own, smaller versions of the ceremonies at home—celebrating the new growth of corn in the early summer and then the new year after harvest was complete.

This journey, however, feels unknowable to Niya. They have a destination, of course—Inola's village. And a purpose, two-fold—bring Inola's sister home while freeing the village from the cultist's grip. Perhaps even prove Inola's innocence along the way, and with the help of Adasi and Nampeyo, bring Tusika home, too.

And beneath that, the strange promise that Niya's dreams seem to hold.

The rest will follow, because it must.

In all too short a time, the harvester bots are settling on the ground as their yutsu tech is powered down. Yona opens up one bot and then the other. He helps Niya and Inola down, ushering them to stay low to the ground.

Voices hushed, they say their *see you laters*. Yona gives them advice both practical and centered on the stomach.

"The warrant will put you both at risk, so stay close to one another and off the main roads—at least until you get further into Keetoowagi lands."

"We will, noosoo—"

"—And be sure to tell Dastinicho that Yona sent you if you find yourselves at the Sleeping Bear Inn. I am certain that he will send you away with some good food—not just for you two but for Inola's family as well!"

Inola, with a hand pressed to her breast, gratefully bows her head. "Thank you," she says, then turns a quick glance to Niya at her side as well. "For everything."

Including allowing your daughter to come with me, are the words that go unspoken.

"Off with you both," Yona says, and Niya sees pride and fear alike in her noosoo's eyes. "Stay low until you reach the small lake. From there, you will find different waterways to follow east. And Niya...remember the things your mana and I have always taught you. Stay safe, keep moving, and for the love of the Creator, don't do anything stupid."

Niya and Inola wave their farewells and head off down the thick rows of the Suwatt family crops.

"How far until we're off the Cahokian daso network?" Inola asks.

They have not been traveling long, but their pace is quick.

Niya stops momentarily, turning to look back behind them to the west.

"I'd say a while yet. Maybe even a half a day. We're sloping down away from the city, and the rise of the horizon behind us is our friend."

At this, she gestures behind them, pointing out some of Cahokia's tallest structures, including at least three that Tusika's noosoo is responsible for designing. The daso networks reach as far as the horizon but no further. Niya glances down at her niisi, anxious for any updates from Adasi and Nampeyo about Tusika's whereabouts. But their messages so far have been vague, only hinting at their progress without implying too much about their true mission, in case anyone is intercepting their communications. Niya vows not to check again until they are near to the horizon or even beyond it—she can always climb one of the tall pines in the area if she needs to reach the signal again.

It is as Niya looks back up from her niisi, as she is turning back to their eastward trajectory, that she catches sight of something that causes her throat to clench and her stomach to drop.

Suyata, spread out in a three-pronged formation and approaching all too quickly through the field of young wheat they'd just traipsed carefully through themselves.

The time for careful steps is gone. Niya throws up a prayer of apology to the Creator, hoping for quick regrowth in their inevitable wake.

"Inola," Niya says, turning and grabbing the other woman's wrist between her fingers in one quick motion, "Run!"

Without hesitation, they both take off running. Their packs bouncing against their backs give an odd, uncoordinated feel to their escape, but they hightail it towards a thick line of trees in the distance regardless.

Inola, slightly faster, ducks through the low brush just ahead of Niya.

"Right!" she hisses, and Niya takes a sharp right as she enters the thick of it after her.

They proceed this way for a harried couple of minutes. Their feet press as quickly and quietly as they can into the forest floor. Breathing as evenly as possible to keep from wheezing their way into their pursuers' arms.

Every few seconds, Inola throws a signed direction over her shoulder before taking it herself. Niya follows. And behind them, the sounds of tracking follow: sharp whistles and the sounds of animals too precise to be anything but imitations, mimics. The yip of a coyote. The trill of a robin. The yowl of a mountain lion. Ever closer, and closer.

Then, just as Niya is beginning to fear that their escape is about to be cut woefully short, she hears it: the hoot of an owl.

As if guided by an instinct beyond herself, Niya surges forward. She grips Inola by the strap of her pack, pulling her to a stop.

And not a moment too soon.

"*Whoa*," Niya gasps.

In front of them and barely two steps on the other side of some thick foliage, they come face to face with a cliff's edge.

"You saved my ass," Inola huffs, her voice low. "But now what?"

Thinking fast, Niya steps right up to the edge. She leans out, listening closely. Her eyes sweep as far around the cliff as she can see.

"Running water..." she says, more to herself than anything else. Her eyes flash up to Inola's. "Follow me!"

She begins running in a low crouch to the north, keeping the lip of the cliff on her right-hand side. Before long, she sees it: a waterfall, splashing down into a growing waterway beneath.

"It's no Mizizibi," Niya says, turning wide eyes on Inola, "but it may give us the cover we need to escape."

In a rush, Inola grabs Niya's hand and pulls her along, dragging them both around the last bend and toward the waterfall's edge. "It's absolutely crazy, that's for sure. But I'm with you."

They reach the waterfall, take sure-footed steps out onto the first few slick stones. The water is gentler at the edge. Strongest in the middle. Absolutely roaring as it rushes over, over, and down—*so* far down. Any sounds of pursuit are being drowned out by the water's violence. If they want to have any hope of evading the Suyata, they must go—and quickly.

"Together?" Niya says.

"Oh yeah," Inola replies.

They squeeze one another's hands tightly, desperately—bravely.

And then they jump.

Niya can tell almost instantly that something has gone wrong.

She breaks the surface, spluttering for air. Little can be heard over the roar of the waterfall as it crashes around her. Treading water, Niya turns back and forth, calling Inola's name. Within seconds, it becomes clear that, while Niya herself surfaced, the other woman did not.

Cursing beneath her breath, Niya inhales deeply, then dives back below the water.

Visibility is good, and Niya spots Inola right away. And the sight causes her stomach to lurch.

Inola's limbs are splayed, the woman clearly unconscious, and she is sinking fast.

Right into a hole in the earth that seems to be swallowing water, light, and everything else.

Niya does not hesitate before kicking hard, surging forward to reach her friend's unconscious arms. She tugs with all her might, looping her arms beneath Inola's armpits. Her legs propel them both to the surface.

Once they hit the air, Niya fills her lungs, deep pulls of breath delivering delicious and much needed oxygen.

"Inola!" Niya manages to keep both of their heads above water, and she begins shaking the other woman. Cursing under her breath, Niya delivers a series of quick, sharp slaps to Inola's face. "Come on," she growls. The weight of the water's pull is intense, and Niya can feel her grip weakening.

As she begins to lean back and propel them out from under the waterfall's sheet of pounding water, Inola bursts into a round of fantastic coughing.

"Oh, wado Creator," Niya huffs, still holding Inola semi-upright, her pack pressing into Niya's front. "Deep breaths," she says, "get it all out."

Inola, now hacking and coughing, lurches forward. She gives an odd belch, and Niya watches with no small amount of mixed discomfort and relief as the woman seems to expel at once much of the water she had swallowed. Her lungs are still recovering, but Niya's chest loosens with the knowledge that Inola is breathing at all.

"Let's get you to land," Niya grunts.

But as they are finally reaching the shallows of the creek's edge, Inola begins hitting at Niya's arms and pointing upward.

"Niya," she croaks, "look!"

Niya looks upward immediately, and her eyes hone in on what Inola has already seen: at least two of the Suyata are peering down over the edge of the cliff from near the waterfall—which means they know exactly where the women are. And there is a third Suyata, unaccounted for.

Niya curses under her breath. Her brain spins—what could they possibly do now?

"The shortest escape attempt ever, huh?" Inola manages to say. Her breathing finally evens out. Niya's arms are still clasped around her.

Shaking her head, Niya disagrees. "No. We've come too far, and we have a lot more to do."

"It's only a matter of time before one of them jumps," Inola says, her voice tilting downward into a despondency that Niya refuses to entertain.

"Think, think..." Niya mutters to herself.

Her mind skips back to home. Back to a basin full of water in her family's kitchen. Activating her Ability, feeling so weary she could collapse.

She remembers wondering what it would feel like, to dive to and fro, beneath and above and between the ancient and deep waters of the Mizizibi in its strongest currents.

Well, this isn't the Mizizibi. And she is uncertain as to the limits of her stamina. But she also knows that this is about promises made and kept, and that she will not let Inola be taken by the Suyata. Not today, not before they have a chance to save her sister.

"I know we haven't known each other long," Niya starts in, "and I know that you only just regained consciousness not even, what, two minutes ago? And I can't believe I'm even thinking of proposing what I'm about to propose—"

"Niya," Inola cuts in, gesturing to the cliff's edge. There is only one visible Suyata now, tracking their progress and keeping tabs, in case they were to make a run for it while their comrades take the long way down. "The point, and quick?"

"Do you trust me?"

Niya blurts out the words, and Inola pushes out of her arms, spinning to face her in the silty shallows.

"I do. What's the plan?"

"There's a hole down there," Niya makes a gesture that would be almost comedic in any other situation, a downward pointing of her fingers, indicating some vague area beneath the water. "A really big one. My guess is that it's a tunnel beneath the land, a series of flooded caves, maybe—I've heard tales of such things before."

"I'm following," Inola says, "but how does that help us?"

Niya's eyes widen in emphasis. "Inola—my Ability."

Inola's eyes mimic hers. "River's Flow!" she shouts,

clapping a hand to her forehead.

"Exactly."

"How long can you make it last?"

"Honestly?" Niya asks, and Inola nods her head vigorously. "I have no idea."

Inola's eyes go dark, and she bows her head. "We're foolish," she says, "your Ability doesn't even account for my own lung capacity."

"That's just it, Inola—" Niya interrupts. "I'm going to breathe for the both of us."

PINATIKINAPA

The smudging motions that have been rote for Niya since childhood take on new and profound meaning as she uses them to activate her Ability—just the way her dream had taught her was possible.

Heart, lungs, mind, body.

As soon as she completes the motions, she can feel the change: her eyesight is almost murky above water but sharp and clear below; her body feels both hers and not, as if it has itself become part of the water; and she can breathe, *breathe,* beneath the surface, mining the river's oxygen and other gasses for her own lungs, and for Inola's.

"Ready?" Inola asks.

"If you are," Niya says with a nod—and her voice sounds odd, almost like it is already underwater. "You know how to equalize your ears?"

Inola nods, showing that she does, then takes a series of slow, deep breaths, beginning to expand her lungs. Then one final breath, deeper than she has perhaps ever inhaled, and she throws her body forward in a dive, aiming for the gaping hole that Niya had indicated.

Just as Niya is about to follow her, there is a magnificent *splash* in the water nearby.

Niya does not take any extra time to assess the Suyata who has just jumped into the water after them, merely sees a mohawk head and a dangerous flash of a magsling about her waist. That's all it takes to spur her after Inola.

Being beneath the water with her Ability activated feels oddly familiar to Niya. Then she places it—it's like flying in her dreams, through the night sky with Owl. In the murky water, the Adanadi mark on Niya's forearm nearly glows.

It's like that, but it's also totally different. And despite the seriousness of the situation, Niya feels *amazing* as she dives after Inola's powerful form. Alongside the wonder and amazement is a very real sense of fear. Niya harnesses it as best she can, swimming full-throttle downward and quickly passing Inola.

Recognizing the strength of her body in this form beneath the water, Niya twists to look back at Inola, grabs her attention, and gestures to her own ankles.

"Grab on!" she shouts. Whatever has changed with her vocal cords causes her words to transfer effortlessly through the water. Inola immediately hears and understands, reaching forward and grasping an ankle with each of her hands. "Hold tight!"

As she pulls them further and further from the Suyata, she hopes that their pursuer does not have a breathing apparatus or, perhaps worse yet, River's Flow or something like it.

The breathing device, which helps prolong a person's ability to stay underwater without surfacing, is handy for exactly a situation like the one the young women on the run have found themselves in. But Niya's plan, concocted of equal parts foolhardiness and brilliance, might meet a speedy end if she does not get moving—and fast. Luckily, Niya learned just enough about using breathing apparatuses at university, back when she thought she might go into hydrology rather than horticulture. She would be shocked if any of the Suyata had compressed air, light as their traveling garb appeared to be, or the more advanced, deep-diving equipment that allowed for long excursions and negation of any nitrogen narcosis that might occur.

This reminds Niya that, when she first breathes for Inola, she must make every effort to harness River's Flow to her intentions—to mine the river not only for oxygen but for the proper balance of nitrogen and overall gaseous exchange to allow Niya and Inola both to breathe while underwater, to keep their lungs from collapsing, and to generally not poison themselves with their own physiological processes.

Maybe River's Flow already knows all this, Niya thinks. *It will protect us both.*

She hopes with all her might that this is true.

Turning away from the sight of the Suyata, twisting about in the water to orient them both, Niya begins to swim now in earnest.

She moves her body in an undulating fashion, almost like the seals of the northern coastal regions, and her speed surprises Niya herself. And it isn't only her own River's Flow-induced underwater efficiency, but the hole beneath them—it acts almost like a siphon. Niya can feel it pulling them along.

A glance over her shoulder quickly shows Niya that the Suyata in immediate pursuit has given up. She is floating, stationary, staring at the pair of them not with anger but with curiosity. Finally, she turns, swimming back to the surface.

Her energy is buoyed by this, and she swims onward.

Before she dips below the edge of the cave-like opening, she grips a rocky ledge and swings herself about to come face-to-face with Inola. The other woman moves her hand through the water, tapping her chest twice and then her mouth. Her cheeks are puffed outward in the effort of holding her breath.

"We'll go under," Niya speaks, that odd, wavering sound piercing through the water easily. "You need breath."

Inola nods.

Niya gulps, but does not hesitate.

Do you trust me? she had asked of the other woman, before partaking of this crazy feat.

Inola had agreed, and their predicament's lack of respect for time meant that they had not had a chance to discuss how exactly this exchange of oxygen was going to happen between the two of them.

But this is it—their last and best chance to test Niya's theory, before they pass the point of no return. And since "no return" in this case will likely spell death for one or both of them, Niya will not proceed before attempting this.

Before attempting to breathe for Inola.

She surges forward, stilling just before her mouth reaches Inola's. She grasps the sides of the woman's face in hands that are gentle but firm. Inola's eyes are wide in what is probably no small amount of justified anxiety.

Then Niya breathes in deeply, filtering the water

and converting it into usable oxygen. She presses her mouth to Inola's, her lips covering her friend's. She breathes out in a slow, deep fashion. And she can feel Inola inhale at the same time.

Niya feels one of Inola's hands come up, and it pinches her nose shut to make breathing only through her mouth easier. Niya can feel her skin prickle as they continue the process for at least a minute or so—exchanging breaths, refilling Inola's lungs, converting her expelled breath back to usable air and vice versa. There is a tension between them, an understanding that one misstep could cause Inola's lungs to fill with water, could cause her to start choking, spluttering.

They have to learn now, quickly and immediately, or else this absurd escape attempt will have all been for naught.

Before Niya pulls away, she gives three taps of her hand against Inola's neck. Inola wraps her free hand around Niya's and squeezes thrice to indicate her understanding.

One more breath, and Inola must make it a deep one.

Niya inhales deeply, then exhales air back into Inola's lungs. It works without a hitch. They separate. Inola gives a nod and a PSL sign of all being well. Niya turns around, Inola grips her ankles, and they descend together into darkness, Inola trailing bubbles behind them both.

— . . . —

Niya can see fairly well through the murky gloom as the light fades. Far better, she suspects, than Inola behind her. The current is swift, pulling them along with a force that Niya exerts her own strength and will along with—the faster they get through this tunnel, this hole, this great, unknowable path, the better off they will be.

As Inola's breath lessens in her chest, she squeezes Niya's ankles. Niya ducks into a slight recess, sheltering from the rushing onslaught of the water.

The lack of stillness here makes the transfer of air even harder than the first time. But they complete it and carry on.

The water takes on an almost pitch-black hue. It is so dark that when they breathe into and out of one another's lungs, they do it almost entirely by feel alone. By feel and trust, and the unspoken promise to get through this madness together.

Niya can feel her pulse racing, has been hyper-aware of it the entire time—from adrenaline, from exertion, perhaps a little bit from terror. But she nearly asphyxiates when she realizes that her breaths aren't coming as easily to her as they had been before. That several blinks aren't causing the gloom to loosen and break into seeable, knowable objects in front of her.

But she does think—or hope—that the darkness is fading a bit. She tells herself that if this water is rushing so fast and so certainly, then it is rushing *somewhere*.

She turns and pulls Inola up against her, throwing caution to the wind, not wasting even a moment more.

Niya presses her lips to Inola's, she allows Inola to exhale the poison air remaining in her lungs, and then she gives the other woman one monumental breath of fresh air. Squeezes her grip tightly against Inola's upper arms, as if to say, *This is it. This is it.*

And if it isn't, then it's been so nice knowing you.

They kick away from the wall together, barreling side by side towards whatever awaits them ahead in the dark.

Within seconds, the rush of water carrying them begins to bubble up, up—and though it is still dark, they break the surface within seconds of one another.

"Ahh!" Inola gasps, gulping great, heaving lungfuls of precious air.

"Ugh," Niya manages to groan. Though less oxygen-deprived, she is weary beyond belief.

"Niya, I cannot believe it! You did it, you really did it! And your aura in the water, it was glowing so fantastically—"

"Inola—"

"The orange and silver of your aura blended with a new shock of blue, and it was so bright I could see everything around us in the otherwise dark. By the Creator, I cannot imagine that anyone will believe us—"

"—Inola, I—"

"I was terrified, I'm not ashamed to tell you that. But you were pulling us so quickly, and I—"

"Inola, please," Niya gasps.

Inola snaps to in the murky dark, grasps ahold of Niya in the warm water. Cool air against their skin causes goose flesh to rise. "Niya?" Sudden worry follows the awareness. "What—?"

"So sorry," Niya says, her voice fading fast, "but I am absolutely going to faint now."

River's Flow having expended Niya's energy reserves to an almost absolute, painful nothing, she does, in fact, faint—right into Inola's waiting arms.

KAWATIKINAPA

When Niya wakes, she has no earthly clue as to where she is, what time or day it might be, or how long she has been out. Even simple facts like her own name come to her as if carried on fog, buoyed by fuzzy lines and irregular shapes. Dysfunctional thoughts leave her blinking long and slow, as if to prolong the time between this and wakefulness would make the world clearer and more even, on the other side of things.

It turns out that Niya is simply very, very dry—from her lips and mouth to her eyes, she feels parched like a desert with tongue rough as sand.

She manages to sit up, and her oasis materializes before her: Inola, walking on steady feet towards Niya's place of rest as if descended herself from the heavens.

"Hello, Niya," she says, and Niya can feel the smile in her words even more than she can see it, eyes still blurry with sleep and dryness. "Tell me how you feel."

When she opens her mouth, nothing comes out but a croak. Inola stifles a chuckle before reaching for one of their waterskins. She helps Niya drink from it. With her throat now at least temporarily soothed, Niya swallows thickly and speaks.

"Like ish," she says. And they both smile at one another. "How long has it been since—"

"Two nights," Inola interjects, saving Niya the energy it would take to get the expected question out. "Nearly three whole days now." She turns on her toes, crouched as she is, gesturing off into the near-distance. "The mouth of this tunnel isn't far from here. You can see we even get some natural light, so we're close to the surface. It's almost like a long, low cavern, leading up from the water's edge where we—well, you know." A smile softly turns the woman's lips.

Niya pulls herself fully into a cross-legged sitting position. Her eyes adjust to the dim light slowly until, it seems, she can see all at once. Inola is still crouched before her, intently watching. Niya scans the area—hears the shushing rush of water lapping up against the edge of the underground shore, sees pockmarks of light above them, feels the faint stirrings of a lost wind tickling its way down from aboveground to where they are sitting.

Inola has set up a camp of sorts, and Niya takes that in, too. It's apparent that she hadn't known when Niya would wake up, because the camp looks well-lived in. Inola must have discovered the intricacies of Niya's pack for herself—how it can elaborately unfold into a sleeping kit, lined with otter fur. Water-repellant, warm. The contents of both of their packs lined up not far away, thoroughly dried out now. Even her daadoo's chunkey spear, which had been lashed to the outside of her bag, made it through the madness of their underwater journey.

"Three days," Niya rasps out, reaching for the gat-printed, foldable cup. Inola places it carefully into one of Niya's hands with both of her own, and Niya thanks her. "Wado, wado...three nights, too. That would be best, don't you think?"

Inola puts both of her hands up, then stands, moving a short ways away to what Niya can see is a fire pit. "Whatever you need, Niya. Honestly—the energy you expended... I cannot even imagine what your body has gone through. Take your time."

Niya nods. "I understand what you're saying, but I know that we need to get to your village. My recovery has already taken us long enough that the Suyata may already have beaten us there!"

"But we are *free*," Inola emphasizes, "and now we have the element of surprise on our side. They can't possibly believe we'll have survived that!"

"Mmm..." Niya hums quietly, sipping water more greedily now that her throat and stomach seem able to take it. "There was one Suyata who tried to follow us. They did not get far. Perhaps you are right—they saw that great, gaping abyss we descended into and wrote us off as dead."

"That would be luck on our side, wouldn't it?"

"Perhaps too much to hope for... but we will hope, yes? Hope and rest, but for only one night more. I won't be the reason you spend any more time away from your home."

Niya finishes, her words going quiet and her body falling still. She settles against the warm otter skins beneath her, pulling the edges up to cover her shoulders. Inola begins to build a fire.

Watching the other woman's movements brings a sort of peace to Niya. It's the ceremony of the thing—of bringing the fire to life. She keeps her eyes open long enough to see that first spark of life, and then her eyes slip closed for longer, and longer blinks. A moment more, and she is asleep, her chin nodding downward against her chest.

— . . . . —

She wakes to the gentle brush of fingertips against her brow. The faint light from above is dimmer now still, and Niya sees primarily by the glow of the fire.

"Have some soup," Inola implores. "Your niisis included a small box of seasoning in their rations. That, some of the meat, some greens that I foraged near the mouth above—it's not a bad meal to fill your stomach, if I do say so myself."

Inola's smile is hopeful. Niya rolls her neck, a crick stuck in it after sleeping so oddly.

"I'm the worst company, aren't I?" Niya chuckles.

"Please, I'm just glad to see your eyes. Come, eat."

Together, they eat using gat-printed vessels and utensils. Inola pulls some baked cornmeal from the stone it was cooking on above the fire, suspended over a low spit. When Niya compliments the soup, her words are true—moreso, for the hunger she feels. And when she tastes the cornbread, she moans in compliment instead. Inola says little in response, her dark skin merely blushing an even deeper shade, smile on her lips and eyes downcast. She murmurs, "You're welcome, my friend," and they finish their meal in silence.

"Let me clean up," Niya says.

"Nonsense and foolishness," Inola snaps back.

"You've done so much!" Niya attempts to argue. "Kept me safe for multiple days, and that is the very least of it. The smallest bit I could do is clean up our dishes."

"I will clean them up," Inola says, her voice low and

pointed, a playful yet serious smile on her lips, "once you fall back to sleep." Fox-like. Like her namesake. Like her Path.

Niya has no fight left in her, meager as it had already been.

"Tell me, Niya—what was it like, using your Ability? Carrying us through the water like you did. What did that feel like?"

With a smile, Niya leans back, takes a deep breath, and tells her.

Or at least, she tries.

Tries to explain to Inola how the water had been less like a foreign entity and more like an old friend. How each breath had felt thick but nourishing, ending in a rush of bubbles, converted by her extraordinarily morphed body. And what it was like, when her Ability began to disappear—how she'd felt her lungs expel the water that had entered them.

But before that, how she had absolutely *flown* through the water. Inola's grip on her ankles had felt like next to nothing, merely a reminder that she was not alone.

"It felt like a miracle," she finishes.

Inola hums. Bites her bottom lip into her mouth. Squints her eyes in the dark with a tilt of her head.

"That's it," she says. "That's what it looked like, from my vantage point: a miracle."

Niya finds herself yawning through her self-satisfied, sleepy grin. Inola chuckles, bumping her shoulder against Niya's.

"One more sleep," the woman says, a low raspiness to her voice that lulls Niya closer yet to dreaming. "One more sleep, then we get going. Yeah?"

"Thank you," Niya whispers, her throat scratchy again and sore. Now that she has recalled the way the water had poured from her lungs, she wonders at the pain in her chest, the barely-there ache of each breath. "Sleep, good."

"Yes—sleep, good," Inola teases, musical laughter chasing away Niya's last conscious thoughts.

She lays down, her head against Inola's empty pack and the sleep kit draped loosely over her.

Inola joins her, before long. Niya feels her arrival, sleep not yet deep enough to miss it. Feels the weight of Inola's arm draping over her side, the closeness of her body heat, pressing against her back. Friendship and warmth and that not-alone feeling that brings peace.

Niya's breaths are full, any tension evaporating. She lets out a small sound, a tiny mewl, as she slips down, down, back into that place called rest.

They awaken together, and it is almost immediately clear that they have overslept. Their mouths are both dry, their bladders are full, and there is bright light streaming down from overhead, doing its best to penetrate the dark around them.

It only takes them a short bit of time to get walking, as Inola had done most of the preparations the night before. When she insists, too, on carrying Niya's pack for her, Niya quickly puts a stop to that notion.

"I assure you, I am well. You have given me ample rest—trust me! I feel pretty much back to normal." Inola gives her a side eye, to which she responds, "I swear to tell you if I need a break. Or my load lightened. Or, I don't know, a foot rub?"

At this, they both laugh, continuing on their way to Inola's village. Each step carrying them closer and closer to her village and its plight.

PIDII

When they get above ground, the first thing Niya does is check her niisi.

"Should've said—" Inola starts. "We're out of daso range. I'm not actually sure how far from the city we got underwater. But while you were recuperating the last couple days, I explored a bit. Found a trail not too far from here. It's running east to west, luckily. So I figure we hop on it, then reassess once we get to the first trailbox. No idea where we are in proximity to any of your noosoo's dining suggestions."

"He'll be so disappointed," Niya says jokingly, and they share a laugh. "Dare I say that this sounds like an actual plan?"

"Let's go, sleepyhead."

Once they get to the trail, they move forward with caution. Their steps are light, and they keep any conversations to a whisper.

They go a couple hours along the path before they come to the first trailbox—strategically placed boxes of rations, with a holographic map and emergency communication capabilities inside. When able, travelers may forage to refill the box, or swap out some of their own supplies and rations for those already available. This close to Cahokia, the boxes are maintained largely by the city. The further the trails and more populous byways get from Cahokia, other municipalities and peoples maintain the boxes.

Even given the common upkeep of the trailboxes, it is never a guarantee that there will be supplies or rations inside. When they open the first box they come across, they are delighted to find the holographic map in good order, a dozen or so packs of various jerkies, about two dozen small bags of assorted nuts, a heaping stash of raisins, apricots, and persimmons, and some freeze-dried apple slices.

First things first, they assess where in the world they are.

"I can't believe it," Inola whispers exuberantly. "Niya—you must have taken us underwater, what... over seven miles? Maybe more, and straight as the crow flies, that's decent headway! We could get to my village tonight." She pauses, tilting her head. "Well, very, very late tonight. And only if we really push ourselves, which—"

"Inola," Niya interrupts with a gentle hand resting on her upper arm. "I am well. Let's get there tonight, no matter how late."

The eyes of Inola Cato shine. She nods, and they take a very small selection of items from the trailbox, most of their own rations from Niya's niisis depleted after their time spent underground.

"Let's eat on our feet," Niya offers, biting into a deliciously seasoned and tender piece of jerky. "Bison, I think, have some!"

As they walk, they talk, keeping each other's spirits high. They talk about their Paths, about their parents; childhood and how it isn't really so far away yet for either of them; adulthood, and what it will look like when it comes, if it hasn't already.

"We're both wanted women now, Niya—me, wrongly so, and you by association. I'd say that's pretty 'grown up' of us, wouldn't you?"

"I'll gladly go back to being considered anything but an adult if it means that we prove your innocence."

They take a few more steps in sync before Inola asks, "Where do you think Tusika has gone?"

Niya slowly shakes her head, hopping over a place in the path where rainwater is washing over the packed dirt lined with stone. She wonders what lengths Tusika might be willing to go to in order to keep her family from finding out that she did not receive an Ability from the Adanadi. Worse yet, she wonders what it is that Tusika would *not* be willing to do.

She swallows hard before answering.

"I don't know. Maybe Nampeyo and Adasi will have news. We'll have to take a climb up a signal tower after we get you home."

"There is one not far from my house—we could certainly head there after getting a feel for the village's current state, tap into the relay to Cahokia. Shouldn't take long at that point, if they had any information to send."

The afternoon fades, and the sun's light along with it. The evening is overcast and cloudy, and there is little light from the sky's nighttime fixtures to see by. Niya and Inola each activate lights from their niisis to guide them.

"We're close, not more than an hour's walk away. I can get us there without using the path."

Since Inola's niisi is on her left wrist, Niya takes the woman's right hand in hers. "I'll turn my light off and follow you. I wish that one or both of us had Second Eyes to see in this darkness, but your knowledge of the land will serve us well. And the stealthier we can be, the better."

They exchange nods of certainty, and Inola turns the brightness of her light just low enough to see a small globe of space before them. Now, they are both trusting in her sense of the area, her gut instincts regarding the terrain.

When they get within a stone's mighty throw of her village, Inola presses her finger to her lips and then turns off her light. The clouds above have shifted enough to allow the great thihan makapoo—the far-away dust of the skyscape above them—to illuminate the night instead. Their eyes adjust quickly, and they approach the edge of the village's borders with the greatest caution imaginable.

"Any night watch?" Niya asks, her voice quieter than a whisper on the wind.

"Two villagers on two different shifts, four hours apiece. They typically circumnavigate the village in a leftwise direction..." Inola trails off, as if waiting for a question or a joke left hanging in the air to resolve itself. Not even a breath later, two gangly young men come walking around the village, but in a rightwise motion. "Unless," she whispers quietly, turning to grin in Niya's direction, "the watchers are Usdi and Ganuhida. They go rightwise for some reason, Creator only knows—and while I do not think they would turn me over to any Suyata, I'd rather not put them in the position to make that decision."

Once the two men meander their way out of sight, Niya says, "They may be all we have to contend with of the village watch. But about the Suyata—do you think they could still be here, or be watching?"

Inola scans the lay of the village before them. She is quiet and keen as she observes the buildings, the smokestacks, the sounds of animals and people alike at rest. After a few long moments, she gestures for Niya to follow her. They begin moving around the village in a rightwise motion, staying always a few minutes behind the watchers, Usdi and Ganuhida, and a few steps within the protection of the tree line. Every so often, Inola stops them for a few moments—waiting, watching. Assessing for the possibility of a Suyata contingent remaining in the village.

Finally, after one complete encircling of the village proper, Inola turns to Niya. "By no small measure of grace, I do not think there are Suyata waiting to surprise us. I think that we can enter my home safely—let's just hope that my mana isn't up doing any of her basketwork."

Niya gulps. "And why is that?"

"Because she is the react-first and ask-questions-later sort, and we do *not* want to startle her in the middle of the night with her weaving supplies in this environment," Inola says, her tone jovial. But then she turns a serious look on Niya, the light of the moon reflecting back at her. "And also because if she is up this late, then it means she isn't sleeping well. If she isn't sleeping well, it is probably because her body is giving her pain... she's suffered from it for years now."

"I'm sorry to hear that."

Inola waves her hand, as if wiping Niya's words away. "It's alright, nothing to be done about it. My noosoo passed when Kas was a little kid, so we've been on our own for a while. My aunties have been living with us the last few years, but that brings more mouths to feed since they've got four kiddos, all younger than me and Kas." Inola shrugs, as if to say, *Anyway, it is what it is.* "I've even seen worry on my daadoo's face the last couple years, which is...well, it's hard to see, that's for sure. My Ability helps, you know, being able to hunt with True Strike."

Niya nods. "I'm sure they'll all be happy to have you back." She reaches out, squeezing Inola's hand.

The woman turns her palm upward, squeezing Niya's hand in return. She turns her eyes on Niya in the dark. "Kas may be another person to feed, cloth, and house—but she is *ours*. She is my sister, and I...I will take care of her. She isn't a burden, with or without an Ability."

In her heart, Niya knows that this is the truth of it. For Inola, gifted with an Ability that helps provide for her family, and Kas, unblessed and feeling unable to help offer something more to her struggling family. How hard would it have been to stay—to see the burden on Inola's shoulders, the ever-present worry of the next meal? But more importantly, how easy would it have been to leave—Ability-less, to follow Gishkiy into an unknown but vibrant future of unlocked Abilities and endless possibilities?

Inola wipes at her eyes and nose with the back of her hand, clearing away any evidence of the tears she has been shedding the last several minutes. Niya reaches out, using the pad of her thumb to wipe beneath first one eye and then the other, before she presses her knuckle beneath Inola's chin, gently quirking it upward. *Chin up,* she doesn't say aloud—but Inola understands the sentiment, her lips drifting into a hesitant but nevertheless present smile.

They don't say more, because there isn't more to say. They'll bring Kas home because they must—but there is work to do than merely that, and Inola knows it.

Turning back to the village, they watch as Usdi and Ganuhida make one last pass in front of them. Once they round a corner and are out of sight, they make their move.

"Follow me—and quickly!"

Inola whispers the command and then bolts off through the night, quick as a fox and blending darkly into her surroundings like she was born to it.

Niya manages to keep up, working her way along the edges of buildings and across open spaces with fleet feet and lithe movements. In a flash that feels like an eon, they reach a back entrance to one of the homes in the village—part mound, part wood, part stone. Even in the dark, Niya can spot gaps around the doorframe, where the entryway doesn't quite properly seal. But there are also wild flowers all along the sides of the home, planted like sentries and clearly tended with loving hands. Some things need attending to while other things take precedence.

Another press of her finger to her lips, and then Inola inputs a code on the door's interface block, the only part of the exterior that looks as if it has been updated within the last few years. The lock clicks, and Inola enters with Niya close behind.

PIDII DOBA WANZI

As silently as mice, Niya and Inola creep to Inola's room. Inola leaves Niya there to quietly change and climb into the bed, while Inola tiptoes off to leave a handwritten message at each of her mana's bedside. The woman is sleeping soundly, a good sign. This way, she will not be startled to find Inola and a stranger asleep in the house—especially considering the warrant that has undoubtedly made its way this small distance to their village.

Hopefully the morning will bring clarity and understanding to the family that Inola has not seen for days.

Niya brushes her teeth without any water, sitting on the edge of Inola's sleeping pallet cross-legged. Her eyes stay shut even after she finishes brushing her teeth, the gat-printed brush handle sort of hanging haphazardly out of her mouth. The day had been long, and though the going had been relatively easy, it was still quite the distance they had walked. If only they'd been in possession of a sunwing fit for two riders, or an efficient personal mobility vehicle for the trails, they could have made it from Cahokia to the village in hardly any time at all! Alas, Niya's family was not in possession of one of the upright PMVs, and it would have been too conspicuous for their purposes.

Either way, they're here now. And they're alive, which feels like a miracle in and of itself.

Niya allows herself to fall backwards onto the bed. The blanket is worn from use, soft. Sadly does she think of the blanket that Inola had left in her room back in

Cahokia, the one that had been stolen by the Suyata, likely on Kaatii Patak's orders. If Niya manages to come face to face with the Suyata who took it, especially once they've cleared Inola's name, she will personally demand the return of the other woman's items.

Her mind is racing with thoughts, racing in that way where sleep is preparing to unobtrusively come and wash them all away without any sort of awareness from the thinker. There, then gone.

In that moment before sleep takes her, Niya hears the tiniest *click* of the door sliding over into place. She opens her eyes, head unmoving.

"Hey," Inola whispers.

"Hi."

"Tired?"

"My eyes feel like stones," Niya answers. But she holds them open, valiantly maintaining eye contact.

"Rest," Inola says, dropping down to her hands and knees on the sleeping pallet, before stretching her body out.

Her long arms go up, up over her head and toward the wall. Her tunic hem rises, a stretch of stomach exposed—slightly lighter in color than her arms and face, but still several shades darker than Niya's. Inola lets out a groan, luxuriating in the stretch of her muscles and the familiar embrace of her bed.

Niya's eyelids flutter as she is taken away, imagining another body next to hers. Tusika, the night before their Adanadi ceremony. Could that really only have been less than a month previous? How things change...

As if sensing the change in Niya's demeanor, Inola curls down and into herself. She looks at Niya through full eyelashes, those light eyes of hers their own sort of miracle, what with how unusually *seen* they make Niya feel.

"I'm glad you are here, Niya. Things are messy right now, but they won't always be. They *can't* always be. You've given me hope that Kas will come home safely and that we can stop Gishkiy from taking anymore people from their homes. I'd like to give you hope, too—that Tusika is not as lost as she seems right now, or at least that lost people can always be found again."

The peace of sleep is coming for Niya, and she answers only with an outstretched hand, resting her palm along the side of Inola's arm. Her pinkie finger thoughtlessly caresses the smooth skin there, and the soft, gentle moment eases Niya right down into a restful slumber.

And though Niya's sleep had been largely free of dreams since leaving Cahokia, this first night beneath the Cato family's room brings dreams aplenty...

The next morning, Niya awakes knowing little besides the presence of the cave. Her dreams were direct, indicating little else besides the importance of this cave on a ridge, surrounded by rocks and ancient trees; two long dead but still standing, their branches weaving together to sit atop the entrance like a thorned headdress. The same cave she's been seeing all along, brought into a sharper focus than ever before.

She sits up in bed, finding herself alone. There is bright light streaming in through a skylight. Niya stretches and begins to undo her two-day-old braids which probably look unconscionably messy at this point.

As she is finishing the fourth and final braid, there is a light tap at the door. It could only be Inola or a family member of hers, so Niya works to still the rapid beating of her chest in response.

"Come," Niya says, sure to keep her voice low.

Inola's head peeks into the room.

"Morning," she says, and Niya returns the greeting with a smile. "I had an alarm set, so that I'd know when you were stirring—I hope you don't mind that I let you sleep late, but I was worried that you still needed time to recover after using River's Flow."

"I feel fully back to normal now, thank you for the extra rest. This last night of sleep was magnificent. I'm more worried that you seem capable of all sorts of bugs and tricks—an alarm triggered when I move?" She smirks, and Inola has the audacity to shrug her shoulders up into a look of faux-innocence that has Niya giggling. "And I haven't forgotten about that biosynthetic tracking powder you used on us back in Cahokia. You've got tricks up your sleeves for days, don't you?"

Inola does nothing to disabuse Niya of this notion.

"Are you ready to meet my family?"

As she finishes freshening up, Niya asks, "I think so. Should I be nervous? Is there a test or a challenge, some sort of battle of wits or strength?" She flexes one arm as a joke, but deflates almost immediately upon noticing that this does not cause Inola to laugh. "Inola?" she asks nervously.

"Not a test, no. But I wouldn't say any of them are in the most sunshiney of moods this morning."

With a gulp, Niya asks, "Are they normally sunshiney in the mornings?"

Inola tilts her head first one way and then the other before answering. "No."

"Oh."

"Yeah."

"Well."

"I know. It'll be alright. I've got your back."

Niya smiles. "And I've got yours."

"Ready?" Inola repeats.

"Ready," Niya says, and she mostly means it.

Inola extends her hand, palm up. Niya glances down for only a moment, then places her hand in Inola's.

— . . . —

Niya isn't sure why she is surprised that the Cato clan seems generally unimpressed with her presence, upset with the way their eldest child has come home. A warrant, issued directly from the Council of Twelve. No solution for finding her little sister. And time spent away from the family, which meant money spent that shouldn't have been, and less hunting than any of the bellies in the house could go without.

The mood around the hearth is cold, no matter how

high Inola's daadoo stokes the flames.

Niya chews her breakfast mechanically, feeling awkward at best and completely like the intruder she is at worst. Despite Inola's attempts to lighten the mood and negate some of the negative energy away from Niya and onto herself, Niya can very much feel the Cato family's ire at her presence.

"You leave a whole fortnight and come back with Suyata on your heels and some Cahokian child you think can solve our problems and you expect me to celebrate, eh?"

This, coming from Inola's mana, strikes Niya right in the chest. She grimaces down into her corn mush as if her own mana had said it. Out of the corner of her eye, she can see Inola biting the insides of her cheeks to keep from responding. Sometimes, the elders need to be given the room to speak their minds. The rest will follow—but it sure can hurt in the meantime.

The woman, whose name is Nakola, has a full head of gray hair. She wears it simply, in a utilitarian fashion pulled back into a knot at the back of her head; one chunky piece of her hair falls loose, and knobbly fingers brush it back behind one ear.

"Your daadoo," she says, gesturing with the end of a bone needle at the elder manning the fire. His bald head, covered with intricate tattoos that gleam out from dark brown skin in the fire's light, tilts toward the girls. His mouth is downturned in a frown, much like his shoulders. Nakola goes back to mending the worn, brown tunic in her lap. "He's been hunting in your place, girl. You know how hard that is on him, don't you? *Winds*, girl, I taught you better than this. But you never stop, you never slow down, you never think!"

"Mana, I *do* think, I haven't stopped thinking since Kas left!"

Nakola *bangs!* her fist on the table. Stillness falls. Any words that Inola had been prepared to say next get choked off in her throat. She lowers her eyes.

"We told you to let your sister walk her path, but you saw malevolence in it, *darkness*. So you went to the tribe's elders, and you didn't like what you heard. So you went to the federation, and you didn't like that neither. Couldn't sit still and wait for the winds to change, so you went to the city—'cause so much good's never come from there, eh?"

With a deep sigh that seems to come from Nakola's core, she deflates. Leaning over the mending in her lap, that loose chunk of hair falls back down into her face. Niya watches from the corner of her eye as Inola heaves a quiet sigh of her own before walking to her mana, dropping to her knees, and pushing the hair back behind an ear once again.

"I know, mana. You always did say that I couldn't sit still to save a life."

"Eh," Nakola grins, somehow making the expression look sad. "My girl, always on the run...if not after your sister, then her after you..."

A tear slides down Inola's face. "Cahokia wasn't what I expected," she says, cutting her eyes across to Niya, who lifts her gaze to meet Inola's, "*at all*. But I've come home with an ally in tow, and that's more than we had before I left."

Niya remains silent, chewing at her soggy mush while trying to attract exactly zero attention from Inola's family.

Which is, of course, when Nakola turns her eyes on her.

"A warrant for your arrest and a stowaway. Hmmph. I'm no fool to curse an ally, but tell me why I shouldn't be worried for first my one daughter and now my other?"

Silence broken only by the crackling fire, over which Inola's daadoo—Wayi is his name—is baking some crusty bread. It smells hearty and filling, and Niya swallows her mouthful of breakfast thickly, wishing for a piece of that bread to have between her hands—something to pull apart, fidget with—instead of just sitting here, staring awkwardly at the hostile presence of Inola's mana and silent, prodding daadoo.

But Inola needs Niya to speak effectively now. And so she will do the best she can.

"I want to thank you first of all for this food. It has been many days since we had the pleasure of a home-cooked meal." Nakola grunts in response, knowing that her hearth's offerings are meager but that the gratitude is customary. "And I want to thank you, too, for raising such a strong-willed daughter—I have not known her long, but she is clearly a force to be reckoned with. She has brought truths into my life that I may have never expected but that I am thankful to have been gifted. I'm still learning what the results of her endeavors may be on my own life and path, but I know that I owe her something of myself in return. I may not be much, but

I have my word, my spirit, and my determination. And I have sworn to help her, so this I will do."

Nakola narrows her eyes as she wets the end of a thread to tie to her bone needle. But before she can open her mouth to respond, the front door bursts open.

Four little ones all run through the entryway, treading dirt and pine needles all over the old deer skin rug at the front of the home. They are all wearing plain leather clothes, well-worn and stained with play and rough use. There are two little ones with pigtails who look to be older, and two with long, wild hair that falls down and into their eyes that must be younger. The two youngins sport identical grins that make Niya smile, the tense moment from before having been broken by their entrance.

"Eh, you lot!" Nakola shouts. Niya hears that there is a softness to her bark, an edge lost when it comes to the children.

"Troublemakers," Wayi snickers from the hearth, patting one little dark-haired babe who stops at his side to pick at the baking bread, risking scorched fingers and all.

"You'd think with eight hands to help, I'd be able to haul in more than one small pallet of firewood, hey!"

This last voice calls in from the open door, and Inola immediately hops up to help whoever it is. Niya moves to stand and help as well, but Inola waves her off.

"It's my auntie, I'll help her and be right back."

Nakola snorts and says, "Wayi, what was it that the girl said just before she took off for the city, eh? Was it

'I'll be right back' or is my memory failing me?"

"Your memory may be failing you, but mine is as long as beaver's tooth—that's what she said alright."

"Hmmph." Nakola looks sideways at Niya as she goes back to hand-threading the needle.

The four little ones continue to run around like dust devils, stirring up messes and trouble. They all four seem to notice her at once and glom onto her like she's their newest plaything. Niya can't help but laugh as they ask her to play dollies or hide-and-seek or any of the other games they shoot off rapid-fire style at her.

"Knock it off, eh!"

Inola's auntie gives a playful shout as she comes inside, Inola close behind. She maneuvers a personal mobility vehicle designed for use both indoors and outdoors, with big, chunky wheels for overcoming obstacles but a tight turn radius empowered by yutsu technology. It's not one of the newer hovercraft-type PMVs, but it does seem decently suited for the terrain of Inola's homeland.

"I am not sorry for their exuberance, but I am sorry that you are their target." Niya stands as the auntie approaches, and they greet one another by shaking wrists. Niya inclines her head in respect, placing her unclasped hand across her heart. The auntie smiles kindly back at her, the warmest gaze Niya has yet felt besides Inola's under this roof. Another ally, perhaps, to help smooth the flawed introduction so far. "Four little ones underfoot, and my wife off on a hunting trip for the village that couldn't be postponed. It was our band's last shot at the bison grounds before the season ends, and they'll hopefully be bringing us all enough back to last a good long time. Even with our current strife—" she turns sad eyes on Nakola, who Niya presumes to be her sister, so identical are their light brown eyes to one another and to Inola, "—I told her we'd manage in her absence. And we are managing, aren't we, sister?"

Nakola grunts her reluctant agreement before rubbing at her lower back. "Managing, eh? Tell that to my back."

"I'm Mistii, by the way, and my wife is Zaka."

"I am Niya Suwatt, and it is nice to meet you and your children. All of my cousins are within a couple years of taking the Adanadi, so it's been awhile since I've been around kiddos of their age." She laughs as the two youngest—who look like they could be twins—duck into exaggerated crouches, stalking their older sisters who are now playing with a pair of corn husk dolls at Wayi's feet, as if to pounce on them at any moment. "I enjoy them."

"You can keep 'em," Nakola grumbles. But there is a smile at the end of her words that Niya spots as a promising sign. Perhaps the return of her sister and the children has lightened her mood, or brought a perspective that might ease the former tension.

"Oh, you," Mistii coos, positioning herself at one open side of the table where there are no chairs. She reaches out and pinches her sister's cheek. "Have you been kind this morning?"

Instead of subjecting her mana to the truth of such a question, Inola cuts in.

"Auntie, Niya was just having her breakfast and

getting to know mana and daadoo. I was hoping to hear what word there has been from Cahokia."

"What word hasn't there been, niece? We had three Suyata sitting at this very table not two days ago, and if that wasn't just about the most unexpected part of this entire thing, I don't know what was."

"What?!" Inola gasps. "The Suyata were in our home?"

"Please," Nakola lets out one of those barks of laughter again, "we've been missing *two* daughters for some time now, haven't we? Suyata on our doorstep, that should have been a gift!"

"By the Creator, what did you tell them?" Inola asks, pressing her hand to her forehead.

"I told 'em that I've got a granddaughter done run off with a mad man, is what I told 'em!" Wayi interjects. "Told 'em they're barking up the wrong tree to be coming after you. Told 'em that if they wanted to arrest somebody, I'd be happy to point 'em right in Gishkiy's direction." This last point, he emphasizes by spitting into the fire.

The family continues to go round and round about the Suyata—how they sent them off without a scrap of evidence or assistance in their search for Inola, of course, and that the small group of warriors of their band and the village over the hills to the south are in communication about their whereabouts. It's been a full day since anyone has seen them.

"If you go looking for trouble, you'll have to be wary of them yet. Who knows if they won't just manage to find their way back to our village. Couldn't get a read on 'em, for how persistent they might be."

"We aren't looking for trouble, daadoo, we're looking for Kas."

Niya's brows furrow as she takes in everything she's hearing. "Wait," she says—and then she repeats herself, since it is clear that no one heard her. "Wait!" she nearly shouts, and just about every set of eyes in the place turns to her. "I'm sorry, but...did you say you could point them in Gishkiy's direction?"

Wayi blinks almost owlishly back at Niya for a moment before saying, "Of course, girlie. He's up in the hills to the north, I'd bet my last nizi on it."

"What nizi?" Nakola and Mistii ask at the same time.

Wayi ignores them. "There's so many caves up there, on that east to west ridge. He and his people, they could be in any one of 'em. If I was a few spins younger, I'd go up there looking myself. Those Suyata, they could look though."

Caves. Niya's breath catches. Her dreams. Owl's flight. The land she's seen now, so many times, from above. *Could it be?*

"Tell me this: does your family put much weight behind dreams?"

Nakola *hmmphs* again. She jabs her thumb towards Mistii. "This one dreams about roads paved with toads every time there's about to be a thunderstorm."

"And my wife has dreamt of morel-hunting, only to find the path laid out richly when she wakes just as it had been in her dream."

"Dreams are as real as anything else in this world,"

Wayi says.

Inola takes the seat next to Niya. She dips her chin and asks, "What dreams have you had, Niya?"

"I think...well. I think my Path animal has been leading me. Not just to here, to help Inola—but to Gishkiy, and to Kas. Every night, I've been flying closer, seeing it again and again. I think I'd know the place with my eyes closed now—a cave, nestled on a ridge with a plunging bluff down to water. Boulders and loose rocks along its entrance. A pair of dead trees to either side of it, twisted in the wind and elements, their branches interlocking just above the cave's mouth..."

"By the Creator," Nakola whispers. The tunic she had been working on falls to the floor.

"Kas!" Mistii cries, clasping her hands over her mouth.

Wayi lets out a peel of laughter, and Inola leans forward eagerly.

"There's a hundred caves within five miles of here, Niya—but those trees you described..."

"Pull up a scratchpad on your niisi, granddaughter," Wayi stands, grabbing a walking stick that Niya had not noticed before as he hobbles over to the table. "I may not be able to climb mountains myself anymore, but I can sure as strong winds and high water draw you a good map to get there yourself."

"—Auntie, let her eat in peace—"

"Inola, the girl can eat in between answering questions, can't she?"

"And you should eat a second breakfast, too, my girl. Skin and bones since we let you go away."

"—I wasn't even gone a month—"

The atmosphere of the Cato household has shifted almost completely. Whereas at Niya's first appearance, it had been cold and nearly downright hostile, now it dares to be hopeful.

"Tell me more about these dreams, Niya."

Niya does tell them.

She tells them about being blessed by her Path animal, Owl. About receiving River's Flow and using it to escape the Suyata. She tells them of the dreams she began to have the night before her Adanadi ceremony, and the way she has felt guided by Owl ever since. A confidence, a calm that falls over her, when she finds herself on the path that Owl has laid out before her in her mind.

"Owl has been in your life longer than that, I'd bet. If you think back on things, I bet she's been watching you for a *loooong* time, girlie." Wayi chuckles, a snorting, snuffling sound primarily through his nose. "Sometimes it just takes us a while to start listening."

Niya and the Cato family sit around the hearth. All ground-level openings are covered to keep out prying eyes. There is a small fire pit in the middle of the floor, and Inola's mana and auntie bicker in a practiced fashion as they lay new logs on the fire to build the small flame into a more substantial one. The fire is good, not too much smoke, but the smoke that it does produce swirls up through a neatly designed outflow above them. It's the kind of fire for a story, the kind of fire to tell tales around.

Nakola brings out three loaves of the bread that Wayi baked earlier. She also brings a small jar out of the kitchen, which she hands almost immediately to Inola to open. When Inola looks down at it, her face crumbles and she immediately looks back up at her mana.

"This is the last of the huckleberry preserves," she says, eyes shining. Mistii reaches over to rest her hand atop her niece's. By way of explanation, Inola turns to Niya and says, "It's Kas's favorite."

Her voice sounds very small—so different from that first night at the Pataks when she had stormed in, intent on gaining Council assistance in rescuing her sister and turning the tide against Gishkiy.

"When your impetuous sister comes home," Nakola says as she slices the loaves for toasting, "she can make more of her own precious huckleberry jam, can't she? Hmmph."

"We'll eat this and think of her." Wayi nods thoughtfully. "She'll know, wherever she is—that we've eaten the last of her best preserves and she better get her ass back here to make some more!"

When the elder laughs, they all laugh too—buoyed by the brief respite of levity.

As the flames ease back towards the hearth, Nakola toasts slice after slice of tasty, nutritious bread. Then Inola spreads a precious layer of the final huckleberry preserves across each slice, handing them around the circle of Catos and Niya. First, Wayi is given a slice of the delicious treat, then each of the children, and finally Nakola, Mistii, Niya, and Inola herself. Everyone gets two slices of bread in this fashion, and while they do, they share everything they have not yet had the chance to share.

"We know where to look thanks to Niya and her Owl," Inola starts, "but tell us more: you've not heard from Kas since I've been gone, is that right?"

"Not a word or a message."

"Have any others from the village left to join Gishkiy?"

"One from our numbers," Mistii speaks up, "but worse yet—three from the Wild Hare Band off east, and more yet from their neighbors to the north, the Otter Band."

Niya shakes her head. "It's spreading."

Inola snaps those startling eyes to hers, her jaw clenched. "Do we know if they've tried again, if they've done whatever it is Gishkiy thinks they can do to gain Abilities?"

Her daadoo hangs his head heavily. "They've sent no bodies down to us from the hills yet, my girl. But I have my fears. There's change in the air."

"Change isn't always bad," Mistii offers, running her fingers through one of her girl's loose hair, carding it through her fingers to twist into braids anew.

"And it ain't always good neither, is it?"

"Hmmph."

They are all quiet for some time. The fire crackles softly. The sun has already begun to set. Inola is staring intently at the map that Wayi drew for them, working to impose his trail lines on top of a map of the region.

Niya watches her, spotting the exact moment that Inola's work is done.

"That's it?"

Inola nods solemnly, pinching outward with her fingers and then swiping outward on the hologram about her niisi, a flickering image now projected out above the fire. The smoke swirls up, up through the map, entangling with the hand-drawn lines from Inola's daadoo atop the topography of their hill-nested homeland.

"If I could go with you..." Nakola starts, not even looking up at the map, instead fixated on the same tunic she's been working to mend all day long. She sounds angry, her voice practically trembling with the force of her words. "I'd bring that daughter of mine back by her braids." She looks up in a snap, grabbing Inola's gaze. "I can't walk up that ridge, not like I could have done half a lifetime ago. So you'll have to do it for me. And I expect you to be careful, and smart, and to watch out for one another." She juts her chin out towards Niya now. "No funny business. You leave Gishkiy be, if you can. If it's not safe...just find out enough to tell me that my girl is alright, and leave it be."

"For now," Inola cuts in. "We'll play it safe *for now*. But we may not have another opportunity like this again, to know where they're hiding out. Niya's dreams have helped us, but we don't know what tomorrow could bring."

"Or the day after that," Wayi says. "Which is why you keep your head on straight and think before you act."

"We all know you good you are at that, my girl," Mistii says, her body bouncing lightly as she silently chuckles.

The sarcasm isn't lost on Niya, as she observes the family's interactions.

She turns to Inola, watches as the young woman takes in all of her family's advice.

"We'll leave before dawn. As the nightwatch is set to finish in the center circle." She turns to Niya. "We'll do our climbing before the sun has a chance to rise high, get as close as we can, see what we can see... and if we get the chance," she says, her tone so resolute that Niya wonders if she wouldn't just follow Inola right into battle, if the lines were drawn, "we bring Kas the hell home."

— . . . —

The night brings fitful sleep to Niya. If she dreams, she does not recall the details in the morning light—only bursts of clashing colors, flashing behind her closed eyelids. Streaks of purple cut through with violent shades of red; splotches of green dripping, dripping through the other colors like so much excess paint. When she awakens, she feels nearly short of breath—swirling red, red, *red,* the only thing left from her restless sleep.

The women dress in silence, all nerves as they prepare for whatever the day holds. They eat in silence, too—the four children of the home are still fast asleep, but Nakola, Mistii, and Wayi solemnly eat with them. Wayi's eyes are closed the entire time, and Mistii quietly tells Niya that he is praying. There isn't much silence after that.

"All sorts of prayers," she says. "He's got a prayer

for everything, has had since we were little girls." She points with her lips at her sister. "Prayers for fleet feet, prayers to keep you from tripping on loose rocks."

"Prayers for scaring snakes out of your path," Nakola joins in.

Inola pipes up as well. "Prayers for clean teeth."

"For smooth river stones at crossings."

"Prayers for blackberries and wild mushrooms, both."

"And for pretty women, too!"

"Eh, disrespectful, you lot," Wayi mutters, not even opening his eyes to chastise the women to their faces.

There is a beat of silence, and then they all descend into quiet giggles that they try poorly to muffle.

Before long, the meal is behind them and the young women are ready to head to the hills, to start their journey towards the cave.

"We'll sneak round to the north, get deep into the woods before cutting properly east."

Nakola says, "Stay away from Thitaga's hut—you know that old crow is always sticking her beak in other peoples' business."

"Oh, yes, we'll avoid her place, and the sightlines of any other early risers, eh?"

Niya watches as Inola whispers something to her mana, and then they head to the back of the home together. Nothing else is said between any of the Catos, and Niya wonders if that is their way—if they purposefully avoid speaking things like goodbyes and good lucks into existence, instead choosing to part with silly advice about a nosy neighbor.

Different from Niya's family, in the way they communicate and show they care for one another, but tough—very, very tough. Niya hopes that when all of this is said and done—when Kas is home and Inola is less burdened, when Gishkiy's clutches are loosened and the sisters' restless spirits settle—the Catos find good times. Or that good times find them and stay awhile.

Armed only with water and some bean-stuffed corn cakes for lunch, Inola and Niya turn to look up at the hills around them, the woods they are set to walk. They keep their voices low, at a volume where only the other can hear them. The sun has not yet risen, twilight laying thinly across the land.

They both turn in tandem towards one another. The air is crisp. The world feels like a promise to be kept. Grins spread across their faces. Niya grips her daadoo's chunkey spear in one hand and reaches out to settle the other on the taller woman's shoulder, giving it a squeeze to accompany her smile.

"Let's go, eh?"

"After you, friend."

PIDII DOBA PIT

About an hour into their hike, Niya looks down at her niisi.

[no new messages]

"Ish, but it'd be good to hear from my friends… or to have one of 'Peyo's drones!"

"It's a bit off our path from here, but there's a communications tower west of home on another rise. We'll get there later, or tomorrow. They'll surely want to hear that you're alive, and that your level-best attempts at drowning the both of us were somehow unsuccessful."

Inola turns back, looking at Niya with a friendly grin. Niya's cheeks flush with warmth.

They haven't talked much about the dark, pulsing deep of the underground river, their mad escape from the Suyata. And Niya hasn't had a chance to think about her Ability and the magnitude of its power. Having only practiced it a small number of times in controlled, escapable conditions prior to the dive, she was able to swim them along several miles with the underground current. The fact that they both lived to tell the tale is miraculous.

"Yes, thank you—they'll want to hear about that miracle. And they may be able to help us more, even from afar."

They press on, climbing the hill that feels more and more like a mountain.

A physical hurdle, and one that is quickly turning into a trial of spirit, too.

— . . . —

The sky is a sliver past midday when they reach the cave. A stone's throw away, the dark slit in the side of the rocky hill feels ominous and unwelcoming.

"This is a place I have not visited in years, not since we were kids. We rarely crossed fully over to the cave, and only the bravest among us would go far into its depths. Do you recognize it? Is this the place from your dreams?"

It only takes one glance to confirm what Niya's gut had already told her to be true. The dead trees at its entrance, branches interlocking... "Yes, this is the place I have visited in my dreams."

This is the place that tried to eat me, she does not say. *This is the place that pushed me to my death—that unlocked my Ability and showed me how to use it.*

"Do you see movement?"

Inola narrows her eyes against the shine of the sun. Niya's heart is beating fiercely in her chest, eager and anxious at once.

"None..." Inola's voice is barely above a whisper, and Niya leans into her side on instinct, to be closer to the sound. "One of those drones really would be nice, eh?"

Niya smiles without taking her eyes off of the cliff face below the cave's entrance. She scans every crevice for signs of a trap, or surveillance that might tip off the cult about their proximity to their hideout. Though she does not see anything, that is no guarantee. Niya had heard enough about the charismatic and resourceful man who had stolen peoples' hearts and minds with his words. Gishkiy is protecting his followers, they assume, and providing for them, to some extent at the very least. What other tricks might he have up his sleeves?

While not eager to find out, Niya is willing to test his limits. When the time comes—if it comes. Hopefully she will not need to do so recklessly.

"Let's get closer."

Inola blurts the words in a righteous hurry, is moving so fast that Niya is almost caught off-guard. And Niya is never caught off-guard.

"Inola—" she hisses, reaching out and pulling Inola back down into their lookout spot just in time. "You can't go like—!"

"But can't I?!" Inola snaps back.

Which is when Niya recognizes the tearful look on the other woman's face. Sees eyes brimming with tears. And as soon as she marks them, catches them out, Inola is scrubbing them away with the heels of her hands.

"It's Kas," she says, voice heavy, "it's my sister."

Niya nods and hugs her friend, pressing her forehead against the side of Inola's head, willing her strength and calm to be of some use to the other woman.

"Yes," she says after a moment, "Kas is your sister. And these are your people, people who know you! They'll recognize you in an instant, and they'll very likely know that you aren't exactly here to congratulate them on their good work." Inola barks out a tearful laugh at this, and Niya smiles. "But none of them know me. Stay here, I'll go take a look—I'll signal you if the way is clear for you to follow."

Inola is still as stone as she considers this, then she nods twice, no small amount of reluctance covering her features. "Alright, Suwatt, you can do this thing for me. But if you disappear from my sight for more than five minutes, I'm coming after you."

Niya's grin is wide, and she does not give Inola a chance to change her mind.

It doesn't not take her long to traverse the rim of the cliff, to approach the cave. She sees almost immediately that her wary steps and cautious approach have been unnecessary.

The cave has been abandoned.

"No..."

Niya curses under her breath, fists her hands at her sides.

Inola is going to be crushed. Their one lead, already gone cold.

She schools her features then turns back toward Inola's spot on the ridge, raises her arms and waves them widely, fanning them out and then in, gesturing as if to pull Inola closer.

The figure that is Inola takes off, crouching low to the ground as she hurries around to the cave herself.

When she gets to Niya, she doesn't bother stopping, moving instead directly into the cave's entrance and beyond.

"No, no, no," she mutters, looking half-frantic, half-despondent.

Niya follows, taking in the scene before them.

The space was clearly occupied not that long ago, by the look of things. A hasty departure was set into motion, causing small bits of food stores and scraps of tech to be left behind, some tables, a sleep kit here or a chewstick there. Scattered bits of lives scrubbed away in a blink.

"Inola," Niya tries.

But Inola is moving further into the recesses of the cave, the light of her niisi turned up as high as it can go. She disappears down a turn in the wall, and Niya can hear the sounds of her footsteps pick up speed. She runs after the other young woman, activating her own light as she goes.

The rock and packed dirt floor is smooth beneath her feet as she runs, and Niya does not stop as she rounds the same left she had seen Inola disappear around, takes a right after that, another left, following the sounds and familiar niisi light ahead of her. Then she rounds one last shift in the rock walls surrounding her, and the cave opens up into a cavern. Though only a fractional size of the place where their underwater jaunt had delivered them, this place is beautiful. A single shaft of sunlight strikes down from an almost perfectly circular hole up above. Water *drip, drips* down in soft pings from above. The space is only slightly larger than the first open area at the cave's entrance.

Across the space, Inola is leaning against the wall. Her body is bowed in half, hands on knees and head towards the floor. Niya does not need to get any closer to see that Inola's back is heaving with heavy breaths, forcing her lungs to work through the panic she seems to be experiencing. She rushes to the woman's side, presses her hands to Inola's back, demands that she breathe with focus and intent.

"Shh, shh, now listen—feel your lungs as they fill. Press them up into my hands. Good, good. Now, out."

Eventually, Inola's body stills enough that she can breathe normally again. She leans her head back against the wall.

"I know that we have options—that there are more places to look, that there must be trails to follow, hope that my sister abandons this foolish notion... but Niya, my heart feels like it's *breaking,* and I can't fathom what on earth to do! Your Owl guided us here, you guided us here, and my hopes were higher than I dared admit..."

Eyes full of tears and cheeks wet with them, too, Inola's chin and lips tremble. Her face seems to shatter, and it is all that Niya can do to hold her—hold onto her tightly, and hold out hope.

"Tell me when you're ready for the plan," Niya eventually whispers against dark, braided hair.

And in time, Inola responds, her voice a quiet whisper interrupting the soothing path of Niya's fluttering fingertips. "Ready."

With each step, Niya ticks a finger upward. "We get out to the fresh air and sunshine and have some lunch. We assess the ground around the cave—they were clearly in a hurry, they'll have left tracks, even if they tried not to. We go slow and keep alert, because the last thing we want to do is rush into things." She ducks down, being sure to catch Inola's eyes. "And whatever we do, we do it together. Yeah?"

Inola reaches forward, clasping her hand with Niya's outstretched one. "The plan is a plan, and I'll take it gladly. Let's get out of here."

Navigating the reverse path back out of the cave is a tad disorienting. There is a small bit of light behind them from the circular room's opening, but it fades quickly. Their niisis give enough light to see by, but the tunnels are largely domed recesses of impenetrable black beyond their little sphere of artificial light. When they turn back into the main room off of the cave's entrance, the sunlight streaming in from the entrance is so bright as to cause spots in their vision.

Which is why they are not immediately able to make out the figure standing in the cave's opening.

"Whoa," Inola says, throwing out her arm to stop Niya in her tracks.

Niya opens her mouth to question the other woman, until she sees what has caused Inola to stop them both.

"Is that a person?" she asks, her voice quiet.

But the acoustics of the space do not lend themselves to secrecy.

"It is," the figure answers back, taking one step forward.

Now out of direct sunlight, Niya's still adjusting eyes can almost make out the features of the individual.

But it's not the face that Niya recognizes first, no—it's that voice. That swagger.

"I was worried that you weren't going to arrive. Or

that you were going to be too late."

"Tusika," Niya gasps, her voice full of recognition and encroaching panic. "Too late...too late for what?"

"Too late to see the cogs clicking into place. Too late to see what Gishkiy's work will accomplish, with the right person at his side—or at mine. Too late to see the effects on the right subject."

Niya gulps, hard. Thinks about their Adanadi ceremony. About how she had received an Ability and Tusika hadn't. Seven generations of Pataks had come before Tusika, all gifted with Abilities. Seven generations of Suwatts before Niya, and not an Ability amongst them. And now, their role reversal. A swapping of fates in the eighth generation.

And the promise of Gishkiy to his followers: power and powers alike without the Adanadi's influence. This information, Niya herself had fed to Tusika in a bid to gain her help in getting Inola before the Council. An Ability, a small price to pay; some untested and unknown ceremony, experimentation; dangerous and foolhardy.

The right subject...

That pride, that confidence—so very Patak of her, but also so very, very Tusika. The young woman Niya has spent her life learning and loving. Willful and stubborn, driven and certain. No Ability, yet still so powerful.

Niya feels her knees quake.

"Tusika, you can't mean it."

"I'm happy though, Niya, happy that you're here. It wouldn't have felt right, you not being here. Well, you can't be with me while it's happening, that much seems all too obvious, what with *her* and all."

Niya cuts her eyes to Inola at her side, arm still outstretched, holding Niya back. Holding herself back, too.

She pushes forward against Inola's arm, makes to move closer to Tusika. But Inola's voice is a sharp whisper, borderline pleading.

"Niya, no—"

"*Niya, no,*" Tusika mimics, her voice slipping into that cruel tone of hers. The tone that Niya has always brushed away before, written off as fleeting, as temporary, as untrue to Tusika's core. And yet, she yields it in moments like this with an effortlessness that leaves Niya weak. "Does she hold the ends of a leash in her hands, Niya? Are you her puppet on a string, her domesticated kitten?"

"Tusika, stop it." Niya's voice is firm, and she takes one huge step closer to the cave's entrance, forcing Inola's arm down and back behind her. She wills herself not to tremble. "Do you hear yourself? You sound rotten, foul. Is this how you treat people? Strangers and friends alike?"

Tusika is quiet. She nods slowly, more to herself than in acknowledgment of Niya's words.

Niya does not say more. She just waits, silent and still. Begging without turning to Inola that the other woman keep still, too.

Her mind, full of racing thoughts, settles on a particular memory.

It's been a long time, Niya remembers, since she last

went hunting with her late daadoo. Not since she was a child, some seven or eight years previous. They'd laid traps, set snares and bait, picked the choicest locations for the best game. The next day when checking the traps, they'd found a bobcat strung up by one ankle and fighting against the restraint for its very life. As if the strength of its convictions, the will it employed to fight against that ill-fated piece of rope, would determine whether it lived or it died. And not only that, but how it would live, how it would die.

She sees that same look now, can almost feel the unuttered, feral *growl* from Tusika's chest across the distance that separates them. The distance that feels immeasurable.

And when Tusika speaks, before she finishes even a single sentence, Niya knows little else besides one absolute truth: the point of no return was breached some time ago. The fallout now is inevitable.

"Before you got here, Niya, I kept telling myself, 'She's coming. She's coming to stop you.' And that didn't feel right, because what I wanted was for you to *be* with me. When you didn't show up, that made it feel all the worse..."

"I had no idea," Niya says, wondering at her friend's words. "Your last message to me, I couldn't decipher it. I didn't know that it meant you were coming to be a disciple of this man, of Gishkiy—the one tearing Inola's sister from her family."

"But we are Niya and Tusika," Tusika says. "You were going to find me one way or another, come to me. We've been close for so long...when I started to think you weren't at least looking for me, then I wondered if you cared at all. And a part of me died when I thought that, Niya."

"I'm glad to have found you—or to have been found by you. I'm not sure which it is or was, but...there are things we need to talk about, Tusika."

"Things, things...what *things*—whatever stories and horrors that girl has put in your head, no doubt. What rumors can I dispel, Kakooni? What nasty truths can I correct for you?"

Niya opens and shuts her fists, takes a deep breath. The tension in the air is real and pulsing. Time feels short, impossibly so. Tusika has always been determined, brash—but this feels different. This feels like desperation. And Niya has to ask the questions or risk never having the truth of their friendship out.

"Was my Ability supposed to be yours, Tusika?"

The question somehow startles even Niya. She had meant to ask about it, meant to inquire as to the impact of Kaatii Patak's childhood friendship with Gishkiy, not only on his Ability-less Adanadi-taking but also his family's exile from the city. But now, in this moment, faced with Tusika's shadow and Gishkiy's propaganda and the very real absence of his cult's presence from this place...Niya feels as if to *not* ask would be to never know. Not ever. And she can't live with that.

"What?" Tusika asks in response, her voice smaller than Niya has possibly ever before heard it.

Another step forward. She hadn't asked it directly before, but she does so now. "Do the Pataks steal Abilities?"

"Do you hear yourself?" Tusika asks, haughtiness hollow in her tone. "What does that even mean?"

"If you've met Gishkiy, then does he know who you are—that you're a Patak? Because we have reason to believe that he blames his lack of an Ability on your mana. Maybe on your entire family."

"And you think...what, that I was going to steal yours?" Niya does not answer, only waits for Tusika to deny it. "Do you still think so little of me, my love?" It isn't a denial, but Niya can feel something in Tusika's voice that sounds an awful lot like heartbreak.

My love. Niya's own heart breaks, too, at the thought that she could truly be that for Tusika. That all of this could be one huge mistake. That Inola and Kas will be reunited and their family made whole once more. That Gishkiy and Kaatii will reconcile, a childhood friendship lost to a decades-long misunderstanding.

"Maybe I had it all wrong. Maybe you aren't out to stop me, to stop us—maybe you're out to join us. Seven generations of Suwatts without, and you've gotten a little taste, hungry for more." She tilts her head, the movement a silhouette in the cave's mouth, dark against light. "No, no...that isn't it, isn't it at all. It's simpler than that."

"Is it?"

"Yes—it's the chase. We've always been chasing one another, haven't we? And we always will be."

"Why?" Niya asks, her voice hoarse from how she wills it not to escape in a scream. Her eyes, adjusting to the gloom, can see a soft smile on Tusika's face now. A small, intense smile that looks so much like the girl

Niya grew up with, the girl she's loved and been in love with for so long—but it also doesn't, doesn't look like her, not even the littlest, most hateful bit. She can feel the sob working its way up her throat from her chest.

"I know you'll keep chasing, because you must. Just as I must run, until I no longer have to."

"Tusika, what are you saying? You can't do this—"

"I can though, can't I? I've come too close to letting my family down, and to letting myself down. And I won't let that happen. You must know that I won't."

"Tusika, don't do this! You don't know anything about this ceremony, this experiment—you don't know what will happen to you. You might die, Tusika!"

"But I don't think I will, Kakooni. And I'm almost always right about these things. Besides, you have to admit: you have an Ability, you both do. You can't understand what we're going through, can you? You'll never understand it, because the Adanadi chose you. For some reason, it chose *you*—not us. Therefore, this is our choice to make now."

Niya clenches and unclenches her fists at these words, true as they are. The harnessing of the Adanadi did not happen in one night or even in one generation. More advancements may come, with time—with thoughtful studying and closely monitored experimentation. Not backwoods pseudoscience and untested ceremony, perhaps lost to time in memorium for a reason.

She takes one step closer to her friend.

"If you're wrong, you're dead. What do you think

about that? What do you think that will do to your family, to... to me?"

Niya's voice cracks, and she thinks she sees Tusika's facade crack, too—just the smallest bit and for only a fraction of a moment. And then it snaps back into place, and she recognizes the young woman in front of her, but she also doesn't.

"You'll be alright," Tusika says, and her smile slips, dips, resurfaces with a punch to Niya's gut. "I know you will. And so will I."

Then, from the edge of the cave's gaping mouth, a man emerges. His white hair practically glows in the light from the sun, and his robes look like waves of blood. Niya cannot see the features of his face well, and she is glad. Standing next to her best friend and knowing the man's power of charisma and persuasion, Niya wonders, worries... if things had unfolded just the slightest bit differently, would she be able to stay put with Inola, firm in their resolutions of dissolving Gishkiy's hold and overthrowing his power? Or might she step forward, going towards the unknown?

How many times has she done exactly that over the years—stepped forward, taken a plunge, fought off the doubts brought forth by the not knowing—because of the love she has for Tusika? They would do anything for one another. That has been their way for so, so long. Even before they were truly friends, there was a sense of duty that came with being in one another's orbit all this time.

But this is different. *Niya* is different.

Isn't she?

The man walks over to Tusika, rests his hand on her shoulder.

"Gishkiy," Inola hisses beneath her breath. Niya already knows, of course, but the name sends shivers down her spine regardless.

Tusika says, "As you like to say, my friend—until we meet again."

While Tusika remains still, rooted to the spot, Gishkiy lifts his hands. A tension pulls tight across his shoulders, and his arms spread wide. The blood-red leather of his garb moves like wings beneath his outstretched stance. Niya can see a trembling in his hands, as if he is exerting some great effort that no one else can properly perceive.

Tusika's eyes do not move from Niya's, not an inch.

Suddenly, the earth emits a rumbling sound, deep and low, and the ground beneath everyone's feet trembles.

"What—"

"Ish!"

"Tusika, *stop him!*"

Niya sees it happening, but it's too late. She can't comprehend it, besides the knowing of it taking place before her eyes.

Gishkiy curls his arms up and inward, as if he is tugging two mighty ropes towards his chest. This effort of his is having an effect on the world around him, on the earth—and on the trees that have stood guard to either side of the cave's entrance for years and years. Gishkiy is not directing others to his bidding, and he has not set off explosives, nor has he utilized some device to cause this destruction. Niya can see that, feel that, smell it in the air.

Gishkiy is moving the earth, and he is doing it as if he has—

"An Ability?!" Inola shouts, finishing Niya's thought.

An Ability.

The man breaks his stance, stumbling away from the opening as it fills in with shale and dirt and boulders from above, the dead, gnarled branches of the two sentinel trees crushed beneath the rubble.

Tusika moves only at the last moment, taking a slow series of steps backwards, out of the way of any possible danger.

Niya runs forward as if to... to...

What? Push her friend out of harm's way? Stop the avalanche from occurring in the first place, somehow? Get one last glance of that face that both is her friend's and isn't?

In seconds, the entire entrance is blacked out. Covered. Impenetrable. Dust fills the air and Niya's lungs, and she is coughing in great, heaving, useless breaths. Hands grip her arms, pulling her back and away, towards air currents that are clean and a darkness that is less haunting.

"No," Niya coughs, the word hardly intelligible.

She would cry, if she could. She would cry, if her heart were broken.

But it isn't broken, it's *gone.*

Those eyes, the eyes that she's known all her life,

had been familiar to her. Up until the moment they no longer were.

And as Niya falls to her knees in the darkness, she wonders if she will ever see those once familiar eyes again. And if she does, will she be able to recognize them at all?

PIDII DOBA TAHOO

From the mouth of the cave, Tusika had spoken something true about their past, their friendship. *We've always been chasing one another, haven't we?* With a painful gut rush of memory, Niya knows that her best friend had spoken the truth.

"We'll never catch them!" Niya despairs, stopping to press her hands into the tops of her thighs, panting to catch her breath.

Tusika slides to a stop a few steps ahead of her. She turns around, a sly grin on her face.

"I know a shortcut," her voice practically vibrates with excitement. She extends a hand to Niya. "You with me?"

And Niya does not answer with her words, only extends her hand with a smile, taking her best friend's fingertips in hers as the invitation they are: one that can lead only to adventure. To excitement. To memory-making and more.

"We'll catch them yet," Tusika says as they begin to run, slipping in and out of Cahokian vendor carts and down this alley and across that expanse of greenway, scaring up turtle doves when they pass by the low-hanging branches of a sugar maple tree. "They'll know better for the future, won't they?" she asks, turning that grin devious, "than to mess with Niya and Tusika!"

Then she crows her excitement into the open air, and they jump across a small stream, splashing in its waters the littlest bit before taking off again. And then Niya sees that Tusika has led them true—Adasi and

Nampeyo are just ahead. Tusika takes them down one last tricky turn through some mound homes, they even climb atop one! At its pinnacle, Tusika shouts, "Trust me!" as she pulls them both into a huge leap through the air. "Duck and roll!" They hit the ground in parallel somersaults, popping up together with laughter heaving up from their spent lungs.

"A-yo!"

A shout comes from behind them, and Niya tosses one quick look back—only to see that they have overtaken their friends!

She turns back ahead, and both girls pick up their pace, the joy of taking the lead propelling them forward.

And Niya glances at the side of Tusika's face as they continue to run, their self-made race through the city drawing to a close with them in the lead. And she sees something that makes her heart beat faster and her face shine with love: ferocity and determination, the spirit of a leader who she would follow anywhere...

Niya chokes on the dust swirling through the air as much as on the emotions that bubble up from inside her at the memory. She had loved Tusika from that moment, had been willing to follow her to ghost country and back, if she had to...

Shaking herself from the stupor of emotional misery enveloping her mind, Niya straightens up. *It won't come to that,* she thinks. *It can't.*

Both women turn on their niisi lights, and the haze of particulates in the air swirls about them like a dust devil. The pull of air through the chamber and the passageways behind them drags the dust thickly past them. Niya and Inola cough through the dust and do their best to shield their faces, mouths already full, lungs aching.

With slightly more wherewithal in the moment, Inola grabs ahold of Niya, bodily hauling her back through the room and to cleaner, easier breaths.

"What do we do?" Niya says, her voice steady enough, even if her limbs feel shaky and her heartbeat erratic. "What do we do?"

Inola, coughing, leans Niya up against a cave wall. She doesn't answer the question though. Not at first. She probably doesn't know what to say. And neither, of course, does Niya.

It does not take overly long for the air to clear and their predicament to sink in.

When next Niya speaks, she does so with a clearer mind, even if her heart is still clouded. Dazed. Lost.

"We have to find a way out of here."

"Unless we learn how to fly," Inola says, gesturing up to where the natural opening far above their heads resides. Far, far out of reach. "That will be difficult. And there's no other exit or entrance, not unless the ground itself has shifted to break something free. When we were little, daring one another to go farther and farther inside, we always made sure not to get turned around. We had to be able to get back to the mouth—there's no other way out, not accessible without wings or gills." At Niya's piqued expression, Inola dashes her hopes before they can pick up steam: "There is running water, but we'd both have to be the size of crawfish to access it. River's Flow can't help us swim there."

Niya turns watery eyes on the other woman. Her voice does not waver when she speaks. "Another way, then. A new way?"

Both women turn to stare up at the hole some thirty feet above their heads. Even if they could grow wings, it would be a challenge. Or if either of them had gecko's skill for adhering to surfaces, perhaps then they could climb to their freedom. But the ceiling's slope is too sharp, only one of them could make the first successful escape, and there simply isn't time. Time to plan, time to execute, time to save her friend and Inola's sister...

If either of them even want to be saved.

Niya swings her bag off her shoulders.

"Your family knows where we are, but if they come searching for us, we risk discovery by the Suyata." She empties the contents of her pack, laying out anything that could offer the littlest bit of use or lend a spark to their imaginations. "So we have to get out of here, we have to do it on our own—and fast."

Inola kneels down, dropping her own small satchel near Niya's things, emptying out the few items she had thought to pack that morning for their simple outing.

"I'm with you," Inola says. "Let's find a way out of here."

Over the next few hours, Niya and Inola try any number of tricks.

First, they fashion a pyramid of sorts to climb atop, inching their way closer to the opening. But it is too far out of their grasp with not enough stones and other remnants from the camp to come even close.

Next, they try using Inola's Ability: a hastily fashioned cave-moss netting and rope combination tied to one end of Niya's chunkey spear. A finely aimed toss up, up through the hole goes the spear. But despite Inola's Adanadi-imparted Ability to aim true and steady, nothing could change the fact that there isn't anything for the spear to impale or the net to catch on once it breaks through the shaft and reaches the surface. The spear clatters sadly back to the ground after the unsuccessful attempt.

After these failures, the young women head back to the first chamber of the cave. They spend some time assessing the compacted rock blocking their way out. They look at it from every possible angle, press against each visible rock, pebble, and boulder to see if there might be the slightest yielding somewhere in the wreck of rubble.

With half an hour gone on this futile task, Niya backs away from the challenge. Not defeated, she tells herself, merely retreating for a time.

Inola continues to make notes, taking pictures from various angles with her niisi then marking those pictures up with some computer-generated mathematical calculations. Pressure points. Spots for leverage.

When Niya asks about the complicated algorithms that Inola's niisi seems to be chugging through valiantly, Inola only shrugs, her eyes not leaving the rockslide.

"I've always been pretty good with numbers. And my auntie always told me that my Ability is a gift best not squandered, and if I thought I could accomplish anything with it, to imagine what I could accomplish with an understanding of the science behind its precision." She bites her lip, and Niya imagines that she is urging her slightly older tech to hurry up. She stands, removing her own niisi and offering it to Inola—who takes it with a surprised grin, coupling the device quickly to her own to boost its computing power. "The way the rocks have fallen tells a story. We just have to figure out how to read it."

"A story, huh?" Niya asks, trying her best to channel even a fraction of Inola's optimism.

"Yep—the story of how we're going to get out of here."

Inola has picked up Niya's spear and is in the process of marking a crevice into which she is aiming to wedge the spear's sharpened tip. But before she does, Niya lets out a gasp.

Inola swivels about quickly, a look of concern on her face. But when she catches sight of Niya, her feelings immediately shift to surprise, then wonder.

"Niya," she breathes, "your aura!"

Niya, however, already knows that something is happening. She can feel it. Can see it, in her mind's eye.

It isn't quite like she is being imparted some sort of new information, no—it's more like Niya is showing herself something her own mind and body already know.

"It's my Ability," Niya says, her voice laced with awe and understanding. "I can do more with it than just breathe underwater. Inola!" she cries. "I can do so much more!"

"By the Great Spirit," Inola's voice is hushed as she drops to her knees in front of Niya. The spear clatters to the ground at their sides. "Whatever it is you are seeing, I think I can see it too." Niya's eyes snap open at this, seeking out Inola's in the gloom of their forgotten niisi lights. But Inola's eyes are roaming across Niya's face, her temples, across her shoulders. "Your colors, they're...pulsing. Strands of color, of silver and gold, weaving together like fine braids. It's like...like your aura is *alive*, Niya! Auras look different when someone is actively using an Ability, but this...it's almost like I can see you *learning*."

Niya sways a bit where she's seated, her eyes fluttering closed. When she moves to stand, Inola rushes to her feet first to help her the rest of the way.

"River's Flow. I used it to breathe underwater because that's how Owl first showed me how to use it." Inola nods her agreement emphatically. "But what it's really about, how the Ability truly works, is through anatomical and physiological change." Her eyes are alight with excitement. "And now I know how to get us out of here!"

A new plan hatches. Inola enlarges her photographs and calculations then projects them out from her niisi, lifesize against the rubble entombing them. Niya surveys the projections with a keen eye for detail, stepping first here and then there, sharing the inner-workings of her thoughts with Inola as she takes in the challenge before them. As she spins her speculations and hypotheses through the air, Inola takes notes and makes alterations to the calculations, and they move closer and closer to action.

They work to select the perfect spot at which to dig. They'll burrow deep into the fallen rock. Then thrust the spear inward, tunneling and leveraging their way right out and into the sun.

With Niya's new manifestation of her Ability, anything feels possible. Even this.

After what feels like an eternity but has really been less than an hour of deliberation, the young women pick their target on the earthen wall.

Inola readies her stance for action.

Niya's eyes slip shut, and she begins her smudging motions.

Mouth for air and focus.

Mind for strength of will.

Chest for pumping blood.

Legs for firm footing.

Arms for power.

Hands for striking true.

"Whoa," Niya gasps, her skin beginning to prick and pull along her spine, creeping outward from one center point.

Her body begins to change.

Her mouth widens slightly, becomes almost cavernous inside her head, and she can feel her lungs expand to pull more oxygen from the air with each breath. The muscles that run the lengths of her legs grow and firm up, and her feet widen to ground her more fully to the earth. A similar process happens to her arms, and they become almost too heavy for her—before her back muscles strengthen and her shoulders widen to accommodate the new weight.

Finally, the bones in Niya's hands seem to shift and melt and regrow, all in the span of seconds, solidifying into rock-hard conical shapes. Ready to bust and break the rocky obstacle before them, her hands glisten and glint in the light cast upon them from Inola's niisi.

"How long do we have?" Inola asks, nearly breathless.

"I have absolutely no idea," Niya says, her voice echoing up and around and back through the halls of the cave behind them both. "But let's do this!"

Inola immediately gives a shout of exhilaration before getting into position. With supreme concentration, Niya focuses on the spot Inola indicates with the point of the spear. As if they are a well-oiled machine, Niya plants her feet and draws back; she swings her body around and her arm forward, and Inola expertly removes the spear, effectively guiding Niya right into the perfect position.

Her newly formed, sharpened spade of a hand drives deep into the debris. A massive *crunch!* echoes back through the cave behind them.

"Woohoo!" Inola crows, levering the spear into the new gap as Niya removes her hand.

"Again!"

They continue, piles of rock and dirt spilling down around their feet. At one point, Inola slips, nearly falling—worse, Niya's attempt to grab her nearly results in Inola meeting the business end of Niya's transformed hands. But they manage to both get upright again with negligible injury.

"You okay?" Niya asks, her arms sort of awkwardly waving about.

Inola catches her breath, looking deep into Niya's eyes. For a moment, they both sit in that strange feeling of wanting to laugh but not knowing how. If this scene had played out but one day earlier, wouldn't they both be laughing now? Instead of answering, Inola picks up the spear and asks her own question. "Again?"

They make the work quick because they must, but it is no small task. By the time they break through and come face to face with sunlight, the sky is sinking towards the horizon.

They climb out of the cave one after the other. Covered in sweat and breathing hard, they collapse side by side on the grass to catch their breaths.

Niya can feel the increasingly familiar bone-deep exhaustion she is coming to associate with River's Flow, but she also feels different this time. Less like she will faint and sleep for days—perhaps her stamina for the Ability has already increased.

"Well," Inola huffs, pulling herself into an upright position with a groan. "Let's not do this again, eh?"

Eyes closed, Niya remains flat out on her back. She manages a lopsided grin. "Not anytime soon at least."

They share a very tired chuckle and then lapse into silence. And it is in this silence that Niya's mind roars back, reminding her of why they are in this position to begin with.

Tusika.

Niya's eyes dart wildly around, foolishly believing for the tiniest sliver of a moment that Tusika might still be here, that she might have waited outside of the cave just to get a glimpse of Niya surfacing. That, perhaps, she didn't go off with Gishkiy after all. A big mess of confusion, that's all any of this has been.

But of course, this is not true. Tusika is nowhere to be seen, nor Gishkiy, nor Inola's sister or any of the other foolhardy cult members.

Niya releases a long, shuddering sigh. She can feel her body settle, easing into the dirt around her as she lets all that stale air go.

It is in this exhausted state that her body begins to morph back into its regular self. As her body resets, so follows her mind, and then her heart.

Tusika...

With great strength of will, Niya sits upright, then hauls herself to a standing position. There is dirt and sweat mixing together, caking all along her arms. She wipes it off, revealing the edges of her Adanadi mark.

"That communications tower," she starts, her eyes seeking out the western sky. "I need you to get me there."

Inola's face is set, firm. "The comms tower. We should be able to get there before dark. You think Adasi and Nampeyo—?"

Niya shakes her head sadly. She stands, brushing

off the seat of her pants—a futile attempt, as the work they've been doing ensures that it will take a lot more than that to get halfway cleaned up again.

"I can only hope that they can help us with our next lead. I don't want to wager anything on dreams, not tonight."

Her voice sounds hollow, though neither woman comments on it as they head back down the mountainside.

PIDII DOBA HAWA

As soon as they get near enough to the comms tower, Inola fires off a message to her family, letting them know that she and Niya are safe. Since they are close to Inola's village, the message goes through quickly and easily. But the messages Niya needs to both send and receive have much further to go—they will have to connect Niya's niisi directly into the terminal that sits atop the tower. Such an endeavor, however necessary, will make them targets.

They must live on the hope that the Suyata are still distracted. Are pursuing them elsewhere. Won't give them the sort of trouble neither is likely capable of dodging at the moment.

Taking the first steps up the comms tower's face, they begin their climb side by side. The stairs are composed of high and tight triangular steps, nearly circling to the top in a dizzying spiral.

With every step, Niya cannot unsee the image that seems to perpetually play in her mind's eye: Tusika, watching on as Gishkiy seals them inside the cave, callous and unmoving and oddly final.

When they reach the top of the tower, they crouch low, keeping close to the rounded edge of the upper terrace. Now that the sun has set, the slightest light from their niisis might give them away to unfriendly eyes in the dark. They sit and catch their breaths side by side.

In the quiet of the evening, with gentle sounds of the earth moving unseen around them in the encroaching dark, Niya feels a quickening in her chest. A tightening rip of a sob. She knows she should not hold it back, knows that to set it free would be the truest expression of her grief, her mourning. But she cannot give it away—not now, not yet.

But the tears do prick the corners of her eyes. And sobs escape from her, but they are quiet, blending into the sounds of the mountain's life beyond.

Not quiet enough, however, to escape the notice of Inola Cato.

"Niya," Inola says, shifting where she sits the very second she hears the sounds of pent up grief and rage and betrayal storming beneath the surface of Niya's chest. She speaks slowly, the syllables filling her mouth like heavy stones, encapsulating the weight of her emotions and care for the other woman before spilling from her lips. "Niya."

When Inola's strong hand reaches out to touch Niya's cheek, Niya flinches away.

"Please don't," Niya whispers.

"Okay, okay," Inola is quick to reassure her. Niya forces her eyes away from the other woman's hands where she is wringing them uselessly in her lap. "Your niisi, I can—"

"Yes, yeah—of course." The words tumble from Niya as she sniffles hard, taking the tears and everything that comes along with them back down. She undoes the clasp on her niisi with fingers that fumble only slightly, handing it over.

"This won't take long. Hang tight."

The faint sounds of Inola's tinkering distracts Niya momentarily. Then a steady stream of synthetic drum beats emanate from the niisi, now connected to the special network that offers connectivity to Cahokia—all of Niya's incoming messages.

Inola kneels next to her, extending the device in her open palm. Niya doesn't respond, instead staring blankly ahead.

Patient and with a steady tone, Inola says her name. "Niya?"

Unblinking, Niya turns her head ever so slightly to the other woman. "She wasn't always like this," she says, still not quite making direct eye contact. "She wasn't always this, this..."

"What?" Inola prompts.

She wasn't always like this, she'd said, but how to finish the thought?

Obsessive over the gifts of the Adanadi, always in charge, tyrannous, dangerously possessive of those around her?

"Ish," Niya breathes out. She presses her palms into her eyes, presses so hard that white spots of light flash behind her eyelids.

But wasn't Tusika those things and those things exactly?

The way she'd responded to Niya's attention turned towards Inola in the club. How Tusika has always seemed to love the Suwatt family more than her own—but has, perhaps, always respected her own Patak clan more. The despair at not receiving an Ability, despite all these many years of telling Niya that it would change nothing between them...calling herself *nothing, nothing and less* for having not received an Ability, without even considering Niya's news, the unlikely probability that she would have received an Ability after so many generations without.

"I've been so blind," Niya cries. And this time when Inola wraps her up in her strong arms, Niya does not push her away. Couldn't, perhaps, even if she wanted to. "How can my heart be so full for someone so callous, so foolish?"

Her tears stream down her face, and Inola rocks her slowly. The woman's voice comes to her on a quiet hush.

"Your capacity for love does not determine another's worth to receive it. It only means you have a lot of it to give."

Niya's tears fall silently. She focuses on the feel of one of Inola's arms and the way it rests across her shoulders. Tunes everything else out, including the heartache. When the tears start to ebb, Inola recognizes the opening and takes her shot at redirection.

"Let's see what your friends have found for us, yeah?"

Nodding, Niya takes her niisi from Inola, cradling it in her hands.

"First things first," Niya says quietly, her voice scratchy from tears. She scrolls through the check-in messages from her family, sorrowful that she's made them wait this long for any sort of indication as to her whereabouts and safety. "I won't tell them much, just that we're alright."

"Definitely," Inola agrees, one hand clasped on Niya's shoulder offering support.

After the check-in with parents, Niya pulls up the messages from her friends. She and Inola lean close to read. The sides of their faces nearly press together as they read.

The first few messages are clearly Adasi and Nampeyo working out the kinks in their program. They argue somewhat nonsensically at times, but Niya can hardly blame them—she knows her friends well enough to understand that this, too, is but part of their process.

[Adasi] the encryption on the closed Cahokian circuit is tough. we'll get there. stay safe.

[Nampeyo] We are close, hopefully an update for you within the hour.

[Adasi] do you think Tusika's mana will take our evidence into account? we should be able to show the locations of Inola and Tusika, and that could clear her name...

[Nampeyo] Rationality often leaves a person's mind when their blood is involved.

[Adasi] that's why we have rules and jurisdictions in place! just being a member of the Council shouldn't mean that Kaatii gets to sic Suyata on whoever, whenever

[Nampeyo] We are in agreement. We are also sitting right next to one another.

[Adasi] good point...hope you're alright, girls. the bulletins are still up. we'll help clear this up soon enough.

The timestamps shift forward a few hours.

[Adasi] will you want the good news or the bad news first? hmmm.........

[Nampeyo] They will read these messages at approximately the same time when they next have a network connection. Therefore, the order in which we send them is only of marginal importance.

[Adasi] ayyy

[Nampeyo] The good news: we locked onto Tusika's position. We also locked onto yours, Niya+Inola.

[Adasi] yo, the bad news: you're all going in the same direction! that can't be good, can it???

Niya sighs, pressing her knuckles into the backs of her eyelids again. This news has already manifested itself painfully enough in their present. Of course Tusika was heading towards Inola's village—she was looking for Gishkiy. She was looking for an alternative to not receiving an Ability. What they couldn't have known when they set out from Cahokia is that Tusika had been doubly successful: she'd found Gishkiy, and in doing so, potentially found the answer she was looking for.

The messages continue.

[Nampeyo] More good news: we could share this information with the Council to show that Tusika left the city of her own accord.

[Adasi] more bad news: all three of you drop off the face of the earth at approximately the same location, separated by only a few hours. so there may still be some amount of reasonable suspicion that Inola...i don't even know, coerced or tricked Tusika into some off-colored shit with devious consequences?

[Nampeyo] And do any of us trust Councilwoman Patak not to turn even the least likely of possibilities into the most likely of occurrences in her mind and the minds of others?

[Adasi] we'll keep fighting… researching

[Nampeyo] Hope we hear from you soon

And then there is a trickle of messages over the following days.

[Nampeyo] Your locations are still turned off, I hope?

[Adasi] things aren't getting quieter here

[Adasi] it's been two days :(

[Adasi] three days what in the Creator's name… praying for you girls

He sends through a little doodle immediately following his message: a coyote howling up at a full moon.

[Nampeyo] Looking forward to an update soon. I am effectively distracting Adasi with the design of a new PMV—imagine if a skimmer met a sunwing. We're printing the parts one by one from our home gats. The wuyis are complicated. Might have a prototype in three days' time or so.

Another day or two in the timestamps, and then—

[Adasi] you said this Gishkiy guy was looking for a way to circumvent the Adanadi process, right? I heard something today from my uncle that sounded almost like it could've been what Gishkiy is getting at, ceremony-wise—if you were looking at the world through a distorted lens or something… I'll keep digging

[Nampeyo] We have your last known coordinates and are considering heading your way soo. It may only be a prototype, but the PMV is coming along nicely.

[Adasi] we're naming Peyo's new ride 'Minaati'—what do you think?! because it demands 'respect', get it? XD

Niya laughs in spite of herself as she finishes reading the messages from her friends. She hasn't learned much of anything new, besides the fact that Adasi might have a lead on a ceremony that Gishkiy is intending to use, to pervert for his own purposes. And that her friends have managed to build nearly an entirely new PMV—personal mobility vehicle—in the course of less than a week.

"Your friends sound optimistic," Inola says. "You better let them know you're alright."

"And you," Niya says, even as she's typing out a message, eyes on her holographic screen. "They'll want to know about you, too."

Niya sends off a quick series of hastily-typed messages. Almost instantly, she is getting responses that interrupt her train of thought. She can't help but smile at the familiar connection to her friends.

[Adasi] you did WHAAAAT through an underground tunnel?!

[Nampeyo] Overjoyed to hear that you are alright! And Inola too. These are good tidings!!

[Niya] We need your help: tell me about this ceremony.

And so they do. Over the next hour or so, Niya's

friends send files along with everything they've surmised from their research.

"This is an amazing start," Niya says, flicking through the drawings and highlighted readings.

Many ceremonies are sacred, not put down on paper—or, if recorded, key elements may be kept out of the documentation in order to preserve the sacred rituals of a tribe. Passed down from generation to generation, the ceremonies that survived the Awis are particularly venerated, having seen the people of Makasing through so much. Even these few, quick glances make it clear to Niya that there are pieces missing here, that this is an old ceremony. And it may not be the only ceremony of its kind, either.

[Niya] I have a thought

[Adasi] look out!!

[Niya] It means more work for the both of you. Possibly a lot more work.

[Nampeyo] What are you thinking, Niya?

[Niya] It might raise suspicions on the Council... Mama Patak might not take kindly to you digging into what obviously has to do with the plight of her supposed child's kidnapper.

[Adasi] who do you know who's more discreet than ME?!

[Niya] Okay, here's what I'm thinking...

Niya lays out her thoughts. That if they found one ceremony whose origins stem back to the Awis, if they found a single ritual whose outcome might offer something that once-upon-a-time resembled the Adanadi

Abilities of today, there could be more. From different lands, nations, tribes, bands. And if there is a common root to the ceremonies—a thematic ingredient, recipe, weather pattern, *anything*—then they might be able to use that information to pinpoint Gishkiy, Tusika, Kas, and the others.

It might be their only chance at circumventing Tusika's headlong rush into danger. Their only hope.

[Nampeyo] We'll find everything we can.

[Adasi] leave it to us, little sister. when will we hear from you again?

Niya turns her head to Inola, and the woman meets her gaze. They've been reading the messages together the entire time.

"We could get back this time tomorrow," Inola says with confidence. "We'll have to be more cautious of Suyata, in case they're tracking incoming messages to this tower."

"You think that's possible?" Niya asks, looking around them in the now-dark with great suspicion and growing worry.

Inola shrugs one shoulder. "I do not think it impossible. Let them know this: if they do not hear from you in exactly one day, then we will return half a day later than that, to try and throw off our tails if needed."

"Perfect," Niya says, already typing out the response, coded in language and parsed phrases that only her friends will be able to interpret as the meeting times she intends.

Niya feels tearful as they sign off and disconnect

her niisi. But it is a remarkably different feeling from when they'd first scaled the tower. Instead of despair and regret, she feels a faint gleam of hopefulness. And a strong sense of homesickness, too.

Sick for the presence of her friends. The bustling streets of Cahokia. The childhood that seems already to be so far away and out of reach. That time not so long ago when Abilities could not be stolen, manipulated, tarnished, or impure.

She said there was no stealing of Abilities by the Pataks, Niya thinks in her head.

Brow furrowed, Niya thinks back to the tense conversation in the mouth of the cave, before Gishkiy buried them.

No, she pauses, recollecting Tusika's response to her direct questioning, *no, she didn't...*

It hadn't been a denial, had it? But neither had it been an admission. Niya hopes she has a chance to save Tusika, to clear the air between them. If she doesn't have that chance, how will she face herself, her friends, or especially the Pataks again? What will the Suwatts do if the Pataks try and force them into exile—like Gishkiy's family before them?

As they walk through dusk to Inola's village, Niya's mind wanders, taking her to all of the places in her mind where the memories of her young life spent with Tusika reside. And she realizes that Inola, in her wisdom and having known Niya only a short relative while, was absolutely right: she *does* have a lot of love to give.

And maybe her love for Tusika is enough to pull the young woman back from the brink.

With this hope, however delusional it may be, Niya's feet carry her onward and into the unknown.

PIDI DOBA ZAPTAAN

When they get to the village, they perform the same dance from before: observe the night watchmen, pick their path carefully, tread lightly. The watchmen are slightly more attentive this time around, so Inola utilizes her Ability to strike true a large, overturned water basin across the square—the dull thud of a magsling bolt on a low setting gives a sound like the thing being kicked. The watchmen lope off in its direction, and Niya and Inola evade them once more.

"Nice shot," Niya says, almost automatically, her voice weak.

"If you think that's impressive, you should see me shoot a walnut off my cousin's fingertip from a hundred paces out. Auntie *loves* when I do that."

As they cross the threshold of the Cato home, Niya sways on her feet.

"Whoa," Inola says, reaching out to steady her. "Let's get you to bed. You've been through a lot today."

Niya isn't sure how Inola means this. Physically? Her body is spent from tunneling them out of the cave with her Ability. Mentally? Her mind is racing, hoping for answers, for clarity, for some hint as to what the right thing is or should be. Emotionally? Wrecked. Still absolutely, miserably wrecked.

Changed and cleaned up and ready for what should be the best night's sleep of either of their lives, Inola moves toward her room, Niya's tagging along with her an understood and unspoken fact.

With the pieces of her broken heart still jangling around inside her chest, Niya realizes that the thought of sleeping near someone who isn't Tusika...it's too much. She will sleep alone or not at all—perhaps sleep will not come even in the quiet of the night with nothing but her own haunted thoughts for company.

As suddenly as the thought enters her mind, Niya bails off, dropping down on the sitting room cushions. At this motion, Inola stops, turning back to look at Niya inquisitively.

Without waiting for the inevitable question, Niya heads the other woman off at the pass.

"I am beyond tired. I'll sleep here tonight."

Inola's brows scrunch down in obvious worry. "Are you sure—"

"Yes," Niya rushes, overly forceful. "And I'll be able to help your family with breakfast first thing instead of sleeping through it, like I did today. Give me a stern poke if I'm not up, yeah?"

Niya affects a smile that she hopes will waylay any further questions from Inola. And she can see it in Inola's eyes, can't she? That the woman sees as much, can tell exactly what Niya is doing, can tell why she is doing it. And instead of calling her out, she lets Niya get away with it.

It does not upset Niya. Instead, it makes her wonder at the friendship they've been able to cultivate in such a short period of time.

All Inola says before turning and treading silently down the hall is the softest uttered *good night* that

Niya has ever heard in her life. She cannot help but wonder how Inola feels about Tusika's path—if she feels any responsibility for bringing the possibility of Gishkiy's way into the Patak household, for putting the idea into Tusika's orbit.

Niya drops her head back onto the couch, her limbs going limp at her sides. She does not blame Inola; she cannot blame her, or anyone else but Tusika. But Niya blames herself, too, for being so wrecked by this.

"Tomorrow is a new day," she mutters to herself. "The girl you love is lost. You have to help her find her way again. And if you can't at least do that, then you've got to keep her alive—and the rest of Gishkiy's followers, too. This isn't over." Niya sighs heavily, rolling over on the cushions, curling into herself. "It can't be."

Niya presses her fingertips against the nearby touchpad that controls the lightstrip above her. They were already dimmed low, awaiting their return, but Niya now shuts them off entirely. The only light left, the fleeting glimpses of starlight through the smoke window in the roof, clouds passing by on quiet night breezes.

As the inevitable exhaustion of the day's events takes over Niya's body and mind, she has enough energy left to shed a few salty tears. But just a few—because tomorrow is a new day, and she will face it. Headstrong and resilient; broken yet undeterred.

Owl does not visit her dreams. But Niya does not feel alone as sleep takes her. Instead, she feels looked after, protected. And her sleep is easy, even if her mind's last thoughts are frantic and full of worry.

Niya wakes up to the smell of crisping meat and fresh cornbread. She is barely able to suppress a moan as she pulls herself up into a sitting position.

"Oh wow," she says, blinking blearily around and to the kitchen area of the Cato home. "Whatever you're making for breakfast smells *amazing*."

Inola's auntie Mistii, gives a hearty laugh before she replies, "This is lunch, girlie—and a late one at that."

Jaw dropping in surprise—and shame at having inadvertently avoided helping with breakfast two days in a row—Niya jumps to her feet. She smooths a hand down the front of the clean outfit Inola had provided the night before, doing her best to press away the generally rumpled look she must be exuding.

"That can't be," Niya says, cutting her eyes across to where Inola is standing, cleaning dishes and pointedly not looking at her. "I told *someone*—" she says in a mockingly sharp tone, "—to make sure I was up to help, didn't I?"

Inola teases back, and it causes Niya's heart to feel lighter and heavier at once. She wonders if her hot and cold emotions are difficult for the other woman to make sense of.

"You were sleeping so peacefully, none of us could bring ourselves to wake you. And the kiddos very much enjoyed putting a feather above your mouth, so they could see how high your snores would push it through the air!"

Niya's gasp is not an exaggeration, and she presses her fingertips to her chest.

"They didn't," she says, voice low.

"They most certainly did," Inola responds with a chuckle.

The youngest of Mistii's children peeks around the doorway that leads to the front entrance of the home.

"You're awake!" she shouts.

Niya's hands go to her hips, her own stout impersonation of aunties everywhere. "You weren't messing with feathers near me as I slept, were you?"

"Ahh!"

The girl screeches and ducks back out of sight. Everyone still inside is laughing, even as Niya lifts her hands to the heavens in playful exasperation.

Another one of Mistii's kids comes careening around the corner from outside, trailing specks of mud all along the floor as they skid into one wall, righting themselves before redirecting right down the hallway and out of sight.

"A-yo!" Mistii shouts, turning away from the hearth and wheeling towards her kids. "Clean feet, clean feet!"

Not more than five seconds later, the kid comes running back down the hallway, dive bombing for the open doorway before their mana can scoop them up and force them to clean.

"How high did my snores take the feather, at least?!" Niya shouts at the kid's back as they disappear.

"Pah!" Mistii scoffs, having just missed her child's scruff.

Like a flash, the kid peeks their head back around the

corner, mischievous grin on their face. "I balanced one a full arm's length above your mouth!"

"Oh, *you*—" Mistii makes as if to dart towards the doorway again, but the kid has disappeared, likely until nightfall this time. She looks exhausted as she moves to grab cleaning items to deal with the children's mess.

Seeing the weariness carried heavily on the woman's frame, Niya rushes forward, taking the supplies gently from Mistii's hands.

"Please, let me."

As she kneels to start wiping away the muddy prints, Mistii's shoulders curve downward and she rests her chin in one palm. Her eyes are directed towards Niya, but it's clear that she isn't really watching her actions. When she speaks, it's obvious enough that her thoughts are with her other niece, Kas. Inola must've informed her family about what they had found yesterday at the cave: remnants of Gishkiy's cult, and a super-powered Gishkiy, too.

"Whatever it is he thinks he's discovered…whatever he's done to himself… *winds*. I just don't know if my sister will be able to bear it, if Kas tries and, and…" Mistii shakes her head, eyes still cast downward.

It couldn't possibly make the other woman feel better, to know that Niya's best friend would apparently be the next person to participate in Gishkiy's experimentation, not Kas. Because it won't matter if they fail or if they succeed—the fact that Gishkiy had come away armed with a power that he hadn't had before would almost guarantee that others would try and try and try again. The only way to save Tusika and Kas is to get them away from the promise of Gishkiy's power—and Niya's emotional wounds are still too fresh for her to truly know if Tusika is capable of being pulled away from something so powerful as this. Maybe they'll have more luck with Kas—if they can find her in time.

Niya rests a hand atop Mistii's knee. "We'll keep trying. Yesterday was... a setback. But we have more information now than we had before. That's something."

Mistii nods her head slowly but does not meet Niya's eyes. Niya suspects that her words have been heard but not heeded. The auntie rolls out of the wide living space and down a hallway without saying another word.

After she finishes cleaning up, Niya takes her place at Inola's side, helping to finish with the cooking. Inola speaks softly to her, even though they are now alone.

"My family... well, things haven't been easy for a long time. And with Kas leaving, one less mouth to feed has felt more like a burden than a boon. Your dreams gave us all hope. I gave them hope, coming back with someone, *anyone,* who believed me and might help. I'm still hopeful that your friends will help us, that Owl will guide, that maybe even Fox will come to me with some clever clue. But until Kas is back home and Gishkiy is stopped, I'm not sure anything will feel okay."

Nodding her head, Niya gives a hum of understanding. "Today is a new day." She moves closer, bumping their hips. "I do wish you had awoken me though. I want to be helpful, not just a lazybones, as my own mana might call me if she saw me sleeping the day away."

Inola cracks a small smile. "Your Ability took a lot

out of you yesterday. It was important that you rest."

Shaking her head slightly, Niya says, "You used your Ability as well, and something tells me that you didn't sleep most of the day away."

Inola makes a sound of mock outrage. "I used my Ability for all of half a minute yesterday, total. You used yours for a much longer period of time, and you changed your physiology to do so! It was no three-day sleep on your part this time, that's for sure—but an uninterrupted half day of sleep was necessary." She reaches out a hand to rest it atop Niya's. "Trust me, yeah?"

As Niya's eyes rest on their held hands, she realizes something that feels important: some people are instantly knowable, while others are known to a person their whole lives long and can still catch one another entirely, shockingly off-guard.

Niya hates that Inola is one and Tusika the other. Hates that Tusika was able to catch Niya back on her heels, despite the signs their whole childhood that this is, perhaps, the way Tusika would always have behaved in the event that their destinies misaligned.

All of this turmoil and angst and danger, and for what? Power and privilege, even if it means Tusika loses her best friend.

How foolish of my heart, Niya thinks, *to love someone like Tusika.*

But that's the problem, and Niya knows it: she loves Tusika for *everything* that she is, even when parts of her hurt.

"Yes," Niya says, her voice catching. "I'm working on that."

PIDI DOBA SAKPI

Niya makes her way alone to the communications tower. Inola stays behind, helping her daadoo with a project. Leaving the Cato household on her own is what Niya needs. Some space to breathe and think is what she needs, and it's easier for her to do that alone. A chance for perspective and to clear her head; to think less about the past or the future, more about the present.

Tusika is on the precipice of a decision that could be disastrous, and she is poised to leap. While Niya knows the truth of her friend's situation, she also knows this: that Tusika could fall, or she could soar. And perhaps she was the first first-born in eight generations not to receive an Ability from the Adanadi, but Tusika Patak remains one of the fiercest, strongest people Niya knows. She is lost in a way, but those who are lost can also be found. And if anyone were to take the leap as proposed by Gishkiy and fly, wouldn't it be Tusika?

Niya shakes her head as she begins the climb up the face of the tower.

If that were to happen, Niya thinks, *it would be the beginning of Gishkiy's rise to power.*

Or Tusika's.

Niya bites her lip as she continues to scale the tight spiral staircase. Would Tusika really allow anyone to be more powerful than her? Niya isn't sure, and the thought makes her stomach churn.

She cannot entertain the possibility of failure and what that would mean for her friend. But neither can she think of what a success might mean for Makasing. The taking of the Adanadi is closely controlled, safe and effective. But Gishkiy's experiments...replicable success could blind many to the risks.

Niya needs to know more about the process—the experiment or ceremony, ritual or rite; whatever it is, she needs to know how it is done. How dire is the situation? And how afraid should she be for her friend's life? For the life of Inola's sister? Knowledge is power, and Niya is hungry for a taste of it at the moment.

As soon as she plugs her niisi into the comms hub at the top of the tower, the potential answer is all too clear.

[Adasi] she won't believe this, cuz

[Nampeyo] Niya was the one to suggest looking for ceremonies with a common denominator component. I suspect she believed it would be possible.

[Adasi] it's cool how messaging each other even though we're in the same room is becoming, like, our thing

[Nampeyo] Is it?

[Adasi] ANYWAYS, what i meant is that she won't believe we've made a connection so soon!

[Nampeyo] Ahh—yes, I expect she will be pleasantly surprised by the expediency of our potential success.

[Adasi] "potential success"—i like your optimism, peyo

There is some more back and forth, which Niya scrolls through hastily, a cautious, nervous smile pulling at her mouth. When she gets to the end of the messages, she types out her response.

[Niya] I love you both! You found something? Please, tell me what you can! I shouldn't stay here long.

[Nampeyo] If I send through a video, can you watch it safely? And privately?

Niya glances around in the dark, purposefully dimming the display of her niisi as she does so. The late evening sky is moving towards night, and the earth is quiet around her.

[Niya] I'm safe. And alone. Ready when you are.

The video takes a minute or two to sync over to her device. When the moving images begin to project in a holographic display about her niisi, Niya narrows her eyes and observes closely. The video is about the size of both of Niya's palms stacked one atop the other. It is clear that her friends pieced together what they could—the first video is a high-definition recording of a lecture being given in an outdoor amphitheater style classroom, the second video is a digital re-enactment, and the third video is low resolution live footage.

[Adasi] voice chat okay, niya?

Niya could shake herself for not thinking of it sooner. She flits through her niisi's digital screens, leaving the video footage paused in front of her while pulling up a voice chat with Adasi and Nampeyo. Before the connection goes through, Niya is sure to put the volume as low as she can possibly get while still able to hear their voices.

The first thing Nampeyo says tells Niya that her overly cautious volume regulation was smart but unnecessary.

"Volume check?" comes their voice softly over the connection.

"Good to go. I'm going to keep my voice at a whisper. Can you hear me?"

"We can hear you, little sister," Adasi responds. "Missed you."

Furiously blinking back tears, Niya smiles so widely that she feels her skin pulling at the corners of her eyes. "Missed you, too." Her voice is thick, and she is thankful when they take back over the thread of the conversation.

"Drag your slider to the beginning of the merged clips," Nampeyo says, "We will narrate for you."

As the compilation plays, Nampeyo and Adasi take turns explaining the three clips that Niya watches.

The first video is a middle-aged scholar sharing the teachings of an ancient band of her tribe. Though no longer in existence as they were hundreds of years ago—long enough ago to predate the Awis—remnants of this particular ceremony have survived. The scholar shares what is known about the ceremony, which is shockingly little, beyond the fact that it must occur when the moon is full, and that the person most central to the ritual's heart must be on the last day of a seven-day fast. She also details the purpose of the ceremony—to bestow preternatural speed and stamina upon the one who receives the focus of the ritual's energy. A sort of Adanadi hack before such a thing existed.

The second video, the re-enactment, is narrated by what sounds to be an elder woman. Her syllables are clipped, sharp, and Niya listens intently as Nampeyo gives supplementary information atop her narration. The digital rendering beneath the elder's words shows the mechanics of another ritual—the setup of the stones, the medicines for the fire, the timing within the lunar cycle, the precise words to speak and how to speak them. It is more detailed than the scholar's lecture, but the elder acknowledges from the beginning that some bits are conjecture. Best-made hypotheses. Guesses in the dark, however illuminated they can be. And this ritual, too, allows the person at its heart to wield a power of camouflage—near invisibility, of a sort—and for a time beyond the ritual's bounds. A semi-permanent change. Miraculous, if successful.

The third video is the hardest to discern. It looks quite old and poorly maintained—perhaps back to the earliest time of video capture in Makasing, and stored in less than ideal conditions before being digitized in the archives. There is no sound. The only narration for this clip is Adasi's low, intent voice, laying carefully atop the actions of the fuzzy figures in the air in front of Niya's face. This one is a performance of a sacred formula, one whose ingredients and directions have been largely lost to time. But Adasi tells the story of the video, and the intent—to imbue the conductor with super-human, parapsychic abilities. Telepathy. Psychokinesis. Mind control.

"And this," Adasi whispers now, his voice hushed and intense. "Is where things get *really* interesting…"

Niya leans in close over the clip, squinting as the

figure completes their motions, speaks their words, and then—*BOOM!*

She does not hear the blast, but she can see its repercussions. Can see the video shake in its frame, can practically feel the tremble of the earth as the person is blown backward. The video device is knocked from whatever surface or support it had been perched upon, and it finally stills, lens skyward.

The video stops, the compilation coming to an end. And in the square frame of the captured image, silhouetted in a night sky some generations before, Niya can see one thing lit up, clear as day in the night around her and unobscured by grainy footage and ill-kept film: a bright, shining moon, full as she can be.

"A full moon," Niya whispers.

Nampeyo and Adasi respond simultaneously: "Yep—a full moon."

"If you'll allow me," Nampeyo goes on, "I can explain the significance of what we have found."

"Please, go on."

Niya is already scrolling back through the video reel, the image of the full moon highlighted in the fallen frame stuck in her mind's eye no matter how far away the clip becomes.

"The scholar details the first ceremony well, and you heard the bit about the moon's phase. The second clip references a ritual that we were able to find in the archives of the city. The only similarity to the first video—other than receiving supernatural abilities?" Nampeyo sets up.

"A full, *ish*, moon," Adasi hisses emphatically.

Niya can feel her skin thrumming.

"And the last clip, the failed execution of a sacred formula…"

As Nampeyo's voice trails off, Adasi steps in. "Besides the obvious danger of this thing," he says, "it clearly shows the sky. We can't find a written record of it. But if that thing isn't full, then I don't know what it is."

Niya feels absolutely frozen in place. Vibrating from head to toe.

"Are you saying…"

She swallows hard, her mouth suddenly dry as a river bottom in a drought.

"Niya," Nampeyo's voice is soft.

Then they are speaking in tandem, directing Niya to do the thing that she has felt too frozen as of yet to do on her own.

"*Look up.*"

When she does, she cannot stop the audible gasp that escapes her.

For the moon above her is full as it can be.

PIDI DOBA PITSIKA

"Are we too late?"

She knows that the moon sits at its most full for at least two nights, sometimes three. They don't even know where to find the cult, and the shape of the moon tells Niya that their time is more limited than ever. Could the ritual be happening as soon as tonight? And where? When? *How?*

With Tusika's ominous proclamation from the day before...

At the thought, Niya's stomach drops sickeningly.

How close are they to losing Tusika? And if they lose her, will it be forever? If it isn't forever, what will the world look like on the other side of things?

Niya's throat thickens with a different emotion now. The tears sting, aching as they are drawn from her. The very real possibility that she might miss her chance to stop Tusika and Gishkiy causes her heart to plunge into the icy waters of dread.

"This is the first night, and it will remain full tomorrow as well."

"Niya, you've got to find her. We have some other data about these rituals, it's possible that we might be able to pinpoint a small number of locations for you to check. There seems to be a theme of oak trees, of a clearing at a low point in the land—line of sight to the moon herself seems to be important."

"Running water," Nampeyo pipes up over Adasi's descriptions.

"Yes, running water nearby," Adasi continues. "Use of a large stone seems common, one with a concave surface? We aren't sure, but we could use what little we know to find some spots for you to check."

Blinking hard, Niya solidifies her resolve. Mouth set in a firm line, jaw tight, eyes sharp, Niya asks, "How long until you have the locations?"

Silence for only a beat, then Adasi's voice. "We'll work through the night. Come back first thing in the morning."

Niya nods, even though she realizes belatedly that her friends cannot see her. Then she feels the blood drain from her face at the realization that this, the first night of the full moon, might be wasted entirely. "Okay," she says quietly. "Okay. With first light. And in the meantime, maybe Inola knows of such a place."

"Be careful, Niya. You and Inola both. Once a ceremony like this starts..." Adasi makes a tutting, anxious sound that reminds Niya of her grandparents. "It shouldn't be interrupted. I've heard things...about powerful rituals getting cut off. Not surviving is sometimes the preferred outcome. For better or worse, it can't start. Or...."

"It can't stop," Niya whispers.

"Niya, my friend," comes Nampeyo's voice now. "Whatever plans Gishkiy has, whatever Tusika's part in them, they cannot end well. These three ceremonies share the full moon, but they share other characteristics besides: a narrow margin for error, a low likelihood of success, difficulty in replication. The odds of someone living through whatever Gishkiy has concocted, let alone manifesting an Ability on the other side...?"

"Miniscule," Adasi pipes up, his tone still somber. "And if Gishkiy succeeded, then the stars literally had to have aligned for him. It's all so volatile—unless he has found some ceremony anew or found a way to stabilize all of the variables, which no one before has managed to do, then maybe he used up all the luck! And the little we've found shows a history of death associated with this type of thing. Sometimes the results of rituals like this can't be undone or given back."

A shuddering sigh, and Niya says, "I know, I know. We have to save her. We have to stop her. Tusika and Gishkiy."

"In the morning," Nampeyo says. "Come back here, and we will have location data to download to your niisi. Alright?"

Another invisible nod, a softly croaked acknowledgement, and the friends begin to say their farewells.

Before the connection ends between them, Niya feels a prickling at the back of her neck. Never one to be snuck up on, she ducks low and spins around. Her eyes search futilely the length of the tower's upper terrace.

"Niya?"

She immediately shushes the questioning voice of one of her friends. She grabs her niisi from its now dangling position beneath the comms port, sightlessly performing a familiar flicking gesture. The terrace is flooded with a piercing light from the device. And Niya would worry about the lack of subtlety if her senses weren't still on high alert.

"I thought..."

With narrowed eyes and a feeling of disbelief, Niya begins to turn back to the portal.

Which is the precise moment when the slightest shimmer of the night air catches her eye, a strange glint from the light of her niisi.

"What the—"

From nothing, the flat side of a war club materializes. Mid-swing, full-tilt, it strikes the side of Niya's head.

All goes dark.

The darkness lasts only a moment in which Niya ends up down on her knees against the hard ledge of the terrace. Though not incapacitated or knocked unconscious, her head still spins.

"Niya—are you alright?!"

She can hear the voices of her friends, calling out to her. But their words swim to her ears on a wobbly current of muffled misunderstanding.

"I..." Niya mumbles, shaking her head. She reaches up to touch her temple. Her fingers move up into her scalp. She hisses at the sensation. Her fingertips come away wet, but she can't see the color in the dark. "What...?"

"Niya!" comes another far away cry. Adasi and Nampeyo, concerned, worrying for an update.

Shuffling about on her knees, Niya sort of collapses down onto her backside, hands lamely managing to keep her from rocking backwards and further injuring her rattled skull.

Looking up, Niya identifies the shimmer again through her sluggishly blinking eyes. She gazes on as it slowly fades away. Like a cracked egg running down the surface, revealing more and more as it goes. The shimmer dissipates, and out from behind it emerges the figure of a man: skin painted in bright, glowing colors; long hair in twin braids down to his waist; a metallic shimmer to his clothes, armor-like; and that war club, poised as if to strike again, if needed.

One of the Suyata who chased them from Cahokia is standing before her now. Niya remembers the Suyata who jumped off the cliff after them was a Haudenosaunee woman with a distinct mohawk. This man is one of her group. All potentially dangerous, armed as they are with such misunderstanding.

"You've been quite the slippery little eel, haven't you?" His voice pitches up and down with his words, craggy and harsh. Niya shivers. "But there's no more running. Too much time has been wasted already. It's not you we want so much as your friend—tell me where she is, and we can end this."

Niya shakes her head in avoidance; the action causes a shooting pain through her skull. She scoots backward, further from the comms port and the frantic voices of her friends. Out of the light from her niisi.

"I don't have time for this. You must tell me where she's hiding."

"I can't...I don't..."

Fighting for words is hard enough with the way her ears are ringing and the splitting agony in her head. But she can't give Inola away, not when they're so close to finding Tusika, finding Kas, rescuing them both from Gishkiy's manipulations and dangerous ploys. Rescuing them from themselves.

"You've got exactly one chance to give her up," the Suyata says, lifting his arm up, wielding the club back above his head. "And then I start coercing you. 'Whatever means necessary', that's the ticket Patak gave us. And I will do what it takes to gain that favor."

It feels futile to lift an arm, to try and block the man's blow that has not yet fallen. But the fog in her brain says to *try, try*—anything is better than nothing.

Before she can do anything—before the Suyata can bring his club crashing down to make good on his threats—he lets out a scream that rends the night air.

Lowering her arm, Niya blinks dumbly at the man, unsure at first as to what it is that she is seeing.

His war club has clattered to the terrace with a heavy series of bounces, skittering right to the edge. And when Niya lays eyes on his outstretched hand, she can see that a magsling bolt is protruding from his wrist. It has pierced all the way through, pinning him to the comms tower wall.

Niya rolls to the edge of the terrace, looking down through the slotted railing. On the east side of the clearing, she sees a light flick on briefly before being doused out just as fast: Inola is there, magsling extended, gaze steady. From her position, now back in the anonymity of the dark, Inola yells up to Niya from the ground.

"Run!"

And Niya does, as best she can.

She clambers up to her feet, taking only a moment to kick the Suyata's club over the edge of the tower, putting enough force behind it that it sails off into the trees somewhere, the opposite direction from the village. Her vision coming back into focus, Niya manages not to stumble as she unthinkingly grabs at her niisi, disconnecting it with a sharp jerk, before taking off down the stairway.

Inola meets her on the final few steps, catching Niya in her strong arms. Niya feels heavy, so heavy—and Inola's embrace feels comfortable and easy, easy enough to stop here for a good long while. But there is no time to stop.

"We'll get this bleeding stopped," Inola says, brushing hair back from the sides of Niya's face. "And tamp down the swelling, too." She reaches into a pouch at her side; she pulls out a small wooden jar and flips open the lid. Dipping her fingers into the aromatic, creamy substance, she applies a generous amount to Niya's head where the war club had made contact. "Can you run?"

Niya looks at Inola, sees past the worry and the fright and the uncertainty. And she sees—

"Fireflies," she mumbles.

Inola's eyebrow crooks comically. "Eh?"

"In your eyes. Fireflies." Niya grins and then blinks overly long, her head still woozy at best and nauseatingly painful at worst.

"Niya Suwatt. I think you might be concussed." Inola

lifts her head, looking up to the top of the tower. Shifts her gaze to pierce the woods around them. Back to Niya, who blinks again, breath coming in exerted gasps from her flight down the tower. "Come—and stay close to me."

PIDI DOBA NISHAAWI

Any element of surprise is long forgotten as the women burst into the village.

"A-yo!" an older man calls from across the way. "Is that young Inola Cato, there?"

Inola throws her arm up in his direction, as if acknowledging and waving him off at once.

"Who's that?" Niya asks.

"No one important, but now everyone is going to know I'm back," Inola grumbles. "We've gone so long without being detected, and now this."

"I don't know a lot," Niya says with a shrug, "but I'm pretty sure the Suyata know already. So."

Inola groans, whether at Niya's obvious observation or the situation itself, it matters little. "Time is short, and this is just another... another... distraction!"

Niya's head grows clearer with every passing step. But this statement has her pulling back, looking at Inola straight on. "Are you saying your impending capture by the elite Cahokian guards is a distraction?"

"Well," Inola says, and nothing more.

With a laugh, Niya goes on. "We'll keep you out of their grasp." She extracts herself from Inola's helpful hold, rolling her neck and massaging at her temples. "But you're not wrong about time being short." At Inola's pointed eyebrow rise in response, she adds, "Adasi and Nampeyo found a lead. But Gishkiy's ceremony—it could be happening as soon as tonight."

"Best to get home—no sense in hiding that that's where we're headed. We can get you cleaned up, figure out next moves."

"Yes," Niya agrees, her mind cruising along a bit smoother than it had even a minute or two before. Inola's salve is working wonders. "That sounds agreeable."

They are propelled towards the Cato home with a renewed sense of urgency. They've mostly snuck inside under the cover of darkness or out through this or that rigged means of escape since arriving. So when they burst in through the front door, they should not be caught off-guard by the surprised scream of her auntie Mistii or the defensive posture and cry of her mana, Nakola—but they are.

Inola skids to a stop with her arms upraised, and Niya winces a bit at the sharp sounds, her head still not fully assuaged.

"What in the whole of Makasing is going on here, girlie? The village alarm was raised, your nieces and nephews were roused just as they were nearly asleep. Is this because of you two?" Nakola tuts her disapproval.

"It must be," Inola says truthfully, for they have not had half a blink even to stop and wonder at the alarm. "Niya was attacked atop the communications tower." She pulls Niya gently forward, at which point her mana gasps dramatically before fussing over Niya's wound and guiding her none too gently down into a chair near the hearth. "There was only one Suyata there that I saw, and I can't count for their actions after I shot them—"

"After you what?!" Nakola hisses through clenched

teeth. "What did you just say, child of mine?"

"—through the arm! I only shot them through the arm!"

"*Only*," Nakola huffs, already distracting herself from her daughter's exploits by whipping up a more substantial poultice to smear across Niya's head wound. "Shot them but *only* through the arm. So glad to hear it." Beneath her mutterings, the woman's touch is firm yet gentle. She cleans away the drying blood, somehow causing very little discomfort in the process. "I see you used a little something on this already, eh? Hmmph..." It is clear that she is trying not to be too pleased with her daughter's actions. Niya can already feel a further easing of pain from the broken skin that had initially stung beneath Nakola's probing fingertips.

Her head, continuing to clear, manages to catch her up not only to what Inola is saying but to what Inola did, back at the comms tower.

"Whoa, Inola—you shot a guy."

"You'd think she wasn't there herself," Mistii mutters, peeking out through a low peephole in the front door.

"Ohhh-kay," Inola drawls, throwing her hands up in surrender. "So I 'shot a guy', but I used my Ability—I didn't hit anything vital. And I needed you to escape! You should have seen his aura. It was *not* friendly."

Nakola surveys her work with a frown that is somehow both satisfied and disapproving. "Winds and water, I think you'll be alright after all. What do you think, eh?"

"Wado. I need my wits about me for what comes

next."

"And what is that?" Nakola asks, standing to clean up the mess. She keeps her eyes averted, as if to give the young women any extra attention would be to acknowledge a possibility that she can't hope too strongly for, in case it all falls short again.

"My friends may have a lead for us. They were going to find out more before morning, but I doubt we can get back to the tower again..."

"The Suyata know you're in the village. With Niya's injury, coming here makes sense, but they'll be unlikely to leave the tower fully unattended. More could be coming from Cahokia even as we speak, what with one among their party injured and the Council's warrants..."

"I'd say we need to hide," Inola says, crossing her arms and pressing the side of her finger to her lips, "but apparently we may not have time for that."

She darts her eyes to Niya, and all eyes follow. Nodding solemnly, Niya repeats what she'd said on their way into the village: that the ceremony could be happening soon. It could be happening tonight.

"There's no more hiding." Niya stands, gratefully squeezing Nakola's proffered hand once before letting it drop. "We have to stop Gishkiy. And this might be our only chance."

Inola begins to pace, her moccasins still on her feet, forgotten, treading softly on the floor. "Since they abandoned the cave, they could be anywhere in these hills. How will we find them?" She stops long enough to lock eyes with Niya. "Your friends narrowed it down to tonight—how?"

Niya recounts everything she can remember from the video compilation that Adasi and Nampeyo had spliced together. The rituals, the details; the risks and the rewards. And that last frozen frame of the full moon against the dark night's sky.

"The moon is full tonight. It's possible that they could perform the ritual tomorrow, but we can't take that chance. With the way everything is happening... We have to assume it could be now."

"And Gishkiy could be planning for a second attempt, if your friend—if Tusika—fails. Another shot at it tomorrow if tonight doesn't go right," Mistii says.

Niya feels her eyes well up with tears, her breath suddenly shallow, like she's been gut-punched. "You're right," Niya says. "I've been so busy worrying about whether or not Tusika will succeed... and what that will mean for her... that I haven't stopped to think about how quickly Gishkiy will move on to his next test subject."

"His next student."

"Or victim," Inola growls.

Nakola lets out a dry, ragged sob, and Inola rushes to her side. Squeezes her hand. Says words that she cannot guarantee no matter how much she would like to.

"Kas will be alright," she says. "We'll save her." A look towards Niya, over the top of her mana's head. "We'll save them all, if we can."

Swallowing hard, Niya says, "Nampeyo and Adasi have a lead." All three women turn towards her, brightening with these words. Niya stands gingerly, holding her hands out before her in an almost placating manner. "It could be nothing," she continues. "But it could also be everything."

With one arm wrapped dutifully, protectively around her mana's shoulders, Inola says, "What is it? What is the lead?"

So Niya tells them all of the details that she'd managed to hold onto, in spite of her head injury.

Oak trees.

A clearing at a low point.

Line of sight to the moon.

Proximity to running water.

A large stone with a concave surface.

Busy worrying at the inside of her cheek with her teeth and with her eyes downcast to the floor, Niya misses the way Nakola and Mistii grab each others' hands.

"What?" Inola barks, and Niya's attention is snapped upward. "You don't know where those things are, do you?"

The two older women are glued together, eyes like magnets. They remain silent.

"It can't be that easy," Niya whispers.

Which is when Nakola gives the other woman one sure, sharp nod, then turns to Niya.

"You're right and you're wrong. Because it *is* that easy—and it is also the furthest thing from easy."

Inola's auntie turns, dropping down onto a cushion.

"This place you and your friends describe, we know of it, it is true."

"We haven't been there in many, many years. Not since—"

"Not since..."

Nakola nods. "A lifetime ago, for our children. Our clan, we don't dare approach it."

Inola's brow is furrowed in confusion. At this last piece of information from her mana, she lets out an exclamation. "Wait! You're not talking about the forbidden hollow, are you? Holy..."

Niya extends her hands, palms out. "I'm lost. What is this hollow, and why is it forbidden?"

"The story is not one told lightly, but our time is short. I'll say only this, for now: there was a death there, back when we were small."

"An accident?" Niya asks, almost hopeful. Because if it was not an accident, then...

"Of a sort," Mistii chimes. "Most of us never fully understood it, just knew to stay away. But too much is making sense, my girls. In a terrible, terrible way. Because the woman who died there, she left behind a partner who perished not long after her, and they... they both left behind their son, who was doing his best at the time to become a man in the village."

The fine hairs on the back of Niya's neck prickle and raise. She feels like she's been electrified, a current passing just beneath her skin from her head to her toes and back around.

"You can't mean...no," she whispers. "Gishkiy? Was

the woman who died there Gishkiy's mana?"

"Ho-ly," Inola repeats, elongating both syllables until they're each their own standalone sentence.

Nakola confirms the revelation. "The elders forbade members of the clan from going there, warned off other clans in the area as well. Bad spirits surrounding such a death. Gishkiy is but one product of that disaster."

Inola steps close to her mana. "Do you think his mana was trying to do the same thing he is doing now?"

Standing up, Niya steadies herself with one hand on the tabletop. "If his stories are true, if the Pataks forced Gishkiy's family into exile from Cahokia…if they had fallen down, disgraced and without support, who knows what they could have thought worth trying."

Mistii speaks up. "We were never told too many details, and there isn't time now to seek out the elders from that time who are still living to find out more."

With a determined nod, Niya says, "Either way, we know the location. We can only assume that it's a generational aspiration, this ceremony. Maybe Gishkiy is out to finish her work, cut short as it was."

"The forbidden hollow…Gishkiy's mana…" Inola murmurs to herself, still caught up in the information overload.

"That's right," Nakola says, striding forward and out from the half-hug her daughter was still draping around her. She reaches Niya, stares fiercely into her eyes. These are the eyes of a mana unwilling to lose a child; hers is the determination of an uncompromising woman, one who will not leave what happens next to chance or fate or even the Creator. "And I'll take you there myself."

Slack-jawed, Niya is about to muster forth a response.

When suddenly, a harried series of knocks sound at the door.

PIDI DOBA HISIKA

For a moment, everyone looks at everyone else. Not a word is said, nor a movement made.

Breaking the hushed silence, Nakola speaks without moving. "Go to Inola's room, both of you. Suyata or not, they will not be able to enter without our say." A sharp nod. Her words are a whisper yet still firm and unbroachable. "I'll see to that. Now, go!"

Quickly and on light feet, they move off down the center of the house and to the entrance of Inola's room. As they duck out of sight, the front door opens. A stony greeting from Nakola, with Inola's auntie planted firmly at her back. An answering voice, calm.

Niya hears a few words and phrases, piecing together what she can: the injured Suyata went rogue, and the third Suyata is taking him back to Cahokia for medical treatment. This female Suyata, she is alone for the time being—but she won't be alone for long, not while Kaatii Patak is as incensed as she is. She says that she knows they're effectively after children, which isn't what she signed up for—might they work together, before things get messier...?

The voice is not threatening, not at all. Instead, there is an almost overly complacent sound to the Suyata's tale. As if she is doing as ordered, but that she lacks conviction.

This is curious to Niya, who had always thought of the elite Suyata guardians as irrevocably loyal to the Council of Twelve. Unswerving in their dedication to their missions, the people they serve, and those they take orders from.

The conversation that she loses track of as Inola shuts the door tells another story—one of less than perfect loyalty, one where the Suyata are able and willing to question their orders, when the situation calls for it.

Niya's head begins spinning anew. So much to take in. The forbidden hollow. Gishkiy's family history. The Suyata, here, *now*. And time—so, so little of it left.

"Hey."

Inola's voice catches Niya mid-thought, the runaway notions of overwhelm scattering as a result. She leans into the wall, her knees quivering. Inola, standing in front of her, steps forward, grabbing her by her upper arms and keeping her upright.

Niya looks up at the taller woman. Blinks in the dimly lit room, only the small bedside alcove's luminescence allowing them to see one another's features.

"We've got so little time," Niya says in reply, nothing else seeming sufficient. The words scrape past her teeth, wobbly and rough. She repeats the words, sinking as she does so more fully into the press of Inola's hand. "So little time..."

"How are you doing?" Inola asks. And her other hand reaches up, delicately touches Niya's head adjacent to the drying poultice. Her eyes flit across stoic features, shadowed lids, the weight of heavy thoughts.

Niya can't help herself: she laughs, presence of mind enough to keep it small, stifled by the back of her hand.

"How are *you* doing? Tusika is my, my...my other

half in so many ways, but Kas is your blood."

Inola nods, her forehead scrunching down in thought. Her lips smoosh to the side in a pondering frown. "I'm calm, honestly. Calm about what we are facing. I want to be on the move, to find my sister, to *do something*. But I'm calm."

And Niya believes it, because Inola may be headstrong and rash—running off to Cahokia, tracking the daughter of a Council member, storming into a stranger's home in the middle of the night all prove it true—but she is as steady as the magsling bolts and arrows and spears she throws. Steady as the power that Fox and the Adanadi gifted her.

"If I could," Niya whispers, voice crackling with unshed tears, "I would grow wings, and I would fly us out of here."

The corners of Inola's lips tilt. "Niya, I don't know." She has the gall to release a quiet chuckle. Niya's mouth dips down into the beginnings of a petulant frown. "You say that as if it were a dream, an unreality."

"It couldn't happen," Niya protests. "I couldn't possibly."

"I haven't known you long, but I've seen you do some truly miraculous things. Never say never, even to flying off into the great unknown."

And Niya feels it, feels it like a seismic shift. Like the ground beneath her is there but is *different*. Like the mechanics that govern all things living have changed, changed in a way so subtle and intense and intangible, that the entirety of Makasing—of Makasing and beyond!—couldn't understand.

The right answer isn't the easy answer, and it may not ever be known. Niya can see that Gishkiy is driven by something real, something important—grief for his lost family connection, hope that achieving what his mana could not might bring her back or give him something that he's been missing his whole life long. Not even an Ability, no, but something like it. Something that makes a person feel like they're part of something bigger.

Niya and Inola and many others, they were gifted by the Adanadi with Abilities. They are lucky in this regard, because science has shown them that luck is so intensely at play. Fickle and fleeting, choosing at random or not at all. Is it fair? No. But it is the byproduct of the Awis, the result they have today, with nothing to be said for whatever the future may hold.

And Gishkiy's methods, the old ceremonies and rituals and lost arts that he is trying to recreate and perfect at once, they could be disastrous. People could die.

But people could also survive.

Niya's breath quickens in her chest. Inola continues to hold her up. The moment washes over her. And she sees it all—sees the different way things could go, as the pieces come together in her mind.

She wants Tusika to be okay. She also wants goodness to prevail.

If Tusika fails, Gishkiy's experimentation may come to a premature but appropriate end. But Tusika might be dead as a result.

If Tusika succeeds and shows that Gishkiy's results

are replicable, how many more will try after her? And how many will die, with hope in their hearts—hope that they, too, could be like Tusika? Blessed with an Ability, not of the Adanadi but of their own making?

"That's it," Niya gasps.

"What?" A whispered response.

"The power is in the choice," she says.

And her choices fall in line before her like giant marbles waiting to be jumped.

The old or the new. Society's innovations or ancient traditions. Longtime loves or friends newly found.

Tusika, who Niya has spent so long loving, being in love with. Ambitious and independent, dark and light at once.

Or Inola, a friend in need, steadying her and lighting the way forward.

Red berries and hemlock; sumac and manchineel and more, she'd thought. *Intoxicating things; toxic in the end.*

A new thought, solid, now. A thought about the girl she thought she knew—the girl she knows all too well. The friend, the love, who turned away from Niya without hesitation or fear.

Sumac. Hemlock. And Tusika.

If they cannot reason with Gishkiy, with Tusika, with the other cult members, then do they let the ritual move forward? Or do they try to stop it?

If it fails, will Gishkiy and his followers stop—or will they simply find new ways and means?

Niya does not know, *cannot* know.

But the power is in the choice.

"The cost now may be less than the cost if he wins."

Inola, despite missing much of Niya's swirling, tumultuous inner thoughts, seems to be keeping up.

"Tell me the plan, Niya. I think I'll follow it—follow you—anywhere. So where am I going?"

Niya does not miss a beat. "We're going to the forbidden hollow. I do not know much, but I know that I must do the best I can. And I cannot do nothing. I will not do nothing. I must try to save every person I can, so long as it is in my power to do so."

Inola swallows hard, licks her lips. "What if the decisions we make tonight…what if they are the wrong decisions, in the end?"

"I don't know, Inola. I don't." Niya lifts her arms, pulling Inola into a fierce hug. "And it scares me beyond belief. I am afraid. I'd be lying if I said I was not. But only the Creator can know. What I know is that I must try and save Tusika. And then I must try and save everyone else, too."

hawa | *the day owl bled & raccoon fled*

PIDI DOBA PIÑA

The sounds of voices down the hall fade. Niya and Inola pull back, both looking at her bedroom entryway.

"Girlies?" Nakola calls softly.

Inola spins toward the voice. "The Suyata, is she—"

"Still here, actually," Nakola interrupts.

"What?" Inola says, surprised.

Niya imagines that her voice only remains as level as it does out of respect for her parent, an understandable impulse, but one that Niya, too, wants to fight against. Because the Suyata should not still be there.

"Not inside the house, of course," Nakola says, throwing her hands up. "But she...well, she refuses to leave, doesn't she? And even though I clearly think her mission is absolute beetle dung, I also can't blame her. You two have given those Suyata one helluva runaround these parts. She's determined to see her mission through."

Swallowing thickly, Niya presses forward. "Then we'll escape out the side of the house, you'll have to draw us a map. We can't let things end like this, we—"

"We won't," Inola interrupts. "We can't. We'll fight her off, if we have to."

"Now, hold on," Mistii proclaims, moving into the room just in time to hear her niece start talking about taking on an elite Cahokian mercenary.

And suddenly, the three Cato women descend into a whirlwind of frenzied whisperings, speaking right up and around and over each other. Niya falls back against the wall, and her mind spins, finding the words she'd overheard the Suyata speak at the front door. About "chasing children" and Kaatii Patak's incensed mood.

About working together.

Niya pushes off the wall and right into the middle of Inola's room, spins about, facing the other three women. They all fail to notice the excitement on her face for a moment. But once Inola glances her direction, the other two quickly follow.

"Hear me out," Niya says, "because I think I might just have a plan."

———·——·——

Some time passes while they work out the particulars. But every minute now is precious, and so they begin to act.

They have two sets of plans: the first dedicated to whatever may happen if things do not go their way with the female Suyata parked outside the Cato home; the second, if they do.

Either way, they are going to do their best to get to the forbidden hollow as quickly as they can. As Niya's time with Adasi and Nampeyo had been cut short at the comms tower, she cannot be certain what time of the night the ritual must take place, only that the full moon must have risen. Night having fallen not so long before, they have little time further to waste, if any at all.

"Oh, I've never liked gambling. And this all feels like gambling to me," Mistii mutters as they move down the hallway.

She leads the way, the others behind her and clad in warmer clothes for the oncoming coolness of the night. Inola has fully reloaded and strapped her mag-sling to her waist. Niya carries her daadoo's chunkey spear at her side. Nakola is rubbing a poultice along her own neck while Inola applies some to her lower back, to fight her chronic pain and also prepare her body for the trek they are about to take. Mistii will stay behind with her children while Nakola leads Niya and Inola to the hollow.

Nakola lets out a string of tittering sounds. "Please, I've seen you make your fair share of bets on persimmon seed shapes over the years."

"That has to do with the weather—it's practically unavoidable, and if I make a few nizi in the process, who's to be bothered with it? As I was saying... I've never *liked* gambling, but here we go a-doing it anyway."

"For the good of the many," Inola says.

Niya turns her head, catching Inola's eye. "I hope," she says, her voice so quiet and scratchy that the other woman essentially has to read the words as they're written small across Niya's lips. "I really, really hope."

When they get to the front door, Inola stretches her tall frame to look out of the clear-sight membrane encasing the gap between the top of the door and the ceiling. Through the view into the night, she attempts to spot the Suyata. Up on the tips of her toes, she scans as far as her eyes can manage first to the left, then to the right, then back again.

"I don't see her," she finally says, dropping back down

onto flat feet. "Maybe she left?"

A triple-knock sounds at the door, and the three Cato women jump. Inola's hand goes to the magsling she now has slung on her right hip, and Niya narrows her eyes at the sturdy door.

Her plan could be crazy. It could backfire spectacularly. She could get Inola bound and escorted back to Cahokia. Niya, too, could be in heaps of trouble for having been a part of Inola's escape from the city and this week-long journey. Inola's family as well—what punishments would Kaatii Patak try to rain down from on high, and how far would her reach extend?

Niya shifts, places her hand atop Inola's, where it rests on the weapon. The weapon she has only witnessed the other woman use once—and to brutal effect.

"Let me," Niya says. Not a question, but there is an ask there.

She raises her eyebrows in a look of acquiescence and resignation. Not resigning herself to Niya but to the situation. "You're the one with the plan. And I trust you. I've got your back."

Nakola and Mistii chime in with their agreement, then silence falls.

Niya steps forward, and she opens the door.

PIDI DOBA KAWANZI

As soon as the door opens, the four women are faced with the Suyata, who is standing stock-still, light on her feet with chin held high.

"Hello," Niya says, without missing a beat. "My name is Niya Suwatt. This is my friend Inola Cato, and her family."

This all seems to very much catch the Suyata off-guard. But the elite member of the Chosen of Cahokia recovers quickly enough.

"I am Pataa, member of the Kolisoo assigned the task of bringing in—" she gestures to Inola, "—well, your friend."

Niya grins at the honesty, and Pataa mirrors her.

"I have a proposition for you, Pataa of the Suyata. If the Catos are agreeable, I'd like to invite you inside."

She turns, and all three Cato women are staring back at her with faces immovable as stone. Because to invite Pataa inside is to invite into their home the will of the Suyata's decree, the warrant of the Council of Twelve, the might of Cahokia, even here.

Nakola touches her daughter's shoulder, and Inola looks her in the eye, nodding once, decisive and unwavering. As a result, Nakola gives Niya a nod of her own.

All four women step back, making way for Pataa to enter.

"Please," Niya says, "come in."

Niya, Inola, and Pataa settle around the hearth, cross-legged on cushions. Nakola brings cups of leftover broth for them all to warm in front of the fire's coals. Mistii watches on with a look of distrust from head to toe—from her stern frown to her crossed arms, she leans back and watches Pataa right down the crooked bridge of her nose.

"We are short on time, so I'll be as quick as I can, if you are willing to listen."

"I am," is Pataa's answer.

And then Niya tells Pataa as much as she can, as efficiently as she can. As she begins to tell the tale, she hopes for some of Inola's storytelling abilities.

She speaks of Tusika's plight, her familial responsibility. As Niya tells of Tusika's lack of Ability, she sends up a little preemptive prayer for Tusika's forgiveness, certain that she must tell this secret in order to protect Tusika in the end. She tells the circle, even those who know already, of Gishkiy's intentions; of the people he has lured from the village, of the research her friends have done, of the danger of the ceremony that may be underway even as they speak. She tells Pataa of the forbidden hollow and that they might still be able to get there in time, if the Suyata and the Council's warrant does not impede them.

Niya tells the Suyata that she can bring her to Tusika. That they share a purpose: keeping the other young woman safe. That time is of the essence.

As Niya concludes her story, she hungrily drinks

down her own cup of broth, the others having started theirs during her accounting of things.

Pataa looks around at each of them before drinking down the rest of her broth and standing.

"I have little interest in bringing Inola back to the Council under the current terms of my Kolisoo's missive. Especially if what you tell me is true, that Tusika Patak can be found, and found safe."

"If we hurry," Inola cuts in.

Pataa turns her head, acknowledging this. "If we hurry," she repeats. "Then—I have nothing more to say, other than this: you have my service, until Tusika is discovered."

"Until she is safely extricated from the ceremony," Niya clarifies. "If we find her and it is too late, the ceremony already underway, we must not interrupt it."

"I understand the stakes." Pataa bows her head. "I will follow your lead, until I can no longer do so."

Niya frowns, uncomfortable with the verbal acrobatics the Suyata is conducting. But she feels that they are on the verge of a more than amenable arrangement, and so she stands, placing her now empty cup to the side. She extends her arm, and Pataa stands, too.

"We have a deal."

Pataa reaches out, grasping Niya's wrist as Niya does the same to hers. "Deal."

Inola unfolds herself from the ground, standing to her full height. Her back is ramrod straight and her chin is up. "Let's go find my freedom, then. And save Kas, Tusika, and the others while we're at it."

Nakola takes the lead. They are all heading across the village square, avoiding as many inquiring looks from out of doorways as they can.

"We will explain," Nakola hisses at another inquiring neighbor, "*tomorrow.*"

"Winds!" comes the neighbor's reply as they shut their door with annoyance.

As the group is about to head out of the village's easternmost limits, following the beginnings of what looks to be an immensely overgrown and disused trail, there is a commotion back behind them. Everyone seems to move at once.

"What the—" Nakola turns suddenly.

"What's going on?" Niya asks.

"It's the night watch," Inola says.

Pataa assumes a fighting stance, flicking both of her wrists to spring forth two short, dual-edged combat knives from out of her sleeves.

Nakola steps back towards the village square, squinting into the dark. She tilts her head, listening hard. "Strangers," she whispers. Then she turns quickly to Pataa. "Did you lie? Was the rest of your Kolisoo lying in wait?!" Her voice is harsh, sharp, demanding.

"Whatever is happening, Suyata are not involved." Pataa shows no sign of being offended at the implication that she may have betrayed them so quickly, clearly calm under pressure. "Could it be the cult leader's people?"

Niya shakes her head, crouching low and moving closer still to the village, keeping a low profile. She peers around one of the water-bringer structures protruding from the earth, reaching with her hearing as far as she possibly can.

And what she thinks she hears is—

"Adasi?!" she chokes out. Incredulously, she turns back, locking eyes with Inola. "By the Creator, I think I hear Adasi's voice. It may be my friends!"

And without any input from the others or consideration for stealth, Niya takes off running for the far side of the village.

When she comes around the corner of the modest council house, her suspicions are confirmed: Adasi and Nampeyo are standing in front of a vehicle, their arms outspread in a gesture intending to show that they mean no harm. The vehicle is vibrating in place, sort of shuddering as if it might fall apart at any second.

"A-yo!" Adasi shouts when he catches sight of Niya's approaching figure in the dim light of the rising moon.

"This is our friend," Nampeyo says, voice only slightly louder than their typical even-keel. "She can explain the situation to you, if you would like."

"Usdi, Ganuhida!" Inola shouts, stepping forward. Niya can hear something resembling mirth in Inola's voice as they recognize the night watch duo who take their route opposite of the rest of the village watchers. "Please, we know these two—they are Cahokians, and they are here to help."

She says this last bit intuitively, for why else would

Niya's friends have made the drive in their experimental new vehicle—the Minaati, Niya recalls—from Cahokia?

"Inola Cato!" one of the watchmen shouts. "What are you doing here?! There have been *Suyata* after you—oh, *look out!* There's one of them now!"

Pataa moves up behind them, looking as non-threatening as a Suyata with weapons drawn could possibly look—her hands are down at her sides, and her posture is ramrod straight. Hardly in a threatening position. At the watchman's words, she raises her hands in the air as if to mockingly surrender. She flicks her wrists lightly, and the two blades slide back into their hidden sheaths beneath her long sleeves.

"She's with us, Ganuhida."

"For now," Pataa adds, unnecessarily.

"For now," Inola repeats with a glare.

"You're *wanted*, young fox—for kidnapping, maybe worse," Usdi adds on, sidling up shoulder to shoulder with his fellow watchman. "Tell us what the city says is untrue."

"It is," Inola says solemnly. "We're off with the last Suyata to prove as much now. And these two are friends. Please, continue on your watch—and get the rest of the villagers back to bed! We'll be gone by the time you get back to this spot."

Nampeyo steps up. "Well, according to my research and the calculations I was able to complete while Adasi drove us here—"

"Niya," Adasi interrupts, a huge smile on his face,

"this machine is *incredible.* Fastest I have ever gone in my life!"

"Really? Because it looks about ready to fall apart," Niya cracks.

"It's got at least two more outings in it," Nampeyo interjects.

"—I expect we will be going off the beaten path. So while you will not see us, you will see this vehicle, as it must remain."

"I'm sure we'll be seeing a lot more of it, since I don't think it's starting back up, eh? Not by the ways of the winds or the water." Ganuhida says, eyebrows raised.

"Junk," Usdi agrees.

"Hey!" Adasi says, stepping forward as if to engage in an actual debate about the Minaati's merits.

Nampeyo clears their throat. "I will have you know, this prototype may not be particularly impressive to behold at the moment, but it certainly got us here from Cahokia in a timeframe that some might consider…what would you call it, Adasi?"

"Absurd," Adasi offers.

"Yes, *absurd.*"

"So please feel free to ignore it," Adasi adds with his own flair, grabbing two small packs from behind the bench seat and handing one off to Nampeyo. "Until we can return to take it back off your hands."

Hastening the young Cahokians away from the underwhelmed but agreeable night watchmen, Inola calls over her shoulder, "Catch you up some other time!"

In a flash, they are all hastening off towards the overgrown trailhead whose start leads, apparently, to the forbidden hollow.

Niya gives her friends brief but warm hugs before they all dash off in earnest.

The Suyata takes one moment to narrow her eyes at the two watchmen—causing them both to cower back the slightest bit—before she turns, jogging to catch up with the others.

They are about three-quarters of a mile into what Nakola tells them is a two-mile hike to the forbidden hollow. Adasi is at the head of the largely unused trail, cutting their way through underbrush whenever needed to continue onward and clear the path for the rest. Pataa brings up the rear of their little party. In between, Nampeyo and Nakola chat intermittently about the flora and fauna of the area. Nakola is doing her best, and Inola watches her closely while the others help her over and around obstacles, her back pain slowing her down and the rest of them with her. Sandwiched between friends and family are Niya and Inola.

Niya marvels about the support that surrounds her. As they keep a brisk pace, she notes that it is becoming easier and easier to see where to step along the way. Not because her eyes are adjusting. But because the full moon is rising, higher and higher above the trees around them.

The two friends are utterly quiet until Niya speaks. She keeps her voice low, as if the night is listening.

"When we get there, I'll need to find Tusika. Maybe on my own."

Inola gives her a sideways smile, and Niya knows she does not have to explain how the other woman's presence might trigger the exact wrong reaction from Tusika.

"And I'll need to find my sister. But we'll all have your back, Niya."

Inola bumps her shoulder against Niya's, and it causes Niya to grin in spite of herself and the tumultuous thoughts catapulting through her mind.

Then she tilts her head, glancing up through her eyelashes and the foliage around them to the sky. Catches a glimpse of the moon overhead. Swallows hard and focuses again on walking quickly, deftly, with great purpose in the wake of Adasi's clear path and Nakola's direction.

Without breaking her stride for even a moment, Inola stays right alongside Niya. And Niya can feel that steady gaze on the side of her face. Turns her head, asks, "What?"

"I feel that I have changed your world," Inola says. "And I do not know if it has been for better or for worse."

Niya shakes her head almost instantly, without further thought. "No, Inola, no—you have only allowed me to see it differently."

"Niya…do you think Tusika will be able to do the same? Do you think she will be able to see the world differently?"

But Niya remains silent, because she cannot know for sure.

She does not answer, and they carry on.

With about half a mile left in their journey, Adasi gives a quiet signal back to the rest of them. They all approach. And they can see clearly where the path they've been cutting through the forest abruptly meets with another.

Nakola gives a single terse nod, understanding what she's seeing as soon as they come upon it.

"Gishkiy's group," she says. "They're ahead of us."

Niya looks up, up to the night sky, trying to catch a glimpse of the moon through the trees. She can't see it, not from here. Tears well up in her eyes without her permission, and she angrily rubs them away.

"We're close. We'll approach silently from here."

No one else has anything to say. Niya takes the lead.

The rest of the going is easy, all downhill as they approach the hollow's basin. Whereas Adasi and Nakola have been clearing their group's path, it seems that Gishkiy's cult—from wherever it is they've come—have trampled the ground thoroughly the remainder of the way to the hollow. Perhaps they've made the trip multiple times in preparation for a night like tonight; clearing the way, delivering supplies, ensuring that their way would not come under scrutiny before the ceremony could be carried out.

Something about that knowledge—that this supreme

act of forethought and determination is leading to one place, one moment, one *person*...a different person for each of them, surely. Tusika for Niya, Kas for Inola, Gishkiy, perhaps, for the Suyata bringing up their rear.

And at the back of Niya's mind, the questions still slither, a snake devouring itself, thought upon thought, chasing one another into a circle that cannot end. If the ceremony starts, will Tusika complete it? Will she fail? Will she succeed? And what comes next, whatever the outcome?

"Aho—!" Adasi yelps.

Niya rushes forward to see what he sees, only to find Adasi near a tall, slender man who blends right into the trees at the edge of the forest. The man doesn't even acknowledge them. He seems indifferent to their intrusion.

Her head on a swivel, Niya takes in the trees around them.

"*Oh*."

They've arrived at the clearing, lit up fully by the moon, now nearly directly overhead. The forbidden hollow. The trees, which cast shadows across those hidden in their midst, make a nearly perfect circle. This chills Niya to the bone—for what purpose was this space originally cultivated? Did the ancestors intend for its use in this ceremony and others like it? Niya's eyes instantly land on a massive stone, tall enough that it would probably come to Niya's stomach. The diameter of the clearing is larger than Niya had imagined—about the length of a chunkey court. But the space is empty, besides the rock...

Where is Tusika?

Niya takes a few steps forward, still within the edge of the circle of trees. She can feel their shadow across her face, can see moonlight on her arms where it pierces the gaps in the foliage.

Gishkiy's followers—for who else could they be?—are everywhere. Spaced out at even intervals around the clearing, tucked away beneath the eaves of ancient branches. The stealth, which the group from the village had so effectively employed until the very moment they arrived at the clearing's edge, seems to have been unwarranted. The cult followers are not paying any attention at all to the new arrivals. Instead, their eyes seem trained unwaveringly on the stone in the center of the clearing. Their postures are universally relaxed, non-combative; they are, simply, waiting.

As Niya continues to look around, taking in as much as she can as quickly as she can, Adasi steps forward. He taps the man closest to them on the shoulder, but the man gives no indication that he even feels Adasi's touch, let alone that he might soon acknowledge them.

Nakola huffs out a heavy breath, and Niya turns to look at her. Her hands are clenched tightly at her sides, and she is looking intensely around, squinting through the dark underbrush. It is hard to see far, except in the places where the full moon's light makes its way through. She looks ready to burst right out of her skin. She shifts back and forth, left to right, silent grimace crossing her face at the pain she must be experiencing after the hike.

"Kas?" Nakola hisses into the darkness. When there

is no immediate answer, she shakes her head and seeks out her daughter. Grasping Inola's elbow, she says, "I must find Kas. I'm going to head this way around the clearing. Signal, if you need me." She turns to Niya, nods once. "Winds and water," she says, as if these words are all she knows how to offer. "Winds and water..." And she turns south, walking off, trying to conceal a limp as she goes.

Niya circles in the opposite direction, moving to the next of Gishkiy's followers that she lays eyes on a woman who looks like she may be only slightly older than Niya and Inola. Inola follows closely, one hand on her magsling where it sits at her hip.

Laying her hand gently atop the woman's shoulder, Niya manages to get the stranger's attention—a slight shift of her eyes, and the woman looks at Niya. But her eyes immediately go back to the clearing, to the rock, transfixed.

Knowing that she is at least able to get the attention of those gathered, Niya speaks, hoping that the woman will deign her worth answering.

"What is it that is happening here?" Niya asks. Of course, she knows at least something of it—but what do Gishkiy's followers think? What do they believe?

An answer comes almost immediately.

"We are waiting for the miracle," the woman says.

One person further along the rightwise ring of the circle overhears this answer, and they take no small slight with it: an older woman, wild gray hair loose and wavy down her back. She turns her head toward the woman who spoke, chastising her with no small amount of vehemence. "Silence! It is not a miracle, you know better than that. We are about to bear witness to highly-focused, skilled work at play. There will be nothing so random as the so-called 'miracle' of the Adanadi, not tonight." With a derisive sneer, she turns back to the clearing.

Niya watches as the first woman who had answered ducks her chin ever so slightly, swallowing hard, eyes now unwavering from the stone.

Stepping back, Niya, Inola, Adasi, and Nampeyo gather together, their heads pressed close. Niya briefly notes that Pataa seems not to be engaging with anyone or anything—instead, she merely seems to be watching things unfold. After all, Niya had promised her Tusika, and Tusika seems to be nowhere in sight.

"What's the plan, Niya?"

"I must find Tusika. After that, I...well, I'm very thankful that you all have helped me get this far. Whatever it is that comes next."

The four friends link arms. Niya locks eyes with each of them. Adasi and Nampeyo grin at one another with stoicism for the moment and pride for the woman their longtime friend has grown into over the years. Inola gives a serious nod, reminiscent of the one her mana had offered minutes before.

"I'll continue on. I've got to find Kas, and—"

"Wait," Nampeyo lifts a hand. Their eyes are on the clearing. "Look."

The friends' eyes all move to follow Nampeyo's gesture.

Niya catches sight of him at the same time that Inola says, "Gishkiy."

Her eyes flash to Inola's form in the dark. They haven't known one another long in some ways, but in other ways, they are connected—the emotion in Inola's voice speaks volumes more than its actual quiet. There is hurt and hate in the woman's tone. Niya knows the difficulties the Cato family faces, how things were worse when Kas left. Her intent—to make life easier, to find answers for questions she supposed were the right ones to be asking—had left the family reeling.

Inola's magsling is no longer in its holster. Niya looks at it pointedly as she speaks. Each syllable of the name of the woman hits heavily in her mouth. "Inola. Remember: he has not hurt anyone."

"Yet. He hasn't hurt anyone *yet*."

"That's right," Niya agrees. "Watch him, don't let him escape. But weigh your actions, as I will weigh mine. And don't forget… he has an Ability now."

Inola drags her eyes away from Gishkiy's slowly moving form, but only for a moment. "We will get Kas back. You will save Tusika. His power will turn to ash."

Niya does not say aloud what she immediately thinks: *one thing at a time.* Instead, she nods in a decisive manner, sure and unwavering.

"Pataa, come with me—there is someone I think you would do well to meet."

Wordlessly, Pataa follows as Inola continues off in a rightwise direction, steps lightly, somehow not stirring the underbrush at all as she turns to go deeper into the woods to keep out of sight. Niya wonders whose side the Suyata will be on, when everything is said and done come morning. She hopes it is the side of right, of good—whatever that means in the end.

Niya is watching their disappearing forms when a wave of awed voices lifts up out of the woods and into the clearing. Rises in volume before crashing back down. Pivoting quickly, Niya's eyes scan the trees in front of her, the clearing, the far reaches of the moon's light—which is when she sees her.

Tusika.

Emerging from a point opposite Niya, Adasi, and Nampeyo, Tusika steps into the clearing like a celestial body fallen from the heavens. She walks slowly, like a Beloved Woman or the highest of Councilmembers, like a legendary warrior of mythical proportions. Her body is draped in silvery, luminescent ribbons, and she looks as if she is a waterfall come to life, or the living embodiment of armor being created. A crash-landed amalgamation of stardust and light.

Niya can feel herself losing the sense of a plan, however loose, that she may have had only moments previous.

"Wow," Adasi mutters.

"Is that *our* Tusika?" Nampeyo asks. And Adasi assures him with a clap to his shoulder.

Ethereal, Niya thinks. *Radiant. Beautiful.*

Intoxicating.

Shaking herself, Niya takes a step forward. She will not be undone, she will *not*.

"What can we do, little sister?"

Niya closes her eyes, taking a moment to look at nothing and no one. Not Tusika, not her friends, not the place in the darkness where Inola had disappeared in search of Gishkiy. She does not perform the motions of her Adanadi Ability, but she does reach deep inside of herself, touching the part of her that belongs to her wholly now—Owl, who makes her bigger than herself alone. And she feels her friends at her back. And she thinks of her family at home, and her ancestors who came before. Of Inola and the mountains she was willing to move to save her sister. Of families who are supportive, in their own way—the Catos, making ends meet, aching for their daughters to be home again—and of families who are not, families a person might hide things from rather than face the truth. For fear, for love.

She thinks, too, of Tusika.

And when she opens her eyes, she knows exactly what she must do.

"Nampeyo, follow Inola. Help her if she needs it. Keep reckless thoughts at bay. And Adasi, find her mana—help find her daughter."

"Is that all, Niya?"

Turning her head, Niya locks eyes with each of her friends in turn. And before she turns to make her way out into the clearing—out to meet Tusika at the stone in its center—she says one last thing.

"Watch my back, will you?"

TAHODII

Niya leaves her pack behind, leaning up against one of the ancient oak trees that surround the clearing. When she walks towards the stone, she walks alone, only her daadoo's spear in her hands, used more as a walking stick than anything else.

But she also knows the most important truth: she isn't alone, not at all. Because her friends are nearby.

And her best friend—the girl she grew up with, the girl she loves—is walking towards her.

They meet at the stone, and Niya is certain that she has rarely, if ever, seen anything more beautiful than the Tusika before her now.

Intoxicating.

Tusika looks even more like a heavenly body, cast down from the stars, up close and personal like this. Her body is a stunning weapon, draped in a material that Niya does not recognize, silver and shining, saturating her vision. Beneath the flowing drapery, she catches sight of skin that is bare and skin that is painted, too—colors infused with diamond flecks that flash and dazzle, as if Tusika herself emanates the light out upon the rest of those gathered. She is not reflecting the moon's light, no—she is making it her own, changing it into something different and hers before casting it back out into the night.

And Niya cannot believe it, but she sees it with her own eyes and it cannot be denied: Tusika's lips are bright, bright red.

Toxic.

Feeling her insides turn, Niya keeps her back straight. Holds her head high, as high as she can carry herself. Tusika has always been taller, but Niya wills herself to grow, *grow*, and fill her own space with certainty and calm, with the presence of mind necessary for such a moment as this. She may be dressed more plainly—in overly long pants that she borrowed from Inola's mana, turned up multiple times at the hems, and a green tunic top. She can feel that even her hair is a bit wild and unkempt, braids pulled at as they had been by the trees and bushes on their hike.

Before a single word is uttered, Niya knows only one thing for certain: she does not know what will come next. But she is ready to face it, and the ripples that come after.

"I knew you'd come."

A test already, then.

Niya swallows, keeps her pulse even in her chest. "How could you have known such a thing? You had us buried alive, remember?"

Tusika's eyes flash at the "us", and her eyes shift away from Niya's face.

"I didn't..." She falters, and Niya's pulse quickens. Tusika looks down, away, then back again—her eyes shine. "But here you are, aren't you? And I'm guessing *she* is somewhere nearby, too."

A derisive look, poisonous. There and then gone.

Niya offers a distraction. "You've got a whole host of onlookers out there, you know."

"Yes, I do," Tusika says, quiet but sure.

"Some of them are expecting a miracle. Some of them are expecting something more than that."

Tusika lets out a low hum from the back of her throat. "And what are you expecting, Kakooni?"

A pause. Niya's brows dip lower for a moment. She takes in the stone between them, with its concave surface. Purposefully strewn about atop it are different items—a mortar and pestle, some sacred ingredients like sage and tobacco that Niya recognizes, some clumps of plant material and tiny seeds that she does not.

"I'm going to be painfully honest with you," she says. Tusika nods, opening her arms in an inviting gesture. "I am expecting this to go terribly wrong. That I'll have to save you, somehow—if I can." She feels her throat catch, and she swallows hard to press onward. "And if something doesn't go wrong, Tusika, then I'm expecting nothing."

Tusika's lips twist. "Nothing?"

"Nothing," Niya repeats, "and that might be the worst thing of all. Because I know you, and I know that this thing you're after... you won't stop until you get it, will you? No matter the cost."

The toxic sheen fades away from Tusika as she ponders Niya's words, and she is suddenly luminescent again, shining and ethereal and otherworldly.

"It is easy for those with the prize already to worry about costs."

Niya forces back a growl of frustration. "I'm not

saying this because I have an Ability, I'm saying this because there is a *reason* that we have the Adanadi. However the people of Makasing take it, we take it at the same time—the peak of adolescence, the turn towards adulthood, the point at which the journey of the rest of our lives begins. And so many people take that journey, on their chosen Path, *without* an Ability, Tusika!" She clenches her fists, wills herself to slow, to breathe, to still. "For the first time in your life, you found yourself experiencing an average existence—the most common way to live, without an Ability—and you lost yourself. You're just *lost,* Tusika."

"That's really what you think," Tusika says, unquestioningly. "You think that I am lost."

Niya shakes her head, not sure of the words that have come out of her mouth before, or of the words that might come next. Deliberately, she speaks. "I think you have been told who to be for a very long time, with expectations placed on you that were unfair. That wasn't right. But the past cannot be undone. I can't speak for your family, or for mine. How my family has gone so long without an Ability, or how yours has been blessed time and time again. Did Gishkiy talk to you about his suspicions, Tusika? That he believes his childhood spent beside Kaatii Patak to be the reason he did not receive an Ability?"

Tusika swallows hard. Niya watches as her friend's lips move undecidedly. When she speaks, her voice is quieter than Niya is used to.

"This again."

Niya interjects. "Yes, *this!* It's the reason any of us

are here! I do not know what it means for some to receive an Ability while others don't. I do not know why I was chosen when you were not—when we were born side by side, grew up together, experienced the Adanadi as one. All I know is that I must do the best I can."

"The best you can," Tusika repeats, her voice lilting and serene.

"Whatever that means," Niya says.

And for a moment, they are just two seventeen-year-olds again. Weeks younger, before the Adanadi. Before everything changed. They are two girls, thrust together by their families. Friends for years but side by side years even before that. They have been there for one another through scrapes and bruises and scabbed knees, broken hearts and kisses and more, days of learning and nights of dancing and a lifetime of knowing one another.

When Niya says these words, there is a pause, and then they both smile. Smiles so familiar as to be heartening and heartbreaking at once.

It feels like a turning point. A precipice. Like maybe, if Niya were to extend her hand, Tusika would take it—would let herself be pulled away from this place, back to something familiar but also different. *Home,* whatever that could be.

Which is exactly when a clear voice rings out across the hollow.

"Imagine my surprise, being summoned out of a closed door Council meeting by a Suyata, told that my child had been found—and found with an Ability-seeking *cult,* at that."

Kaatii Patak steps out of the woods like an apparition. She is clothed in rich robes of burgundy, buttons down the front from her neck to past her waist. Her moccasins are black. And her dark hair is twisted and piled into an elegant updo more appropriate for a Council of Twelve event than traipsing through the woods. Niya watches her approach just long enough to confirm that her presence is real before she looks back to her best friend—and she watches the blood drain from Tusika's face.

"Mana, I—"

But Kaatii raises that imposing hand of hers, gestures her only child into silence as easily and simply as if issuing a decree to the entirety of the Free Lands and beyond. Tusika's lips snap shut; her head lowers. Niya feels her heart beating wildly beneath her breast.

Then Kaatii performs another gesture, too, one that Niya has seen the woman perform only a handful of times her entire life. With her arms outstretched, Kaatii wraps them into a circle. She lifts her encircled arms up, up above her head, fingertips touching. Her lips move soundlessly, her eyes shut. And then she gently breaks the connection between her fingers. As she does, a red orb fills the space around her. As she brings her arms out and down, it expands. She rotates her wrists, now pushing, pushing outward. The red glow rushes out, encapsulating now only the hollow and none of the woods beyond.

Niya recognizes the Ability, which can be used in different ways. In this form, it allows everyone inside of it absolute privacy amongst themselves; it seems that Kaatii is about to say some things that she does not wish the onlookers to hear.

"Drones," Kaatii says as she approaches. Her steps are measured and slow. She moves like someone who has been in charge their entire lifetime, maybe longer. Like she has nowhere more important to be than right here, and everyone else better keep up—or else. "That's how I knew where to find you, once I had the information I needed. The Suyata was not mortally injured by any stretch of the imagination—" here, she cuts her eyes across the hollow, as if she can see into the dark of the treeline, can spot Inola Cato and identify her as the one who pulled the trigger. "But he certainly had a story to tell."

"Oh?"

Kaatii's eyes slice the air as they travel to her daughter. Niya can see where it comes from, that venom that Tusika occasionally wields.

"It wouldn't take a genius to put these pieces together, Daughter." She positively strolls now, taking her time, moving to and fro at her leisure. "Some girl shows up from the countryside with tales of an Ability-seeking cult. The name Gishkiy gets thrown in my face as if to spook me—ha! Memories from childhood, ghosts. And as my daughter's Adanadi window closes, she disappears, and the country girl along with her—and her best friend, too. Hmm..."

Niya watches as Tusika's shoulders begin to heave with the efforts of her breathing. Her nostrils flare and her brow draws down sharply with her frown. "Mana, please, I don't think—"

"That's *right*," Kaatii interjects like a viper, "you *don't*. This girl received the Ability that should have been *yours*, Tusika Patak." With an arm thrown wide, Kaatii gestures at Niya, and Niya feels the ground give way beneath her. "All you had to do was follow orders. All you had to do was obey. And the rest would have worked itself out—has done exactly that for how many years now, how many generations of Pataks?! Pah! The Suwatt blessings could have been yours, should have been ours, but no—you let your emotions get the best of you, and now our line is broken."

She throws her arms up now, as if disgusted. Turns away from the girls. She knows exactly what she has said and done—knows that she has spilled the family secret, the very secret that Tusika had denied three different times to Niya's face.

Tusika turns wildly about, looking for Niya across the expanse of the large concave stone between them.

"Niya, listen..."

Disgust is the wrong word for what Niya is feeling, though it is close.

"Stop."

"You misunderstand her, this is not what it seems—"

"Don't try and poison my mind, Tusika! Is what she says true? *Are the Pataks stealing Abilities?* And have you... have you known all along?!"

"No, no no no," Tusika steps forward, moves closer to the stone. When she makes as if to step around it, Niya pivots, keeping the same distance between them. Tusika's face softens, breaks, then hardens again. "I didn't know, Niya."

"Until you did." Kaatii's viperous voice again, striking another death blow to Niya's heart.

Tusika shakes her head but doesn't voice any denial.

"Since when?" Niya asks, tears building in her eyes. "When did you know—that I was to be but a sacrifice to continue the line of gifted Patak first-borns, huh? When, Tusika—?"

"Three years!" Tusika screams, cutting Niya off. And Niya does feel cut off; she feels *cut*. Sliced open and bleeding, hemorrhaging away any life that she had known before this night. "Three years ago, she told me...I...I guessed as much, because of some writings I found in her office. Some things I had heard, and seen, and...I asked, and she told me. And then things had to change, because of it, and—"

"By the Creator," Niya gasps. "You found out that you needed to be closer to me, and that's when..." She thinks back to their childhood, how they had always been at one another's throats. Until they weren't. Until things changed—they started working together more, engaging in a less competitive and more challenging, complex, fulfilling way. Had all of that been part of some great cosmic scam? "Has it all been fake?"

"No." Tusika says it so forcefully that Niya almost believes her. She slams her palms flat against the stone, and Niya winces at the impact. "No, Kakooni, I—" Tusika's voice cracks. She lets out a cry, sounds like a trapped, caged animal, as she tries to give voice to whatever is inside of her, trying to escape. "You are my best friend, my everyth—"

"Be careful what you say, Tusika." Niya's voice comes out cold, colder than she's ever heard herself before. But her words have the intended effect: Tusika stops, pauses, shuts her mouth and clears her throat.

When she speaks, she is calmer than before, steadier. "I followed my mana's directions, but everything between you and me—every experience, memory, adventure—all of it was real."

"And you were supposed to receive my Ability. Or... *whatever* it is your family does, whatever manipulation is done, you were supposed to take it from me."

"It's about potential," Tusika says, her voice deathly quiet. "The Suwatts...your family hasn't had an Ability in seven generations. Do you know how much potential is stored up in you, Niya? You can be *glorious* with it all."

"It should have been *ours*," Kaatii snaps. "Just like Gishkiy's potential was mine, and my mana's best childhood friend was hers, and so on and so on. But Tusika, my inept, foolish child, had to go and break the one cardinal rule: the one thing that cannot be done, if the magic is to run its proper course."

"And what is that?" Niya asks against her better judgment.

"Mana, *no*—" Tusika starts. But Kaatii pays her no mind.

"She fell for you. Fell in love. And the magic changed course, flowed in the wrong direction. So instead of tapping into all of that delicious potential, all my daughter did was unlock it. But not for herself, not for the Pataks—for *you*."

The world could stop spinning, and Niya wouldn't even notice. Not with the way her heart is beating and her breath is catching and her mind is racing, racing, *racing*.

"Is it true?" It's all Niya can find within herself to ask. And, knowing everything that has happened over the past few weeks—knowing the truth of the Pataks' Abilities and Gishkiy's power and Tusika's disappearance—Niya knows that the answer may break her, whichever way it comes.

Tusika puts her hands to the edge of the stone, breaking her eyes away from Niya's. She looks at her ingredients and then up at the night sky above her. The full moon throws her face into stark relief. Niya inhales sharply. Tusika drops her line of sight back to Niya, and Niya watches as a single tear slides down her best friend's cheek.

"Of course it is," Tusika says. "And I'm so, so sorry for that."

"Tusika..."

With a tilt of her head and a lift to one corner of her mouth, Tusika smiles the saddest smile Niya has ever witnessed.

There is so much left to say, so much that has gone unspoken, all this time.

But Niya is out of time. And Tusika might be, too.

With a suddenness that stuns Niya, Kaatii, and everyone else in the forbidden hollow, Tusika lets out a warlike shriek.

"Aayyyyyyyaaaooohhh!"

Her high-pitched, ululating scream rips through the air. Kaatii flinches, covering her ears, and the red haze of her Ability bursts and dissipates like nothing.

Effectively distracting everyone, Tusika hardly even lets the echoes of her cry fade before she darts forward.

In one of her hands, she snatches up a bundle of sage leaves, in the other, she grabs for a sprig of flowering hemlock. She brings them together in front of her, held in crossed arms and cradled like a blessing. Her eyes slip shut, and she begins to speak.

And just like that, the ceremony begins.

TAHODII DOBA WANZI

Niya is a passive bystander, regardless of how much she would prefer to be acting. Her limbs feel heavy, frozen; she is thankful for her daadoo's spear, which she is leaning upon heavily. When Tusika begins speaking, Niya looks at her as if she is a stranger—a magnificent, terrifying stranger. Niya feels a tug at her spirit, anchoring her to the ground, and to the young woman standing across from her.

It is immediately clear that Tusika has been practicing—using that expansive, sharp memory of hers to get down not only the proper words and languages for the ceremony, as concocted by Gishkiy, but also the feel of the thing.

After a minute, Niya believes that she has heard at least eight or nine different languages. Her own Tsalagi. Some Ojibwe, Lakota, Siouan, Algonquin. Muskoke, like part of Inola's family. Some Anishinaabe, like she's heard Nampeyo and their family speak from time to time. A phrase or two of Dinadayapi that Niya recognizes but cannot translate.

And Tusika is signing, too. The language used primarily upon the Great Plains. Short, clipped terms and phrases. Her movements are dance-like, almost obscuring the sign language by mixing it with the movements of the ceremony. But Niya sees signs like *sage* and *cedar*—and, more concerning, signs like *blood* and *spirit* and *darkness*.

Focusing on Tusika, Niya can hear little else. Like the rest of the world has had the volume turned down. A susurrus of wind through the trees does not exist outside of this moment but is instead an integral part of it—like Tusika's planted feet and moving arms, her twisting fingers and hands, are directing the world around her. Niya even feels herself swaying, caught in the rhythm of it. There is a hum, low and almost nonexistent, but Niya can hear it and knows instinctively that it is coming from Gishkiy's followers. An odd background dirge, like a lament for those who came before.

Or for those who come next.

As Tusika continues to chant, reciting her spell—her recipe, her ritual, the ceremony, in its entirety, over and over and over again—she prepares the sacred medicines atop the stone. The grinding sound of her work is but another instrument of the night. The smells from the tobacco and the sweetgrass, the cedar and the sage; they combine to make something holy and right. They smell familiar to Niya, comforting; like home, like safety, like smudging and the protections and spiritual cleanliness they offer, have always offered.

But then Tusika begins to grind up other items altogether, and the smell changes. Niya tries to open her mouth to protest but finds herself incapable; spellbound.

No, she thinks, powerless to act as she sees—

Red berries of the holly bush. Spring hemlock leaves. Smooth-edged sumac. Supple green manchineel.

Tusika lights a small fire at the center of the stone, large enough to catch and stay lit, but small enough not to obscure her every motion. Small enough to not be a distraction, but substantial enough to give off a bit of light, a small tinge of warmth.

The girl Niya grew up with, this woman before her, performing something altogether new and holy, old and foul—she begins adding the ground-up medicines to the fire. As they catch and scatter on the light wind, Niya can almost taste them on her tongue, at the back of her throat.

But something odd happens as each ground up item touches the fire: colors escape, like small-scale explosions of light and sound and energy.

The tobacco emits a blue brighter than the most beautiful summer sky.

The sage lets off a striking violet hue.

The cedar showers the space over the stone with an impossible orange, burnt and bright.

The sweetgrass goes silver, looping up and around itself, light woven into braids before exploding delightfully.

Niya still wants to scream, as the sacred medicines seem to conclude and the other items come into play.

Poisons.

The red berries turn the air thick as blood.

The hemlock casts a putrid yellow tint between them.

The sumac causes a burst of color undeniably vile, like a wildfire consuming everything in its path.

The manchineel lets off a slow-dissipating cloud, bile-green.

And then the air stills. The fire goes on burning. And

Tusika's voice falls silent.

When she speaks again, it is in Kag Chahi, but there is another language there—looped around it, tighter and tighter, as if to cut off its supply of oxygen.

Tusika extends her arms, raises them slowly with her words. Tilts her head back, and back.

Faster than a lightning flash, quicker than Niya could have ever comprehended, Tusika lowers her head back down. Grabs Niya's eyes with her own. Tosses aside the silvery material of her garb to grab hold of a ceremonial dagger—the blade black as night and just as cold. A silvery shadow of an indentation runs down its center.

Niya finds her voice, then.

"No!" she screams. She drops her daadoo's chunky spear to the ground and begins running at Tusika. But she meets an invisible wall that keeps her from reaching the young woman she loves.

And she is too late anyway. The words have been said. The ceremony has been carried out, nearly to completion.

What remains, only this: Tusika draws the blade efficiently across her upper arm, ending with the tip pressing directly into the base of the wound.

Her blood flows. Fills up the indentation, pools neatly in the dagger's center.

Niya continues to push forward, aching to stop Tusika's blood from touching the fire. But something is there, in front of her, in the empty air—and it is pushing back.

"Tusika—" Niya tries. But her throat is a stopped-up

mess. She can barely form the syllables.

And Tusika, her face tells Niya one thing and one thing only: Niya could cease breathing in this moment, could fall over and drop stone-cold dead in between heartbeats—and Tusika would be none the wiser.

"Ish," Niya gasps on a wince, tears coming to her eyes. Her hands clench so tightly as to draw blood. Maybe she'll see the little half-moon cuts in her palms later and remember what true anguish had felt like. "Tusika, nooo… *please.*" She manages to summon the air into her lungs to nearly howl these words, desperate and out of time.

The air is alive. And everything stills, the moment before Tusika's blood drips, drips from the blade's edge. The trees are still, the oaks waiting. No animals speak or skip. Gishkiy's followers fall silent, Niya's friends are, perhaps, nowhere at all.

Then a drop falls.

The flames of the fire lick upward, embracing Tusika's blood like a hungry mouth.

And then, Niya knows little else besides light and pain and insufferable, unending silence.

Because the world as she knows it explodes.

TAHODII DOBA PIT

The breath is knocked from Niya's lungs. She is shoved backwards with such force that her vision bursts into multifaceted colors before fading to black. The blast leaves her entire head feeling pillow-stuffed, like she's buried in sand. Sound is muffled, she can see nothing, and then—

It fades in a flash. Like a hologram with the power switched off—there, and then, suddenly, not.

Niya opens her eyes.

Wherever she is, it isn't the forbidden hollow.

Well, it is.

But it isn't.

Not unless she lost half a day, as the sun is bright and unmoving in the center of the light blue sky overhead. No clouds. No birdsong. Nothing.

And it is the hollow, but it stirs within Niya a feeling unlike any other. A feeling that is forever unfamiliar until named, disconcerting in how commonplace yet unusual it is. That feeling of something that has already been seen, of living through it for a second time. She has been here before, but she has not. It is the forbidden hollow, but it is not yet forbidden.

Niya sees movement at the edge of the woods, just out of the corner of her eye. She snaps her head in that direction, and she sees a most curious sight.

A stone—*the* stone—is being mightily pushed out of the line of forest and into the opening. Niya watches its curious progress. After a few moments, the stone draws even with her. Then it begins to pass.

Pushing it is Raccoon.

A mighty huff contorts Raccoon's face as she passes Niya. She sneers as she stops pushing the stone.

"Well," she chirs, "you just gonna sit and watch all day, then?"

Niya turns slowly, looking first over one shoulder and then the other. She points to her chest as if to say, *Who, me?*

Raccoon gives another great huff, rolling her eyes skyward. Then she goes back to pushing the stone.

Suddenly, from out of the woods opposite Raccoon's entrance comes Fox.

"This nonsense again," Fox chirps with her squeaky voice. "Haven't we convinced you better yet?"

Raccoon grumbles. Niya approaches with interest and caution.

"Always trying to tell me what to do...mind your own business, why don't you try that for a change?"

Fox begins jumping around in little circles. "Why mind my own business when yours is so interesting? Anyway, she'll be here soon."

Raccoon ignores this. Once she has the stone precisely where she wants it—right where it is in the forbidden hollow in Niya's time and place, Niya notes—she waddles back off into the woods.

Fox tilts her head at Niya once Raccoon disappears. "She's not normally this grumpy, I'll have you know."

Niya simply raises her shoulders in a shrug, perplexed

look on her face. This seems to be enough for Fox, who turns back to the stone. She hops atop it, turns and turns in circles, then settles down into a ball of red fur, the white tufts of her ears just visible.

Soon enough, Raccoon reappears. She is walking on two feet, a smooth, round rock in her front paws.

"Get, you!" she shouts at Fox, who obliges with a flourish, springing from atop the rock and to the sweet spring grass below.

Without any pomp, Raccoon climbs atop the large stone and begins grinding the smaller rock into its surface.

Niya walks closer, only to see that the large stone is not concave on its surface, not at all—not like it is as she knows it.

Not yet, at least.

For a while, Niya and Fox simply sit side by side. Watching. And waiting.

"I have to get back," Niya says.

"Do you, though?" Fox replies.

Niya blinks back at her.

"I could wait, I guess."

And so they wait some more. No sound but the soft grinding of Raccoon's rock against the great stone's surface.

Eventually, a new sound enters the hollow: the disconcerting screech that Niya recognizes as hers. As Owl's.

"Told you she'd be here soon," Fox chirps, bouncing

a bit in place before running around the stone a few times.

Owl careens into the hollow, magnificent and silent wings spread wide. She glides towards them, low and fast, before landing lightly on the edge of Raccoon's stone.

Niya's heart picks up to a gallop in her chest.

Racoon repeats Fox's words, "Told you she'd be here soon," but in a snide mockery.

"Play nice, you two," Owl chides.

Raccoon grumbles but says no more.

"Don't know what makes you think this will work, Raccoon," Fox rolls over onto her back, paws dangling in the air. "It hasn't before, what makes this time different?"

Snuffling, Raccoon shoots a quick, sharp glance in Niya's direction. Niya almost believes she has imagined the look—but then Owl turns her great white and orange framed head about on her shoulders, looking directly in Niya's eyes.

"Yes," Owl says. "That may do the trick."

"She won't give it willingly," Raccoon grumbles.

"Well, she's here, isn't she? And that's always been your trouble," Owl replies. "No patience. No faith."

"What *about* me?" Niya asks.

"Come closer," Owl says, "and I'll show you."

Without hesitation, Niya steps forward, comforted by the presence of her Path animal. Once she is a few steps from the stone, Owl extends her mighty wing.

And she touches Niya's temple.

Everything comes into her mind at once.

"Me?" she asks. "Why?"

She can feel tears forming in the corners of her eyes. One breaks loose, tracking down her cheek. Owl touches it with the tip of her wing, absorbs it into her feathers.

"When two people are linked, there is a power in that. You are hers, and she is yours."

"Do you mean—?"

"Yes, to her, too," Owl cuts her off.

Niya's brow furrows. She shakes her head.

"The ceremony is...too dangerous. I can't be a part of it."

"You already are," Fox pipes up from her side.

Raccoon grumbles, "It's actually better this way, loathe as I am to admit it."

Niya looks down at her, understanding in that moment that Fox is right. Raccoon, too.

"You can do this the hard way," Raccoon grunts, still grinding away at the stone, "or you can let them die."

"What, there is no easy way?" Niya asks, in a moment of confusion and desperation.

"Look at me," Raccoon hisses, "would I be doing this if there were another way?"

Owl tilts her head, looking first at Raccoon and then back to Niya. "Dear girl, darling heart—getting here was the easiest part of all. It's the choice that is hard."

"The choice," Raccoon interrupts with another grumble, "is everything."

Owl continues, unconcerned with Racoon's interruption. "The action is simple."

"The rest, as they say," Fox lolls over onto her side, staring serenely up at Niya's face, "is up to you, girlie."

"Will it hurt?" Niya asks.

"*Will it hurt,*" Raccoon grouses.

"Only as much as your most painful memories," Owl says. "And only for a short time."

Niya thinks of her most painful memories.

Falling and breaking her arm when she was twelve years old.

The first time she saw Tusika kissing another girl.

When her daadoo died.

Tusika's face, before the rock wall crashed down into place, burying her and Inola in the cave.

"And my actions here..." Niya wonders aloud.

"Will save those connected to you, if they can be saved."

"And if they can't?"

Owl's feathers ruffle. "Then none of this matters."

"Do we look like creatures who enjoy wasting our time?" Raccoon barks. "Get on with it, time's shorter and shorter still."

With a shock, Niya sees that the stone has been worn down into the familiar concave surface from her time and place. How long has she been here?

"I will help," Niya says, decisive and sure.

"Of course you will," says Fox.

"Your hand," Owl says, extending her claw.

Niya moves to place her hand into Owl's open talons. She does so unwaveringly. Owl's grip is cool to the touch, and she jerks Niya closer, pulling her whole arm out and over the stone.

"Happy thoughts," Fox trills, running circles.

"Still, Child, you will soon be gone from here," offers Owl. Lowering her head, she nips over and over again at the flesh of Niya's arm. Blood begins to well up to the surface, but nothing seems to hurt, not like Niya had expected. "Other arm." And Owl repeats the motions. Blood covers both of Niya's forearms. Her palms face upward, to the sky. "Now, clench your hands into fists. Curl your arms upward. Bring your chin low."

Niya follows Owl's directions, and her blood begins to drip down to the stone's surface. So much blood drips down that it begins to pool in the center, sure to leave a red, unbleachable stain, unable to be lifted even by years and years of sun pouring down upon it.

With her head low and her eyes closed, Niya misses Raccoon's movements. For the creature has stood on her hind legs. And she lifts the smaller rock high above her head.

"Happy thoughts," Raccoon hisses, so much differently from Fox, who flinches now but stays stoically near the stone all the while.

"Sorry, darling," Owl coos.

"For wha—?" Niya begins to ask.

But Raccoon crashes the stone down against her skull, and Niya relives all of the most painful experiences of her life at once, falling, falling into darkness once more.

TAHODII DOBA TAHOO

The pain is terrible, excruciating, an amalgamation of every horrible thing she has ever experienced. *Only as much as your most painful memories,* Owl had said—but Niya had remembered so many at once, just at the suggestion. And she was feeling them all, wasn't she? *Only for a short time,* Owl had also said. And the pain begins to fade.

Which is when Niya realizes that she is not back, not yet. Not to her right time and place. She is still somewhere else, somewhere unknown, or unknowable. She is screaming, but she isn't. She can hear her own hollow voice, but she also can't. There is a veil between who she is and who she should be—the Niya *there* is suffering, but the Niya *here* is trapped in between. Experiencing it but not. Living it or remembering it, she can't be sure.

But she is not alone.

"Niya?"

Turning abruptly at the sound of her name, Niya spins to come face-to-face with Tusika. She gasps out the other girl's name, finds herself moving forward automatically. She is drawn by something more than her best friend's presence—she is drawn by something growing out of the look on Tusika's face. A look in the dark, a willful hunger.

It's all Niya can do not to crash her lips against Tusika's, to still her body enough that she doesn't surge forward of a volition not her own, pressing their hips and chests together until she feels nothing but Tusika.

She manages to stop herself. Inches away from the young woman she so loves, Niya asks, "Where are we?"

Tusika shakes her head, as if she is unable to speak. It's then that Niya can hear another scream, mingling with that of her own body, on the other plane as it seems to be. Here, in between reality and unreality, the screams seem separate from them, somehow. Like the pain that draws forth their cries is happening to someone else entirely. It is, but it isn't.

"I don't know," Tusika says.

Her voice, so soft and small. Normally so bright and sure, Niya feels an intense desire to protect Tusika wash over her—as if the reason for their being in this situation in the first place doesn't matter. And it doesn't, does it? Not here, not know; nor there, maybe not anywhere. Impossible, in this place, for Tusika to hide behind one of her many masks. Here, in this place, with the young woman who loves her and who she loves back, the one always able to see behind her masks.

"I..." Niya's voice trails off, not knowing where she had been going to begin with. Then her heart fills in the blank space left by her mind. "I've loved you for a long time."

Tusika does not look away. The background cacophony of their otherworldly screams somehow plays like a soundtrack to this terribly odd pronouncement.

"I know," Tusika whispers.

"You betrayed me, lied to me. Tried to take something special and sacred from me."

Tusika does not look away as she answers, the volume

of her voice minutely higher. "I know."

"Do you regret it?"

"That, and so many other things besides," Tusika grimaces, glancing down at her outstretched hands for a moment. Then she brings her fingertips up, touches her own lips. Her eyes slip shut as her fingers brush along the length of her downturned mouth.

"Are you sorry?"

A shuddering breath, and Tusika stills. Her eyes open, and her pupils are so round and full as to give them the appearance of being wholly black. "You'll never know how much. But I can't take it back. Time is, well—" she looks around them pointedly, shrugs at the strange veil-like there-but-not membrane between them and... *them*. "Time isn't on my side, I'm afraid."

Niya nods, taking a step forward. Again, her words come from her heart to her lips unbidden but not unwanted. "I love you still."

Screaming, screaming, screaming.

"Oh, Niya," Tusika says, her voice breaking over a heart-wrenching sob. "I know."

There is a pause, a silence between them, filled only with the hammering beats of their young, strong hearts, and the palpable heat of their mixing breath. Even the ethereal screams from their lips a world apart fall silent for a moment. And then their mouths are on one another, and the fate of anything outside of the two of them is entirely, blissfully forgotten.

Niya distinctly remembers three particular kisses throughout her young life. Not her only kisses, but three that echo through her memory like ripples in a pond.

The first was with a little boy in her primary school class. It was an agreed upon kiss, ordinary and silly and forgotten by the next day's noontime meal.

The second, she recalls with piercing clarity. Her first time, and one of the only times, that Niya had used mind-altering chemicals at a dance hall. The colors had been so vivid, and the music so fiercely pulsating, and the girl across from her so carefree and alive. Niya did not even know her name, just that they kissed, and kissed, and kissed. Until one day became the next, and Niya—present and present and present—became someone totally different from who she had been before.

The third...well. Tusika's mouth on hers, possessive and domineering and everything and nothing of what Niya had been craving for years—years! A kiss borne of desperation and a breed of loneliness that Niya has only now begun to understand. She'd wanted Tusika to be something different, maybe her whole entire life. But Tusika had wanted Niya to be someone different, too—someone there, there, always there.

This kiss, so different from any kiss, ever, experienced by anyone in the entirety of the known world. It has to be. Niya believes this to be true.

She can feel it, right down to her bones. But mostly in her chest and her throat and certainly in her wobbly, fuzzy brain. Chemical signals shooting off like sparks from a blaze, faster than comprehension.

With their foreheads still pressed together, Tusika speaks words that Niya can practically taste. "You asked me if I regret it."

"Yes," Niya breathes as she moves her lips against Tusika's again. Tasting, feeling, living.

"There's something I regret even more. I didn't think it possible, but it is."

"What? What do you regret more?"

Tusika sighs, and warm tears drip down her face. Niya presses her cheek against them, feeling the warmth and the wetness, making them her own.

"Not doing this. *This.* Kissing you, more, before it was too late."

Niya's eyes flutter open. Her eyebrows draw down. A shadow catches in the corner of her eye, and Niya turns her head to look at it. But it's gone, gone—until she turns back to Tusika.

That's when Niya sees it: a creature of indescribable blackness, a perfect silhouette around her best friend. Laying across her shoulders like an unholy blanket, a putrid darkness that has Niya wanting to run, run, *run.*

"Tusika, what do you mean? Before it's too—?"

Crash!

With a thunderous clamor, the two girls are thrown apart.

"Ahh!"

Her vision spins, images somersaulting round and round, dizzying and awful.

"Tusika…!"

Her throat is raw from screams that she does not remember screaming. But the screams are still coming, rending the air around them.

The screams are coming from Tusika, from the young woman that Niya loves still with her whole heart. Hellish and horrifying. Niya shakes her head to steady her mind, rips open her eyes.

She finds herself back in the forbidden hollow. The right time, the right place. But everything feels so horrifically wrong.

Tusika's screams fade into warbling bursts of pain, rising and falling on the tides of whatever is happening inside of her. And in the valleys of her pain, Niya can hear other things.

From the woods, outside the edges of the clearing, she can hear bouts of commotion. The clashes of fighting. Shouts in the night. A short, blood-curdling scream that fades as quickly as it comes on. Magsling bolts being discharged. The slicing of knives through the air, of war clubs clashing.

And through it all, Tusika, sounding as if she is boiling from the inside out.

Niya lifts herself halfway up, crawls on hands and feet to Tusika's side. But Tusika is thrashing so violently in the grass that she cannot approach.

With a full-body cringe, Niya notes that all of the grass beneath Tusika's body is dead. Blackened, almost charred. But Tusika—she still breathes. How else could she make these sounds? Her lungs are working spectacularly, her body clenches into itself and back out, over and over. She lives, she *lives*.

And that's it, isn't it? Tusika is alive—and if she is

alive, then the ceremony… it had to have worked.

Was it Niya's blood? She wonders if this could be true. If the story that played out in her mind was real or imaginary or something altogether new.

But she is here, and there are pockmocked scars along her forearms and inside her wrists, and it had *felt* real, hadn't it?

And Tusika is alive, Niya keeps telling herself. *And that kiss was anything but make-believe.*

Whatever battle is being fought in the forest rages on in the background. It fades from Niya's mind as Tusika's body falls still—or as still as it can be, with all the trembling. Stiller, at least, and something like a miracle unto itself.

"Tusika?" Niya whispers, crawling close. Pressing her lips down near the other young woman's ear. "Tusika, can you hear me?"

The answer comes as if from a great distance. "Yes," Tusika whispers. "Niya. Yes." Her voice cracks until it breaks, and something inside of Niya breaks too, as a result.

Suddenly, the commotion spills over, filters into the clearing like a dam broken. Inola's voice rises above the noise, and Niya looks up and around, searching for her.

"No! He's getting away, we can't let him out of our sight!"

Then she sees the man from the cave's mouth: Gishkiy. Looking frazzled and fraught, he stumbles but keeps his feet. He is shirtless despite the chill of the night air, and his brown skin shines from sweat. His long, white hair is wild around him, caught in a storm all its own. He is barefoot and unphased by it. He looks back over his shoulder once before breaking out into a much steadier run, straight for Niya and Tusika. From some distance, Niya watches as he catches sight of Kaatii Patak. He lets out an animalistic growl at her, cursing her in a language that sounds ancient. Kaatii's body lifts into the air, flying up and up and up. Gishkiy performs an action with his body, almost like an archer drawing back his bow and then releasing it. As he does, Kaatii's body goes flying—at least thirty paces into the forest. She goes silently, as composed as the Councilwoman somehow always manages to be. And just before Niya loses sight of her, that same red haze from before surrounds the woman.

Niya can't help but wonder if the red bubble Kaatii has always manifested for privacy, or spying, or whatever else suits her, might also offer physical protection of some sort.

But she doesn't have time to think about it long, because Gishkiy turns back to Tusika and covers the remaining distance between them in a few short, powerful strides. Reflexively, Niya moves to shield Tusika with her own body. But when Gishkiy gets to them, he sends her flying with little effort. As if she weighs nothing. With a groan, Niya lands hard on her back. For a few terrible moments, the air is knocked completely from her lungs.

When she regains her breath, Niya wheezes her protest at the man. "The...hell...get away from her!"

But Gishkiy ignores her completely. He pushes close

to Tusika, the knees of his pants getting soot-stained from the grass that had burnt to a crisp beneath Tusika's writhing body. He cradles her head in one of his large hands, using the other to pull her closer by the opposite shoulder.

"Tusika," he says. The syllables each sound sharp to Niya's ears, strange and unfamiliar and wrong in his mouth. "Tusika, tell me now: did it work?" Niya aches with how badly she wants to know the answer herself.

She does, and she doesn't.

And to her utter horror and fascination, a macabre smile spreads across Tusika's lips, familiar but not.

"I think so," Tusika answers.

"No," Gishkiy hisses. With dread and a sickening clench in her stomach, Niya watches as he pulls tight at Tusika's wild hair, tight enough that her neck elongates and, for a moment, she winces. Then he relents, loosening his grip, smoothing his fingers along her brow and down the back of her skull. "No," he says again. "It worked, or it did not work. Which is it?"

Niya watches Tusika swallow and swallow hard, shutting her eyes, furrowing her brow.

When she opens her eyes again, Niya is certain that whatever remained of the Tusika she once knew is no more.

"Yes," Tusika says. Fire glints in her irises. Niya imagines that she sees smoke emanating from her mouth, snaking up from her lungs in her chest to the air outside of her. "Yes, it worked."

Gishkiy wastes no time.

"The nonbelievers are trying to take our people." *Our people?* Niya struggles upright, gaining her feet. "We must stop them, stop this before it goes any further. At least one has already returned to the village." *Could it be Kas? Kas with Nakola?* "This girl, they've been following her for some reason. And she brought Suyata to our midst." One long finger with a sickeningly pointed fingernail shoves straight at Niya's face. "End her, and we will be free to escape."

"*End* me? You can't be serious," Niya says, on the verge of hysterical laughter at the thought.

But Tusika brooks no argument with him, and Niya feels the air leave her lungs again and her heart clench at the inaction.

"Tusika, what are you doing?" Tusika moves to stand, and Gishkiy extends his hand, helping her to her feet. "What are you doing, my love?" He moves to stand behind Tusika, just over her shoulder. And the look on his face is pure evil: Niya knows this because he does not look evil at all. But his words are poisonous, contaminating Tusika's already fragile psyche. The Adanadi did not give her an Ability, and he has preyed on that perceived weakness in her—in all of his followers. "Tusika, please. We are not enemies."

"No," Tusika says, her voice quiet but strong. "We're so much more than that, aren't we?"

When Tusika's lips twist upward, curling into another macabre mockery of the girl Niya used to know, Niya feels something pull apart and burst inside of her.

Tusika came back, we both did. We made it through the ceremony—but what came back from the in-between with her?

And another question, somehow worse, still: *And what did Tusika leave behind in its place?*

"Please," Niya begs. She is ready to drop to her knees, if only it would bring back her love.

Tusika, however, is unmoved. "You would have this ceremony lost to the annals of history, would you not?" She gestures to the stone. Now that Niya is standing, she can see the horror for what it is: Tusika's blood, pooled in the center of the stone's bowl. Tusika's blood, pooled now as Niya's had been in her dream, or vision, or whatever unreality she'd found herself in with the Path creatures before.

Niya hardens her heart enough to speak her truth. "I would have no part of this dangerous ritual, this ceremony that has taken lives before and will again, if you let it loose. This is blood magic, and that's a danger we cannot abide." She feels her voice crack before she hears it.

"Hypocrite," Gishkiy hisses, low and quiet.

"Hypocrite," Tusika says, her voice growing louder and louder.

Inola appears in Niya's periphery. She can see the woman, magsling clenched tightly in her hand at her side.

And Niya realizes that they are not wrong, but neither are they right.

"I did what I did so you would survive," Niya implores. "There are no guarantees in this madness!"

"If you try and stop us now that we have unlocked

this power, then I will be forced to disabuse you of any such notion of control."

"Do it *now*," Gishkiy hisses. "Do not give her that chance!"

Tusika turns her head, speaking over her shoulder. "But I—"

"Do it!" Gishkiy screams.

Another voice enters the fray. All eyes snap to Kaatii Patak as she limps back into the clearing. Her clothes are disheveled, and there is a madness to her. But still a regalness that cannot be imitated or denied.

"Do it," Kaatii says in a whisper that only the few of them closest together in the center of the clearing can hear, "if you can."

This, Niya knows, is the final say in the matter. She does not know what Ability Tusika Patak has stolen from the other side, from the in-between place they had found one another, but she fears for everyone in the forbidden hollow.

Everyone but herself, even if she should be the most worried of all.

Tusika's eyes are wide and bloodshot as she turns, unblinkingly, from her mana back to Niya. Her face is frozen as she steps forward.

And Tusika does as Gishkiy has commanded—as Kaatii has goaded.

Niya barely sees the small, intricate hand motions that Tusika is taking before she feels the stinger's barb of excruciating pain inside her mind.

"Ahh!" Niya screams out in pain. She falls to one

knee, and the pain already begins to fade. "Ish..." She whimpers, and she feels more than she sees Inola running to her side.

"Monster!" Inola yells, putting her body between Niya and Tusika. She wraps her strong arms around Niya, pulling her up onto her feet, legs wobbly and insecure, like a newborn fawn. "She loves you, don't you know that?" Inola asks, the vehemence in her voice palpable. She turns back to Niya, pushing back her hair, slick with sweat that Niya did not know she had been making. "What a waste."

That foul look in Tusika's eyes, it grows fouler still upon Inola's utterances. "How *dare* you—"

Niya's eyes focus just enough that she can see the twisting of Tusika's fingers, can recognize them now for what they are: Tusika's method of activating her newfound Ability. Whatever it is, it punctures the mind, causes damage to a person's very core, their spirit.

"Tusika, wait!"

It works enough that Tusika pauses, drops her fingertips back to her sides. "What, why? For *her*? You can do better, Kakooni."

A subtle flick of Tusika's wrist, a slight twisting of her fingers, and Tusika wrenches a guttural scream from Inola's throat.

"Winds!" Inola cries. "By the Creator...what monster have you become?"

She falls to her knees, trembling, and Niya throws herself between the two women.

Kaatii looks on, somehow coming off as disinterested.

On the other side of Tusika from her, Gishkiy is watching on, too—but he looks like his very existence hinges on whatever it is that will happen next.

"You will not hurt anyone, Tusika. Not while I still stand."

Tusika looks contemplative and calm as she replies. Casually enough to be immeasurably cruel, she says, "Then I will put you back on your knees."

Even before Tusika begins those small, intricate movements of her fingers, before she can prepare the wasp's sting to plunge into Niya's mind and bring her to her knees—or worse—Niya begins motions of her own.

The memory of Owl surfaces, speaking to her, telling her what to do.

Clenched hands. Chin down. Arms out, then curled forward.

Niya remembers Raccoon, bringing the stone down on her head. On her mind.

On her very thoughts.

And when Tusika sends out her psychic spear, Niya is ready. As she curls downward, she catches sight of her Adanadi mark, sees its wingtip lit up by the moon's glow and is strengthened by it.

Because Tusika is not the only one to have developed something new from the ceremony.

"Oh shit," Inola gasps behind her. And because the woman can see auras, Niya does not have to wonder hard at what Inola must be seeing.

She can feel it: a wave of energy, a barrier to just such an attack as Tusika is throwing her way.

Tusika growls in frustration, and Niya lifts her head, the invisible armor firmly in place. Tusika's motions grow larger, more furious. She leans forward, planting her feet so firmly in the ground that Niya fears she might sink through its surface. Niya can feel the barbs of each and every attack coming at her—there is pain, but nothing compared to what that first attack had felt like.

"Tusika, you must stop this."

"No, no, no!"

With each shout, Tusika takes another step forward. Another thrust of her arms. Another invisible projectile, any one of which might have killed Niya, without the protection of her stony, unseen armor; her protected mind.

"Tusika, *please*." Warm blood trickles from Niya's nose as she continues to fight.

"I can't go back, I can't go back," Tusika begins muttering, her voice a shattered mess. Tears are streaming down her face. "I *won't* go back."

Inola groans from behind Niya, pushing herself up into a standing position. Niya glances back only for a moment, and she sees Inola lifting her magsling, steadying one of her hands with the other, ready to defend herself and Niya alike from the onslaught Tusika is throwing at them.

"Tusika!" Niya screams. In the moment, Niya isn't sure if she is warning Tusika about Inola's coming attack, or if she's begging her to stop. It's all so mixed up, and she is so very tired. She licks her lips and tastes blood.

Turning her head, Tusika prepares to unleash her mental attack against Inola, which Inola sees coming—reflexively, she fires all of her remaining magsling bolts toward Tusika, which should strike true. Despite using her Ability and flinging the shots towards Tusika's extremities, they are deflected with apparent ease. Tusika's warped Ability of the mind, powerfully intercepting the bolts, tossing them aside like childrens' playthings. And Niya knows what she must do.

As Tusika makes to shift her fury, Niya propels herself forward with as much force as she can. She moves up and into Tusika's line of sight to Inola. And she *pushes back* with her armor, does not merely allow it to absorb the barrage this time.

With incredible mental strength, Niya ricochets the attack back upon the young woman who unleashed it, sparing Inola in the process.

Tusika screams. So similarly to that hellish nightmare of a scream that she had emitted at the conclusion of the ceremony.

But this one, Niya fears, will never end.

"Niya, come." Inola pulls at Niya's arm, trying to drag her away from the clearing.

A war cry echoes across the hollow, and Niya sees the silver-haired woman from earlier, now armed with a war club, wielding it overhead with a strength that belies her age but shows clearly her intensity and, perhaps, her madness. Pataa dashes out, engaging the woman—apparently deeming the fight worthy of entering now. They exchange blows, disappearing back into the cover of the trees. But more are coming.

"But Tusika, she—" Niya falters. Inola catches her.

"Tusika has chosen her path. I'm sorry, Niya, we must go."

Niya's feet catch again on the ground beneath her, and she goes down on one knee. Inola's hands are quickly on her shoulders, checking to see if she is okay.

Tusika continues to scream, and Gishkiy kneels at her side. He does not look in Niya's direction, not at first. But once he sees the pain writ large on Tusika's face—once, Niya believes, he realizes that the outcome of the ceremony may now be jeopardized—he does turn.

And he looks at Niya with fury and rage and murder.

As he charges across the clearing towards her, he announces as much, if it wasn't clear already.

"I'll kill you for this!" he screams. "You'll pay!"

"No—"

Niya moves to extend her arm outward, to try and push his maniacal rage away from her. Weak, exhausted, utterly spent. Perhaps if Gishkiy were rushing her with his power of telekinesis, Niya could manage to harden her mind against him. But Gishkiy has picked up a stone bigger than his considerable fist and is wielding it like a war club of his own. Niya can tell he's going to come for her head, attack her brain physically where Tusika's mental assault had failed. She closes her eyes, using the last of her strength to raise her arms above her head, to try and deflect the inevitable blow.

But the blow never comes. Niya hears rushing steps in the grass, a heavy breath, the sounds of exertion. Then a thunk, a scream, the thud of a body falling…

She opens her eyes only to see that Inola has found her daadoo's chunkey spear, grabbed it from where Niya had discarded it as the ceremony had begun. And she has used her Ability to strike true—right through Gishkiy's chest.

The world slows. Someone from the trees gives out a scream at seeing their cult leader fall.

Without another word leaving his soothsayer lips, Gishkiy collapses forward, onto his chest, driving the spear further into his broken heart.

A small number of cultists are coming out of the forest, falling to their own knees. But there are far fewer than there had been earlier in the night. Just beyond them, Niya catches sight of Kaatii as she steps backwards, enveloped by the shadowed woods.

Niya does not see Nakola or Inola's sister, Kas, all of whom she presumes left before the ceremony's conclusion. Whether that was Kas's choice or not, she cannot know.

Adasi and Nampeyo come running full-tilt towards her. Adasi is in the lead, and he immediately begins to support Niya when he arrives. Nampeyo looks past their small group, taking in Tusika's form in the grass, the hopeless way she is clutching her head, digging her nails into her skull. How utterly alone she appears to be, even in the midst of the flurry of hands and voices assessing her for physical damage that they will not find.

"Tusika..."

Their friend's scream finally begins to abate. They watch on as several former followers of the now late

Gishkiy hurry forward to help. As they do so, Inola keeps two small daggers at the ready, held firmly in her grasp. Some of Gishkiy's group glance at her nonplussed, while others bare their teeth towards their adversaries, a few even looking as if they are desperate to fight on. Seeing that they are outmatched, that this is a battle that they have lost but that, perhaps, there is a war left to win, they do not engage. The defeated followers get Tusika up onto her feet, manage to steady her. But her head remains low, held tightly in the grip of her trembling hands.

They hasten to the opposite side of the clearing. As they reach the trees, in the moment before they disappear, Tusika turns back, still supported by the many hands of others. From across the distance, Niya can feel her intense gaze. For whatever it is worth, Niya feels the *goodbye* of it.

But Niya never says goodbye. She won't let Tusika say it now, with words or without.

Stepping out of Adasi's and Inola's arms, Niya takes three shaky steps forward. And then she summons whatever strength is left in her body to project her voice across the distance between them. And she shouts, "Donadagohvi!"

Until we meet again.

Tusika's eyes never leave her as she does this.

And then Tusika turns, disappearing into the forest with the small few remaining of Gishkiy's cult, now hers. At Tusika's back, Niya sees a shadow where one should not be, lit up by the moon's face as it is.

Silence falls.

Oddly enough, the first person to break it is not Niya or one of her friends, but is Pataa, covered in blood spatters and sporting several blooming bruises.

"Well," the Suyata says, stepping forward. "I think I have seen enough tonight. It is clear that Tusika Patak was here of her own free will. And you, Cato—you defended your friend from someone intent on murder. As the two of you are of the same people, you will have to report to your tribal council for this life taken."

"I will," Inola says, head bowed and voice low. "Of course I will."

"The warrants and bounties for the missing Patak girl will be canceled as soon as I get back to Cahokia. You have my word."

Nampeyo steps forward. "We can get you there quickly," they offer. "If you would let me take you back on Minaati."

Pataa agrees. Adasi and Nampeyo rig up a makeshift stretcher, onto which they carefully load Gishkiy's body.

They all begin the walk back to the village, Niya and Inola bringing up the rear of their group.

Before they leave the clearing fully behind, Niya stops on its edge. She replays the night in her mind. Surreal, that it happened at all. Unkind, that it has ended as it has.

The moon's descent has begun. And the sun is following her lead, rising on opposite ends of the earth.

"Intoxicating," Niya huffs, beyond exhausted.

"What?" Inola asks from behind her, where she has

turned back from following the others down the path towards the village.

Niya continues, pulling her eyes from the far away stone and locking onto Inola's expressive face. "Power. Everything about this night. It's intoxicating, and I am afraid of what comes next."

Inola cocks her head to the side. Her lips quirk upward into a soft smile. "You've surprised me since I met you, little owl. I think...whatever comes, you will be alright."

Niya nods, solemn and quiet. "I know that wasn't an easy spear to throw, but...thank you. You saved me."

"I'm not proud of what I did. But I would do it again, if I had to." With a tilt of her head, she sighs heavily and says, "Now, please—stay close, if you would. I feel about ready to pass out, and if I need a shoulder to lean on—"

"Oh yeah, of course. You know we've got your back."

They exchange quiet, weary smiles. Eventually, Niya turns away, leaving the forbidden hollow behind. But she leaves something of herself behind, too, there in the clearing, something that she isn't quite certain she'll ever get back.

But she can't help but imagine, with each passing step, whether or not she might someday return to try and reclaim it for herself. If, perhaps, she will meet Tusika there, too—when the time comes.

TAHODII DOBA HAWA

Tuboo Sokobi is bustling with activity. Adasi and many others will be graduating tomorrow, going on to tackle their next adventures—in agriculture, trading, economics, astronomy, and many other areas besides.

Niya has decided to change her course of study. Again.

Her parents were not thrilled with her decision, but what they *were* thrilled by was her return home—safe and sound, if not entirely whole.

So Niya walks around the university isles, watching as her peers prepare for their next round of schooling, or to embark on their next journey, or to prepare to live the next great legend of their people.

And she knows that stories are already being told. Changed and magnificent, warped but true. A song to sing, a story to tell. *That of Niya and Tusika, of Owl and Raccoon.*

But a legend is a story that grows, with time. Even once it is finished.

Not that Niya believes their song is truly finished. Not yet.

Not yet.

Meandering along the Mizizibi's edge, Niya revels in the birdsong. She sees a pair of river otters playing amongst the docks, Adanadi-tinged fur violet in the day's glorious sunshine, and she smiles. And when she reaches the place where she had docked her own canoe, she finds that she is not alone.

Inola's voice is sweet as she greets her. "Niya."

"Inola! What are you doing here?!"

Niya rushes to her, throwing her arms around the fast and forever friend and squeezing her tightly.

"My tribal council has made a decision on my sentence."

"Oh." Niya's breath falters. "I did not get to speak with them, to speak on your behalf. To tell them you saved me, and—"

"I would not have let you," Inola stops her. "It was an unnecessary pain to put you through. But they have decided that I will undergo a three-month exile and term of service."

"With what tribe?" Niya asks, curious.

"The farthest reaches of the Haudenosaunee Confederacy, if you can believe it. I think they are going to try and turn this sentence into an ambassadorship opportunity. But I do not have to leave for three more days. And I hear that Adasi is graduating tomorrow."

"This is true," Niya says. "You can distract us all with details of your upcoming voyage."

"Yes, and then I'll be heading home tomorrow to make the most of my time with Kas and my cousins before I have to go. Still a lot of work to do there, you know."

Making the most of things, Niya thinks to herself, *before they go changing again. Changing forever.*

But change is part of being alive. And Niya is grateful to have that honor. Even if she does not know what changes the new day may bring—what darkness, or what light.

"Let's go dancing," Niya says, struck suddenly by the thought. "What do you think?"

"A-yo!"

"Hey, girls!"

Adasi's voice, followed by Nampeyo's, greets them from farther along the shore.

The young women turn to wave at their approaching friends.

"How does a night of dancing sound to you two?" Inola asks.

"One last night to be wild and free?" Adasi says questioningly. He pauses for dramatic effect before saying, "Sounds like my kind of night!" Then he gives several coyote yips, which Nampeyo does a more than halfway decent job of mimicking.

In a daze of laughter and good spirits, they all head across the Mizizibi together. Niya allows herself to be warmed by the promise of it all. And of course, she aches, too. But she knows that will pass—toxins clear a person's system, even if they leave scars behind, sometimes invisible.

But things have worked out so far. Even though Niya wakes every morning with an aching chest and a heavy heart, imaginary kiss-bruised lips and tear-stained cheeks. She has to believe that Tusika is out there, that the shadow at her back can be conquered, discarded, overcome.

She must believe it.

By the grace of the Creator—and her friends, and their gifts, and their insurmountable spirits and love—if by no other way.

DONADAGOHVI

ACKNOWLEDGEMENTS

Hemlock and Sage exists because of the efforts of so many people.

To my editor, Heidi Billy: you helped me take this from a decent story to a lasting legend, and it wouldn't have been the same without you. Thank you for your endless patience, expert scuba insight, kind words, and thoughtful direction. If a promise was made but not kept, it's solely my fault! I'm truly, truly thankful that you were tasked to help me make the story of Niya and Tusika (and Inola, too) shine—I believe we were successful, and that's pretty dang awesome.

To Connor Alexander, the creator of Coyote & Crow: I wrote an email one day on a whim, not knowing that it would end up pulling me into this amazing community of content creators, Indigipunk badasses, and creative spirits. The world of Makasing is revolutionary, but it also isn't—it's a revolution in that it encompasses a beautiful, futuristic world for Indigenous peoples, a world wherein we are who we are, and that's not only enough, it is *everything*. But it also *isn't* revolutionary—because all you did was ask the simplest of questions: "What if?" Thank you for this opportunity, and for letting me play in the sandbox of Coyote & Crow for a while.

To Mackenzie Neal, the cover artist for *Hemlock and Sage*: words cannot express how thankful I am to have been able to watch you bring these characters to life. You created something truly stunning. The cover for this book is exemplary on the outside of everything I meant for it to be on the inside: luminous, Indigenous, and indicative of the power that lies in choice. *Thank you.*

To the creative team of Coyote & Crow: you did the heavy lifting. You reimagined a Cahokia that could have been, turning it into a vibrant, lush landscape of Indigenous opportunity and life! You created entire languages, technologies, economies, creatures, governments, and more! You invited me in with open arms, and I'm thankful to all of you in Basecamp. Whether it was brainstorming Cahokian cuss words, creating Kag Chahi for all of the chapter titles, or thinking through the intricacies of a world untouched by colonialism, you all always delivered. This is a better book because of you, too.

To the We Need Diverse Books Native Children's and YA Writing Intensive: to every single person who attended as part of my cohort and to our faculty mentors, I thank you. I was able to attend during the writing of *Hemlock and Sage,* and your passion for kidlit and the telling of Native stories—in all of their forms—was inspiring, humbling, and powerful. It's an experience that I still think about every time I sit down to write. Because who am I doing this for, if not for the young version of myself?

To the Writing Folks: you idiots are the loves of my life, every single one of you (don't tell Bridget). Thanks for all the distractions, commiserations, and love—but also for the butt-kicking when I needed it. Our weird little family is a liferaft in the tumultuous ebbs and flows of the nonsensical adventure that is writing and publishing, and I wouldn't want to float through it with anyone else.

And to Bridget: I'm quick to tell people that you're my first, last, and best reader. But you're so much more than that—you're my inspiration, my voice, and my reason. You fix my plot holes and point out when I'm being crazy (or lazy). You push me, and you make me *better*. Porch Kitty, Hazel, Cha-Cha and I—we're all so very lucky to have you. (And don't worry, the Writing Folks know you're the real love of my life.) Thank you for everything, everything, everything.

Coyote & Crow

Visit coyoteandcrow.net to find out more about the world behind *Hemlock and Sage*, purchase the core rulebook and other products, or connect with the Coyote & Crow community via Discord, Twitter, Instagram, and YouTube.

ABOUT THE AUTHOR

Tali Inlow is an author of queer speculative fiction. This is her debut Young Adult novel. Read more at taliinlow.com, and join her mailing list to find out about upcoming releases as well as how to stay connected.

Made in the USA
Thornton, CO
11/28/22 17:22:30

e5714a00-c198-4785-9518-193a43066d13R01